KHAMSIN

Khamsin

by

Denise Robins

Dales Large Print Books
Long Preston, North Yorkshire,
BD23 4ND, England.

British Library Cataloguing in Publication Data.

Robins, Denise
    Khamsin.

    A catalogue record of this book is
    available from the British Library

    ISBN   978-1-84262-814-0 pbk

First published in Great Britain
by Hutchinson & Co. (Publishers) Ltd. 1948

Copyright © Denise Robins 1948

Cover illustration © Jill Battaglia by arrangement with
Arcangel Images

The moral right of the author has been asserted

Published in Large Print 2011 by arrangement with
Patricia Clark for executors of Denise Robins' Estate

Dales Large Print is an imprint of Library Magna Books Ltd.

Printed and bound in Great Britain by
T.J. (International) Ltd., Cornwall, PL28 8RW

For my son-in-law
CHARLES MURRAY SUTTON

KHAMSIN

Yesterday the *khamsin* came...
Like a demented spirit from the desert
  waste–
A bitter savage wind from hell, it raced
And in the cloud of swirling sand and dust
Through Ismailia's quiet streets it rushed;
Tearing the purple jacaranda flowers,
Tossing the flamboyants in scarlet showers
About my feet.
Oh, breathless heat!
Then suddenly there came the rain, the
  blessèd rain.
And I could dream I walked in London
  streets again.

D.R.

Khamsin – from the Arabic *Khamasin,* fifty
days of storm and wind.

PART 1

1

It seemed to Phillida that she had waited so long and struggled so hard to get a passage out to the Middle East in order to join her husband that when the troopship finally docked at Port Said the whole thing fell rather flat.

It was, she supposed, a sort of anti-climax ... and in her deep, rather serious way of thinking, she also supposed that it is one of life's ironies that when you want a thing madly and hopelessly it is the most desirable thing in the world. But when you've achieved it ... well, it doesn't seem quite so marvellous after all.

Not that Phillida was really a cynic. Far from it. She was much too young for that, and at twenty-three she still had an almost childish capacity for enjoyment and an enthusiasm for beauty in art and nature. But she was, perhaps, a bit more thoughtful and analytical than most girls of her age. She had been in the Services – the W.R.N.S. – for the last four years of the war. Service life made a girl think a bit ... knocked off a few of the

11

corners … took away a few illusions, perhaps. Phillida – more generally known to her in-mates as 'Phil' – had seen a good deal of men and of life in general during those arduous and at times harrowing years of hard work, night watches, rationing and bombardments.

It had been a marvel to herself, as well as to those who knew her, that she had managed to retain so much of that disarming innocence which seemed still to cling to her life as a charming aura even when she achieved the dignified status of 'married woman'.

This morning, early February in the year 1947, Phillida, clutching an old Service zipped bag in one hand and with her hand-bag under the other arm, plus a rug and a couple of books, stood at the ship's rails and regarded Port Said with an expression of anxiety rather than excitement on her face. An essentially young sensitive face with a fair skin that blushed easily, framed in long fair hair which did not curl but which she wore madonna-wise, parted in the centre and coiled into a neat shining bun at the nape of her neck. She had wideset eyes, grey rather than blue – a little weak. She had had to wear glasses for close work since she was a child. She was not strikingly beautiful, but she was slenderly built and graceful and had lovely long legs. Her chief assets were that smooth pale gold hair and a beautifully shaped mouth with its sweet, serious expression.

At first sight some people thought her rather prim – even haughty – but on closer acquaintance became aware that Phillida was merely shy and a most kind and friendly person – almost too generous at times. She had deep reserves and an inferiority complex. Service life had really been purgatory for her. She could not bear noise and a slapdash communal existence. She loved to curl up in a chair with a book, or listen to music; she adored the country and used to help her father in his garden before a stray bomb had wrecked home, father and mother in a single night.

That night (Phillida had been away stationed in Portsmouth at the time) was one of the black dreadful incidents of her life which she did not care to remember, but which still haunted her imagination, even though it had happened four years ago. She had so loved home and parents. Being an only child, she had basked always in their love, too, and accepted their devotion as part of a happy, easy existence.

To be bereft of all in a single night had been a harrowing and bitter experience, and it was just about then that she had met Rex Maltern and soon afterwards married him.

One of a large crowd on a heavily laden ship, Phillida now stared at the unusual scene before her and wished that she could feel wildly excited. But she really felt afraid. Disappointingly enough, it was not a bright day; there was none of the heat and sunshine that she had expected to find in Egypt. It was unusually cloudy with a threat of rain, and at this early hour – seven in the morning – it was quite cold. Phillida shivered in the wind that blew strands of hair into her eyes and cut through her camel's-hair coat.

Port Said looked rather gloomy and depressing, she thought. There were a number of ships in the harbour and many small craft. She could see a lot of boats full of natives trying to sell their wares. She was almost deafened by the noise ... the hoarse screaming voices which filled the air with discordant sound. The wily Arabs flung ropes up to some of the troops on the lower decks, who caught them and hauled up all kinds of merchandise; anything from leather goods to oranges, food, sweets and nuts in small baskets. There was a good deal of haggling going on, of laughter and derision from the troops, of barter and protest and a flood of unintelligible Arabic from the men in their boats.

Phillida leaned over the rails and stared down at the dirty white gowns of the Arabs; at the red tarbooshes, the variety of turbans, the mixture of black races; she tried to be interested and amused but was faintly repelled by the smell – the odour of the East with which she was not yet familiar. And she was not a little apprehensive.

Here she was in Egypt at last. Would Rex be here to meet her? Would he have got the cable which she had sent to the Army address he had given her, telling him she was sailing?

What would her life be like out here as the wife of an Army captain? Personally, she knew more about the Navy. It seemed queer to her at times that, after all those years as a Wren, she had married into one of the other Services.

She had met some charming Naval officers in the old days and had had numerous proposals – like all good-looking girls whose work had flung them into the company of war-weary, woman-hungry men. But somehow it had been Rex who had won the day… Rex who had met her at the psychological moment so soon after that disaster to her Exeter home. Phillida was a Devon girl and came of a family who had lived in Devonshire as far back as they could trace the name Millverton.

Rex came from London. He was a mixture of Irish and English with a dash of French thrown in – his maternal grandmother came from Nice. It was from her, Phillida imagined, that he had inherited his facile charm and those gay almond-shaped brown eyes which most women found so attractive.

It was three years since Phillida had seen him. Sometimes it frightened her to think what strangers they were, for she had only known him for a month before they were married and had spent only ten days with him as his wife – ten days crammed with passionate excitement and the intense happiness of loving and being loved after all the tragic misery of losing her house and beloved parents.

They had been given no real chance to get to know each other properly. Phillida had lived on letters – and memories. Letters were unsatisfactory things and Rex's particularly, because he proved himself a poor correspondent. Rex, when you met him, was a born orator, had tremendous powers of expressing himself, but he seemed unable to write anything more than scrappy notes which Phillida had found so disappointing. It wasn't enough for her just to be told that somebody 'missed her'. She wanted to know what he was thinking and feeling deep down. And Rex had never told her any of these things. He wrote about his parties, his tennis, his riding, but of himself, personally, only in the most vague fashion.

For the last two and a half years he had been in Burma. He could, she knew, from what she had been told by other people, have got back to England now, but he

16

seemed disinclined to return to a cold climate and the austere conditions at home. He had said as much in one letter to Phil and had 'wangled' a further posting to the Middle East. Much better, he wrote, for her to join him, than for him to go back and 'moulder', as he put it, in some dull English station. He liked the life out East, the sunshine, plenty to eat and drink, and so on.

Secretly Phillida deplored this attitude. She was essentially a home lover – English to the core – and she had a grandmother still living and with whom she had made her home after her own had been demolished, whom she had hated to leave.

'Gamma,' as the old lady was always called, was the only one of Phillida's family left to her and they had clung together after the awful disaster which had robbed Phillida of both parents and Mrs Millverton of a much loved son and daughter-in-law. Gamma was nearing seventy and none too well these days. Phillida had been loath to leave her alone in the tiny cottage in Alvercombe which had belonged to the Millvertons for a hundred years. She knew, too, what it had meant to the old lady to see her go ... each of them had been afraid that they might never see each other again. But Rex had written:

You can't hang on to your grandmother for the rest of your life, darling, and it would be darned

17

selfish of her to expect it. My parents don't expect to hang on to me, and now you are a soldier's wife you have got to like travel and change.

Well, Phillida didn't think she would ever learn 'to like travel and change'. She was a creature of habit ... hated to be uprooted. While she was in the W.R.N.S. every fresh posting had been a torture to her. She was so shy and found it so difficult to make new friends. But there had always been darling old Gamma and the cottage to go back to on leave.

What a long way away Alvercombe seemed now, Phillida thought, as she looked with her wide serious eyes at Port Said. How lovely it was ... the little whitewashed cottage, the garden full of old-fashioned flowers, and that view of Alvercombe Bay and the sea. At this hour Gamma would still be asleep. But Phillida knew exactly what she would be doing in an hour's time; she would put on her electric kettle for an early cup of tea, then go down to cook her solitary breakfast, and then, when Mrs Brothers, who 'did' for her, came to clean the cottage, Gamma would take her stick and brave the poor weather – and her sciatica which had given her so much trouble lately – and trudge forth to buy the day's food.

Of course it was absurd that she should be

missing Gamma and Alvercombe when she was here about to meet her husband and at last start with him that married life for which she had so ardently longed.

But, she thought ruefully, she hadn't really wanted to begin that life in married quarters in the Middle East. She had foolishly built up a picture of Rex in a home job, able to live out ... in a cottage in the country (Devonshire for preference), leading the quiet life she had always led; only with Rex at her side.

'There I go again,' she thought. 'I must snap out of it and face up to the fact that it will be years before Rex retires and I can have my cottage in Devonshire – or settle down...'

Besides, Rex wouldn't want her to 'get settled'. *He* was so much the opposite. He adored change and adventure and he was not country or cottage minded. A flat in London for him if anything at all in England. And a fast car to take them down to a racecourse for a day's meeting, or out for a night's dancing. (Rex was a marvellous dancer and if he had any pretensions to being artistic at all, he was musical. He could play 'swing' like a professional.)

What would he be like after three years in Burma? How would he look? she wondered. He had sent her snapshots but they had never really told her anything. Occasionally a brother officer had come back and looked up 'little Mrs Maltern' who was still in the W.R.N.S. and given her the sort of news that has no meaning … *'Old Rex is as fit as a fiddle…'* or *'Rex always enjoys life … dickens of a chap'* or *'Your husband told me to give you this parcel … silk stockings, I think…'* or *'I saw him in the bar at the club the night before I left Rangoon. Full of beans,'* and so on.

None of that had brought Rex any closer to her. It merely inferred that he was enjoying life.

Whilst Phillida, despite her work which kept her occupied until she was demobilised and the sweet tranquil leaves at home with her grandmother, had not really been enjoying life at all. Marriage and that short honeymoon with Rex had made her more in love with him than ever and she had felt desperately lonely and unfulfilled all these years. For a long time she had had her name down on a list of 'wives' awaiting their turn to join their husbands abroad. But the waiting and frustration seemed to go on endlessly until she had reached this present stage of feeling estranged from Rex and half reluctant to sail when at last the chance was offered her and she boarded that troop ship at Southampton.

She tried to tell herself that once she saw him all the old marvellous love and excitement would return and he would make her forget England and Gamma … that she was just a bit muddled in her mind and emotions for the moment because they had been separated so long, and that it would all pass the instant she set eyes on him.

She heard a voice behind her:

'Oh, Phil! I've been looking for you everywhere...'

Phillida turned and saw a dark-haired girl of her own age, also laden with bags and parcels. Just behind her, carrying a suitcase, was a tall, fair, nice-looking man in uniform which was wet and glistening, for it had been raining hard until a few minutes ago.

Phillida's anxious face relaxed into a smile. This girl had been one of the eight with whom she had shared a cabin on the rather tiresome journey from England. Her name was Mrs Cubitt. Everybody called her 'Steve', which apparently had been her nickname since her childhood, and with her rather strong features and short curly hair she looked like a boy, particularly in the slacks which she was now wearing.

Steve was the only person with whom Phillida had really become friendly on board ship.

'Oh, *hello*,' Phillida said. 'I wonder how long it will be before we go ashore and can find our husbands.'

Steve proudly tucked an arm through that of the tall man beside her.

'I've already found mine. Isn't it lucky,

Phil? Geoff's been in Port Said for the last forty-eight hours on a job, and has just managed to come out in one of those R.A.S.C. motor-boats to find me.'

'Oh, what marvellous luck! I am pleased for you!' said Phillida, and shook the hand which Major Cubitt extended to her.

The three of them talked for a moment.

'I don't suppose you've seen my husband or know him,' said Phillida wistfully. 'He's Captain Maltern – in the Midland Regiment – he's at G.H.Q. in Fayid.'

Geoffrey Cubitt grimaced.

'Poor chap! Is he indeed? It's a bit tough out there in the desert. No, I haven't come across him, I'm afraid.'

Steve Cubitt gave a friendly smile at Phillida, whom she liked and admired more than any girl she had met for some time.

'But isn't it wonderful, Phil? We shall be quite near you because Geoff is stationed in Cairo at the moment, but everybody's moving out, and we shall all be down in the Canal Zone by the end of March, so we are bound to see each other.'

Geoffrey Cubitt also smiled.

'Yes, I've been telling Steve she will only have a few weeks of civilised life in a nice *pension* in Cairo and then it will be a bedsitting-room for her in this Married Families' Camp they are putting up in the desert fast and furiously to accommodate

22

G.H.Q. officers and their families.'

'But Rex is working in Fayid already,' said Phillida.

'I expect he's in the advance party,' said Cubitt. 'The married quarters aren't ready for the women yet. He'll be living in a tent. But I dare say he has got you a room in Ismailia.'

Steve asked her husband the question which was on Phillida's lips. 'And what's it like in Ismailia?'

'Quite the nicest spot in Egypt,' volunteered Major Cubitt. 'Full of Suez Canal Company families – about fifty miles from here by road, and about twenty-eight from Fayid. Delightful little place – all green trees and flowers.'

'Oh, that will be lovely!' exclaimed Phillida, who had secretly dreaded life in the desert. Rex had warned her in one of his letters that the married quarters that were being put up in G.H.Q. were blocks of rooms – and a 'quarter' meant one bed-sitting-room for the wives of all officers under the rank of Brigadier, with communal public lounges, dining-rooms and bathrooms. It did not sound like home life to her.

Geoffrey Cubitt leaned over the rails to look at the harbour. The sun was breaking through the straggling clouds now – that hot penetrating sunshine which was never long absent here. In another moment it would be very warm. The water was taking on the colour of a sapphire. Port Said, with its big white buildings along the front, looked stately and much more inviting.

Phillida said to Steve:

'How awfully nice your husband seems and what fun his being able to come on board to fetch you!'

'It's grand,' said Steve Cubitt, and her strong face – not pretty, but attractive with the firm white teeth and bright hazel eyes – looked very tenderly at her husband's broad back. 'Just think, Phil ... four whole years since Geoff and I were together!'

'And you don't find him much changed?'

'Not at all. The moment he grabbed hold of me and kissed me, I felt we'd slipped right back to where we were when we said good-bye.'

Phillida sighed.

That sounded promising. Perhaps it would be like that with her and Rex. Steve looked so happy! She had a poise and assurance which Phillida secretly envied her – she had noticed it once they became friends and talked a lot together... She seemed so certain of herself, of life and of her adored Geoffrey.

'If only I were as sure of myself and of the future!' thought Phillida.

It was that touch of timidity in her nature which she knew was a weakness to be conquered, for life these days was hard and events moved swiftly – there was no place for the weak or ultra-sensitive. Rex had said that once during their honeymoon when she had shown hesitancy; been unable to make up her mind about something as quickly as he wanted to. Rex was impulsive. He always liked to act on the spur of the moment. Sometimes his impulsiveness almost scared Phillida. Several times during this voyage she had decided that she must try to be as strong and forthright as Steve. Rex would like it.

'Oh, Steve, I do hope we shall see more of each other,' she said.

'I am quite determined that we shall, my dear,' said Steve. 'Now look ... I think they are sending out the tenders. We shall all be ashore in a moment, and then you'll find your Rex waiting for you.'

Phillida looked down at the harbour. She saw the first tender coming out. Her heart began to beat faster. Her spirits rose. She felt much more enthusiastic than she had done a short time ago. She forgot about the country and the beloved grandmother she had just left. It would be wonderful to see Rex ... to feel his arms around her again. He had such complete mastery of her. In those arms she felt so secure. There was no need to be afraid of life; no need to be uncertain of her own attractions. He had told her a

25

hundred times that he found her lovely and most desirable, and that she was the only girl he had ever wanted to marry. It was marvellous to think that he felt like that about her. Her gay, handsome Rex who was run after by so many girls. He had told her that he had been a confirmed bachelor until her met *her!*

The Cubitts said good-bye... Steve was to have the privilege of being taken off by Geoffrey in the R.A.S.C. launch, straight away. She and her husband would be catching the boat train to Cairo, but they'd keep in touch, she said, as she kissed Phillida good-bye.

Then they were lost in the crowd. Once again Phillida was alone with her own thoughts, standing there, waiting to go ashore. And while she waited, she looked back to that first day of her meeting with Rex.

2

It had been in the month of June, on one of those wet windy days which the long-suffering English people call summer. She had been to Torquay to see old Mr Brockle-bank, the family solicitor who was winding up her father's estate. They had had a melancholy lunch together. She was on compassionate leave, staying with Gamma. She knew now that she had left to her her father's life insurance money and the war insurance which would eventually be paid on her demolished home. In all, perhaps, she would have an income of £50 or £60 a year for the rest of her life and that was all.

She had never had to worry about money. Mr and Mrs Millverton had not been rich. But before the war George Millverton was a dentist with a good practice and they had lived in a delightful little house and garden. Phillida had gone to a good school and would have been sent abroad but for the world-shaking events of 1939. After the second year of war Mr Millverton had a stroke, after which he was never able to work again. He had sold his practice and they had afterwards spent most of their capital, but none of this had affected Phillida financially. She had her pay as a Wren and her doting parents or her grandmother had seen to it that she always spent the most lovely leaves with one or other of them.

But to be alone in the world and homeless except for Gamma's cottage was another thing. So, with Mr Brocklebank's help, Phillida had had to turn her attention to banking accounts and so many details of the kind that had never troubled her before.

She had decided to hitch-hike back to Alvercombe. Mr Brocklebank dropped her in his car at one of the main crossroads. It was late afternoon. She stood in the rain, a lonely, rather pathetic young figure in her blue uniform ... long legs looking longer and slimmer than ever in black silk stockings, Naval hat perched at a rather drunken angle over one eye; the long fair hair looped back as usual into a sleek bun.

Then a car came along – a racy-looking old Alvis tourer, hood up, torn mica windows flapping; a young man in grey flannels, hatless, cigarette between his lips, at the wheel.

Phillida held up her hand.

The Alvis slowed down with a slurring of tyres and a grinding of brakes. The young man leaned out. Through a blur of rain they had looked at each other, Phillida and Rex. She had thought him marvellously good-

28

looking with his thick chestnut hair and those sloe-dark eyes – a striking combination – and he had given her a most engaging smile. He – so he had told her afterwards – had thought she looked a comic little thing, bedraggled by the rain, but with those incredibly beautiful legs, and that was why he had stopped. He made no bones about it. Rex was nearly always frank, if at times embarrassingly so.

The next moment she was sitting in the Alvis beside him and they were roaring along the wet road. He always drove too fast; her first impression of him had been that he was overwhelmingly vital and high-spirited. But he was the sort of man she had dreamed of ... he didn't make her feel self-conscious or shy like so many of the gauche young Naval officers who were often as tongue-tied as herself. He put her at her ease in a moment, gave her no time to think. And he was disarmingly brazen.

'Of course I stopped when I saw those marvellous legs!' he chuckled when she humbly thanked him for pulling up when he was in a hurry.

And later:

'I have had a hell of a day with the C.O. at a demonstration. He's an awful old woman and loathes me. However, I little knew the gods were about to send me a dream in Wren's uniform to soothe my shattered nerves.'

Phillida had started to giggle. He was such fun after Mr Brocklebank and all the dreary business of wills and those awful revived memories of Mummy and Daddy and seeing the heap of rubble that had once been her home.

Captain Maltern went on talking in his gay fashion; he told her that he was stationed quite close to her grandmother's home on a course, but was going out to Burma at any moment. He had just got out of uniform and was about to meet a pal at a favourite pub of his, about five miles from here. Why wouldn't Phillida join them? Phillida was the hell of a pretty name; and how strange that their surnames both began with an M. It was a good sign. How long was she to be on leave? He expected to be in Devonshire another month. He would like to see more of her. And so on; taking Phillida's breath away. She had plenty of experience, in a mild way, with enamoured young N.O.s, but Rex was the fastest worker of them all and the most irresistible.

It all ended with him breaking his appointment at the pub and going back to the cottage with her. There he made himself excessively agreeable to old Gamma, whose heart he won instantly. Rex had 'a way' with old people. And with tradesmen and servants too; a most ingratiating way. Later, when she got to know him better, Phillida realised that it was all part of an egoistical make-up and his tremendous vanity. He liked to be liked. He would go to any lengths to gain popularity, but she saw nothing unattractive in that for the moment. It all seemed part of his charm.

He sat until dark in Gamma's pretty oak-beamed sitting-room, talking and drinking, the whisky which Gamma had brought out much to Phillida's delight (she kept it locked in a cupboard for what she called medicinal purposes).When she told Rex that he roared with laughter, showing his fine white teeth, and said:

'Then I'm permanently in the doctor's hands, Mrs Millverton.'

And he pleased her by showing a superficial knowledge of gardens and her rockery, which she took him out to examine as soon as the rain had stopped. And admired her collection of lustres which were her passion. He was boyishly appreciative of everything, and all the time kept looking at Phillida, who had hastily got out of her damp uniform and put on a cotton frock.

Later he said:

'You look an awful kid in that short pink-and-white thing. And I love those grave eyes of yours and that wonderful mouth dimpling with laughter. As for your hair, I have an absolute passion to take the pins out and see it all tumbling round your neck … you wouldn't look so demure or prim, I bet!'

And it made him laugh, he said, when she gravely put on her glasses to look at any close work, and turned herself into a prim little old-fashioned schoolmistress with her fair 'bun' of hair.

He had shaken her heart when he had talked of pulling down her hair. No man had ever said anything quite so intimate to her before. He had held her hand in a firm possessive clasp at the garden gate, standing by the Alvis.

'I want to see you again, little Phil,' he said; 'there is something about you which appeals to me.'

She wanted to see him again, too.

After he had gone, she and Gamma talked a lot about him. He was in the Regular Army. He had two homes, he had informed them. He had made them laugh about it although old Mrs Millverton thought it rather tragic. He was the son of divorced parents. His father had a flat in Jermyn Street, a retired Regular, too old for service in this war; Rex could get a bed there whenever he wanted one. His mother was married again, and had a house in Roehampton. She was smart and amusing, Rex said, but he couldn't get on with his stepfather, so he didn't stay with them very often.

They were always telling him to get married to some nice girl who'd look after him, he said. He was twenty-eight, and had had lots of love affairs but had never met the right girl, and so he spent his money on new cars and having wonderful leaves.

'But I think he's rather lonely, don't you, Gamma?' Phillida had said thoughtfully, and felt sorry for him. (Phillida liked to feel sorry for lonely, unhappy people.) Gamma agreed that under all that gaiety and swagger he was probably a rather solitary and unsatisfied young man. He had been through Dunkirk, and now he was going out to fight those beastly Japs and might get killed. How awful, Phillida had thought, even to imagine Rex Maltern being killed, and shut her eyes and recalled his lithe figure and the brownness of his skin, and the shatteringly open admiration in those narrow eyes whenever he looked at her ... no man had ever looked at her in *quite* that way before.

She was certain that she would never see him again. It was just a chance meeting. He would never bother to come back ... she was depressed at the thought.

But he did come back. That very next day, as soon as he was free to get away from camp, he rushed over in the old Alvis and took her out. They had tea together in a hotel, and then walked on the cliffs in the sunlight, and later Rex spread his coat on the grass and they sat there talking, talking,

33

talking. It was marvellous how he made her talk. She had never before found so much to say for herself. And she heard a lot more about *him* ... he told her thrilling stories of Dunkirk. She was quite sure when he had finished that he had been awfully brave and ought to have had the Military Cross, but his courage had been overlooked ... of course there were so many brave men and they couldn't all get medals. And it was so wonderful to think that he had not even been wounded.

When he wasn't talking about himself he discussed her. He said he thought it 'pretty decent of her' to have joined the W.R.N.S. They worked them pretty hard – he knew that – and then when he learned what had happened to her parents and home he was genuinely distressed for her and took her hand and held it against his warm brown cheek.

'Absolutely grim for you, my poor little poppet,' he said.

Her big grey eyes filled with tears. The sight of her wet lashes, the pulsing in her young white throat and the slenderness of her pretty hands and feet enchanted Rex. And suddenly she found herself in his arms. He was kissing her with slow, experienced kisses to which Phillida responded with all the ardour of her own passionate young being. For there was both fire and passion in

Phillida under that gentle cool façade, and Rex within forty-eight hours managed to fan her emotions into a bright flame which threatened to burn up commonsense and reason – and reserve!

Just somehow she managed to keep her head, and after a few more of those intoxicating kisses, she insisted upon going home.

She wouldn't go out and dance with him that night as he wanted. Nothing would persuade her to. Phillida had a lot of control and she used it now. Rex Maltern said he had fallen madly in love with her. Perhaps she was madly in love with him, too. But this was where their temperaments differed. This was where her slowness to act and that touch of hesitancy in her make-up served to good purpose.

Phillida went home and stayed home and Rex went back to camp, disappointed and frustrated. He was used to easy conquests.

Phillida was not as beautiful or seductive as many of the women he had known. She was not really amusing. He let her talk about books and art and music but he had no time for any of these things. He was used to the sort of girl-friend who could sit on a high stool at a cocktail bar and put down a succession of quick gins with him; the very modern sort of girl who knew the ropes and could play the love-game as lightly and as efficiently as he could himself. And he liked a girl to be 'alive'. Phillida was a little too quiet; not really his type. But that quality of reserve, of virginal purity – of innocence despite her life in the Service – coupled with those lovely legs and long-pointed hands, began to hold an incredible fascination for Rex. Having once held her in his arms and kissed her he wanted to repeat the process. He wanted more. He wanted to pull down that shining hair and thread his fingers through it. He wanted to teach her all the things she didn't know. And in a vague sort of way he thought her pathetic as well as sweet, with nobody in the world belonging to her except that old grandmother. He called her 'my little orphan, Phil'.

She returned to duty at Portsmouth. He got leave and went to see her and take her out. Later he worked things so that they both got a week's leave at the same time and wangled an invitation to stay at the cottage with Gamma where he could see and be with Phillida all day long.

He went on making love to her. She was by then desperately in love with him, frightened at the mere thought that he might go out of her life. She was another person when she was with him – a vivid, laughing, happy Phillida under a spell.

They spent the long, lovely, summer days bathing and pick-nicking. Gamma encouraged it all, glad that her poor little Phillida had found a nice boy-friend at last, and was so happy after all she had been through. The old Alvis was there to take them out in the evenings; just for a drive in the starlight, or into Torquay to dance – Rex was a marvellous dancer. They spent wonderful enchanted evenings together.

Just at odd moments queer little tremors of anxiety about his character shook her. Sometimes he did things which jarred on her – very slightly. Such as when they were together in a restaurant one evening, and she was studying the menu, he had seen a brother officer come in and hastily whispered:

'Take off your glasses. That's old Pumphrey who's in my mess. I want him to see how good-looking you are and I hate those specs...'

Yes, that had jarred a little. It made her embarrassed, as though she were being shown off, and he ought to like her just as much with her spectacles on as off. On the other hand, she was conciliated by his obvious appreciation of her and his anxiety to introduce her to his friends. She forgave him. Just as she forgave the evening when he lost his temper with a waiter. Any public exhibition of that kind horrified Phillida, brought up as she was by a gentle courteous father who had always been particularly patient and pleasant with servants.

That night she had very nearly decided that she was not so much in love with Rex after all. But he had been so contrite, apologised so humbly, put it down to a hard day's work and the fact that his nerves were strained because he was going through an arduous course and about to take an examination. And after the meal, taking her home, he had stopped the Alvis, caught her close to him and whispered against her ear:

'There's something about you which is so wonderful, so different from all the other girls. I absolutely adore you.'

So of course Phillida melted and forgot all about his exhibition of temper. She could not, she decided, live without him.

When at the end of that month he finished his course and got his orders for Burma she immediately worked herself into a panic because she thought he might be killed or taken prisoner by the Japs; with all her emotions at fever heat, more than confident that she loved him and that he was the man for whom she had been waiting all her life, she thought of nothing, nobody else, day or night.

Rex, too, had the unpleasant and perhaps natural dread that he might die a hero's death in the Far East and thought it would be nice to leave a wife, if not a child, behind him.

Shortly after hearing the news that he was to go at once on embarkation leave, he rushed down to Portsmouth to see his 'little orphan'. He suggested an immediate marriage. Without hesitation, Phillida complied. Gamma liked him; had never seen him in any guise but that of a charming, amiable young man. Phillida got compassionate leave, tore round London, bought the best trousseau that coupons and very little money could procure at a moment's notice, and married Rex by special licence in the dear little Norman church in Alvercombe.

Rex's mother sent a handsome cheque and a hastily written letter explaining that she could not possibly get down to the wedding because 'dear Jack' (her husband) had a war job in Edinburgh and would not allow her to come south during the bombing. So Phillida did not make the acquaintance of her mother-in-law. Rex's father also sent a cheque and a telegram, but although he genuinely wanted to come to his son's wedding, he was prevented from doing so because he was in a nursing-home at that time being treated for duodenal ulcers from which he suffered regularly.

Phillida and Rex went to see him after they were married. From her point of view old Major Maltern was a disappointment. He was a selfish, complaining, disagreeable old man. He made the most of his ills and was

39

disinterested in his son or his son's wife. Phillida realised how completely a divorce could ruin the relationships between children and parents. Rex, in his way, was as motherless, fatherless and homeless as herself, which awakened in her an additional tenderness and sympathy for him.

That ten days' leave before he left for Burma remained in her mind like a feverish dream. They were both strung to concert pitch. Rex was at his best, a passionate but considerate lover. She did not find it difficult to break through that barrier that he laughingly called her 'Puritan streak'. With all his experience, his tremendous vitality and charm he roused the dormant woman in her and was – he told her – completely satisfied with his 'little orphan'.

He was generous to the pitch of extravagance; bought her presents such as she had never had before. They stayed at the Dorchester. They were both too young and too much in love to bother much about the raids, and there was still plenty of fun to be had in London.

Then came the parting. The awful morning when Rex sold the Alvis and had to go and get a strong drink because he was so upset at parting with the old friend. A final dinner and dance … a last poignant, feverish night when neither of them slept much and they said all the things that probably thousands of others in their position had said before them.

'I'll always love you, darling. I'll never change...' 'I could never forget this ... it means absolutely everything... I'll be faithful to you. There won't be anyone else until we meet again.'

From Phillida, with a white face, drenched with tears:

'Promise me you won't stop loving me, Rex...'

From him:

'I swear it. You're my wife. This is quite different from anything else in my life...'

And so on until his departure. Then Phillida, numb and sick with grief, back in her W.R.N.S. uniform, journeying wretchedly down to Portsmouth, looking at her little gold wedding ring through a blur of tears. Oh, this terrible war ... this awful waste of time and life and love! She loved Rex so much that her heart was breaking.

She did not hear from him again for nearly six weeks. Security forbade him to communicate with her until he reached Burma, from whence he sent her a cable.

After that the months seemed to drag by, slowly at first, and miserably, and then with astonishing rapidity. Phillida slipped into a rut. Life became a routine of work at her depot ... of leaves spent with Gamma ... of going out with her girl-friends, and sometimes with young men. But she had little time for the latter. She was Mrs Rex Maltern now … and had a future with Rex to look forward to.

But that future seemed a long way off. And there was nothing for her hungry heart and taut nerves except letters … those disappointingly scrappy letters which he wrote irregularly from Burma.

There came a time when it was hard for her to remember the sound of his voice and only his photograph and the snaps he sent reminded her of what he looked like. It was as though she were married to a stranger. Everything became dulled by time … even her first frantic fears that he might be killed. Lethargically she waited for news. She wished at times that there had been a child born of that first feverish union with him, then her marriage might have seemed more concrete; she would have had something more in life than her old grandmother and Alvercombe. But there had not been a child. There was nothing but this interminable and intolerable waiting.

When Rex was posted to Egypt it brought him a bit nearer, but she was terribly disappointed because she expected him to come home on leave, and he did not seem anxious to get back. He had lost touch with England, he said, and (so she secretly dreaded) he had lost touch with her. The war was over. He had borne a charmed life and come through it all without a scratch. He had taken a Staff Course in Palestine. He seemed to be getting good confidential reports, and now had a good job. He settled in Cairo, which he described as 'wizard', and he had recently bought another car which had taken the place in his heart of the old Alvis.

He seemed content.

But Phillida, three years older – war-weary, tired out like so many Service girls, sick of the monotony of her existence – was utterly unsatisfied and lonely. She was a wife yet not a wife. Materially she had benefited – spiritually she was bereft. She drew a marriage allowance ... she was able to help old Gamma, who had been hard hit by the increased taxation and the fact that her small private means had been hopelessly reduced. Phillida was, at twenty-three, after being demobilised, her own mistress and had saved quite a little nest-egg with her gratuity and the money Rex gave her.

But these things did not count with Phillida. She wanted her own home ... she wanted Rex back again; wanted those wonderful, intimate days when they walked on the sands together at Alvercombe, when they dined and danced and kissed and were so feverishly happy.

She wrote to him:

43

We can't go on like this ... it's getting me down,
darling... Why can't I come out to you? Surely
wives can get out now. If you put my name
down for a passage my turn will come...

He wrote back and said that he would apply
for her but that there was a ban on wives
going out to Egypt for the moment.

After that, more long weary months of
waiting and of doing nothing but help
Gamma run the cottage, and hoping with
every mail that came she would hear that
her passage had come through.

Meanwhile Rex seemed to be having what
he called the 'whale of a time' in Cairo. He
sent her food parcels and nylon stockings
and beautiful shoes and bags. Occasionally
he remembered to write something really
tender and lover-like. But he did not seem to
be able to carry on with that sort of thing
after their long separation. It was she who
struggled to keep the flame between them
alight. Subconsciously the effort left a mark
on her – a profound hurt. Although she
would have died rather than admit the fact
to her grandmother, she was secretly convinced that Rex was not as anxious to get
back to her as she was to go to him. And that
was an awful thing to think ... she tried to
argue herself out of it ... and failed. In consequence she grew more shy and reserved

44

than she used to be before their marriage.

During these years she did not even have the pleasure of a happy relationship with either of his parents.

After the end of the war with Germany and the cessation of bombing, Mrs Spikes – Rex's mother – came back to London. Phillida lunched with her once or twice. She was a handsome woman from whom Rex had inherited his looks; still young for her age and extremely smart. Her two passions in life were Bridge and clothes. She had no time for anything else, and only the most superficial feeling for her son.

'We never really hit it off – even when he was a child. He has my looks and his father's nature,' she told Phillida.

Sincerely Phillida hoped that was not true, for on the few occasions on which she had met old Major Maltern he struck her as being an egoist and rather stupid.

Through the gradual decrease of blind devotion, she continued to cling piteously to her faith, to her fervent hope that she had done the right thing in marrying Rex Maltern; and that they had only to come together again and all would be well.

It was with these high hopes that she sailed from Southampton, and so, with the long, difficult years behind her, reached Port Said today and awaited her reunion with her husband.

3

They were ashore at last.

Going through the Customs was a nightmare. Skinny black hands grabbed Phillida's luggage from her. She found herself in a jostling crowd of passengers almost as dazed as herself, and Egyptian officials. She wondered if she would ever see her things again. She was bitterly disappointed because most of the other women seemed to have been met by their husbands, but hers was not here. She had long since lost sight of her one and only friend, Steve Cubitt. Anxiously she searched the crowd in the Customs House in vain for Rex's familiar face.

By some miracle, all her luggage turned up again. She was eventually cleared through the Customs and found herself outside. By now she was in a panic. Rex could not have got her cable. What ought she to do now? She was being surrounded by half a dozen Arabs all jabbering harshly, their Arabic interspersed with a few words of English, all trying to sell her something, or get *backsheesh* of some kind.

'Lady want hotel ... *kwayiss* ... I take you.'

46

'Port Said very nice ... show you round, lady...'

Dark, grinning faces ... hot sunshine ... traffic horns blaring ... all the noise and bustle of a busy port, and suddenly Phillida felt frightened and looked around her in despair. Oh, why hadn't Rex come? She hadn't the least idea where to go or what to do now.

A black urchin with a woolly head thrust three oranges at her, demanded a *piastre* each. A tall man with a dirty white gown and turban appeared mysteriously from nowhere with a tray full of rubbishy silver ornaments, and endeavoured to attract her attention. A shoe-shine boy wanted to smarten up her shoes. Then a couple of better dressed Egyptians pressed forward to look at her, their gaze full of bold admiration for the fair-haired English girl.

Phillida shrank back, her cheeks hot and pink with embarrassment.

'Oh, please go away!' she said helplessly. 'Go away and leave me alone, *do*.'

Then suddenly a strong clear English voice said:

'*Yalla ... Imshi*, the whole lot of you.'

The motley circle disappeared like magic. Phillida saw the tallest man she had ever seen standing in front of her. He was well over six-foot-four, she decided. He was a typical Englishman – he wore grey flannels which bore the unmistakable cut of London. He had a thin, tanned face with strong bones – and thick fair hair almost as fair as her own. She could not see the colour of his eyes because he wore dark glasses.

Flustered, but grateful, Phillida stammered:

'Thanks awfully ... that was wonderful... I was getting simply *desperate.*'

From his great height, Martin Winters looked down at Phillida with a kindly smile.

'You'll get used to it,' he grinned. 'You've just come off the troopship, I suppose?'

'Yes.'

'Isn't anybody meeting you?'

'There ought to have been ... I mean, I cabled my husband ... but it was all such a rush ... you know what it is. I only had about forty-eight hours' notice that there was a berth for me on this particular ship ... but I *did* cable Rex...'

The tall man laughed.

'Oh, you don't know this country; all kinds of queer things happen here. The post and telegrams and so on are pretty erratic.'

'But I cabled to his Army address,' protested Phillida.

'Which is where?'

'G.H.Q. Fayid.'

Martin Winters whistled. 'Aha, well, there's a lot of fun going on there. G.H.Q. is just in the process of moving from Cairo. I dare say his cable got held up between the two places. I wonder if I know your husband?'

'He's Captain Maltern ... Rex Maltern ... the Midland Regiment. He's got a staff job – something to do with what he calls "Q", but I can never understand these Army terms.'

Martin Winters laughed again. How young and slender and sweet she was, he thought, very shy-looking and defenceless. He had not heard of Rex Maltern. He explained to little Mrs Maltern that he personally was a Lieutenant-Commander in the Navy, working here in Port Said at Navy House.

Phillida's eyes brightened suddenly. Her taut young face relaxed into a smile which he found rather touching.

'Oh, *are* you! I've just been demobilised from the W.R.N.S. – sir!' she added with a little giggle.

He drew himself erect. They saluted each other and laughed. He took off his dark glasses. She saw now that his eyes were a clear deep shade of blue. They smiled at each other again. Contact had definitely been established.

'Not very often the Wrens marry into the Army,' he observed.

'No, I know!'

'Very disloyal, I call it!'

Phillida laughed again, entirely at her ease

and much less lost and lonely.

'What sort of job were you doing – where were you stationed?' he asked.

They chatted for a moment. He discovered that she had worked under an old friend of his in Portsmouth. This conversation would have developed, but the advent of another circle of would-be vendors brought another flow of Arabic from the Lieutenant-Commander, who hastily added:

'Look here, I must get you out of this. I've got my car parked a few yards away. I'll take you along to the Officers' Club and we'll put a call through to your husband and see what's happened.'

Enormously relieved, Phillida allowed Martin Winters to take control. She was at home with the Navy. And Martin was typical. There was something fresh and wholesome and nice about him. And she had to admit that he was a striking-looking man, with that tremendous height and those blue eyes ... eyes with a little network of wrinkles around them, as though he constantly screwed them up. She had noticed so many sailors who looked like that after the long hours of watching the high seas.

Lieutenant-Commander Winters had a small shabby Morris. It had done fifty thousand miles and was creaking, he told her ruefully. It 'ate oil' and needed a 'rebore', but it was still on its legs. If anything happened

50

to it he wouldn't be able to afford another. *'Malesh.'* (That was a word Phillida was to get used to out here. *Malesh.* No matter!)

'Life's darned expensive in Egypt, Mrs Maltern, as you'll find,' said Martin. He threw a few rapid orders at a couple of Arabs who hastily piled Phillida's luggage into the Morris.

Driving with him to the N.A.A.F.I. Officers' Club, she relaxed and began to concentrate on the water-front of Port Said and take some interest in all the life and colour. She exclaimed at the beauty and colour of the brilliant bougainvillaeas, at the lovely trees, the blue sky and the sunshine. It was all so different from home. It had been grey and cold in Alvercombe when she left.

Martin Winters said:

'Oh, there's quite a lot about Port Said that's all right, but the life's very limited here – and everywhere – these days. Chaps like myself who had been here for a year are a bit sick of it, but you'll find a lot that is interesting and I agree with you that the vegetation couldn't be lovelier.'

'I do so love flowers!' said Phillida.

He took a quick glance at her as they drove along. It struck him long afterwards when he thought about her that those words were symbolic of Phillida Maltern. She loved flowers. She was like a pale flower

51

herself. He discovered later on that it was typical of her, too, that the first thing she should notice about Egypt were the flowers and the trees, rather than the shops. In that she was different from other women he knew – most refreshing.

Martin Winters at the age of thirty-three had – like most men in the Senior Service – a certain amount of experience with the opposite sex. There were always parties ashore; guest nights on board; dances, duty and otherwise. Women instinctively liked him because he exuded kindliness and good-humour, and was good to look at into the bargain. He had what might be called a 'success' with most women. But he had loved only one: a girl whom he had met in the early days of the war, when on leave in England following a hard year in the North Sea. Those difficult, dangerous days of war – mostly spent in a destroyer – had left a mark on Martin. His ship had been sunk in the Baltic and after hours of exposure and exhaustion he had ended up with pneumonia and a patch on one lung. But with a passionate love for his profession he had refused to give in. He had recovered, but with a chest weakness and some sinus trouble for a legacy, which left him with bad intermittent headaches. During this last winter in Port Said, however, he had been well, and was at the moment feeling particularly fit.

Under his cheerful exterior, Martin, however, was a strangely solitary being of close, deep reserves. Two women had meant more than anything in the world to him – his mother, who had died while he was still at Dartmouth (her death had affected him for a considerable time), and Bridget, the girl to whom he had been engaged.

It gave him a curious pang to see little Mrs Maltern sitting beside him in the car today with her fair demure bun in a snood, that blue-and-white silk scarf, and camel's-hair coat around her shoulders. She looked like Bridget – they had the same slight fragile build and long expressive hands. There was something in her shy smile which was Bridget's smile. God, how he had loved Bridget, and how perfect life had been when they had been together! Like this, she used to drive with him, and he had always felt tender and protective towards her and felt so big and clumsy. She was so slender and graceful. She had appealed vastly to his sense of chivalry.

But he had lost Bridget in an even more tragic way than his adored mother. He could scarcely bear to recall it... It was at the end of his summer leave in 1942. They were to have been married before he rejoined his ship. Her trousseau was ready and he had bought the licence and the ring. Three days before the wedding Bridget fell ill and was rushed to hospital with an emergency appendix. It must have always been her heart that was weak. She had tried to join the W.R.N.S. several times but they had turned her down. But nobody guessed how dangerous her condition really was. After the operation they knew ... because Bridget had left them all very suddenly ... she never came round from the anaesthetic. All the sweetness and youth of her had been extinguished, the bright flame blown out at a single gust.

Martin had torn up the licence, put away the ring, and gone back to sea a brokenhearted man. He learned to smile again, but there was a deep hurt still inside him, and only very recently time had salved the wound sufficiently to give him back a real enjoyment of life.

But there was nobody else after Bridget. Her photograph remained in his cabin, with his mother's. He was quite sure he would never ask another girl to marry him.

This stranger – Mrs Maltern – had a strange look of Bridget which pulled uncomfortably at his heartstrings, and the poor little thing was so disappointed that her husband had not turned up. He felt that his dearest wish at the moment was to get hold of the fellow and see that she was really happy. 'Little thing,' he kept thinking, but, good lord, she wasn't as small as all that.

She was rather a tall girl. He always forgot what a height he was himself. Six-foot-five-and-a-half in his socks.

They reached the N.A.A.F.I. Officers' Club. Martin took Phillida upstairs, installed her in a chair on one of the verandahs overlooking the harbour, and suggested that she should have a cigarette and a cup of coffee while he put through the telephone call for her. He knew it would take some time. The Signals were still working on the telephone lines to Fayid.

'I can lock the car up with your luggage – it will be quite safe,' he said.

So Phillida found herself sitting comfortably in a basket-chair, drinking the first cup of Turkish coffee she had ever tasted, watching all the movement on the glittering waterfront, of which she had a wonderful view from the Club balcony. It was going to take her some time to get used to the blueness of that sea and of the sky, she thought. There were so many lovely strange trees, and those funny old *gharrys* drawn by lean-looking horses – and sleek motor-cars – lorries, jeeps, a variety of Army transport ... W.D. cars – moving up and down the tree-lined road below.

It really was rather exciting and so different from England... She was beginning to feel more confidence ... a big thrill of happy expectation. That nice Commander

55

would get Rex on the phone for her, and she would speak to him at last, and he would know that she had arrived and would come rushing to Port Said to fetch her, and oh! it really would be marvellous to feel his arms round her again, and see those handsome eyes of his, brilliant with passionate appreciation of her.

'Rex, darling...' she thought, 'I do love you. I do so want our marriage to be a success...'

The tall, loose-limbed figure of Lieutenant-Commander Winters appeared on the balcony. He said:

'Just as I thought – an hour's delay.'

Phillida's face fell.

'Oh dear! An *hour!*'

Martin flung himself into a chair and stretched out the ridiculously long legs which always got in the way of things. He grinned.

'That's nothing in this country. The first lesson you will have to learn is patience. Nobody hurries here.'

She laughed.

'Well, perhaps that's a good thing. It isn't that I'm so fond of high speed in any shape or form. In fact I always used to like the verse which begins: *"What is this life if full of care..."*'

'*"We have no time to stand and stare..."*' Martin finished for her quickly. 'I couldn't agree more. I'm all for a nice lazy life sitting in the sun.'

'Oh, but don't you have to get back to work? Oughtn't you to leave me?'

'I'm quite sure I ought not to,' he said, with his wide attractive smile which brought a few more wrinkles around the blue eyes and cut two deep lines on either side of his mouth. 'Anyone who looks like you and has only set foot on Egyptian soil for the first time needs an escort, so why not a Naval one at that?'

Her cheeks grew pink and her long silky lashes fluttered a little nervously. Phillida was always embarrassed by flattery. But she was pleased and she thought this man was awfully nice and she really did not know what she could have done without him. Frankly she told him so.

He responded by saying that it was a pleasure for him, and added:

'After all, we have to look after our personnel, even when they are "ex".'

'Well, it's terribly nice of you,' she said. 'I'm sure Rex will be most grateful.'

'It's bad luck he didn't know that you were coming. I'm sure he would have been down at the water's edge at crack of dawn.'

Phillida gave a little sigh and finished her coffee.

It was rather marvellous to sit in the sun without a coat in February, she thought – it was like a warm spring day at home. She was beginning to learn how quickly the weather could change out here. When the troopship had docked it had been quite cold.

During the hour whilst they waited for the Fayid call the tall Naval officer and the slight fair girl seemed to find a lot to say to each other. Reminiscences of her days in the W.R.N.S. – of his war service ... of her meeting with Rex and subsequent marriage... They discussed, to begin with, as strangers will, all the most attractive things that had happened to them both. It was only towards the end of the conversation that either made mention of hidden griefs.

Martin, unaware that he touched a sore spot, asked Phillida if her parents were in England. Then he saw her expression change. Her head drooped. She told him quickly that a bomb had wiped her father, mother and her home out of existence.

Martin looked uncomfortable. He felt desperately sorry for her.

'What a ghastly show!' he said. 'You poor child!'

She grimaced.

'One gets over these things I suppose.'

He thought of Bridget, and looked stonily for a moment at Phillida's slender fingers with the glistening rose-varnished nails. (That was the colour *she* used to use.) His lips twisted. He said curtly:

'I wonder if one ever does. In a way, yes. One couldn't have disasters like that and go on feeling them acutely – or one wouldn't want to live. As a matter of fact, the girl I was going to marry died three days before our wedding...'

Phillida looked at the man's strong kind face and was instantly full of compassion.

'Oh, I'm terribly sorry! So you've been through it too...'

He could not bear her pity and quickly clapped his hands to a passing *suffragi*.

'We mustn't get morbid. I think I shall abandon Naval traditions and sink some beer, because it is too early for my pink gin!'

Her spirits rose to match his. A moment later they were laughing together again. But Martin, drinking his beer, looking thoughtfully at Phillida's serious face, felt secretly rather annoyed with her for reminding him so painfully of his lost buried love. Abruptly he set down his glass and rose.

'It's past eleven. I'll go and see about that call...'

He returned with a grim smile.

'More delay. Oh, don't worry, I tell you you'll get used to it in the land of the Pharaohs.'

'I wonder if Rex is there,' she said anxiously.

'If he's working at G.H.Q. he should be – at this time of the morning.'

'How long will it take him to get here?' she asked.

'Has he got a car?'

'Yes, an old Studebaker he bought in Cairo a month ago.'

'Well, that ought to fetch him here in an hour and three-quarters.'

Her soft grey eyes sparkled.

'Oh, it would be wonderful if he could get here for lunch, and we could have drinks together. I want him to meet you ... you've been so awfully kind...'

His heart melted to her. She was so young and artless. Ten years younger than himself. Much younger than Bridget, who had died just after her twenty-fifth birthday. *She* would have been thirty now ... this girl seemed a mere child. She had been married for three years; and she had had ten days of married life. A poor show. The war had mucked things up for all these young people. And God knew how many marriages were going adrift. He trusted this one would be all right because the girl was sweet. He hoped the husband was a good fellow.

He looked at his wrist-watch. How big his bones were, thought Phillida – what a big strong wrist, with the large watch on its wide white band. He said:

'Hmm. Well, I think I'll ring up the ward-room and tell them that I won't be back to lunch. No, don't worry, I shan't be hauled up in front of the Admiral, or anything of that sort. Actually I am starting a couple of days' leave, and was thinking of going sailing when I saw you. So my time's my own.'

'Oh!' exclaimed Phillida, 'then I've ruined your morning...'

'Not at all. You've made it. It's rather jolly to meet someone straight from home, and hear all about things. I haven't been back for a year. What's more, one gets tired of the same old faces, you know. It's extremely pleasant sitting here talking to you like this... Tell me some more...'

Happily she launched into a further description of Alvercombe and Gamma. Martin watched and listened. He began to see that he was right in his assumption that this girl was different from others – completely devoid of vanity or that feminine instinct which he had seen in so many women he met, which was to score a hit with a chap as soon as she got to know him. Phillida made no effort to 'impress'; she was shy and even naïve, and probably a lot of chaps he knew wouldn't think her 'good fun'. There was something quite homely about her ... he could see her in her grandmother's cottage doing odd jobs about the house and her bit of gardening. Lord! how the child loved flowers! She was describing the herbaceous border she had made for the old lady last autumn, and giving the plants their Latin

61

names in a manner which commanded his respect. She was rather old-fashioned ... yes, that's what she was ... a sort of Brontë girl ... she might have come straight out of *Jane Eyre*. What a comic little Wren she must have been, he thought. But he was sure she had done her job efficiently.

She did not bore him ... on the contrary, he was curiously attracted by her personality. He had no use for 'glamour girls' who knew they were glamorous! Above all, he respected her obvious love for her husband, her desire to settle down to straightforward married life.

A bed-sitting-room in the desert, and Army life, didn't sound to him quite her cup of tea. He was quite sure that she felt it too. She dreaded it. She was the sort to be lost and lonely in a place like Fayid ... in the Army crowd. He knew the sort of homesickness that would descend upon her. It had descended upon *him*, man that he was, with a Naval career behind him. Once he had wanted a home and a garden of his own, and somebody to love very much – somebody who would love him in the same wholehearted way.

He kept wondering what Rex Maltern was like.

The Fayid call came through ten minutes later.

Phillida, cheeks bright pink with excitement, stood beside Martin as he took the call. Her heart thumping, she knew suddenly that the 'anti-climax' feeling had gone. She was in love with Rex – terribly in love, as she used to be. She wanted badly to hear his voice. She held out her hand for the telephone.

Then she saw Martin shake his head and heard him say:

'Oh, I see. Hold on a moment...'

He covered the microphone with his hand and turned a face that expressed disappointment – for her.

'I'm awfully sorry, Mrs Maltern. Your husband isn't there.'

The heartbeats slowed down. She said:

'Oh ... he's out... He'll be back... Shall we leave a message for him to ring me here?'

Martin spoke into the telephone again. Then he said to Phillida:

'No – he isn't expected back until to-morrow.'

Now Phillida's heartbeats were slow and painful. The bright colour faded. The soft eyes grew cloudy. Martin thought that she looked like a disappointed child. She said:

'Oh dear!'

'Just a moment,' said Martin. 'I'm speaking to one of the chaps in the office. I'll try to get some more information ... or would you care to speak to him?'

'No – you do it for me – if you will.'

63

A moment later they were back in their chairs on the balcony overlooking the sunlit harbour. Martin said gravely:

'It appears there *is* a signal waiting for him with his mail. That is probably yours.'

'Then he never got it!' exclaimed Phillida.

'No.'

'But where is he?'

Almost apologetically Martin answered:

'They just don't know. He's on leave. He's been on a week's leave. He's probably in Cairo.'

Now Phillida looked aghast.

'In *Cairo...!* Good heavens, I'll never be able to trace him, unless I could go there and enquire at the various hotels.'

'You can't possibly go knocking around Cairo alone, my dear child,' said Martin quickly.

'Then what shall I do?'

'Well, this chap seemed to think Maltern is due back at work tomorrow, so he'll probably be in Fayid tonight.'

She brightened.

'Oh – then it's the *end* of his leave!'

'Fortunately.'

'And he *might* be in Ismailia tonight?'

'Quite possibly.'

'Then I'd better go there at once.'

Martin gave her a thoughtful look.

'Yes, it's the best thing. Has he made any plans at all for receiving you? Rooms booked, I mean?'

'He didn't actually know what date I'd get my passage. It isn't his fault,' she said. (He thought her apology for her husband was touchingly loyal.) 'Especially if he didn't get my cable.'

'So you've no rooms arranged or anything?' he said.

'N-no,' she said doubtfully. 'Won't it be easy for me to go into some hotel in Ismailia?'

'There are only a couple of hotels there worth going to and they are probably full. The place is packed now the Army is moving down to the Canal Zone.'

'Rex talked a lot about the French Club.'

'You can't stay there. They don't let rooms.'

'Oh dear, what do you suggest?'

Martin frowned. He would have liked to suggest that Phillida stayed here, in Port Said. Conscious suddenly of his own loneliness, he wanted to take her out tonight ... enjoy a little longer that fresh shy sweetness and honesty which he found so attractive. But a Port Said hotel was no place for a young girl, alone. Better she should go straight to the place where she stood a chance of contacting her husband.

'I tell you what,' he said suddenly, 'we'll get Fayid on the 'phone again – leave a message in case your husband turns up there, then I'll give you some lunch here if you'll allow me to, and afterwards I'll drive you to Ish...'

'To … Ish?'

'Ismailia.' He smiled.

'Oh, but you're going sailing – I've already spoiled your day off. I can get a train...' she said with a dewy, grateful look which made Martin Winters feel he would have sacrificed a good deal more than a day's sailing for the sake of pleasing Phillida.

'I shall drive you into Ish,' he said firmly. 'It will be a good excuse for me to take a nice drive along the Canal Road – it is a good road. You'll enjoy it. I know George … a delightful Greek chap who runs the French Club. He'll suggest something for you – some nice rooms with a French family, perhaps. Then we can have some tea and maybe a drink later on, and more than possibly your husband will turn up this evening. Especially if you say it's his favourite haunt.'

Phillida's spirits began to rise again.

'Oh, it really is good of you, Commander Winters… I'm terribly grateful.'

He grimaced.

'What about dropping the title … just "Martin"?'

'And call me Phillida, please, or Phil. Everyone does.'

'Not Phil. It's a shame to spoil that lovely name.'

She laughed. He clapped his hands for the *suffragi*.

'Now for my pink gin,' he added cheerfully.

She sat back in her chair, relaxing, trying not to worry about Rex and whether or not she would find him in Ismailia tonight. She felt very safe with Martin Winters. Trust the Navy every time, she thought, with all her old Wren's pride in the service. She was chatting to him again cheerfully when the *suffragi* brought the pink gin for Martin and a lime-squash for herself.

4

Phillida thought that she had never driven along a more fascinating route than that which runs beside the Canal between Port Said and Ismailia. Martin was an interesting companion, pointing out all the places of interest as well as the names of the various trees and bushes, with which he seemed familiar. He was obviously a Nature lover.

It was very still and warm after lunch when they drove those fifty miles and Phillida was amazed by the heat of the sun and by the fabulous blue of that slender shining stretch of water – the Suez Canal. It looked incredibly narrow and yet some of the biggest ships in the world passed through it. On one side, the sandy waste of the desert as far as the eye could see; on the other, the fertile, cultivated land. Half-way to their destination they came to Kantara, to the ferry that goes across the canal into Palestine.

Phillida now received her first impression of this strange, violent country, made habitable by that ancient river, the Nile, and by these man-made wonderful canals. She saw the cotton plantations, the sugar-cane, the melon plants, the date palms and the tall dry pampas grass. Slow-moving, velvet-lipped camels, the copper-coloured *fellahin* toiling in the fields; grey patient donkeys, tethered oxen; and the black-gowned women with their veils, their primitive gold ornaments, and the tall jars of water or baskets which they balanced so superbly on their heads. She had her first glimpse of an Arab village, of mud huts, of primitive cafés crowded with beturbaned men, wearing white or striped gowns which Martin told her were called *gallabiahs*. She watched small white herons flying low over the water, and sinister black vultures poised under the blue sky waiting to swoop down on an un-suspecting chicken or some heap of rotting bones. She had little doubt, from such sights and from the accompanying odours, that there was a disagreeable side to life in this country as well as a glamorous one.

Once Martin stopped the car and let her watch, with youthful excitement, a big P. and O. liner moving slowly and proudly through the Canal. It was crowded with people leaning over the rails. They waved to her and Phillida waved back with her scarf, and suddenly felt a lump in her throat. In spite of Martin and his niceness and her hopes of seeing Rex tonight, she wished passionately that she were on that ship going back to England and to Devon.

Martin, with a pipe stuck in the corner of his mouth, watched the varying expressions on the girl's serious young face, and ventured to guess what she was feeling. Gently he said:

'You'll get used to it out here, you know. One settles down, but I remember when I was first posted to Port Said the first time I saw a home-bound ship passing down the Canal I damn' nearly jumped in and swam out to it and said, "Hi, give me a lift!"'

Phillida sighed and smiled.

'Do you think everybody feels like that?'

'Surely you know the old poem, *"Breathes there a man with soul so dead who never to himself hath said, 'This is my own, my native land,'"* etc. But we're perverse people, you know, because when we're in England we spend a lot of time wishing that we could get out of it.'

'I never much wanted to travel,' she confessed, as Martin started up the old Morris, and they drove down the sunlit road. 'I'd like to see France and Switzerland, but I've always rather hated the idea of the East. It's Rex who loves it. He could have got a job at home if he'd tried when he left Burma, but he wanted to stay abroad.'

'Some fellows do,' said Martin.

But he fancied that this was a sudden insight into the character of Rex Maltern. He must have known that this girl had deep roots at home, and would have preferred to stay there. But he had made her come out here. Well, perhaps he thought it was good for her to broaden her outlook. Martin repeated:

'You'll get used to it.'

'Oh, I'm enjoying this drive terribly,' she said with enthusiasm, 'and you must think me awfully silly.'

'I assure you,' he smiled, 'that I do not, and that everyone you meet out here after a time wants to go home again. Only you've started that way. Well, I don't mind telling you that I'd give my soul to change this road for one of those twisting turning ones over Exmoor for instance. Or do you happen to know North Devon at all ... that lovely road that winds round between Dulverton and Exbridge, overlooking the Exe Valley ... on the borders of Somerset?'

'Oh!' exclaimed Phillida, 'of course I know it. My father used to stay at the Dulverton Arms when the mayfly was up. He was mad about fishing.'

'I like it myself,' said Martin, 'and there's many a time when I've stayed at the Dulverton Arms, and many a good trout I've landed there. Yes, I'd give a lot to exchange all the things one can do out here – sailing and swimming and tennis all the year round and so forth – for one of those soft cloudy afternoons in Dulverton when you put on a

71

pair of waders and stand in the middle of the stream and watch an unsuspecting fish rise to the fly you have thrown. Then with two or three speckled beauties in your bag, you go back to the pub and have a couple of beers and a pipe, and a chat with that nice fellow in the tap. And later in the oak-beamed dining-room – roast beef and Yorkshire pudding, and apple tart, and...'

'Oh, don't!' Phillida's voice interrupted on an imploring note.

He gave her a sidelong glance and laughed.

'There you are! You see how homesick *I* am!'

'You've drawn such a wonderful picture of it. You've made me think of Daddy ... he simply couldn't wait for his fishing holidays.'

Martin said:

'My father was rather keen on dryfly fishing too. He's dead now. But while he was still alive, and after my mother died, we used to spend most of our holidays in Scotland. The old man liked to kill a salmon, and we stayed in Ayrshire with my Aunt Kate, my father's sister. One of the angels of this world is Aunt Kate. She married a Mackay – a grand old laird. They have an estate in Ayrshire. The old laird joined his forefathers just before the war, but Aunt Kate's still there. She never had any children but she's sort of adopted me. I'm more of a son than

72

a nephew. She's crazy about her home – Killoun Castle – and I am, too. It is an isolated spot up on top of a hill. It's got all the romance of Scotland still clinging to it, and they don't seem to have been touched by the war up there. I used to go back on leave and feel that I was still living in a world in which there was no such thing as an atomic bomb, and very nice too!'

It was Martin's turn to talk and Phillida's to listen. She had a vivid imagination and she felt she could almost see the grey old castle standing on the summit of that hill, half hidden by tall trees ... the broad bubbling waters of the river running at the foot of the hill ... and the old laird in his kilt, teaching the young Martin, home from sea, how to fish for salmon, and of the battles royal they used to have with the great leaping fish.

How nice it all sounded! And no wonder Martin – if he was that sort of man – fretted in a shore job at Port Said! How she wished that Rex felt that way ... and that his one desire was to go back to a day's fishing in the old country! But it wasn't. One thing that she remembered most poignantly about Rex was his thirst for travel and ill-concealed contempt for English life. But hastily she trod on these thoughts. It was disloyal to want to change Rex. She had fallen in love with him just as he was and she mustn't want him to be different.

They came to Ismailia. Once they had passed the big camp, which Martin told her was for the Indian troops out there, they reached the Sweet Water Canal – then a small town of broad pleasant roads flanked by green trees; French-looking villas surrounded by gardens that were vivid with flowers. English flowers – roses, stocks and marigolds. And in contrast, long avenues of small graceful palm trees, and the violent cerise of magenta of the bougainvillaea, tumbling in a cascade of colour wherever Phillida's gaze turned.

'Oh, it's a *lovely* place!' she exclaimed.

He nodded. He wasn't going to depress her by telling her how soon the 'loveliness' would pall. That she would soon get tired of it, because the life here was so limited. He would let her enjoy the beauty of the place, which was indeed, at first sight, intoxicating. He explained to her that these fine villas with their exotic gardens belonged to employees of the Suez Canal Company – many of them French or English pilots who brought the great ships through the Canal. The place was, in fact, largely populated by Europeans, although there was an extensive Arab quarter.

He turned into the one main shopping street known as the Negrelli. Phillida looked with interest down the long, narrow, crowded street. The shoppers were a cosmopolitan crowd – a mixture of all races, with a large sprinkling of khaki; and suntanned, hatless girls wearing essentially English clothes – obviously 'the wives', some of them pushing prams, or holding small children by the hand. Phillida smiled when she saw them; they were so *unmistakably* English, and a contrast to the local beauties, who were ultra-smart, sleek-haired, heavily made-up.

'You'll find every type here,' Martin told her. 'Egyptian, Syrian, Maltese, and a mix-up of the lot.'

Phillida was looking at the shops now. She had never seen so many beautiful shoes and bags – such glittering window displays – everything that had been unobtainable in England for so long, and all without coupon restrictions. As for the chocolate … she just had to make Martin stop and let her go into one of the shops and buy some sweets – a whole *pound*, and she could have had more. She made Martin smile by her enthusiasm when she displayed the box to him.

How young she was, he thought, and how completely unspoiled. Rex Maltern had something very precious here … and it was to be hoped that he appreciated it.

It was nearing four o'clock when they reached a pleasant green square surrounded by a succession of low-built bungalows with covered arcades in front, through which one could walk in the shade. On one corner of this square stood a more imposing building in front of which Martin stopped the old car. With interest, Phillida looked at the brass plate which bore an inscription in three languages.

'*La Cercle* ... in other words, the French Club,' announced Martin.

At once Phillida felt at home. Rex had rarely forgotten to mention in those short notes of his that he 'had been down to the French Club for a drink'. He had always said that he patronised the bar here rather than the N.A.A.F.I. Officers' Club, which was farther out of the town on the Suez Canal road. She was surprised to find that she was quite cold when she entered the Club beside Martin. He saw her little shiver and said: 'Yes, it's early in the year yet – the Egyptians still call this winter. And after sundown it can be very cold, so be warned and carry a coat with you for another month, after which you'll find it a good deal warmer and more settled.'

'Ah,' said Phillida, with a little laugh. 'And beware of tummy attacks, too. I know all about "gippy tummy" – Rex has had it. It's the sort of colic the English get out here, isn't it, and you have to be very careful of chills.'

Martin bowed with mock solemnity.

'You are well instructed. Allow me to add

that you might get this well-known malady not only through cold but food. You want to watch out for raw salads that aren't properly washed, or too much fruit, which no doubt you will want to eat, having had none for years.'

'I'll remember and try not to be greedy,' she laughed.

They had entered a large bright room in which there was a ping-pong table. Through tall French windows Phillida caught a glimpse of a pleasant courtyard full of small shady trees, and in the centre a smooth stone dance floor which looked exciting.

'Yes, they dance out of doors in the hot weather,' Martin continued with his course of instruction, 'but not as a rule until the end of May.'

Now they passed through into the Club proper, which had a bar at one end, and was full of small tables and wicker chairs. To Phillida this all looked rather vast and unfriendly. With its many doors and French windows and stone floor the atmosphere struck chill. There was to come a time when she was not only to grow accustomed to this place but even attached to it. But looking at it for the first time, today, she found it strange, and a sad contrast to Gamma's homely little cottage. She was filled with a sense of dismay. Was it really here, in a place like this, that she must spend her spare time with Rex? Must she, who more than most girls dreaded meeting strangers and disliked new surroundings, become a Club habitué? What an awful thought!

There were few people here at this time of the afternoon. One or two French couples and two officers of the Egyptian Army, with khaki uniform and picturesque tarbooshes, sat drinking Turkish coffee. It was all very bright and white and spotlessly clean. Several waiters moved busily around; a Sudanese *suffragi,* a waiter with an ebony-black face and amiable smile, all of whom seemed to know the tall Naval officer and welcomed him with a salute and the word '*Saïda*' (the Egyptian greeting), to which Martin replied. He was often here. It was his custom, he told Phillida, to drive to Ismailia to many of the pleasant concerts which were given by a German Prisoner of War band, and he had friends, also living in Ismailia, with whom he dined regularly at this Club.

Now a tall, broad-shouldered man wearing a grey suit came towards them. Martin whispered:

'Here comes George who runs the Club.'

Phillida was introduced. The big debonair Greek had a charming smile and a way of making the members of the Club feel at ease. He put Phillida at her ease very quickly too. When he heard her name, he thought a moment and then said:

'I believe I know Captain Maltern, madame.'

'Oh, do you?' exclaimed Phillida eagerly. 'Oh, do tell me...'

George thought again.

'He has dark eyes and is very vivacious, is he not, madame?... I think he wears the badge of the Midland Regiment.'

'Yes, yes, that's my husband!'

George bowed. He looked even more thoughtful, but said no more. He was discretion itself. Phillida added:

'Oh, do you think he'll be in here tonight?'

'I have not seen him for a few days, madame ... but he comes often.'

Phillida turned to Martin with that hopeful devoted look in her grey eyes which he found so touching.

'Then if he's back from leave, I know he will, I feel that he will turn up.'

To himself Martin Winters said:

'I really think I shall murder this fellow if he doesn't.'

Then began the essential task of finding somewhere for Captain Maltern's newly arrived wife to stay.

George was grave. Ismailia was packed, he said. He knew that the Y.W.C.A. hadn't a room because he had just tried for another lady. There was not a room in the Ismailia Palace Hotel or the King George. The English *Pension* was full. But he would do anything to oblige Lieutenant-Commander Winters, who was always so delightful and, in George's opinion, a fine example of the best type of English Naval officer. He was not quite sure that he could say the same about Captain Maltern. But that was not his affair. He would like, however, to help the very young-looking, fair-haired wife of the Captain.

'If you'll give me an hour, I think I know somebody who might help. It is essential for madame to go where she will be properly looked after, especially while she is alone. Anyhow, I will do my best.'

Phillida said that she thought it would be only for one night because she was sure that Rex had fixed something as a permanency.

George left them. The cheerful little black waiter whom everybody called 'Hassan' was told to bring tea for two. Then Martin and Phillida sat down to the second meal they had had together that day.

At the end of the hour, faithful to his word, George reappeared. He had found a room that madame could have for tonight or longer if she required it. A double room in a villa in the French quarter – that nice green flower-filled part of Ismailia through which Phillida had just been driven. The villa, he explained, belonged to a Monsieur and Mme Martial, whose family had grown up and gone away, except for one small boy, and who had rooms to spare. Mme Martial did not really like strangers in the house, but to oblige George she would take in Mrs Maltern – for the moment, anyhow.

Tea over, there was yet another journey in the old Morris for Phillida. Kind and comforting and nice though Martin was, she was beginning to feel very tired and her spirits were drooping again. She had been up since dawn when the troopship had berthed at Port Said, and reaction was setting in now – the fear that Rex would not come into his favourite club tonight for a drink and that she might have to wait another twenty-four hours for him. And she had banked so much on her reunion with Rex today. She could not bear the thought of spending the night in a strange house in a strange town. Besides, her knowledge of French was slight, and Mme Martial, according to George, did not speak any English. How difficult it all was, and so disappointing after the glorious picture Phillida had built up of her arrival in Egypt, and of being taken at once under the wing of an adoring husband. How bitterly she envied Steve Cubitt, who by now would be settling down in the Cairo *pension* with her Geoffrey.

The villa to which Martin drove her (as directed by George was in one of those quiet tree-lined avenues leading off the Rue Mohamed Ali – the broad road of the glorious flowers and palm trees flanked by the Sweet Water Canal which Phillida had admired so much when they first reached Ismailia. Now the sun had vanished. Cold and tired, Phillida sat gloomily beside Martin without speaking.

The man looked sideways at her and felt immense sympathy but knew that he could do nothing to alleviate her gloom. Only the arrival of her husband on the scene could do that.

'He's a lucky fellow,' Martin thought not for the first time.

He waited outside in the car whilst Phillida interviewed Mme Martial, who proved to be an olive-skinned dark-eyed woman with Italian blood in her, who must once have been a beautiful girl. M Martial, whom she addressed as 'Emile', was much older than she … a dapper, typical old Frenchman, with a sense of humour. He spoke broken English, and could make himself understood and interpret nicely for Phillida, who stuttered and stammered her schoolgirl French. The villa was also typically French, full of the *'meubles anciens'* of which the Martials were very proud, and which they had brought from their native France. Monsieur in his youth had worked for the Suez Canal Company. They had lived here in Ismailia for over twenty years.

Finally, after much talking and a certain

amount of misunderstanding each other, Phillida was shown into a vast bedroom, which contained a huge bed, a magnificent suite in glossy walnut, a fine Empire mirror and many gold-framed photographs of the Martial family adorning the pink-papered walls. It all seemed foreign and rather depressing to Phillida for the moment – like her first impression of the Club; she was not used to all this space, or the polished wooden floors, which were bare except for one or two beautiful rugs. Mme Martial was proud of what she called her *'belles tapis'*. The windows were shuttered. Contrary to English taste, these people seemed afraid of the sun and proud of the Stygian gloom and chilled atmosphere in which they lived.

'It is the coolest villa in Ismailia,' M. Martial said proudly, and pointed out that they faced the desert on one side from which blew a cooling breeze, even in the hottest weather. Phillida timidly suggested opening some of the shutters, but Mme flung up her hands in horror. The flies and the sun must be kept out. It was not until later in the year that Phillida realised why those who lived here grew to dread the sun for which the European visitors – starved of it – so ardently longed.

All this darkness and the complete change from the dear cheerful little cottage in Alver-combe served to increase Phillida's sense of melancholy and her immense longing for someone who knew her – whom she knew – and *for Rex.*

The Martials were very hospitable. They only let the room with breakfast, but they offered to give her an evening meal if she was too tired to go out again. This Phillida refused. She must go back to the Club and wait for Rex. Having deposited her luggage and spread one or two things on the enormous bed in her room, she said that she must rejoin the Lieutenant-Commander who was so patiently awaiting her in the car.

Madame, who was fond of a joke, darted a mischievous look at the pretty English girl from her almond-shaped eyes, then nodded her head in Martin's direction.

He was a *beau 'garçon'*, the big blond officer of the Navy, she said. Not her husband, *hein?* Then when Phillida said no, that she was married to an Army man and that she hoped he would join her tonight, Madame said *'Bien'*, and that there would be plenty of room for both.

Driving back to the French Club, Martin Winters looked at the girl's downcast young face.

'Not up to expectations?' he asked.

'Oh yes – they're awfully nice – I'm sure I shall be comfortable. It's wonderful of you to have helped me to find that room!' she said.

But he heard a suspicious tremor in her voice and was aghast. The poor kid was just so homesick it was pathetic, he thought. What an idiot that fellow Maltern must be not to have got some more information about her passage and made quite sure that he *did* meet her. Altogether a poor show.

And now what could he do for the poor little thing – who looked so like Bridget that it had wrung his heart – except offer to stay and look after her a bit longer?

'We've had two good meals – let's have a third and dine together,' he said cheerfully. 'That is if you're not sick of the sight of me.'

Phillida conquered the most ridiculous desire to weep, and managed a laugh.

'Of course I'm not. You've been simply marvellous and I want Rex to meet you.'

She meant it.

She was, indeed, grateful to Martin for all he had done for her since she had set foot on Egyptian soil. But even his kindness and knowing that he would stay with her for dinner could not really cheer her up. She was beginning to nurse a secret fear that Rex – on this the last night of his leave – might stay in Cairo and not come back to Ismailia at all. Which meant that after Martin left her she would have to go back alone to that big cold bedroom, and feel utterly cut off from everything and everybody she had ever known.

5

It was seven o'clock.

Martin Winters had ordered a table for dinner at the Club. Now he sat up at the bar with Phillida. He was enjoying his customary pink gin, but the girl had refused everything he suggested except tomato juice. She did not drink; she did not smoke. It all seemed in keeping with her character. He wondered how she would get on out here where everyone – including the women – did a good deal of both drinking and smoking.

And still Rex Maltern had not arrived.

Martin surreptitiously watched Phillida's demure head turn continually towards the door. It was as well, he thought grimly, that he was not a chap out for 'fun and games' with a pretty married woman who had as much freshness and quaint charm as this one. Phillida was wholeheartedly in love with that husband of hers. Yet he was neither bored nor annoyed because she seemed unable to concentrate on what he was saying. The question was – would Maltern turn up? Martin was beginning to feel doubtful.

Phillida secretly shared those doubts. While she sipped her tomato juice and talked in a desultory fashion to Martin, she was in a veritable panic of anxiety in case Rex failed to visit the Club tonight after all.

The place was filling up. All the stools at the bar were now occupied – mostly by men in the Army and Air Force. Martin had told her that there were many big R.A.F. stations in the district and a large number of outlying Transit Camps.

Many inquisitive and admiring looks were thrown in Phillida's direction. She was a newcomer, and prettier than the average girl, but she looked through the men who stared at her in a blind sort of way. There was only one face, one figure, that she wanted to see.

She heard Martin say: 'Would you forgive me for a moment if I go and say a word to a fellow over there?'

'Of course,' said Phillida.

He moved across the room and joined another man in Naval uniform. Phillida's gaze followed the tall lanky figure. She thought miserably:

'What a dear he is and how awful I'm being … he must think me so dull and uninteresting … but I just *can't* be gay tonight!'

Next to her a red-haired girl in her late twenties sat drinking a cocktail and eating potato chips. She had a great deal of mascara on her lashes and a big, vividly red mouth. She eyed Phillida for a moment, then said:

'Filthily cold tonight, isn't it?'

Phillida blinked and laughed.

'Good heavens! I think it's quite warm, though I admit when I first came here it struck chill.'

The red-head dug her hands in the pockets of a grey flannel coat, under which she wore a yellow polo-necked sweater.

'Well, I'm frozen. But then my blood's getting thin, I've been out here two years. You're new, aren't you?'

'Yes, I only landed this morning at Port Said.'

The red-haired girl grimaced.

'Straight out from the old country, eh? And I bet you've had a rotten winter with queues and coupons and everything freezing up. I hate England. Unluckily for me, my husband's being demobilised and we go home in March, but I'd like to stay here for the rest of my life.'

Wide-eyed, Phillida looked at her.

'Would you really? I didn't want to come out a bit, except that my husband is here. I like it at home.'

The other woman drained her glass then pushed it across the counter to the bartender.

'The same again,' she said. She offered a packet of cigarettes to Phillida, who refused, and lit one herself.

Frankly, Phillida did not like this type. She had met it in her Service career ... the type of woman who could drink and smoke as much as a man, enjoy a pub crawl, tell racy stories, was never without a cigarette between her lips, was smart in a way, and yet always looked rather dirty, with a smudge of rouge on the side of her mouth, or chipped varnish on her nails, or a stain on her dress.

The red-head continued to talk to Phillida in a confiding fashion. Mainly about herself. Her name was Mrs Riccard – Victoria Riccard. Everybody called her Vic. She'd been christened Victoria, but God knew, she said, she was no Victorian. Her husband was a Flight-Lieutenant, stationed in Ismailia. In civilian life he had a job connected with 'the Dogs' (Phillida couldn't make out what sort of job – Vic talked so rapidly with a mouth full of potato chips). Frankie (that was the husband) could not wait to get back to 'the Dogs', she said. She took a dim view of that. She was having such a wizard time out here. Absolutely bang-on. Dances, parties, lots of fun in Ish, small place though it was, and last year in Heliopolis (that was a suburb of Cairo) she'd had an absolutely dizzy time. Phillida would soon stop wanting to go back to England.

Phillida, slightly bewildered, listened and made one or two polite comments, then Victoria Riccard further observed that a girl with any looks could have all the fun she wanted with the chaps. To this Phillida replied:

'But I rather like my own husband, you know.'

The red-head seemed to think this funny and laughed.

'Oh, that needn't stop you having a wizard time with somebody else. Husbands go to work, don't they?'

Phillida began to feel slightly nauseated.

'I don't think that's quite my cup of tea,' she said coldly.

Nothing daunted, Vic added:

'Well, I don't know about the Army, but you can certainly have fun in the R.A.F. We must meet for coffee some morning at Antoinette's – the cakes there are bang-on. And if any of the chaps I know come in tonight, I'll introduce you.'

Phillida melted. In spite of her vulgarity, the red-haired Vic seemed of amiable disposition, and meant to be kind. She was continuing:

'And I can't *tell* you what a hotbed of gossip it is around here. So just watch out. The place is so limited – you can't have a party with a chap and not be seen by somebody. There are one or two major shows going on now, I can promise you. Myself, I like a good time, but I wouldn't let old Frankie down. But there's a chap in our crowd – a Squadron-Leader, too, who has got himself married to a Syrian

Jewess. She's the hell of a good-looker but they run to fat and go off, and I think poor Kipps – that's the Squadron-Leader – he's always called Kipps – is beginning to rue the day. His beauty is already painting the place red, having the whale of an affair with an Army Captain. Everybody knows about it except Kipps. The girl's a – you-know-what – because she openly boasts that she's living with this Army chap, and he's got a wife in England, too and ... well ... what do you expect from a beauty Kipps picked up in Palestine?...'

She stopped. At that moment the tall figure of Martin advanced across the room towards the bar. Phillida felt relieved. Mrs Riccard's sordid gossip rather disgusted her. But Mrs Riccard was not one to be snubbed and quickly managed to get herself introduced to the good-looking Lieutenant-Commander.

'I've often seen you in here,' she said cheerfully. 'Let's all have a drink. I'm waiting for Frankie. He's due back from Abu Sieur any moment.'

Phillida and Martin eyed each other significantly, but there was no way out. The gay Mrs Riccard was an expert gatecrasher. Sheer politeness forced Martin to pay for the drinks she ordered.

At that moment Mrs Riccard, glancing over her shoulder, suddenly gave Phillida a violent nudge.

'I say – just out of interest,' she said in a loud whisper, 'here comes that Syrian girl I was telling you about and the chap she's living with. Poor Kipps is in Palestine for a fortnight, so Rebecca is making hay. Everyone knows she and the Captain have been in Cairo together this week, because he's on leave. I must say he's a smasher – I don't blame her for falling for him – but it's bad luck on his wife...'

The sibilant whisper died away. Mrs Riccard added:

'I say, what's the matter ... are you ill or something?'

Martin looked sharply at Phillida. The girl had gone dead white – so white that she looked as though she were going to faint. Her large grey eyes were staring at the 'Army Captain' and his companion, who were sauntering slowly towards the bar.

Martin, who had heard all that the singularly indiscreet and unattractive Mrs Riccard had been saying, felt a sudden thrill of horror. *Good lord, surely it couldn't be* ... but yes, it was ... for Phillida, tightly gripping the side of her stool with both hands, and with an expression which he was not to forget for a long time, said in a small dead voice:

'How extraordinary! Here comes ... my husband.'

Martin tried to answer but could not. He

took another quick look over his shoulder at the approaching pair; the good-looking young Englishman who wore a grey pin-stripe suit, and the rather plump Jewess who was with him.

Rebecca wore a short skirt which showed a lot of shapely leg. Her shoes had very high heels. She had a short white fur coat over her shoulders, and a green chiffon scarf around her neck. Martin recognised her. He had often seen her about the place with an R.A.F. chap. Obviously she would run to fat in time, but now, in her early twenties, she was strikingly attractive, with huge brown eyes, magnificent lashes, an olive skin and sleek black hair cleverly dressed into a very high Edwardian 'bang' ... hair as sleek and black as a raven's wing. She wore large green earrings which matched her scarf. She was laughing up at the handsome young man beside her. He had obviously just said something to amuse her.

Victoria Riccard, very red in the face, gave Phillida a look of real dismay.

'Is he your *husband* ... Rex Maltern?'

'Yes,' said Phillida in the same dead voice.

Mrs Riccard choked over her drink and hurriedly set down her glass.

'I say! I couldn't be more sorry. I *have* put my foot in it.'

'Yes, you have,' Martin answered for Phillida in a low, furious voice.

Mrs Riccard stammered:

'Oh, but ... I dare say I am mistaken ... you know what these rumours ar ... I don't suppose there's anything in it. Oh lord! how could I guess that he was *her* husband?...' and she slid off her stool and walked rapidly away – anxious to make herself scarce.

Martin could willingly have murdered her. Ye gods! What a thing to have happened ... what an atrocious thing! Why the hell had he ever left Phillida's side? It was just that he had been trying to get that chap on the 'phone for days and wanted to talk shop. And he had never dreamed that Phillida would be made the victim of a coincidence like this! A catastrophic one. Damn that red-haired female for pouring her poison out without bothering to find out to whom she was speaking, thought Martin savagely. And now he knew why Maltern hadn't been there at Port Said to meet his wife. Damn *him*, too!

Now Rex Maltern saw the slim grey-eyed girl, with the Jaeger coat over her shoulders, her fair hair in that familiar snood, and the pale, serious young face. And he stared at her as though at an apparition, his jaw dropping. For a fleeting moment he was completely dumbfounded, unable to move or speak. Then he gave a convulsive swallow. With the red blood flushing his tanned handsome face, he made a somewhat theatrical rush forward, both arms extended.

'Phil! Good lord! Of all the staggering surprises...!'

He broke off, shaking his head as though he couldn't think of anything more to say. Phillida faced him equally dumbfounded. But her heart beat in a painful sort of way. She was so confused and horrified by the naïve and tactless bombshell that a perfect stranger had exploded at her feet, her brain refused to act normally. She only knew that the red-haired Mrs Riccard had accused Rex, her husband, of being the lover of this girl whom he had brought into the Club with him. Her impression of the said girl was equally confused. Usually cool and observant, if anybody had asked her at this moment what Rebecca was like, she could only have said that she had enormous eyes, looked rather like a cheap copy of a Hollywood film star, and was flashily dressed.

And deep down inside Phillida the voice of her heart kept repeating:

'It isn't true ... it isn't true ... it *mustn't* be true...'

Now she felt Rex's hands, rather hot and moist, gripping hers. She heard him speak again:

'What a *marvellous* surprise!... Phil darling ... where in the name of all that's holy did you spring from?'

She made an effort to answer:

'I arrived this morning ... I cabled you...'

'This morning!' repeated Rex Maltern, blankly. 'Then the cable's probably in my office. I haven't been back ... I've been on leave in Cairo...'

'Yes,' said Phillida, 'I know.'

'How did you know?'

Nothing would have induced her to tell him there and then what Vic had said. She replied that another Captain at G.H.Q. had told her that he was on leave in Cairo. She had telephoned to Fayid from Port Said. Lieutenant-Commander Winters had helped her. He had been so very kind ... Rex must thank him...

Stammering, and with two hectic little flushes on both cheek-bones, Phillida now turned to Martin and introduced the two men. For the fraction of a moment she caught the full gaze of Martin's very blue eyes. They looked grave and compassionate. She wanted to sink through the floor. *He had heard.* Of course he had heard what that vile red-haired girl had just said. Pride came to the fore. Some of the confusion lifted ... the first acute feeling of dismay in Phillida died down. She must not allow a mere stranger like Martin to imagine that she believed this monstrous allegation against her husband. She must pass it all off as a joke. Whatever she felt, whatever her suspicions might be, they must not be made public.

She saw Rex and Martin shaking hands.

96

Rex said, with the same touch of exaggeration:

'Thanks a million, sir, for looking after my wife.'

'I was glad to be of use,' Martin said coldly.

And he knew in that moment that he disliked Rex Maltern at sight. He was more sorry for the little Phillida than he could say. He admired the courage with which she was trying to pass this thing off. She was actually laughing now.

'You are an old pig, Rex ... enjoying yourself in Cairo and letting your poor better half land in Egypt alone and terrified. I don't know what I would have done without my Naval escort ... and we only met by chance...' (More laughter ... an appealing glance at Martin as much as to say: *It's all right, I don't believe a word of it ... and you needn't either.*)

But Martin Winters believed every word of the gossip that had poured from the red-haired female's lips. Two things convinced him of it. One – the quick significant look which he had intercepted between Rex and the Syrian girl just now ... a warning look from Rex ... a knowing one from her ... and the other – the concrete fact that he had often seen Rex Maltern in this Club with this very girl. He recognised them both. Maltern was a good-looker and no doubt fascinating to women, but he was pretty much of a bounder. What in heaven's name had induced that shy flower of a girl to have married him? Perhaps a matter of contrasts … people married their opposites … and she had been lonely after the tragedy of her parents' death. Yes, it wasn't really difficult to understand.

Rex was now introducing Rebecca to the circle.

'This is Becki … her husband, Kipps, Squadron-Leader Rendledon, is a great pal of mine… Becki … isn't this grand? … my wife's actually got here at last…'

Now Rex had his arm around Phillida's shoulders. Her slight body was trembling. He did not notice it. He was looking at Rebecca. Her huge black eyes were brilliant with anger, however. With a pretty foreign inflection, but speaking good English, she said that she was 'enchanted' to meet Madame Maltern, then shook hands with the tall fair Englishman, the Lieutenant–Commander. But her eyes were only for Rex. Her big scarlet mouth turned down at the corners. And Maltern thought:

'This is a nice mess … for crying out loud, what the hell did Phil want to turn up like this without warning, blast it!'

Phillida said:

'We … must all have dinner together.'

She was giggling now, in a rather hysterical way. She could not stop trembling. She was glad of Rex's arm holding her. Blindly she looked at him. He was just as vividly good-looking as ever ... more deeply sunburned ... that was all. All the old memories rushed back on her ... memories of their first love and brief passionate honeymoon. And yet he was a stranger. A man whom she did not know at all, whose arm supported her, at this moment, and who called her his wife. There were three long years between them ... three years in which he had lived a life about which she knew nothing.

Martin's voice intervened:

'I don't think I'll stay for dinner, if you don't mind. Now your husband's turned up, Phillida, and I know you're safe and sound, I think I'd better get back to Port Said. I'm quite sure, after all this time, you'd like to dine alone, you two...'

He said those words rather grimly, for the benefit of the black-eyed Mrs Rendledon. He caught the resentful look she flickered at him through her magnificent lashes. Her physical good looks left him unmoved. He had absolutely no interest in her or her type. The Middle East was full of such women and he wondered if this one had married the wretched Squadron-Leader for the sake of a British passport rather than for love.

They were all speaking at once now. Phillida timidly begging him to stay ... Rex (rather too heartily) endorsing her suggestion, Rebecca sullenly announcing that after a drink she was going back to her flat for dinner.

In the end they all stayed to dinner. Martin because he had no real excuse for abandoning the table he had already reserved; although he had little wish to remain and watch Phillida struggling rather like a butterfly that a cruel schoolboy had pinned, while still alive, to a board. And he hotly resented for her sake the fact that the Syrian girl remained, looking at and laughing with Rex in a familiar way that spoke volumes. Whilst for Phillida the whole meal was an agony. It was, in fact, one of the most distressing parties she had ever been forced to attend. And so different was it to the magical *tête-à-tête* she had dreamed of with Rex on their first night in Egypt – their first together for so long – that it was almost laughable.

Everybody seemed uncomfortable and ill at ease. There was a lot of laughter and joking and frivolous conversation in general but with it an undercurrent of unease and furtive looks, one from another. Rex had said at the beginning:

'This dinner is on me, folks... Where's George?... George, we must have a bottle of champagne to celebrate my wife's arrival...'

And later, he said:

'What a damn' shame old Kipps isn't here

to join in … isn't it, Becki?'

The Syrian girl twisted her red lips and agreed.

'Oh yes, it *ees* a pity!'

Martin Winters sat back and looked and listened and thought: 'They're both lying…'

And he had Rex privately taped now as a hypocrite as well as a bounder. Nevertheless he was 'doing the grand host' … the champagne wasn't enough … and he ordered wine as well, and liqueurs after the meal… He kept up a running flow of conversation with his wife. (He did most of the talking, Martin observed.)

'What sort of voyage did you have, darling?… Can't think why that last letter of yours didn't reach me saying that you expected your passage… As for me being on leave when your cable came … it was the *bottom* … and it's only by the grace of God that I came in here tonight… I nearly stayed in Cairo, then decided to look in at the Club here and see if old Kipps had got back from the Holy Land. But they told me at the door that he wasn't there, so I went round and fetched Becki along for a meal…'

(More lies, decided Martin.)

He listened as Rex went on chattering. One glib phrase and excuse after another poured from his lips. Did Phillida believe him? Martin had his doubts. She still had that awful wounded look in those soft grey eyes. He found it pathetic. But she appeared on the surface to be content, and she said things like:

'Marvellous to be here... Egypt's so wonderful... You're looking so well, Rex ... you haven't changed a bit...'

But she would have none of the champagne. Rex, with a glass in his hand, turned to Martin.

'I can't make my wife take to drink. It's something for me to live up to, you know, this teetotal business. But she'll have to learn to sink a bit in this country, won't she, sir?'

'I don't think it's strictly necessary,' said Martin. Then, in order not to appear ungracious, added, 'Though, speaking for myself, I don't think a little alcohol does anybody any harm.'

'Trust the Navy,' said Rex, 'Ha! ha! ha!'

Everybody laughed. Phillida too. But her head was beginning to swim with fatigue. She was so overwrought and strained, she hardly knew how to get through the long-drawn-out meal. Would it never end? Used as she was to rations, to one supper dish with Gamma in the cottage, she could not have tackled this dinner, course after course, with ease even had she been in the best of moods. But on this particular occasion she had no appetite. She felt rather sick. All nerves, of course, she told herself;

but she did feel so very strange. She could not *believe* that she was actually here with Rex again. He was drinking more champagne than anybody else. Now and then he put out a hand and pressed her knee, or murmured something about how 'thrilled' he was to have her here.

'But you really could have bowled me over like a ninepin when I saw you here at the bar this evening,' he exclaimed. 'And oh, lord … what about a room for you? I haven't got anything fixed. I'm still leading a bachelor life in a tent. I've been looking out for a flat here for us like the one Kipps and Becki have got, but nothing has turned up, and you see, I thought I had another few weeks…' He broke off.

And once again Martin intercepted the look that passed between Maltern and the Syrian girl, and he was more than ever convinced that what Vic Riccard had said was the truth.

He was horribly sorry for Phillida.

It might have been Bridget sitting there … little Bridget whom he had loved so much, and that she should have been hurt like this was unthinkable.

Phillida began to explain to Rex how and where she had found a room in Ismailia.

Martin was glad when that dinner ended and he could get away with the suitable excuse that he mustn't leave it too late to drive back to Port Said. The lights on the old Morris were not too good; and it was a darkish night.

He looked at Rebecca.

'Perhaps I can give you a lift home, Mrs Rendledon?'

She gave him a sulky look through her lashes and showed glistening white teeth.

'Thank you, but no ... my flat ees just a moment's walk...'

Martin inclined his head with cold courtesy, then turned to Phillida. She looked so white and exhausted that his heart ached for her. Gently he took her hand.

'Well, good night, I've so enjoyed meeting you. I'm quite sure we shall run into each other again. Anyhow, you and your husband must dine with me ... we must have a return of this magnificent party... I expect you're on the 'phone ... most of the Canal Company have telephones. I'll look up the Martials' number and ring you.'

Rex put an arm round his wife.

'Very decent of you, sir, and thanks again for doing my job for me. I'm most grateful and it was a tremendous piece of good luck that Phil ran into you.'

Phillida slowly drew her fingers away from Martin's. How tall he was, she thought dully. She had thought Rex tall, but Martin towered over him. And suddenly she was sorry that he was going. Going and taking with him that sense of security that he had given her all day. Why should she feel that she was no longer secure ... that she was afraid ... more afraid than she had been when she got off the ship and found herself alone in Port Said? ... such an awful desolate sinking feeling; yet her own husband stood here with his arm around her.

She watched Martin go out of the Club. Rex gave a long sigh.

'That's better. What an old stick that fellow Winters is! Puts up the hell of a formal atmosphere.'

Phillida said quickly:

'He was awfully kind to me.'

Rex laughed.

'Oh, don't run away with the idea that lonely men go round Egypt being "kind" for the sake of kindness, my dear Phil. I dare say Winters was only too pleased to be of use to a pretty blonde.'

Phillida flushed. That sounded rather cheap. It put Martin's chivalrous conduct to her all through the day in an unpleasant light, which instinctively she resented. Rex added:

'I can see you haven't changed...' He turned to Rebecca ... 'My wife's full of high ideals ... always thinks the best of everybody. She's got a lot to learn, and she'll soon put Winters where he belongs ... on a plane with all the other fellows out here who are trundling around looking for a girl-friend. Don't you agree, Becki?'

Rebecca shrugged her shoulders. She was bored. Rex added:

'Let's have another drink.'

'You have such good ideas, Rex,' said Becki, now flashing her huge eyes at him.

But suddenly Phillida put her arm through Rex's, and said:

'If you don't awfully mind I'd like to go home. I'm terribly tired.'

Rex said:

'Oh, you want a drink ... I always tell you that... You wouldn't feel tired if you had a double whisky. Come on, let's go up to the bar... Becki wants one, anyhow...'

Then Phillida experienced one of her rare moments of anger ... sheer ice-cold anger which shook her from head to foot. She repeated:

'I'm sorry, but I'd like to go home.'

Rebecca stared at her, shrugged, and looked bored again. Rex coloured slightly, then he, too, shrugged his shoulders.

'O.K. I'll get the bill. I expect you *are* tired. You landed pretty early. Now look here ... will you take this cash? Pay the bill for me, darling. Let me leave you in George's care for a moment. I must run Becki back. She can't go home alone. And there isn't an inch of room in the car for three of us. I exchanged the Studebaker for an M.G. two-seater while I was on leave, you know. One of the Midgets. You just can't squeeze in a third.'

Phillida looked at him. It was so like Rex. The Rex of the old days. Always mad about cars and always changing them. He had told her once that the Alvis was the only 'bus' he had been faithful to for more than six months.

Perhaps his was not a very faithful nature. Perhaps Mrs Riccard's gossip was founded on fact and Rex and Rebecca ... but Phillida's thoughts carried her no further ... she felt sick.

Rebecca, with rather obvious rapidity, accepted Captain Maltern's offer to drive her home – an offer which, when it had come from Martin Winters a few moments ago, she had refused.

Now her red lips parted in a dazzling smile and she was in a better humour. She extended to Phillida a small plump hand on the third finger of which there was a colossal imitation ruby.

'I see you again...' she said.

Phillida rose and forced herself to smile back and shake hands with the Syrian. Rex was singing facetiously under his breath.

'"*Whenever Spring breaks through again*" ... we've gone all Noël Coward ... *Bitter Sweet* and all that... By the way, Phil, you must hear my new piece of swing. We must get a flat with a piano. I'm on the track of one actually... Hi, George!' he hailed the manager, who was passing by. 'Keep an eye on my wife. I'm just running Mrs Rendledon home...'

George bowed. His face expressed nothing, but perhaps he felt a little sorry for the newly arrived wife of the Captain, because in his gentle and courteous way he asked her to sit down again and have some more coffee.

Dumbly Phillida shook her head. She sat there clutching two or three of the dirty Egyptian pound notes which Rex had pressed into her hand. She was watching Rex and Rebecca walk away. George, to distract her, pointed out the big coloured map of the world which formed an amusing mural on the wall behind the bar. He was explaining to her about the design ... indicating the *'vin du pays'* of all nations.

But Phillida could hardly see the painting, for her eyes were blind with tears.

6

Rex Maltern left his wife alone in the French Club a good deal longer than he had intended to. He had that sort of character; in the first instance his intentions were good, but invariably trailed off in a less worthy direction. He was not wholly bad. He had a lot of endearing qualities. He was generous, and anxious to please, by virtue of the fact that it satisfied his ego to be thanked and appreciated. But his nature was a shallow one and his egotisms and vanity on occasions led him to sink to measures which – having sunk to them – he really deplored and which afterwards made him abashed. But he never found it easy to give up something he wanted.

Once he had wanted Phillida. So deeply had her fair and virginal beauty combined with that touch of prude in her attracted him that he had resorted to marriage in order to get her. And he had lived with her such a short time that he had not had a chance to be bored, although at times there was a quality of cool dignity in her which irritated him, and he had felt deep down that it was an irritation which might increase were they to see a lot of each other. She could never really 'thaw' or, as he called it, 'let herself go' sufficiently to satisfy him. But so quickly had they been separated by the war that he had left her believing that he had found the right wife, and chafing against their enforced separation.

But year by year the memory of her attraction for him had faded. His emotions were on the surface. For Rex, propinquity was the thing. It was not in him to understand or experience a deep abiding love for any human being. He was too impatient to wait for anything long, and too wrapped up in himself to bother much about the feelings of others. (That was a side he had inherited from his father.) And he had grown up to know his mother as a spoilt selfish woman, so that love and sacrifice had never really come within his sphere.

He had been as much in love with Phillida as his capacity permitted. But he had been away from her too long. There had been hectic exciting leaves during his Burma tour during which he returned to the old status of the attractive bachelor. Most women 'fell for' Rex Maltern. He had a way with him and the love and attention of pretty women, and drink, were sheer necessities to Rex – stimulants which he could not do without.

Within six months of his marriage he was involved in a scandal over a pretty nurse in one of the Base hospitals to which he was sent with bad fever. It resulted in the nurse being sent back to England in disgrace, and Rex was severely reprimanded. In a vague way he had been sincerely sorry that he had helped to ruin the life of a nice girl to whom he had made passionate love without even telling her that he was a married man. But he soon forgot her. And once having broken his vows to Phillida, he found it easy to go on breaking them. He devoured her sweet and devoted letters eagerly only for a time. The poor little thing missed him and was so lonely ... he was sorry for her. And each time she wrote *'Come back to me soon'*, he formed a new resolution to be loyal to his Phil and to love and protect her always. Then shortly afterwards he would meet somebody else ... and another pair of long-lashed eyes or shapely ankles beguiled him from the path of virtue again.

After the episode of the nurse came leave in India, and another scandal over the wife of a Government official ... an unhappily married and very attractive woman ten years older than himself. He got himself into a lot of trouble over Irene, because his own passion was short-lived and hers had all the frenzied persistence of a woman who knew that she was fast reaching an age when she would no longer be able to attract men. Irene pursued Rex remorselessly and he was nearly drawn into a divorce case as her co-respondent. But he was lucky. He had really had a lot of luck in his life, he decided, one way or another. The injured husband chose that psychological moment to go down with some fatal and obscure disease which carried him into the Better World from which he had no jurisdiction over his faithless wife or her reluctant lover.

And that was also the moment for Rex to make a getaway, which he did rapidly – disappearing once more into the Burma jungle. It was the last the lamenting and widowed Irene heard of him.

There were others ... not necessarily grave scandals ... but lesser and lighter love affairs... In Rangoon when the war with the Japs ended, and in Cairo, once he was transferred to the Middle East.

And all the time Rex grew more estranged from the girl he had married and whom he had never really known very well. He was even sorry that he had been so crazy that summer in England as to give up his liberty. A chap really had a better time in the Army without a wife, and living apart, as he was from Phillida, there was no financial gain ... rather the reverse.

He had begun to dread going back home and being asked to settle down to a hum-drum married life. Too many of his friends – temporary officers who were demobilised, or Regulars whose tour came to an end – wrote to him, saying what a devil of a mess the old country was in. Whisky and decent food and accommodation unobtainable … cost of living high … and petrol still rationed. No, Rex decided that there was no future in England. He had only the vaguest desire to return to his wife. He saw, however, that he must make some effort to carry out his duties as a husband and put this marriage into which he had rushed on to a more concrete footing. So he had 'applied' for his wife through the official channels.

Once down in the Canal Zone, away from the attractions in Cairo, he was bored and in need of fresh excitement. He even began to look forward to seeing little Phil and setting up in a home with her. (He had quite decided not to join in the communal life in the desert camp at Fayid). He had a car … and a bit of cash. He could take a flat in Ismailia with Phil. He began to revive some of the attractive memories of his honeymoon. He was impatient for her to arrive.

And then Rebecca came into the picture.

Kipps Rendledon was the friend of a friend of Rex's. The Squadron-Leader and his wife met Rex at a dance at Abu Sieur; Kipps was then newly married. But from the very start it was a 'thing' between Rex and Becki. Kipps was a plain, fat, good-natured little man. Becki was thoroughly bored with him. Rex found that out very quickly. With his experience of women it did not take him long to discover how bored the beautiful Rebecca was. That she was greedy and worthless he also knew. But she had an extraordinary fascination for him. Other chaps out here spoke of Becki as 'good value'. Certainly he found her extremely amusing when she had a couple of cocktails. She danced divinely. She was tremendously vital. Much too vital for poor old phlegmatic Kipps, who followed her meekly around trying in vain to please her. And she treated him like dirt. But to Rex she behaved differently. He was the most handsome of the English officers she had met in the Middle East, and the most gay. She liked that touch of French blood in him ... his superb insolence, the high spirits which matched her own. They were like two live wires coming together.

Within a very short time of meeting Becki, Rex wanted her. Wanted her with that usual ruthless egoism which had no pity for her stupid and unsuspecting husband, and little respect for the girl herself. But Becki did not want respect. She was crazy about Rex as he was crazy about her ... well, it was simple ... because Squadron-Leader Rendledon's job often took him away.

The affair was at its height when Phillida arrived in Egypt.

Rex had been genuinely shocked at the

114

unexpected sight of his wife tonight. He had expected and hoped her passage would be indefinitely delayed so that he could pursue this affair with Rebecca. That supple body, those wonderful melting black eyes, the long black hair that fell about her like a cloak, her broken English, the way she could sing little German and French songs, in a husky voice, had become a fascinating habit which he could not break; which, indeed, he did not want to break. And it was so satisfying to his vanity to see the way she refused all the other fellows and was, in her fashion, faithful to him.

Now Phillida ... his wife ... was here in Ismailia. He could see there'd be the devil to pay.

Full of champagne and *bonhomie*, however, he drove Rebecca round the corner to the block of flats in which she was quartered with other R.A.F. wives. He stopped the M.G. outside the entrance, switched off the engine and began to apologise feebly for what had happened this evening.

'You know I meant it to be *our* evening, Becki, my sweet ... but what can I do? It's all very tricky.'

Becki's black eyes flashed at him in the dim light of the little car.

'You do this to upset me ... you knew she was going to be at the Club ... you think it funny, eh?'

115

'My dear, don't be absurd!' he said with a laugh. 'You must think I'm nuts. Didn't you see for yourself what a shock it was to me? And there's nothing very "funny" about walking into a club with one's girl-friend and finding one's wife ... who was supposed to be thousands of miles away.'

'You said she couldn't get a passage...' Rebecca glowered.

He put out a hand, caught one of hers and kissed the palm of it.

'M'm ... luscious perfume,' he murmured. 'What is it?'

'The last bottle you gave me,' she said sullenly. 'Jean Patou's *"Moment Suprême"*.'

Rex Maltern gave a short laugh and drew the long points of her scarlet polished nails softly across his cheek.

'"Supreme moment" all right in that Club tonight... I'm still suffering from shock, my sweet.'

'Why didn't you *know* she was coming?'

'Because, my dear, her cable went to Fayid whilst you and I were in Cairo. *Voilà!*'

Rebecca drew a deep breath.

'Now she ees here in Ismailia ... she is your wife. I hate her!'

'You needn't. Phil's very innocuous.'

Rebecca threw him a sulky look, flickering her long lashes. 'I don't know what that means.'

'Innocuous, darling ... glass of milk ...

116

whilst you ... you are like the champagne, sparkling and somewhat intoxicating.'

A suspicion of a smile dimpled at the corners of Rebecca's mouth. 'Oh! Then why you marry the glass of milk?'

Rex Maltern frowned. He had asked himself that question once or twice lately. He shrugged his shoulders.

'I was young and foolish and on a boring course in Devonshire, and I was sorry for her ... and everybody at the time was telling me to get married and settle down.'

Rebecca snuggled close to him and rubbed her cheek against his shoulder.

'And are you settling down, *mon amour?*'

She spoke in that husky provocative voice that never failed to 'get' Rex. He caught her close and kissed her throat.

'No, you know damn' well I'm not ... but it's a hellishly tricky position all the same.'

'Why you not leave her, and I'll leave Kipps and we run away,' murmured Becki.

Rex received this monstrous suggestion as though it were a tremendous joke. He roared with laughter. Becki was full of those sort of ideas.

Physically he was mad about her, and in some queer way her complete lack of morals, coupled with her *penchant* for himself, appealed to all that was worst in him. He had long since decided that playing the good and chivalrous husband to a pure

117

girl like Phillida was hard work, whereas a love affair with Rebecca was a glorious pastime. And a fellow's nerves got ragged out here... (His own were unusually bad at the moment. Probably he had been too long in the East.) One's sense of values changed; unless a fellow kept a grip on himself he could soon go to the devil. But in his way Rex was a good soldier ... he loved his job, just as he liked the goodwill and appreciation of his commanding officers. So he had done quite well since being posted to G.H.Q.

He was mad about Rebecca, but not for one moment was he prepared to start a serious scandal. And now that Phil had come out here he reckoned he must do his stuff. Besides, there was old Kipps in the background ... they had only been married three months. Becki couldn't quit him cold.

'Look here, Becki darling,' he said, 'I can't stay and talk things over with you now. I've got to get back to Phil; you understand, don't you? I'm damn' sorry about tonight, but there are just no two ways about it. As for me leaving my wife and you walking out on Kipps, well, you know that is impossible.'

Rebecca did not agree. But she was an astute young woman. For all the fact that she was only twenty-two she knew a lot about men and how to handle them. She quite saw that this was no time to tackle her handsome English Captain, but she had no intention of letting him go altogether, and in a few honeyed words told him so.

Heartily Rex agreed.

'Of course we're not going to say good-bye, angel. Phil and I are a modern couple. She's quiet but quite broad-minded and we agreed long ago to have our own pals. That Naval chap she was with ... you saw for yourself, she's not above having a boy-friend. We can still see a lot of each other. I'll fix things, you wait.'

He spoke convincingly enough. He knew perfectly well that every word he had just said about Phillida was untrue but he had to find some quick way of mollifying his Rebecca. And without bothering to think too deeply he had also rapidly decided that he would be able to carry on with this intrigue without too much difficulty. As he said to Becki, once he got Phil installed in a flat he could always get away for some reason connected with his work. Oh, it wasn't going to be as easy as it had been while they had only Kipps to contend with. But he'd fix something.

'You know that I couldn't live without you now,' he whispered, holding Rebecca very tight.

Her lips parted to meet his kiss.

It was an hour before he got away and back to the Club.

119

By this time he was a little fed up with women in general. His good humour had evaporated, and he felt annoyed because the sight of his young wife sitting there so pale and still and weary made him feel ashamed. He hated to feel ashamed.

'There's something the matter with that damn' car,' he said with a scowl. 'The ignition wants looking at. I would have been back half an hour ago except I couldn't start the damn' thing up once I'd got Becki home. Had to get a couple of Arabs to push it.'

Phillida stood up, hands in the pockets of her coat. Her head ached violently. It seemed to her years and years since she had got off that boat at Port Said this morning. Not a fraction of joy in her reunion with Rex remained. The awful things that that red-haired girl had said at the bar tonight had reduced her to a state of misery and doubt. This last hour, waiting alone for Rex to come back to her, had been the finishing touch.

She said:

'I was just going to get a taxi and go back to the villa.'

'I'm awfully sorry, Phil, but I couldn't help it, could I?'

'No, of course not.'

After the events of the evening he felt that he badly needed another drink, but had the grace to submerge this desire. He felt heroic for so doing.

'Oh well, come on, darling,' he said, putting an arm through Phillida's. 'I'm sure you must be fed up.'

'I'm so worried,' she said, 'because these people who have given us a room probably go to bed early and I'll have to wake them up.'

'Didn't you ask for a key?'

'I'm afraid not ... I imagined we'd be back earlier ... or that I would if you didn't turn up, and then Martin was waiting and...'

'Who's Martin?' interrupted Rex.

Phillida coloured.

'The Lieutenant-Commander who brought me over to Ismailia. You know!'

'Oh, I didn't know his name was Martin,' said Rex, yawning. 'Is he your latest boy-friend?'

They were walking through the Club towards the entrance. Phillida's colour deepened.

'How absurd! I only met him for the first time this morning.'

'I suppose you've got the old boy-friend tucked away somewhere in England, though?'

'No. As a matter of fact, I haven't. I don't go in for "boy-friends".'

Rex yawned again. He had forgotten what a serious, good little thing she was. But now it was all coming back ... he could see her in her W.R.N.S. uniform standing in the rain waiting for a lift ... and how after he had got to know her she had amused him with her quaintness ... and later – after their marriage – how moved he had been by her innocence ... what a sweet pupil she had been to his passionate tutoring. He began to see what a lot of harm had been done by their long separation, their lack of contact. It was the devil, really. It meant starting all over again. He didn't know what *she* felt, but he knew that *he* was three years older and wiser and a good deal more cynical than the Rex who had 'beaten it up' in the old Alvis during that course down in the West Country; the boy who had found those long walks over the cliffs and on the sands at Alvercombe with the young Phillida a satisfying way in which to pass the leisure hours. Now he really needed something a bit more sophisticated, someone like Becki to excite his rather jaded senses. He was a bit alarmed to find that the sight of Phillida left him cold; that he got as much kick out of seeing her again as he would have done a young sister. He felt rather sorry for himself ... caught in the toils of matrimony ... however, tonight he was generous enough to be sorry for her, too.

'I really am awfully sorry I wasn't at Port Said to meet you, Phil, darling,' he said. 'But it wasn't my fault, was it?'

122

'No, of course not, Rex.'

'Good thing that Naval chap was there.'

'Yes,' said Phillida in a low voice, and thought gratefully of all that Martin Winters had done for her today.

'Decent of old George to find these rooms for us.'

'I thought you'd have something fixed.'

'I didn't have a chance. I only come to Ish in the evenings or at week-ends to do a bit of sailing. I've been living in a tent in Fayid myself. But I did intend to have a flat ready for you, Phil. It's all a bit of a mess-up.'

'Yes,' she said.

She felt unutterably tired and depressed as Rex opened the door of the M.G. for her. It was a night of velvet sky, of luminous stars. A warm beautiful night such as she had never experienced before. But as far as she was concerned it might have been raining, she was so dispirited. Rex forgot about her and looked at his car.

'Hell of a nice little bus, isn't it?'

'Yes,' she said, 'awfully nice,' and had a choking desire to burst into tears.

'Do you know the way back to your French villa?' he asked, as she got into the car.

'No, I don't think so,' she said helplessly.

Rex, who would normally have received this with good humour, felt unaccountably irritated in this moment.

'Well, that's a lot of use.' He sat back in his seat, pulling out a cigarette angrily, and lit it. Phillida was almost blind with fatigue and depression. With an effort she pulled herself together.

'I ... you see, we drove there in the daylight ... but I think I might remember if you can get me on to the road that runs along the Sweet Water canal. It's a sort of bungalow right at the top there in the French quarter.'

'I don't happen to know the French quarter,' said Rex coldly. 'You haven't changed, Phil. You never did have a bump of locality.'

And then, out of sheer nerves and misery, she began to cry. Big tears rolled silently down her cheeks. Rex saw them and was immediately abashed. Damn it, the poor little thing had had a miserable reception in Egypt so far, he thought remorsefully. It was up to him to play up to her a bit; after all, he'd married her. In a way he wished to goodness he hadn't met Becki Rendledon. It had spoiled things with Phil, definitely spoiled them, and he was the first to admit it.

He threw his cigarette out of the car and quickly put an arm round Phillida's shoulders.

'Don't cry, Poppet ... we'll find the place... I'll nip in and ask George to give me directions. And do you know you haven't kissed me yet? Darling, it really is lovely to see you again.' He introduced some warmth and enthusiasm into his voice which, coupled with the use of his old pet name for her, reaped a rich reward. Phillida flung her arms around his neck and clung to him, trying to stifle her sobs.

'Oh, Rex, Rex ... darling, it's been so long ... I'm so glad to see you. Honestly I am. It was so awful not finding you at Port Said ... everything seems to have gone wrong ... and I was so looking forward to coming...'

He held her close a moment, stroking her head. The fair silken hair was like a child's, he thought ... very different from that coarse vital cloud of hair that rippled down to Rebecca's knees. And he had forgotten how slight Phillida was. Too thin, of course. Probably the poor little thing hadn't been eating enough, while he and Becki and the others were out here guzzling on the fat of the land. He felt none of the old wild passion for his wife – that seemed to have gone – but with brotherly affection he held and petted her.

'There, there, don't cry, poor little Poppet ... everything will be all right,' he said vaguely. 'Now dry your eyes and smile at me and just hang on a moment, angel, and I'll pop in and get those directions. We'll soon have you tucked up in bed and asleep. I know it's been a rotten day for you.'

She was comforted. This was the Rex she

had loved and in whom she had put her confidence. The Rex whom Gamma had thought such a 'sweet boy'. And if the passion was missing in his kiss, she was too distraught tonight to notice it, too exhausted to want anything more than tenderness. She made a tremendous effort to smother her suspicions, that sense of total loss and even horror that she had experienced when she first saw him enter the Club with this Syrian girl.

While he had gone to find George, she quickly dried her tears and dabbed some powder on her nose. When he returned, he was still feeling remorseful and ready to treat her with great kindliness, and she felt altogether better as they drove through Ismailia and the French quarter to the Martials' villa.

The Martials were waiting for them. M. Martial opened the door, called 'Sophie' to his wife, who came running out to greet the couple, and put Rex in the best of humours by telling him that their garage was empty and all ready to receive the Captain's car.

Sophie Martial's soft almond-shaped brown eyes beamed at Phillida and she said:

'You are happy now, *hein?* The husband has arrived. *Mais comme il est beau!*'

And she tactfully intimated that he was even more 'beau' than the Naval officer who had brought Mrs Maltern here earlier. Then

126

the Martials, in their hospitable fashion, invited Captain and Mrs Maltern into their private sitting-room and suggested that the Captain might like a whisky-and-soda, which Rex accepted. He was quick to win the kindly French couple by talking to them in excellent French and in particular made Madame's heart glow by the charming little flattering speeches he made to her.

Once again the exhausted Phillida sat watching drinks being poured out and thought wistfully how much she would like a cup of tea. But tea-drinking did not seem to be a habit in this country.

Madame whispered:

'He is so handsome, *très amiable, Monsieur le Capitaine.*'

'Yes, indeed,' said Phillida, but wished secretly that Rex would stop showing off and let her get settled for the night. Her eyelids were burning. She felt positively weak with fatigue. The whole day with its sequence of events had been too much for her. And after a while as though through a haze she heard the excited voices of the Martials and Rex, all gabbling French together rapidly (Phillida did not understand one word), and her head began to nod and swim again. Suddenly, as from a long way off, came Sophie Martial's voice:

'*Mon Dieu! Madame est malade...*'

And then from Rex, jumping to her side:

'I say, darling, you're not going to faint, are you?'

She dragged herself back from her haze of fatigue and whispered: 'No, no, I'm all right.'

But the kindly Sophie saw for herself that the English girl was worn out. It was she who bundled Phillida off to the big pink bedroom at once and helped her undress. Rex said that he would just 'say good night to Monsieur, and have another quick one'. And while he did so, he felt fresh remorse about Phillida. He decided that he would be extremely gentle and solicitous from now onward. She hadn't much stamina, poor little Phil – none of Becki's exciting vitality (that was a regretful afterthought). And what a mercy he had his suitcase with him – still in the car – when he and Becki got back from Cairo this evening! He'd better go to Phil now and make sure she was all right.

He met Mme Martial coming out of the bedroom.

'She is well now, *la pauvre petite ... elle est très fatiguée, c'est tout.*'

'*Bon soir et merci, Madame,*' said Rex.

'*Bon soir, Capitane.* Tomorrow I will take madame her breakfast in bed. And you?'

'I have to get off early,' he said. 'Got to be at Fayid by eight-fifteen and do a spot of work. My leave's at an end.'

'*Bien, Capitaine.* Perhaps you would like

an omelette with my husband and myself and our little son, Pierrot, who also gets up early and goes to school.'

Rex assured her that that was an excellent idea.

Whistling under his breath, he walked into the bedroom.

For a moment he blinked at the pink walls and big Empire mirror and then turned to Phillida. She looked small and desolate lying in the middle of the vast bed, her hair in two fair silky plaits. It struck him in that moment almost with a sense of shock that this wife of his was almost 'schoolgirl' in comparison with the experienced Rebecca Rendledon, although in actual years she was younger than Phil. In the light which burned over the bed Phil's face looked pale and pinched. She lay with the clothes tucked up under her chin as though she felt cold. She was, in fact, shuddering despite the fact that the Egyptian night was a good deal warmer than it had ever been at home. She was on the verge of collapse. She would have given anything for a hot-water bottle, but it was so late and Mme Martial had explained already today that the only form of heating here was primus stove in the kitchen. There was no hot water. Tomorrow there would be a hot bath – Madame would light one – but not tonight.

It had been Madame who had found the

nightgown – an old 'relic' of her trousseau, already torn and mended – and helped Phillida into it. But Phillida was too tired to care. And yet she remembered that she had bought such a lovely length of artificial silk georgette in London, and Gamma, who, despite her age, embroidered beautifully, had made her something really lovely – for the occasion of her reunion with Rex.

What a grim failure it had been! she thought wretchedly. She opened her heavy eyes and saw Rex sitting on the bed, taking off his coat. He was yawning and ran one hand through his thick hair.

'I'm whacked,' he said.

She had heard him say that so many times. She had seen him thread his fingers through his hair like that, with that quick nervous gesture. It was all coming back ... every memory of her honeymoon in England when she had been so happy with him. If only he had met her at Port Said! If only she had never met that awful Mrs Riccard in the Club or heard what she had to say! If only Rex hadn't come into the Club with Rebecca! So many 'ifs'!

Then Rex bent over her, took her two fair plaits and pulled her by them gently up into his arms.

'Poor Poppet. You're more whacked than I am. Go to sleep. I'll have to leave you early, but I'll be back as soon as I can, and we'll talk our heads off.'

She lay against him, almost too exhausted to lift her lashes.

He kissed her on the mouth. But it was like his other kisses tonight, without passion. He said:

'I'd like you to look for a flat ... see if George knows of anything going. Get Mme Martial to go round with you...'

'Yes,' whispered Phillida.

The next thing she knew was that he was in the big bed beside her and had switched out the light. He had pushed open the shutters. The bedroom was suffused with the soft milky light of a million stars. They could hear the steady chirping of the crickets.

Suddenly, desolately, she clung to him, and cried under her breath:

'Do you love me like you used to ... oh, *do* you, do you, Rex?'

'Go to sleep, Poppet,' he said.

She could not see what lay in his eyes – or in his mind. It did not seem to matter any more. She passed swiftly from that brief, impassioned desire to be loved by him into a profound slumber from which she did not awake until long after he had gone the next morning.

7

The first thing that Phillida did that next morning was to write to her grandmother. She knew that the old lady would be anxiously awaiting a letter. After all, she was all that Gamma had left in the world, and this parting had not been easy for her.

Mme Martial settled Phillida in the garden in a basket-chair, under the shade of a large mango tree, and gave her a little wicker table on which to put her writing things. Phillida had put on blue slacks and a short-sleeved jumper. She had pinned her hair rather hastily on top of her head instead of in the usual bun. She still felt tired, but it was restful in this green garden although Phillida could not quite get used to the strangeness of it – and it was so unlike the garden at Alvercombe Cottage. It had a distinctly Continental flavour, with its paved pathways and little formal beds, its big pots of ferns and fringed palms, its many funny little trees to which Phillida could not put a name. Only one, an apricot, could she recognise. The drooping grey-green leaves of the mangoes lent a tropical air to the place. The sky overhead looked incredibly blue. The sun was deliciously warm. Phillida had to put on smoked glasses.

Mme Martial had given her a good breakfast in bed, and she had been introduced to the third member of the family, the twelve-year-old schoolboy whom they called Pierrot. He had proudly displayed his somewhat scanty knowledge of the English he learnt at school, and made her laugh. He had the almond-shaped eyes of his mother and very black satiny hair which he kept brushed down with a rather powerful-smelling lotion. He was vain and self-possessed and amusing. Phillida liked him, and obviously he looked with favour on Phillida because he brought her two roses from the garden, and said proudly:

'Eenglich rose...'

Strange how those roses had given her a pang of homesickness, for they were, indeed, like the ones Gamma grew – not in January but in late June – at home.

So far, at eleven o'clock this morning, Phillida had written only a few lines about the voyage, of things out here. She just did not know what to say. The last thing she wished to do was to indicate to her grandmother that her reunion with Rex had been so bitterly disappointing. It would only distress the old lady and what could she do all that long way away? What could anybody do? One must, Phillida thought, work out

133

one's own destiny. But it seemed a sorry and ironic thing that one could never be really frank about oneself for fear of wounding the feelings of another.

What would she have written to that adored grandmother had she been able to speak the truth? She would have said:

Nothing is as I dreamed or hoped it would be... My first day in Egypt was awful... Had it not been for Martin Winters' kindness I would have been sunk. Rex has changed ... he looks the same, and all his words and actions and his personality in general are familiar. But he has changed and I don't think he is in love with me any more or that he really wanted me to come out here. Last night was a nightmare, that awful dinner with that girl Rebecca looking at Rex all the time and Rex drinking too much. I have a ghastly fear that what Mrs Riccard said has some truth in it. Am terribly anxious. I don't know what to do. I'm not very good about human relationships – not clever. This sort of thing confuses me so terribly. I don't know whether I ought to ask Rex outright whether it's true about Rebecca, and see what he has to say, or keep quiet about it. I can feel that the balance between us is disturbed and that everything is so delicate that the least wrong touch might send our lives completely out of tune. They are out of tune, and it will want a lot of fact and patience and understanding to put them in harmony again. But I don't know how to do it. Life frightens me out here. It isn't the sort of life I'm used to or that I want to lead... I've only been here twenty-four hours, and from what I have seen there isn't much else to do but go from one bar to another ... or at least that's how Rex likes to spend his leisure. This French family are delightful and I like them all, but it isn't my home, it's theirs. I couldn't stay here. Maybe if I had a home of my own it would be better. I must find one. Rex wants a flat. Perhaps that will be the answer ... he will settle down into home life with me in a place of our own. But if he has stopped loving me and is having an affair with this other woman ... I won't be able to bear it. I want to believe in him, and I will try ... and yet ... I want to know where I stand. I want to know about that other girl ... I want to know...

Those were the words that were turning round and round in her mind ceaselessly. Dark frightening thoughts destroying any real pleasure she might have had in the unaccustomed warmth and beauty of the Egyptian morning.

The rest of the letter remained unwritten until Hassan, the Sudanese who was the Martial's *suffragi*, brought her a cup of Turkish coffee. She took the cup and smiled at him. He was a young, pleasant-looking boy whose broad brown face bore scars of those deep gashes across one cheek which

135

form part of the ritual of his race, and are inflicted during infancy. He wore a white *gallabiah* and a red tarboosh on his woolly black head. He grinned back at her and after he had gone she sipped the strong sweet syrupy drinks (so different from Gamma's milky coffee) and thought:

'Everything that happens out here will be different ... I'll have to get used to perpetual change...'

It was a thing that hundreds of people prayed for ... would find exciting... So many of her own friends and acquaintances would willingly change places with her, come out to Egypt. Well, perhaps she would have liked it all better if Rex had met her at Port Said, she thought ruefully.

There had been nothing of the old lover about him last night.

She had felt rather dismayed when she had woken up and found that he had already gone. Madame had said that he told her to give Phillida his love and say that he had not wished to disturb her but would be back from Fayid at about six o'clock tonight.

So she had the whole day alone in which to brood and wonder about Rex and herself and Rebecca.

Every time Phillida thought of the Syrian girl she felt indignation and resentment. She was wicked – that Rebecca – with her flamboyant beauty and heady sex-appeal. She had a husband of her own. What right had she to go round the place with Rex?

And then Phillida thought miserably:

'Perhaps if a man is away from his wife as long as Rex was away from me, he needs a girl-friend. And perhaps I ought to excuse it...'

Perhaps it was all because Rex and she had met and married in so short a space of time and been parted so quickly ... and this sort of thing was the outcome. While she was in the W.R.N.S. she had seen a good deal of life ... the married difficulties and troubles of others ... men away at sea for long duration ... pretty wives left at home... She remembered talking one day to a girl who was in the ranks with her, and whose husband, a petty officer, had not been home for three years. This girl, Betty, had started a love affair with an American in Plymouth, where Phillida had been stationed for a short time. Betty had tried to justify herself in Phillida's eyes.

'Why shouldn't I have a good time while Eddy's away? I know he's got a girl-friend in Malta because he's admitted it. But I'm not going to ask him any questions and he needn't ask me any. And so long as things are all right when we come together again it doesn't matter ... we're only human, aren't we? We can't live like nuns and monks, with all the strain and stress of war going on, plus the monotony of Service life.'

That had shocked Phil. The conversation had taken place about a year after Rex went overseas. Phillida had protested hotly.

'I don't agree. If one loves a person enough to marry them, one should stick to them. Marriage vows were not made to be broken. I don't want another man in my life until I can have my husband again...'

Betty had grimaced at her.

'You are an awful idealist, Phil,' she had said. 'I rather admire it, even though I can't live up to it myself. But I wonder if your precious Rex has the same ideals, and will stick to you for years and years. You wait, my dear. I'm older than you and have had more experience of men. In every letter Eddy writes from Malta he says how difficult it is for a chap to go straight in these outlandish countries. The climate makes people nervy ... they've *got to have an outlet...*'

At the time Phillida had thought it rather beastly. She did not for a moment believe that Rex would need an 'outlet'. And she had no intention of lowering her own standards. She was not a prig, neither did she consider herself particularly virtuous, because she had no inclination to be otherwise. Her love, her emotions, were focused on one man only. She pitied girls like Betty who *had* to find relaxation and amusement in a series of promiscuous affairs. But then, apart from the moral aspect, it was dangerous for two people living apart to 'go their own way'. Once one relaxed principles – anything might happen. On the other hand, one might begin a harmless flirtation and find it ended in a serious affair. No – one must keep rigidly to the rules.

It was queer, but she was thinking of Betty this morning, and her arguments. She had a horrid sinking feeling that perhaps Rex belonged to the Eddy class ... perhaps *he* had found that the climate and the loneliness in the desert had played havoc with his nerves out here and so he had plunged into an affair with Rebecca.

Doubts and worries and suspicions went on turning in Phillida's head.

It was only sheer love for her grandmother that forced her to write her a short, and what she felt to be a somewhat insincere, account of her arrival, to keep the old lady from being anxious about her. But when she added the words *'Of course it's marvellous to be with Rex again,'* she felt a hypocrite, and rather wretched.

The morning seemed endless. Mme Martial came out and chatted and asked if she would like to be escorted down to the town to see the shops, but Phillida had a sudden wish to do something that would please Rex. She must stop thinking and doubting and let this business of Rebecca slide. Yes, perhaps it was all grossly exaggerated by Mrs Riccard. Rex and Rebecca might have been going about together a bit, but how could anyone know that there was anything in it? If she loved Rex she must trust him. Last night had been a fiasco because Rex had been on leave and had never had her cable, and they had both been tired – herself in particular. Tonight it would be better ... quite different. She would not lay her cards on the table and ask Rex about Rebecca. She would try, like Betty, to be broad-minded. Whatever Rex had done while she was away, she would shut her eyes and ask no questions. Now that she was here he would be hers again. Probably he wouldn't see Rebecca any more. And, anyhow, the Squadron-Leader was due back in Ismailia shortly.

'I won't say a word, I'll try and make everything wonderful for Rex tonight,' thought Phillida, with a sudden burst of enthusiasm; a profound desire to re-establish her old happiness with her husband.

He had asked her to try to find a flat. She would find one.

She put away her writing materials and asked Sophie Martial if she would be good enough to telephone for a taxi.

'Maybe you would come too and help me look for an apartment, Madame,' she said, with that shy smile which brought her

140

serious young face so suddenly alive.

Sophie spread out her hands. She indicated that it wasn't going to be easy, but said that she would be delighted to accompany Mrs Maltern and give her assistance.

It was then that Phillida remembered that Rex had said last night that 'he was on the track' of a flat but she had not asked him where and he had forgotten to tell her, and perhaps, indeed, he had just been doing some talking. Rex was like that. She felt that it might be best to get ahead with the job.

Mme Martial did her best, and they spent several hours in the search, but it ended in finding nothing. Ismailia was full. Only one man – a Greek – hinted that there might be an apartment vacant in a week or so, and that he would let Phillida know. With that she had to be content. Mme Martial tried to put her at ease by saying:

'You can stay in our room until you are fixed, so do not worry.'

But the one point on which she was firm was the subject of food. She did not wish to start feeding her lodgers.

Phillida lunched alone at the Club. It was the first time she had ever eaten alone in her life. She was so used to being either at home with her parents, or grandmother, or with friends, and used to Service life during the war, where one was never alone.

She sat at a small table in the Club dining-room and was dismayed to find how lonely and homesick it made her feel. The place was full; mainly with employees of the Suez Canal Company, some alone, some with their wives. A great deal of noise and clatter was going on. And Phillida watched and listened and felt what she was ... a total stranger ... an exile from her own land.

All desire for food seemed to leave her. She had to struggle through the first two courses and refused the third. She thought dejectedly of Rex. He would be bringing her here tonight. Being with him would be better, but she hoped to goodness that she would feel nearer him ... that somehow he would make her feel that it was all worth while.

Suddenly she felt that she could not sit here a moment longer. She called one of the waiters and gave him an Egyptian note. Rex had left her some on the mantelpiece.

And now there was the whole long afternoon to get through. Sophie had told her that shops shut from now until four o'clock. This was the time for a *siesta*. Phillida was tired. But she did not want to sleep. However, there was nothing else to do.

She walked down the beautiful Rue Mohamed Ali, back to the Martials' villa.

The family was obviously resting. The house was shuttered, dim, and very still.

Phillida entered her bedroom and closed

the door. She had a horrible choking desire to burst into tears. She struggled not to give way to that longing. Whatever happened, she must not face Rex tonight with swollen eyes and upset him. Inevitably she remembered the brilliant-eyed beautiful Rebecca, and with a bitterness new to her she tried to use that memory as a spur. If it were true that Rex was interested in Rebecca ... it was up to her, his wife, to be more beautiful and brilliant, and so divert his interest to herself.

Desperately she sought distraction, crushed down the sensation of sick loneliness, and unpacked a few more clothes, then decided to wash her hair. Rex used to like her hair after it was newly washed, because it looked so fair. It had got sticky on the boat. She needed a good shampoo.

She washed the thick fair tresses and then sat out in the garden to let them dry in the sun.

It seemed a long time before four o'clock. And even then there was no sign of life from the Martials and no suggestion of tea. Phillida pinned up her hair and changed from her slacks into a light grey flannel suit and fresh white piqué blouse. She decided that another walk into the town wouldn't do her any harm. She just must have a cup of tea. She would find a place. And now she remembered that awful woman, Mrs Riccard, had mentioned the name 'Antoinette's' and said that the cakes there were very good.

She would ask her way to Antoinette's and trust to luck that Vic Riccard would not be there.

She found the little shop in a side street. It was full of English, mainly men in uniform with their wives or girl-friends. Feeling very much alone, Phillida sat down and ordered tea. At least it was good, she thought that everybody seemed to speak a little English in Ismailia.

But once again she experienced that awful oppressive sensation that she was exiled in a foreign land. She told herself desperately that she would get used to it, of course. This was only her second day in Egypt, and it was bad luck that she had to spend it by herself – atrocious luck that Rex had had his week's leave just before she arrived, and would not get any more for some time. And, of course, everything would have seemed so much better if she had had a different welcome. It was no use pretending otherwise.

Once more she returned to the villa. The Martials were in evidence now. Madame sat out in the garden, under the mango trees with a basket of mending in front of her. Pierrot was home from school, careering round the paved garden on his bicycle. Monsieur, who was a bird fancier, was busy in another part of the garden with his aviary.

Phillida rather thankfully sat down beside Madame, glad to have someone to talk to, even though it meant a struggle with her French. And then it seemed only a short time before Rex would be back, and she hastened to brush her hair again, painfully anxious to look her best when he came back tonight. She was determined to shut out the memory of last night. She had every intention of giving him the benefit of the doubt – she would throw herself into his arms and he would hold her close and tell that the whole of yesterday had been just a nightmare, and that he loved her as he used to do, then she would not feel alone or homesick any more.

She even began to jeer at herself.

'Pull yourself together, Phillida Maltern. You've been wanting to get to your husband for the last three years, and now you've got here what are you worrying about?'

She sat on the edge of her bed filing her nails and revarnishing them, her window open, listening for the sound of the little M.G. car that would bring Rex back from Fayid. It was already dark, and much cooler. These February nights were quite cold although warmer than anything she had experienced in England for a long time. It was at this sort of time that she saw little beauty in Egypt; when the mango and the apricot trees assumed queer sinister shapes, and the distant sound of a donkey braying, or the yelp of a pi-dog from the desert, were melancholy sounds and she would have given a whole lot to have been sitting in front of a log fire in Gamma's cosy little sitting-room, where everything was so dear and familiar; where in lieu of this swift transition from light to darkness there would be the gentle blue dusk of twilight which would gradually envelop the dear little garden and the surrounding snow-covered fields and woods.

Then came the sound of a car racing down the street. Phillida knew that it was Rex in the M.G. Nobody would drive at that speed in a country full of Army lorries and dangerous drivers except Rex. With a half-smile she remembered what Martin Winters had said about the need for care here, and how quietly the old Morris had ambled along from Port Said.

She took a quick look at herself in the mirror, decided that she looked all right and had actually caught the sun this morning when she toured Ismailia. Good! Rex liked her to be sunburned. During that summer they had been together in Devonshire he had repeatedly told her that he adored her blonde hair with a brown skin.

She had never more ardently wanted him and his love and approbation.

She must be able to feel once more that

everything was well between them.

She ran out into the darkness to the gate to meet him.

'Rex!' she called his name softly.

His voice came back to her and she saw a lean shape emerge from the little car.

'Oh, hello … you're there, are you, Phil?'

She took a little step forward, her heart fluttering, her face burning with the unusual emotional upheaval.

Then to her intense disappointment she saw another man in khaki get out of the M.G., and realised that her husband was not alone. Rex announced:

'I've brought Jimmy Angus back with me… His wife, Doreen, is in Moascar Garrison Hospital. They had a baby a fortnight ago. She's coming out next week… I've asked old Jimmy to have a meal with us tonight. I think we ought to drink to the occasion, don't you?'

Phillida's heart sank like a stone. Rex was making the introductions now.

'Captain Angus – Jimmy to everybody – my wife…'

Politely Phillida extended a hand. She could not see Captain Angus well, but had a vague impression of a short, broad young Scotsman with a chubby boyish face and Glengarry on the side of a red head.

Rex tucked an arm through hers and they all walked towards the villa. Rex was doing all the talking. What a hell of a day in the desert! Too much work. Old Jimmy worked at B.T.E., but he had a flat in Ismailia. He'd only just found it in time to get it ready for Doreen and the kid next week. Phil, he said, must make friends with Doreen. She needed a bit of moral support; she was homesick.

'Poor wretch,' Phillida thought, and grimaced at the idea that *she* could give moral support to anybody, feeling as *she* had done today.

No doubt Captain Angus was a very nice fellow and lonely while his wife was in hospital, she reflected. But why, oh why must Rex ask him back tonight? It was tactless, to say the least of it. He must have known that she wanted him to herself. She was rather hurt that he didn't wish to be alone with *her*.

But she tried to make the best of it, and hoped that Captain Angus would go home early, leave her to talk to Rex alone at the Club for a little while at least. Just anything rather than wait to go back to that large, dim pink room wherein, instead of talking, he would probably fall asleep. And then all the waiting and misery would begin again tomorrow.

'Are you ready, Poppet?' asked Rex.

'Yes – I have only to get my coat,' she answered.

'Look here,' put in Captain Angus, 'there won't be room in your little bus for three of us. I'll start walking.'

'Oh, we can squeeze in,' said Rex cheerfully. 'Phil's just a wisp these days, and if you don't mind more or less sitting on Jimmy's knees, darling...'

She felt her cheeks suddenly burn in the darkness and a slight constriction of the throat.

In that vague and quite unpredictable fashion of his Rex had forgotten that only last night he had maintained that there was not room in the car for three people. But, of course, he had wanted to run Rebecca home alone.

She felt Rex's arm pressing hers against his side.

'Poor old Poppet ... been alone all day. Never mind. We'll go down and drink to the health of young What's-his-name...'

'Doreen wants him to be called William after her father. So I expect young Bill it will be,' said Jimmy Angus.

Phillida drew her arm away from her husband's and ran into the house to fetch her Jaeger coat. There was a cold wind blowing from the desert, rustling the mango trees. Searchlights from an Egyptian Army camp beyond circled and flashed across a sky that was already luminous with stars.

The heart of Phillida felt dead again. Another night's drinking at the French Club! How disappointing it all was!

Her acute disappointment stifled all the gay, eager expectation with which she had run out to meet her husband. She knew she was going to be thought quiet and tongue-tied and stupid by him tonight, and she wouldn't be able to help it. Last night there had been Rebecca ... tonight Jimmy ... every night perhaps there would be a fresh cause for celebration, and never a moment in which to get to know and understand the man she had married.

She was profoundly depressed as she climbed into the little car, wedged her slim body into an uncomfortable and crouched position, and lay half across the little Scots Captain, who kept aplogising, and was obviously as embarrassed as herself.

8

'You didn't have much to say for yourself tonight, Poppet,' said Rex, with a prodigious yawn as he unbuttoned his khaki tunic and then pulled his shirt over his head.

Phillida looked at him. She had not yet started to undress. It was eleven o'clock. She was tired and rather cold. She longed for a fire – for some hot water – and there was neither. She was also worried because she was so tired. What was wrong with her? But at dinner Jimmy Angus, who seemed a kind little man, had told her that it was the change of climate, and that Doreen hadn't been able to keep awake the first week she arrived.

Rex, on the other hand, brought out the old grievance:

'What you want is a stiff drink, and I can't think why you won't have one.'

She had made no answer and again the little Scot had come to her rescue and murmured that Doreen didn't drink, either. They would have a lot in common, he had said.

Driving home, Rex, with a touch of acidity, observed that he hoped that his wife hadn't got anything in common with Doreen Angus, for it was no compliment.

'She's the most dismal little mouse of a thing, and spends her whole time belly-aching. Can't think why Angus ever tied himself up to her. Hasn't even got looks. A snub nose. Saucer eyes. I suppose the big eyes got poor old Jimmy.'

To which Phillida had replied:

'I say, Rex, that's not very kind. The poor girl may have something in her that you don't see. Anyhow, Jimmy seems devoted to her and the baby.'

'*Chacun á son goût,*' said Rex, 'and Doreen isn't my "*goût*", and I'd just as soon people didn't think *you* were like her. She loathes Egypt and the Egyptians. She loathes Ismailia. Always grousing. She leads old Jimmy the hell of a life and he's mug enough to stand it. If a woman nagged me like that I'd soon quit.'

Phillida had spent the next few minutes reflecting on this remark in silence. Rex was a complete stranger. He seemed to bear little resemblance to the charming and sympathetic boy she had married. Why should three years of service abroad coupled with gay bachelor leaves have hardened him so? He *was* harder ... that was easy to gather from every word he said. He obviously had no sympathy for the weak and miserable. He was strong and buoyant himself. He had no

152

time for the less fortunate. During dinner at the Club, after a good many unnecessary toasts to young Bill had been drunk, Rex held forth about life in general.

Jimmy had let fall a chance remark that Doreen had an older sister, Peggy, who was quite pretty except for the sad fact that one of her legs was crippled; she had been like that from birth. She was very conscious of the malformity and made everybody else conscious of it. She had a slavish adoration for Doreen and wanted to come out here and stay with them. Jimmy didn't mind, but wondered if it would be a good thing because poor Peggy would never dream of appearing on the Plage, for instance, in a bathing-suit, nor be able to dance, and it was embarrassing for everybody in a place like this, where people continually met in public.

Immediately Rex said:

'Good lord, old boy, I'd keep her firmly at home. It's awfully sad and all that, but personally I can't stand deformities. They make me sick. I mean you don't *have* to have your sister-in-law to live with you, so why put up with it? I believe in being kind and all that, but one gets taken advantage of once you start pitying people.'

Phillida had not joined in that conversation. But it had interested her. It had also slightly shocked her. It put Rex in a poor light. Men were very different, she had reflected. Rex seemed to perform acts of kindness only with an ulterior motive. She was fast being brought face to face with the blunt fact that she had married a supreme egoist. But a man like Martin Winters – surely, in Jimmy's position, *he* would have asked the crippled sister-in-law out here to enjoy the sunlight; anxious to help her, let alone please his wife. And no doubt Jimmy Angus would eventually get her here, but Rex, in his shoes, would use every argument against. Clever sort of arguments, vindicating his own point of view. He had added:

'"Beware of Pity" … that book of Stefan Zweig points out how dangerous it is to pity people, and if you started being nice to a girl like that she might think you were in love with her or something. It doesn't do.'

Hands on either side, pressing down upon the bed, a slender, rather desolate young figure, Phillida watched her husband divest himself of his uniform. He was so very good-looking, she thought. He ran his fingers through his thick, tousled hair, a cigarette dangling from his lips. But there were many lines under his eyes and slight heaviness about the jaw. She noticed suddenly that Rex was beginning to put on weight.

He caught her gaze.

'Were you always as quiet as this?' he

154

grimaced at her. 'I honestly can't remember – it's so long since we beat it up together at home.'

Did they ever 'beat it up'? she wondered. Certainly they stopped occasionally at the little country pubs so that Rex could have a beer, but there was none of this heavy drinking going on. But then they hadn't been in a place like Egypt ... they had laughed and loved each other in a more gentle sunlight by the blue Devon sea ... not such a violent blue as the Suez Canal. Nothing was as violent or as curiously frightening at home as it was out here.

She made an effort to smile at Rex.

'I was always rather quiet, darling.'

'Oh, well, keep your chin up,' he said vaguely, and began to whistle as he stepped into cream silk pyjamas and brushed down the thick chestnut hair. He paid no further attention to her for the moment. With her spirits at zero she thought:

'He hasn't kissed me once ... he seems so far away from me... It's going to be hopeless like this.'

Rex lit another cigarette and then sauntered over to the bed and lay down, lacing his hands behind his head.

'Didn't you have any lucky flat-hunting, Poppet?'

'No none. Madame Martial helped me. But there's nothing.'

Rex Maltern thought of the smart, modern little flat in the Greek quarter of Ismailia occupied by Squadron-Leader and Mrs Rendledon. He scowled.

'Well, we can't stay here, obviously. I want to entertain. Life in a bed-sitt. is my idea of hell. We must find something. I'll go and see a chap I know tomorrow. I knock off at 1.15 on Saturdays. We'll spend the week-end trying to get fixed up. There's no room here for my clothes – or yours...'

Hers, she noticed, were an afterthought. What did he think *she* felt about 'life in a bed-sitt.'? Perhaps he imagined that coming from Gamma's simple cottage, and her recent life in the Services, she wouldn't mind 'pigging it'. He did not bother to enquire. He only knew that from his own angle it was unattractive.

He flicked his gaze in her direction.

'Aren't you going to get undressed? You're sitting there like a little figure of grief.'

She went suddenly hot and resentful. She swung round at him. 'I wonder if you realise that I haven't had a chance to talk to you at all ... not since I arrived in Egypt?'

He took his cigarette from his mouth and stared.

'My dear Poppet! We were talking the whole evening.'

'In front of a stranger.'

'Old Jimmy's not a stranger. He "liaises"

156

with Fayid. I see a lot of him.'

'But I don't. He's a stranger to me. I think he's very nice, personally, and it's sweet the way he fusses about his wife and is getting everything ready for her ... in fact, I think Mrs Angus is rather lucky.' The words tumbled out, welling up from Phillida's sore young heart.

Rex suddenly burst into laughter.

'Am I being ticked off or something? Come here, you funny little thing.' He put his cigarette in the ashtray beside him and held out his hand to Phillida. 'Come here and be kissed.'

But to his astonishment she was not so easily to be cajoled. There was a streak of pride in Phillida – a stubborn streak – which he had yet to learn about. She felt bitterly disappointed because of the sequence of events in the past forty-eight hours. She felt neglected. She had not been considered in any way by him, and she was not ready to go to heel the moment he whistled.

She sprang up and with trembling fingers began to unbutton her blouse.

'If you don't mind, I'll get undressed,' she said, in a choked voice.

Rex was annoyed. He didn't like being turned down. But he had some sort of a con- science, and it was still pricking him. He waited until Phillida had undressed, watched her brush the fair silky hair and then plait it,

157

watched her take off the blue quilted silk dressing-gown which he had not seen before – it made him realise how long they had been apart; he recognised none of her clothes. She came towards him looking utterly dejected and touchingly shy, in a thin peach silk nightgown which had only the slenderest of satin shoulder-straps and a touch of cream-coloured lace over the bosom. She met his critical gaze and suddenly, for no reason, blushed hotly, sat down on the bed and covered her face with her hands.

'Oh, I wish I'd never come!' she said in a muffled voice. 'I don't believe you want me any more. Something's happened, it isn't a bit like it was...'

Then he was aghast at himself for the brute he was. He was a person of impulses – both good and bad – and this was one of the good moments. He sprang out of bed, seated himself beside Phillida and put both arms around her. She was cold and trembling. But he said:

'Poppet, I'm frightfully sorry. You've had the hell of an awful time since you got here, and I really am sorry. Things will be all right. Don't get yourself all worked up. Come to bed and get warm, you little icebox.'

She did not know whether she loved or hated him. She only knew that she must be comforted because she could not bear her sense of appalling loneliness and disappointment. She let him draw her closer, surrendered herself completely to his caressing hands, and pressed her tear-wet cheek against his. She asked that question which she had asked last night:

'Do you still love me, Rex?'

And this time he answered:

'Of course I do, darling.'

Rex Maltern was easily stirred, and if he was no longer crazy about this wife of his, he had not lived with her long enough for his feelings – even though superficial – to have reached the point of complete satiety. Perhaps the spirit of Becki lingered in the background and laughed in derision, but he was content to ignore it for the moment. He was anxious to put himself right in Phillida's eyes. He had a childish wish to be thought wonderful by everybody, and besides, he could not have Phil writing back and telling that old grandmother of hers that he was unkind.

His kisses, his caresses, which were at first gentle and comforting, burned suddenly into something more like the old desire he had once had for her. Inspired by that passion he was able to lie with the greatest of ease:

'I love you, my little Poppet. You're as enchanting as ever... Kiss me ... tell me you forgive me if I have seemed different, but I'm not really ... just thoughtless. I know you hate this pub-crawling. Now that you've come I won't need to spend all my time soaking. Things will be like they used to be. Kiss me, darling, and tell me that *you* haven't changed, either...'

She lay close to him, her arms about his neck, her own senses stirred to meet his passion. Somewhere deep down inside her lay the nagging little wish to ask him now, at this moment, if that story about Rebecca was true ... just for the sheer pleasure of hearing him deny it. But something held her back ... the fear, perhaps, to spoil this moment which was doing so much to lift up her morale and restore some of her self-confidence.

So she answered his question – pathetically eager to please.

'I've never stopped loving you, Rex. Oh, my darling, *darling* Rex!'

And it seemed before she slept that night as though the nightmare was over and everything in Egypt was going to be as she had dreamed and hoped for. She belonged to Rex and he to her. She was ready to forget all her disappointments, and to criticise, or suspect no further.

She awakened to early breakfast with Rex, feeling on top of the world, a complete transformation from the miserable Phillida of yesterday. Rex was charming to her and it was like a continuation of their honeymoon.

'Meet you at the French Club for lunch, darling. It's my early day,' he said, as she saw him off to Fayid.

'I'm going to rush round Ismailia the whole morning and find a flat, darling. Just wait and see.'

'That's the girl! Never mind the rent. We'll manage.'

She smiled at him.

'Are we well off these days?'

He grimaced. A captain's pay and allowances were by no means sufficient to satisfy his luxurious tastes. Secretly he thanked heaven that his mother had married a rich man and could send him the odd cheque. He had had a handsome one for his birthday last month. And there was always that couple of hundred a year, free of income tax, which old Uncle Reginald had left him. (Praise the lord Mamma had christened him after the old So-and-So, and that he had remembered to write to Uncle Reg every Christmas until he died. And there was always an overdraft … and the money that was coming to him when Papa popped off.)

In the best of moods, gratified by the new devoted, happy look in Phillida's eyes, he kissed her good-bye and disappeared down the Rue Mohamed Ali roaring up the engine of the M.G. But as he went he was thinking:

'Damn and blast ... old Kipps comes back tomorrow night. *I must see Becki some time today.* Why the dickens a chap can't have two wives, I don't know. There's a side of me that Phil could never satisfy, and that little devil Becki is in my blood. I'll just have to be clever and tactful about it and keep them both happy. *"The Man with a Load of Mischief"* ... that's me! And very nice too. How dull life would be if one didn't have some *divertissement!*'

He whistled gaily as he drove along the Suez Canal road towards G.H.Q.

When a telephone call came through from Fayid to the Martials' house later that morning, telling Phillida that Captain Maltern had to go to Suez on business and wouldn't be back until half past four, and that she was not to wait lunch, Phillida received the news quite cheerfully. Even though it was a little disappointing, it never for an instant entered her head that it wasn't true.

The world seemed so much brighter to her today. It was one of those brilliant Egyptian mornings with dazzling blue sky and hot sun tempered by a cool breeze, which made the spring out here so attractive. After last night she seemed to view everything with a new eye – even the prospect of being alone until this afternoon. Rex had been so marvellous last night. She was so happy again. She had firmly shut out the memory of Mrs Riccard's

162

ugly gossip. She was determined to believe completely in her husband again. She was under the spell of the old enchantment, and this time she wrote to Gamma on a much more sincerely contented note. She wrote also to some of her W.R.N.S. friends and a particularly long letter to Patsy Luddon, who was the daughter of the Rector of Alvercombe, and her particular friend. Patsy was getting married this summer to a Naval officer to whom, in actual fact, she had been introduced by Phillida. A nice young Lieutenant who was due back from a Mediterranean cruise in June.

Phillida wrote:

Ask Oliver if he has ever come across an awfully nice Lieut-Commander called Martin Winters, who looked after me the first day I landed in Port Said.

She added, with quickened heartbeats:

It's so wonderful being with my husband again, and I do hope Oliver is as marvellous to you as Rex is to me…

Having completed the letter, and with her thoughts focused upon Patsy and her N.O., she once more recalled Martin and wondered if and when she would meet him again.

She completed her morning's correspondence by dropping a note to Steve Cubitt in Cairo telling her to hurry up and come down to the Canal Zone so that they could meet.

Later she walked down to the Club and thought what a huge difference love made in a person's life ... how good it was to be alive and out here in the sunshine with Rex, and that it was stupid of her ever to have felt so homesick or wretched.

The first person she saw at the bar when she walked into the Club was Martin Winters.

He was wearing grey flannels and a dark blue blazer, and had a pipe in the corner of his mouth. He sat on a stool talking to an attractive elderly woman with ash-blonde hair, and a bald-headed man who wore uniform with red tabs.

Martin saw the slender, fair girl as she walked down the long room and his face lit up. He was genuinely pleased to see his protégée again. And – as before – there was that somewhat painful tug at his heart at her strange resemblance to his lost love.

'Why, hello, Phillida! How nice to see you!' he said.

Phillida, also pleased, gave him her hand, which he held for a fraction of a moment. Then he introduced her to his friends.

'This is Mrs Maltern ... she has just come

164

out to join her husband, who's at Fayid. Phillida, may I introduce you to Brigadier and Mrs Pentyre? You remember I told you, Phillida, that I had some very good friends living here. Mrs Pentyre and her husband were stationed in Malta before the war, when my ship was there, and some very fine times we used to have.'

'We did indeed,' said Mabyn Pentyre, and smiled at Phillida, who thought she had never seen such a blue pair of eyes – which, with her sunburned skin and ashen hair, made Mrs Pentyre look absurdly young for a woman who, she later discovered, was twice a grandmother. The Brigadier said:

'Those were the days. Malta before the war, eh, Martin? But give me anywhere except this infernal country. Buksheesh, malesh, haseesh ... a lot of rogues!'

'Oh, but I *like* Egypt!' exclaimed Mabyn Pentyre, 'and I *love* the sailing. You must come sailing with us, Mrs Maltern.'

'Yes, by jove!' said the Brigadier, with an admiring look at Phillida.

Mrs Pentyre grimaced at him and then at Phillida.

'Beware of my husband. He has a passion for pretty girls.'

'And why not?' said the Brigadier, lifting his glass and regarding it with satisfaction. 'My only regret is that they haven't got a passion for me. Too old and too fat. Infernal

165

country! Look at the stomach I've produced. Couldn't get on my old mess kit if I tried.'

'You shouldn't eat so much, you greedy old man!' said his wife.

They all laughed. The Brigadier shook his head sadly.

'I'm bullied by everybody. What'll you have, Mrs Maltern ... gin and something, or sherry ... or...'

'She doesn't drink, sir,' said Martin.

Phillida smiled at him.

'You've remembered that, have you?'

Martin remembered quite a lot about that day with Phillida. In fact, he had thought about her quite surprisingly often during the past forty-eight hours, and had hoped that when he came over to spend the day with his friends he would run into her. He wondered how things were going with her husband, and if there had been any trouble with the Syrian female. He was pleased to see that Phillida looked happy ... very much happier than she had been at that dinner party the other night, poor little thing. As before, he took an aesthetic delight in watching the grace with which she moved those lovely hands, and heavens! he thought, what a long, slender neck she had. The small head was exquisitely sculptured. Freddy Pentyre was making her laugh. She had the most infectious laugh, and a dimple at the corner of her mouth which Martin had not noticed before. When she was animated like this she was really very pretty, he thought. It would be a crime ever to allow her to be sad.

The Brigadier exclaimed:

'The child comes from Alvercombe, Devonshire, by gad! That's a poor show. Bitter enemy of mine. I'm a Cornishman. *Of course* I am with a name like Pentyre.'

'Don't take any notice of him, Mrs Maltern,' put in Mabyn, her blue eyes twinkling at the girl; 'he's got the name but I'm the Cornishwoman. Freddy's only been to Cornwall once in his life. He's a Cockney, born within the sound of Bow Bells, and he's no more Cornish than the cream you get at Groppi's.'

Phillida blinked.

'What on earth's Groppi's?'

'A big luscious shop in Cairo where you buy cakes and make yourself sick,' said the Brigadier. 'I'll take you there one day if you're a good girl.'

Phillida sipped the orange squash which had been ordered for her by Martin.

'Oh, I do look forward to seeing Cairo!' she exclaimed.

'Nasty, smelly place...' began the Brigadier, but his wife interrupted.

'Now be quiet, Freddy, and stop grumbling. You know you adore being out here, and you'd be having a horrid time if you were at home, where you can't get anything to eat,

167

and whisky's rationed.'

Brigadier Pentyre grinned at Phillida. 'See how she treats me – no respect. I've spoiled her. I'm just a slave. Let's have another gin … Martin, you'll have the same again, won't you?'

'Well, if you insist, sir,' said Martin.

Phillida thought:

'They're no different from Rex … they all drink out here. It doesn't seem to matter.'

And she had a sudden wish to be loyal to him in her heart, and also to let Martin know how things were with her, for it had been so awful the other night when he had heard what Vic Riccard had said, and then realised that Rex had been the man concerned.

She said:

'Rex was to have been home to lunch, but has gone off to Suez on a job. I do so wish he were here.'

Mrs Pentyre began to question Phillida about her husband, his work and how long they had been married, and so on. Upon hearing what Phillida had to say, and being the kindest of women, she was at once anxious to play the fairy godmother, as she had always done with the junior 'wives'.

She would have a party for Phillida, she said, and introduce her to everybody. Why not bring Captain Maltern to their place for cocktails this evening? They had one of those nice houses in what was called the 'Bayswater Road' in Moascar Garrison, which was all part of Ismailia. She explained to Phillida that the Brigadier was at B.T.E. (that stood for British Troops in Egypt).

'Oh dear,' Phillida laughed, 'what a lot of initials standing for lots of things in the Army!'

'You'll get used to it when you've been in the Army as long as I have,' Mrs Pentyre assured her. 'Twenty-two years' service.'

'Of which we have only spent about ten together,' put in the Brigadier.

'With nineteen moves,' said Mrs Pentyre triumphantly. 'Oh, we have ever such a good time in the Army!'

'Now, Mrs Pen,' said Martin, cocking an eyebrow, 'don't scare the poor child like that. You know you wouldn't be in any other Service.'

'Except yours, Martin dear. But then I shall marry you in my next life. You're so tall. I adore tall men, and you play such *beautiful* bridge, and you're such a comfort when things go wrong.'

The Brigadier whispered loudly to Phillida.

'Between you and me, Mrs Maltern, I suspect my wife of having a schoolgirl crush on young Winters, and I don't think I shall let it go much further.'

Martin grinned and knocked the bowl of

his pipe on his shoe.

'If it wasn't for the scandal, sir, the honour of the Navy and all that, I'd march off with Mrs Pen tomorrow.'

'There you are!' said the Brigadier with a lugubrious sigh. 'That's what I have to put up with. Goings-on right in front of my very eyes. When she's a great-grandmother, Mabyn'll be doing the same, and I'm not even allowed to look twice at a pretty girl.'

'But you *do,* dear,' said Mrs Pentyre sweetly.

Phillida chuckled. She was feeling so happy now and rapidly losing the shyness which had enveloped her when she first met Martin's friends. She would like Rex to meet them this evening. The Pentyres were taking Martin back to their house for lunch. Mrs Pentyre asked Phillida to join them, but she felt that she might be intruding on a party already arranged, and refused this.

When the Brigadier and his wife moved away from the bar, Martin lingered to say an additional word to Phillida.

'In confidence and all that,' he said, smiling, 'I've just heard that there is a very good chance that I may be posted from Navy House to Fayid to do a liaison job.'

Phillida looked up at the big, tall man with genuine pleasure.

'Oh, that would be nice; we'd see more of you.'

'I think it's pretty certain,' he said.

'Will you be sorry?'

'On the whole, yes. The desert doesn't appeal to me as much as the sea. On the other hand, there is some good sailing at Fayid, and there's always the old Morris to bring me in to the French Club, and as you know from personal experience, one gets accustomed to moves. No use having roots.'

Phillida sighed a little.

That had been true when she was a Wren, and yet she had never quite got over that homesick feeling every time she left her parents while they were alive and, later, Gamma and the cottage at Alvercombe. And now it seemed even more imperative that she should have some sort of security and settled life with her husband. She sighed again.

Martin heard that quiet sigh and wondered... He wished more than a little that he knew how Phillida had reacted to the unfortunate events of the other night and what Maltern had had to say for himself. Now that he saw this grey-eyed, fair-haired girl again he was surprised at the interest and even the curiosity she roused in him. He said:

'I would very much like you and your husband to dine with me here one night next week. Perhaps you'd suggest a date.'

'Oh, I'd love to!' she exclaimed. 'I'll ask

171

Rex. But we'll be seeing you tonight at the Brigadier's, won't we?'

'Do you think you'll be coming?'

'I hope so.'

'Well, till then...' said Martin, and put his pipe in his coat pocket and reluctantly left her.

On his way out he saw the red-headed woman who had done all the damage with her sordid gossip on the night of Phillida's arrival. He passed her with a feeling of apprehension and hoped she wasn't going to repeat her foolishness.

Victoria Riccard was with a woman friend, but immediately she saw Phillida sitting alone in the dining-room she rushed up to her.

'Oh, *hello!* How are you? My dear, what must you have thought of me the other night? I just hadn't a clue! You mustn't mind me – I'm always making *gaffes* – and I always get mixed up. It wasn't your hubby I was discussing at all, you know.'

Phillida, who had just put on her horn-rimmed glasses and was studying the menu, took her glasses off. Her face flushed scarlet, but her eyes looked up at Mrs Riccard without expression.

'Please don't bother about it,' she said, in a frozen voice. 'I didn't take the slightest notice of what you said.'

Mrs Riccard was not one to be snubbed

easily. She said:

'Come and lunch with me and my friend, who is one of the "wives" out here.'

'Thanks all the same, but I've started my lunch,' said Phillida, and hurriedly put on her glasses and returned to the menu.

Mrs Riccard shrugged her shoulders and moved away. Phillida saw her whispering to her friend, who looked much the same type. A little of the happiness which she had been feeling this morning evaporated. It was horrid being reminded of that beastly rumour about Rex and Rebecca. It was best forgotten.

Later she returned to the Martials' villa and hoped for the time to pass quickly so that Rex would come and be charming and lover-like to her as he had been last night and dispel the clouds. She looked forward to telling him about her meeting with the Pentyres. It would be fun going to drinks with them and nice seeing Martin again. He really was a very pleasant person, and she would like Rex to think so too.

9

Rex was an hour later than he had said he would be. It was a quarter to six before the little M.G. pulled up in front of the gates of the Martials' villa. Phillida, already dressed to go to the Brigadier's house, had with care put on her one and only smart three-piece. It was suitable for the cool spring evenings here, being of a light wool material, and the soft shade of green suited her. She wore with it a small pearl necklace which had belonged to her mother, and Rex's badge brooch, set in paste and enamel, which he had given her when they were first engaged.

When Rex arrived she was sitting in the Martials' salon looking at the small model fleet of cars, jeeps and aeroplanes which young Pierrot collected, and which were the pride of his life.

Eagerly, Phillida ran out to meet her husband.

He walked up the garden path looking, she thought, a trifle gloomy. He greeted her with the faintest smile.

'Hello, Phil. I'm just about done. Had a puncture on the way home. I'll either have to get a new car or some new tyres.'

'Oh, what bad luck, darling!' she said sympathetically, and put an arm through his with a gesture of confidence and affection. Once they were in their room, Rex let his khaki canvas haversack slip from his shoulder on to the floor, tossed his cap on to the bed, and unbuttoned the tunic of his battle-dress. He hardly glanced at his wife. She eyed him anxiously. What was wrong? Surely a mere puncture would not put him in such a poor humour.

She said, 'What a shame they made you go to Suez on your half-day...'

'Oh, I lead a dog's life,' he muttered, then added. 'Get that bottle of whisky out of the cupboard and give me a drink, will you, Poppet?'

'Poor old Rex ... you do look tired,' she said, and hastened to get the bottle, a glass, and a jug of water from Madame.

Rex tossed down a drink, then announced that he was going to wash and get into civvies, after which he returned to the bedroom, and both looked and felt in a slightly better frame of mind.

The job in Suez' had, of course, been Rebecca. When he left G.H.Q. at one o'clock he had picked Becki up outside the R.A.F. mess at Deversoir, which lay on the Canal Road half-way between Ismailia and Fayid. She had induced someone in the R.A.F. to give her a lift there. She had brought a picnic lunch, and they had eaten it together under the beautiful faroa trees, in a secluded place well known to them both – a few hundred yards away from the glittering blue waters of the Canal and out of sight of the road.

Rex had gone to that meeting with a rather half-hearted determination to break with Becki and do the right thing by his wife. The determination petered out within half an hour of his being with the Syrian girl. She was adept in her handling of men and she knew Rex. She knew exactly what 'got him'. She was at her most gay and amusing, teased him wickedly, and rejected his first effort to kiss her. After the picnic was over she lay on the rug which they had spread on the warm ground, her hands laced behind her head, glancing at him slantways out of her brilliant eyes.

'Rex must be a good little boy now, *hein?*' she murmured, with a mocking smile.

Rex looked at the wonderful supple body which he had so often held in his arms, and at the big, provocative, crimson mouth. At once he felt challenged.

'Since when have *you* decided to be good, my sweet? I thought you said the other night that you didn't wish my wife's arrival to make any difference to us?'

She gave a little gurgling laugh.

'It eees too difficult, perhaps – no?'

'*No,*' muttered Rex, 'nothing's too difficult, if you want it enough.'

She laughed again.

'I theennk the little wife will keep you in order now?'

Rex scowled. If there was one thing calculated to destroy his good intentions towards Phillida, it was the idea that he was being 'kept in order' by her. He took another look at Rebecca's tempting lips and those large, wicked eyes of hers. It was the devil, he thought ... how she fired his senses every time. There was just something about her that Phil hadn't got, and that was all there was to it. He suddenly bent over Becki, gripped both her hands and pinioned them down on either side of her.

'If you think you can get away from me as easily as all that, you're mistaken,' he said savagely.

She tried to get away now – but not very hard.

'Rex ... you're hurting me!'

'I'll beat the life out of you if you start telling me that I'm going to settle down to being henpecked, by my wife or any other woman.'

The magnificent eyes glistened at him.

'I don't know what ees "henpecking"?'

He ignored this.

'Are *you* going to start being ordered about by Kipps when he gets back?'

She giggled.

'Yes! Becki is going to be a little angel. I would suit wings, eh, Rex?'

'Wings be damned!' he said through his teeth, and kissed her fiercely, until gradually the laughter subsided, the lustrous eyes half-closed and the Syrian girl surrendered voluptuously to the man's embrace.

After that there were no more arguments, nor even a suggestion that either of them should submit meekly henceforth to the rules and regulations of married life.

But the hours sped by far too quickly and Rebecca didn't want to go home at half past four, and sulked when Rex insisted on leaving their green and shady retreat to take to the road again. But she must be reasonable, he said. It was his half-day and he couldn't leave Phil alone too long. He didn't want to arouse suspicion or 'start anything'. He wanted some peace in the home.

As he drove Becki back to her apartment he had the sensation that he was perforce 'coming to heel'. Had Phil not been there he and Becki would have spent the whole long languorous afternoon together, and then danced tonight at Fayid at the Officers' Club.

And that girl's dancing was a miracle. Sitting opposite Phil at the French Club talking about nothing wouldn't be much fun. Of course, there was a dance on *there* tonight. He had taught Phil to dance in England.

Admittedly she was light and graceful. But Becki's dancing held all the sensuousness and excitement of the East ... he had never known any woman who could move as she did.

Rex had never been good at doing things that were against his wish. He came back to Ismailia and his young wife reluctantly and, therefore, in a bad mood.

He was also genuinely tired. He flung himself into a chair and poured out a second whisky.

'Time for a quick one, and then some food, Phil,' he said. 'I think we'll nip down to the Greek Club tonight. I don't particularly feel like dancing. We'll come home early and go to bed.'

She stood before him, a slight feeling of anxiety creeping over her.

'Oh, are you frightfully tired, darling?'

He did not meet her gaze but mumbled, 'Yes.'

He then had the grace to remember that she had been alone all day and asked what she had been doing.

'Nothing much,' she said slowly.

An uncomfortable feeling of disappointment was creeping over her. He wasn't easy to understand, this handsome young husband of hers. How terribly moody he had become! There was none of the passionate tenderness of last night in his present attitude. He hadn't even kissed her yet.

Then she remembered the Pentyres and Martin. She said:

'Oh, Rex, we've been asked out to cocktails…'

He raised his head, looked at her and saw how smart she was.

'What's all this? Who's asked us?'

'Do you know Brigadier and Mrs Pentyre?'

Rex frowned and blinked.

'Never heard of them…' Then: 'Oh, ye gods! Not old Penwiper from B.T.E.?'

'Yes, if that's what you call him,' she smiled.

'Where in the name of fortune did you meet *them*?'

Phillida explained.

'They're awfully nice … not a bit stand-offish just because they're so senior, and Mrs Pentyre asked me to take you along to their place this evening. Do let's go.'

Rex set down his glass on the table.

'Really, Phil, you do make the most extraordinary friends!' he said. 'I don't know Penwiper or his wife personally, but he's got a reputation for being a silly old fool. Anyhow, I loathe having to be on my best behaviour, and it isn't as though he's my Brigadier or the slightest use to me. I really can't be bothered to drive all the way to Moascar just to say "Yes, sir" "No, sir" to Penwiper.'

Phillida's heart sank.

'I see,' she said.

'Do you want to go?' He frowned at her.

She coloured slightly.

'I thought it might be rather nice because I ... I liked them.'

Suddenly Rex put his tongue in his cheek and burst out laughing.

'Aha! Now I've got it. Your beautiful big Naval Commander is going to be there. You want to go and talk to *him* – not the Pen-wipers.'

She went crimson.

'Don't be silly, Rex.'

He pursued this line. It amused him. It also made him feel better about this afternoon.

'O.K., O.K., my angel! There's no need to look like a scared rabbit or be ashamed of "having a thing" about someone out here. I'm not locking you up, you know. But I thought there was something in it, and you all dressed up ... looking the tops. Good old Poppet!'

She felt suddenly furiously angry.

'I won't have you talk like that. It's not right! It's nothing to do with Martin Winters. I like him – I like him very much – but it was the Brigadier and his wife who asked us and who wanted to meet you and...'

She broke off, her eyes full of stormy tears.

She almost felt that she hated Rex for twisting the issue like this. She added:

'I'll go and telephone and tell Mrs Pentyre that you can't come. I told her I wasn't sure...'

He knew that he was being thoroughly selfish and disagreeable, and in consequence was annoyed with Phillida for making him feel so.

'I'll go if you insist,' he said darkly, 'but I really can't say it would be much of a party with the Penwipers and that smug stick Winters.'

'I don't think he's smug or a stick,' said Phillida.

Rex began to laugh again.

'I think you really have fallen for him.'

With a gesture of exasperation she turned and walked towards the door, conscious that her lips were quivering. Then, turning her head, she looked at him with resentful eyes.

'The "smug stick", as you call him, asked us to dine with him next week. I said we'd probably see him this evening and make a date. What message shall I give? He is spending the night with the Pentyres.'

'Oh, tell him we'll see him some time,' said Rex airily. 'I don't want to be pinned down.'

Her heart sank.

'Isn't that rather rude, Rex?'

He shrugged.

'O.K., tell him you will have dinner with him on my next late night.'

She stared at him unbelievingly.

'Rex, really?'

'Oh, tell him whatever you want!' snapped Rex. 'Make a date for us both for dinner. I'll sit through it and watch you enjoy yourself. I couldn't care less. But I loathe being nagged at the moment I get home.'

Speechlessly she left him and made her way to the telephone which stood in the hall. Once again her world of illusions and hopes came tumbling about her ears. This was not the Rex she had married. It was not, *it was not* ... oh, she couldn't bear it if they were going to disagree like this over everything.

Somehow or other she managed to get Mrs Pentyre on the line and make her apologies for this evening sound ordinary – casual.

'My husband had already made an appointment and I didn't know. I'm *so* sorry.'

'That's too bad,' said Mabyn Pentyre, 'but we'll make another date. I'll give you a ring, my dear.'

Slowly Phillida hung up the receiver and then returned to her room. She had sent no message to Martin.

Rex was lighting a cigarette. He put the burnt match in the ashtray and gave her a more friendly look.

'Did you put them off?'

183

'Yes.'

'Well, that's good,' he said, relieved; 'I really am too tired to stand a formal party. You must forgive me for being so selfish, darling.'

She felt confused and unhappy, and made a gesture of bewilderment.

'I didn't particularly want to go ... and what you said about Martin Winters is simply fantastic. I hardly know him.'

Rex grinned. Now that he had got his own way, and after three whiskies, he was feeling better.

'O.K., Poppet. I was only ragging you. But don't tell me that Winters isn't shooting a line with you, because I'm sure he is.'

'Well, I'm sure he isn't,' said Phillida indignantly.

'I don't mind if he is, my sweet. I'd hate to think you were the sort of girl no other chap admired.'

She stood silent, unsmiling. She completely failed to understand this new Rex. If he was in love with her ... surely he would hate some other fellow to 'shoot a line'. What sort of marriage was theirs to be? Did he really want it to turn into the sort of 'you go your way and I'll go mine' affair ... the sort of relationship which her friend Betty had favoured? The mere idea appalled Phillida.

'Come on, don't look so fed up,' Rex said;

'we'll go down to the Greek Club at seven. There's a very good bar there.'

Bars … drinks … bars … that was Rex's idea of a good evening – not being a guest in the house of nice people like the Pentyres. Rex slid a careless arm around her.

'You like going out with me alone, don't you? You used to like it.'

Immediately she responded to his friendly overture.

'You know I love being alone with you. It's what I want…'

But they wouldn't be alone in these bars where he knew a lot of men, and perhaps girls. It could just be another drinking session. She was anxious to please him … desperately anxious to recapture the happy feeling of being close together, which she had had last night and this morning. She hid her feelings.

'I'll just powder my nose and then we'll go, darling,' she said, trying to be cheerful.

He dropped a kiss on her cheek.

'Good old Poppet.'

She wasn't difficult to handle, he thought. Nothing like so difficult as Becki, really. He wondered if Becki would be at the Greek Club. She told him that she was going out in a R.A.F. party tonight. He wished he were going as her escort. Married life was a bit of a 'bind' and no mistake. He put an arm around Phillida and made a slight effort to get back into her good graces. 'You're looking lovely,' he said. 'I like you in that dress. I'm feeling better now. Perhaps when I've had a meal we won't come home early. We'll go on to the French Club and dance. Would you like that?'

Her spirits began to rise again. She used to like dancing with him.

'It would be lovely, Rex.'

'You wouldn't rather be going out with your N.O.?'

He asked the question out of sheer devilment and with a vain wish to hear her deny it. He was pleasantly flattered when she affirmed hotly that there had never been any question in her mind of preferring to go out with Martin.

When they reached the Greek Club he was pleased both with her and himself again.

The bar was crowded with R.A.F. and a smattering of Army. And sure enough Rebecca was there sitting on a high stool with a cocktail in her hand and a small circle of junior pilots around her. The moment Phillida saw her she froze, but Rebecca, with a swift, significant look at Rex, greeted Phillida gaily and with a flashing smile.

'Hell-o!... How nice to see you! Come and meet some of our boys.'

Rex, hands in pockets, said casually:

'Hello, Becki! How are you?'

One of the flying officers pushed a stool forward for Phillida. Everybody talked at once. Phillida caught no surnames. There was 'Sam' and 'Pete' and a red-haired, freckled boy whom everybody addressed as 'Jock'. Everybody seemed to be drinking, and everybody expressed surprise when Phillida said that all she wanted was a tomato juice. Then Rex added:

'A bit odd, my wife, isn't she? Prefers tomato juice to gin. Can't understand it...'

Everybody laughed again. Phillida joined in the laughter, but it didn't really seem very funny. 'The boys' were being very nice. She was young and fair, and pretty, and they were delighted to meet her and include her in their fun, and she knew how to talk to them... Through the war years she had served with men, and understood their language. But the atmosphere in general seemed to her artificial, as though everybody was trying to be gay but just now and again they told the truth. They didn't like Egypt. They were sick of the sun and the sand. They wanted to go back to England. Only Rex said he didn't want to go back.

With his bright, almond-shaped eyes mischievously slanting at Rebecca, he said:

'England's "had it" as far as I'm concerned. It's me for the Middle East or even the Far East again, if I get the chance. I don't think Phil and I will ever have a settled home. Even when I retire I think I'll go on travelling. It's lots of fun.'

The red-haired boy looked at Phillida. He thought she had the most beautiful grey eyes he had ever seen. But they were sad eyes. He was a Celt and he sensed that sadness. He said:

'Do you like travelling, Mrs Maltern?'

She caught Rex's eye. To please him she perjured herself.

'Oh yes, Rex and I both like it,' she said valiantly.

'Well, I'm a Scot,' said Jock, 'and my home's in Oban. I've a wee lassie waiting for me over there, and it's Scotland for me when my tour ends out here, praise the Lord.'

Phillida remembered that Martin had told her about the laird, his uncle: about the salmon-fishing, the purple-heather-covered moors, the grey, melancholy mists and weeping rain. Then the sun, breaking through the ragged clouds, lighting up the green crags, making a ribbon of silver out of the swift-moving river. She looked wistfully at the young Scots pilot, and said:

'Do please tell me about Oban...'

He told her, delighted to find someone who would listen to him because none of these others wanted to hear such things, nor would they understand the deep sick need of home that was within him. For until he

188

was drafted out here he had never been away from his native land. For a little while he was completely happy. He could have hugged this slender, wistful-eyed girl as he would hug a sister. And now he knew that she had not spoken the truth when she said she loved travel, and that she had only said it to please that good-looking Army chap to whom she was married.

Rex was no longer concerned with Phillida or what she was doing. He stood as close to Rebecca as he could get, and whispered:

'You look gorgeous...'

She wore pale yellow and looked subtle and rather Spanish tonight, with her sleek black hair parted in the middle and twisted into a knot at the nape of her neck. She coquetted with him, fluttering her long, glistening lashes.

'Did you get into trouble for being late?' she asked, in an undertone, the rim of her glass against her lips.

He retorted with a swagger:

'Certainly not. I do what I like, *when* I like.'

'I've had a wire from Kipps,' she said; 'he'll be back here tomorrow afternoon.'

Rex grimaced.

'Oh well, see how the land lies, and what his movements are, then ring me at the office.'

Rebecca set down her glass and looked at Phillida.

'She ees pretty, your wife, *hein?* I am jealous.'

Rex whispered fiercely in her ear:

'You know damn' well you've no need to be...' Then raising his voice: 'What about another round? This one's on me.'

So the drinking began again. Jock, the Scots boy, had a date and reluctantly left the Club, for he had been happy talking to Phillida Maltern, who was, in his private opinion, too good for Maltern, whom everybody knew was a helluva chap for drink and women. Another of the flying officers attached himself to Phillida. But he only wanted to induce her to exchange her tomato juice for something stronger. He was a flippant, rather stupid young man. An hour of it and Phillida was not a little bored and rather hungry. That was the worst of not being able to drink cocktails or whisky, she thought wryly; you wanted to eat but the others were happy to go on drinking.

At half past eight Rex was still standing in the crowd getting through a lot of money, and the party was centred around him – and the beautiful Rebecca. There was a lot of amusing backchat going on and everybody was laughing. Phillida felt suddenly resentful because not once had her husband asked her when she would like to eat, nor was he paying her the slightest attention. She slid off her stool and moved to his side.

'How about dinner, darling?'

He was in an affable mood and grinned at her.

'No hurry, honey. Have another of those tomato juice things you're so fond of.'

'I'd really like some food,' she said.

A frown replaced the grin.

'There's no hurry, Phil, is there?'

At once she became conscious that Rebecca's lustrous eyes were focused on her, and, in fact, all the rest of the party was watching and listening. She was horribly embarrassed. But she held her ground.

'Well, lunch seems an awfully long time ago and I didn't have any tea.'

Now Rex was conscious of Rebecca's somewhat mocking scrutiny. He did not want to be unpleasant to Phillida. He really liked to please everybody. But he was not going to be thought a henpecked husband, so he put down his glass on the bar and called for replenishment.

'We'll go and eat in a moment, Poppet. Have some nuts or chips... Becki, another drink... Pete, what about you?'

So it began again. And Phillida fancied she saw triumph in Rebecca's eyes.

The blood rushed to Phillida's cheeks and then faded, leaving her very pale. But she could do nothing about it. Rex was being stubborn and inconsiderate in the most charming way possible; offering her salted peanuts and potato crisps, loudly urging her to try a gin instead of a soft drink. She could not complain that he was inattentive to her. But her heart felt like a stone. She could see that the fact that she wanted to go and have dinner was not nearly so important to him as his own (and possibly Rebecca's) wish to remain here.

Then at last Rex decided that he, too, was hungry. But there seemed no question in his mind of dining *à deux* with Phillida.

'Shall we all go and have some food?' he suggested, and looked out of the corners of his eyes at Rebecca.

But Rebecca already had an escort and he didn't happen to like Rex Maltern. He was a friend of Kipps Rendledon's and a nice friendly boy. He said quickly and coldly:

'Afraid you must leave us out of it. Becki is dining in my party.'

Rex shrugged. Rebecca smiled. She liked men to quarrel over her. She said sweetly:

'See you sometime, *hein,* Rex? And you, Meeses Rex...'

Phillida murmured something unintelligible. She suddenly disliked Rebecca Rendledon exceedingly. She disliked the whole crowd. But she tried not to betray her feelings when at length she sat down at a small table beside Rex. She gave him a timid smile. But he did not return it. He was sulking. He was annoyed because that young flying officer fellow had appropriated Becki. He studied the menu and then handed it to his wife without speaking. Phillida put on her glasses. He stared at her resentfully. Why had he ever found her attractive? She looked like an insipid schoolgirl, reading the menu through those disfiguring horn rims, he thought. He saw no beauty tonight in the fair, smooth head or graceful hands. He was much too conscious of the strong physical allure of Rebecca ... Becki ... who was sitting somewhere in the restaurant ... in another party. He kicked one heel against the other savagely and called for a passing waiter.

'*Esmah* ... come on ... come on ... let's get on with the b—y dinner.'

Phillida looked at her husband over the rim of her glasses. Her face was very pale. She knew that he had had too many drinks. She said in a low tone:

'Don't shout, Rex... I – I hate people to look at us.'

'Don't teach me what to do!' he snapped.

She bit her lip and returned to the menu. But she could not see what was written on it. She was blinded by sudden bitter tears. She knew in that hour, beyond all doubt, that it was that Syrian girl, Rebecca Rendledon, whom Rex wanted ... not her, his wife.

10

Chaos reigned in the little flat which Captain James Angus had taken for his wife Doreen and the new baby.

He had fetched them from the Families Hospital at Moascar Garrison early this morning. It was now five o'clock. The baby lay in his new cot screaming his head off, waving small fists frenziedly in the air. He was hot and he was hungry; he had on far too many woollies and blankets.

His young mother lay on her bed face downwards. She, too, was crying, beating her small hands against the bed.

Jimmy Angus stood looking around him, his round, red face almost comical in its dismay. His nice blue eyes were bewildered. He had not the least idea what to do, nor whom to comfort first – his weeping wife or his howling son.

He had just come back from Camp and found everything in this state of misery and disorder. The little flat had been recently built and was not too bad – so he had thought – although he knew it would be hot in the summer because it was high up under the roof, and a long climb up the stairs for a woman with a baby. But he had had no choice, and had been considered lucky to get this place as all the other flats had long since been let. The furniture was simple and if not very adequate was new and clean. The walls were newly painted, the floors polished. There were blue-and-white cretonne curtains and dark green shutters. But there was no fly-proofing yet, so the rooms were full of the 'plague of Egypt'. And it seemed that the Sudanese boy whom Jimmy had engaged to come and 'do for' Doreen had not turned up. She had had to struggle alone all afternoon – so she told him between choking sobs – and had left little Bill with a kindly woman downstairs and gone out to buy food. She did not speak the language nor did she understand the money. (She made little effort to learn either.) She maintained that the brown, grinning faces and clawing hands of the street vendors terrified her, and she was equally afraid of the smooth and wily Oriental gentlemen in some of the shops, who spoke her language but looked so lasciviously at her English charms. She was by no means well yet, nor capable of looking after herself, let alone a new-born child. At the moment she was feeding the infant, but because she had 'been in a state' young Bill had, at midday, imbibed her chaotic mental condition, and cried dismally all the afternoon. He would not let her sleep. She was so tired that now she was rapidly becoming hysterical.

'I hate this place! I hate it! I want to go home!' she wailed.

Jimmy Angus was a placid soul, not easily disgruntled. He was anxious and troubled, but by no means defeated. He cast an eye at the cot which trembled every time the infant shook with a fresh spasm of grief and fury because he was neglected; then sat on the bed and tried to soothe his wife.

'Don't cry like that, Dorrie darling ... you aren't fit yet ... you'll make yourself ill ... it'll be all right ... it's only because that devil of a *suffragi* hasn't turned up, but I'll find you someone else. Now don't carry on like this, please, darling. Listen to Bill ... he needs you. Pull yourself together, do, Dorrie darling.'

This only served to fling her into a further frenzy of despair. She edged as far away from his hands as she could, great hiccoughing sobs convulsing her. She was not strikingly attractive. She was too short and would later run to fat, and for the moment she had not yet recovered her normal figure. But she had pretty fair hair, close-cropped, curling about her head and a very white skin, and when smiling she was what the Scots called 'bonnie' with her big blue eyes, cheeky little nose and a small pouting mouth. She had small feet and ankles. At the moment she looked bedraggled and plain. Her face was blotched with crying. She wore a not very clean dressing-gown of artificial blue satin, which was fraying at all the seams and had a grease stain down the front.

'I shall never be able to stand this!' she moaned. 'It's all very well for you ... you men get away from the place, and everything's done for you. You don't know what it's like for a woman trying to cope with a baby and a flat in a strange country.'

Jimmy gave a sigh.

'Oh, I'm sure it's difficult for you, dear, until you get used to it, but when you've got a servant...'

'I don't like black servants,' she broke in, 'I'm afraid of them.'

'But, darling, there's nothing to be afraid of. They're all quite friendly, and the Sudanese make the most faithful slaves. This one just didn't turn up but...'

She interrupted again:

'I can't speak Arabic, either. I'll never be able to give orders. He'll be able to do "do" me and thieve to his heart's content, and I won't be able to stop him.'

'Darling, on the whole the Sudanese are honest,' Jimmy persisted gently.

She sat up, running her fingers through a damp tangle of curls, and looked at him with her swollen, resentful eyes.

'I don't know how to cope with babies... Bill never stops crying. If only we had a nurse it would be different.'

The faithful and loving heart of Jimmy Angus sank a little.

'Afraid I can't afford a nurse as well as a servant, darling, but you'll learn about the nipper, won't you? Didn't the nurses show you...?'

'Yes,' said Doreen sullenly.

He tried to take her hand again, but she snatched it away, adding: 'I don't want to be pawed.'

Jimmy flushed, stood up and walked across to the baby's cot and stood staring at his son. The canvas cot was without trimmings. He knew that Doreen had meant to put fresh white, organdie frills and blue ribbon around it, but during the last six weeks before Bill was born, living in a local hotel, Doreen had grown so miserable and listless she had hardly done anything. And she had groused without ceasing since she arrived here three months ago.

He knew that she oughtn't to have come. Her parents had been against it. They had wanted her to stay on in her old home, where her mother could look after her until her baby was born. But she had insisted upon joining him in Egypt. Out of three years of marriage they had had only two months together. He was not a Regular, but he had another year's service to get though. She had wanted to spend that year abroad with him. When he had written home to say that he had enough points to get her out under the Married Families scheme, and could book one of these flats, which were then being built in Ismailia, she had been all eagerness to come. She would have the baby in hospital out there, she said, and enjoy the good food and sunshine, and everything would be wonderful. That was so typical of Doreen. She always wanted her own way, and then when she got it found the thing that she had craved was no longer so desirable. Jimmy had, from the beginning, dreaded uprooting her from English life and ways. But she had persuaded him, and he had applied for her.

In spite of his Scottish name and descendancy he had been born and brought up in the South. Except for a few relations up North he had no interests there. Before the war he had been articled to a firm of solicitors in London. They were holding the job open for him and he hoped to return to civilian life as a lawyer and eventually get a partnership. While he was still a bachelor he spent a lot of his spare time tinkering with cars, which were a passion with him (it was the subject of cars which formed common ground between him and Rex Maltern when they first met in the Middle East), and as a sideline he bought and sold quite a number. During the war Jimmy's family had been bombed out of their London home, and old Angus, a retired civil servant, bought a small suburban house and garden in Welwyn Garden City. The Palmers – Doreen's people – lived next door. During the first leave which Jimmy spent in his new home he saw a lot of the curly-haired Doreen and her crippled sister, Peggy, and a very nice elder brother, Dick, who was in the Marines.

Looking back on those days of his lightning courtship and marriage to Doreen and the subsequent leaves spent with her, Jimmy was always rather bewildered by the complete metamorphosis which had taken place since she joined him out here – the change in Doreen's outlook and conduct towards himself.

She had seemed so much in love in the Welwyn days ... so anxious to please. And he had been crazy about her, she was so sweet, always prettily dressed and so beguiling with those big blue eyes that looked up at him so adoringly and that small, pouting mouth raised thirstily for his kisses. Of course, he had not bothered then to wonder how domesticated she was or whether she would make a capable wife (he was used to being well looked after by a capable Scottish-born mother). They had never had a home together. Doreen's home was well run by her own mother, and all their leaves had been easy and lovely. He had looked forward to a most successful married life with her.

As for the baby ... it had been Doreen who had wanted that, too. In his slow, cautious way Jimmy had suggested that it might be better for them to wait until he could return to civilian life and they were more settled ... but no, she had insisted ... in one of her transports, that strong urge for something she hadn't got ... and here was young Bill. But from the moment Doreen landed in Egypt she had opened his eyes to that other girl whom he had never known, and whose faults had been so cleverly hidden from him by her doting family.

Now she was unfolding before his sight as a discontented incapable young woman. A difficult, exacting Doreen, with whom he found it hard to deal despite all his patience, and almost impossible to love because she seemed to have taken a physical dislike to him. So worried had he been by her antipathy a month ago that he had gone, miserably, to the M.O. and had a talk with him. The M.O. had patted him on the back and told him not to worry; that it was her pregnancy which had changed Doreen and that once the baby was born she would be her old loving self again.

While she was in hospital he had hoped forlornly that this was so because she had seemed so pleased to see him when he visited her. She had produced young Bill with comparative ease and enjoyed her 'lying in', spoiled and surrounded with flowers and with gifts both from him and the other 'wives' whom she had met out here. He had hoped for ... so much. And he had meant tonight to be a great celebration ... he was enormously pleased with his son and anxious to feel that all was well between Doreen and himself again. But this didn't look like much of a celebration, he thought ruefully, as he stared round the disordered room. And here she was moving away again when he so much as touched her...

Helplessly he looked down at the girl. The baby's screams rose to a crescendo. Strong though his nerves were, Jimmy felt them suddenly fray.

'For the love of Mike pull yourself together, darling, and see to young Bill,' he said, speaking more sharply to her than he had intended.

Doreen looked shocked and then burst into fresh tears. He didn't love her or he couldn't speak to her like that. What would Mummy and Daddy – or Peggy – have said if they had heard? She wished she had never come out to Egypt. It was the end.

With a long-drawn sigh Jimmy sat down

on the bed and without further ado pulled the reluctant body of his wife into his arms and firmly held her there.

'You're a ridiculous little thing and you know it. You know I love you very much, and I've been looking forward like anything to having you out here. Now don't cry any more, Dorrie darling. Things will be much better when you've had a chance to get used to this new life. Just you wait – we'll have some lovely times together.'

With difficulty he soothed and cajoled her. Finally her weeping subsided. She wiped her streaming flushed face and controlled herself sufficiently to walk to the cot and attend to her three-weeks-old son, who had by this time changed his own tactics and lay with half-shut eyes in a slightly stupefied comatose condition.

Doreen, bending over the cot, muttered:

'The water in the tap's not hot. Put the kettle on for me, Jimmy. I suppose I must bath the poor little soul.'

Jimmy brightened and rushed to put on the kettle. He began to whistle cheerfully as he helped his wife prepare the bath. While he worked he tried to comfort her with a few words of hope and encouragement.

'I've asked Rex Maltern and his wife to come round and see us later on this evening. I told you what a nice girl she is. She'll be a good friend for you, darling.'

Doreen sniffed and blew her nose. She was not really in the mood to accept comfort, but she was so glad to have her husband back, helping her, that she allowed him to try and lift her out of the depths of despair which had engulfed her while she was alone. She hated being alone in this frightening country. Somehow when she was in England she had woven in her mind a fabulous and quite unauthentic picture of a romantic Egypt wherein she would find luxury and glamour; a palatial residence, a retinue of fawning and well-trained servants and nothing to do but clap her hands and give orders. She was given to creating a world of illusion, and she had always been spoiled by her adoring parents because she had been a delicate child and they had sacrificed everything for their family. Because Peggy had been born with that malformed hip they had been terrified that something would happen to the second daughter. Doreen had, in fact, been a martyr to asthma, which had kept her out of the Services during the war. So the spoiling had gone on until she met Jimmy Angus. His round, cheerful face and obvious adoration had decided her that he would make a good husband and she had snatched at him when he proposed marriage.

As a matter of fact she had been in better health with little Bill on the way than she had ever been before, and in the hospital she had been told she was perfectly fit and able to nurse the infant. But she had no great wish to resign from her former position as the 'fragile little thing' who needed a great deal of pampering.

She had been more than slightly horrified to find what conditions were like for Army wives abroad these days. She was of poor courage and lacked the pioneer spirit. Such was her disappointment that she made Jimmy the scapegoat. *He* was responsible for landing her in this hard life in a country which she had begun to loathe. For the moment she was out of love with him and out of countenance with the world in general.

She dragged herself round the flat and tried to put up some show of remembering what the nurses had told and shown her concerning the welfare of her baby. But it was Jimmy who, with tunic off and sleeves rolled up, did most of the work. Clumsily and tenderly he held the pathetic squirming little body of his son while Doreen sponged him. It was Jimmy who cleared everything away while Doreen fed the child.

'Poor little skinned rabbit,' he thought. 'What sort of a world have we brought him into? All the nations at each other's throats. I hope to God we haven't merely produced cannon-fodder for the next war...'

And he fell to dreaming about the better world he would like to build for his son. Whilst Doreen, once more calm, nursed Bill and brooded as to how soon she could get away from Ismailia and take the child back to England with her. She worried over this problem without a scrap of consideration for her husband or as to how he would feel, parting with her and the child so soon. Her feelings were purely egotistical. She wanted to get home where her mother would do all the work for her and Peggy would help look after Bill.

The snag was, of course, money. She had only been out here four months. Jimmy had nothing but his Army pay and allowances, and there was young Bill to consider now, and save for. Jimmy wouldn't really be able to pay her passage home now; besides which he had taken a lease of this horrible flat, and was on the list for a 'quarter' in the Garrison. And she couldn't get her father to pay for her ticket because at the moment he had put all his available cash into a new branch of business which he and a friend were opening – an estate agency – which he hoped to turn into a good thing. She was cornered. She could see it, for the moment, anyhow, and it was that feeling which made her antagonistic towards Jimmy.

As soon as the baby was replete and asleep, and all was quiet in the flat, Doreen wearily changed from the blue satin dressing-gown into a dress. Then she began to forage round the little kitchen and open tins for supper. The long list of complaints reopened.

'You said we could eat out. I never expected to do any cooking. You know I hate it. Mummy always did it at home. I oughtn't to have to do any work now when I'm just out of hospital. It's disgraceful. If they could see me at Welwyn tonight they'd break their hearts…'

Jimmy, who hadn't stopped working since he arrived back in the flat and now had a tea-towel tied round his waist and a pipe in his mouth, dug the point of a tin-opener somewhat violently into the lid of the Spam which she had handed him.

'I'm damned sorry, darling. I know you oughtn't to be working,' he said, 'and it wasn't what I meant. You know I had the boy all lined up. I'll wring his neck if he turns up, the so-and-so. He was supposed to be here first thing this morning and Phil Maltern said she'd come along and look at you. But Rex was on the 'phone from Fayid this morning to say she was laid up or something.'

Doreen brooded over this. She had met Rex Maltern once or twice and thought him very handsome and charming, but goodness only knew what the wife would be like, and she didn't want some woman who would just come and criticise and want entertaining, when she herself was feeling so awful.

Jimmy added:

'You'll like Mrs Maltern – I'm sure you will. She's a sweet girl, and actually I think Maltern bullies her a bit.'

'All men are bullies,' said Doreen bitterly.

Jimmy shook the moist, pink Spam out on to a dish, then eyed his wife with a wry smile.

'Darling, I don't bully you, do I?'

Her lashes dropped.

'No, but you expect a lot of me.'

'I don't expect anything,' he said gently.

'But you oughtn't to have let me come out knowing what Egypt is like.'

'But, angel, you insisted on coming. I did write and say that it might be better for you to wait until after Bill was born, but you begged so hard for me to put in my application. I even told you that our quarter at Moascar wouldn't be ready for a few months, and that I'd have to get a flat for you. I'm sure you'll be much better when we get our quarter…'

She interrupted:

'You keep pointing out that I insisted on coming. It looks as though you didn't want me.'

'Dorrie darling, don't twist my words. You know I wanted *you*, but I was afraid of this sort of thing…' He made a gesture of the hand. 'And it's all much worse because all my plans have gone wrong and the *suffragi* let us down. But don't let's argue any more. I'll always do my best for you – you know that – and tomorrow we'll get a boy, by hook or by crook.'

Doreen walked to the window and looked down at the street. It was quite a nice street in the centre of the town with a narrow strip of green, shut in by railings and a row of green trees, running down the centre of it. Most of the buildings were clubs, hostels, blocks of flats or small hotels. It was a busy thoroughfare, and now, after dark, with lights glaring from all the windows and doors, it presented a strange and sinister aspect to Doreen after her quiet home in Welwyn Garden City. It looked to her like an inferno, with street vendors haggling shrilly, native music blaring from one open door, the sound of a modern dance tune on a radio from another, little Arab boys, dirty and ragged, in their long gowns, racing after each other with gaunt, odd-looking dogs at their heels. Immediately below an ancient native led an overloaded donkey; a constant stream of private cars and Army vehicles passed each other. The pavements were crowded with a mixture of races – Egyptians, French, Syrian and a large smattering of British troops.

With a shudder Doreen drew back and

eyed her husband with her large resentful eyes.

'It's an awful, evil place. I hate it. And you are going to get up early and leave me in the morning? Shall I be left to cope with Baby *and* the shopping again?'

He bit his lip.

'No, darling; even if I have to see my C.O. and explain the position, I'll get the day off and help you. I won't let you be alone.'

His patient kindliness seemed to incite her to further abuse rather than touch her heart.

'I think it's awful the way the Army treats wives. You're a Captain. I ought to have more consideration. Mummy's sister, my Aunt Dorothy, was married to a Captain and she had a most wonderful time in India. When we were children I used to hear about it. She had a marvellous bungalow and lived like a queen and never did a stroke of work. Her bearer used to pick up her handkerchief if she dropped it.'

This reduced Jimmy to sudden laughter. Poor little Doreen! She looked such a funny, pitiful little thing standing there in one of the new, pretty dresses she had brought out (made by Peggy, who sewed marvellously), a dark blue with a V neck and short sleeves which showed the milky whiteness of her throat and arms, that lovely white skin which with her golden, curly hair had so fascinated him when he first saw her. He had not noticed then, nor did he see very plainly now, that she had a selfish, spoiled mouth, and that the snub nose and small chin belonged to a weak, stubborn character. He remembered only that she was the girl whom he had made his wife and with whom he was still deeply in love, and that she had just given him a son. But he had to laugh.

'I don't see what's so funny!' she flashed.

He grew serious again.

'But, Dorrie darling, it's so absurd to compare the life your aunt led long before the war with this post-war existence we're leading. I know chaps in India at the moment, and I assure you life isn't much easier there these days than it is here. The Army rates of pay are all lowered, or if they're not they are going to tax allowances. Nobody but the high-ups live these days like a Captain *used* to live pre-war. Life is changing for everybody, darling, and not only for folks in the Army. It'll be the same for me when I'm a civilian again. We're all having to accept a lower standard, unfortunately.'

Doreen seized a loaf of bread and began a hopeless search for a knife that would cut it. She didn't know where to find anything. She hardly cared. She thought of Welwyn; of the good supper Mummy would be serving up for her father and sister, and Mrs Ealing, their char, who would come in and do all the washing-up tomorrow morning. Of course, there was rationing, and it was bitterly cold; there were electricity cuts, too, and a shortage of fuel, and everybody grumbled. But it was better than this sinister, fly-ridden country, she thought.

She felt her husband's hand on her arm.

'Don't be too miserable, Doreen darling. I'm terribly sorry if you're disappointed with what you've found out here. But I assure you it won't be too bad later on. We shall have our quarter in the Garrison, and it will be a nice one, whereas fellows of my rank with a wife only get one room in Fayid. And for us it isn't for ever. Only for another year.'

'A whole year!' moaned Doreen, dropping the loaf of bread and bursting into tears again.

Jimmy was exasperated, hurt and quite incapable of dealing with the situation. If he tried to kiss her or comfort her she accused him of wanting to make love to her, and being 'beastly'. If he left her alone she said that he was neglectful. He supposed that it was having this baby and being so far from England that was affecting her. Privately he was of the opinion that if Peggy could get a tourist visa and come out and help Doreen with the baby it would be all to the good. Peggy was a cripple and four years older than Doreen, and had none of her appeal.

But she was a most sensible and capable girl in her way, and she worshipped Doreen. Jimmy registered a mental vow to write to his mother-in-law tomorrow and suggest that if they could all scrape together for the fare and get the visa, Peggy should come at once. He was really getting worried about Doreen.

He was a hungry man after his day's work, but he had to be content that night with a very scrap meal. And it was he who finally prepared it, made some coffee and waited hand and foot on his young wife, who had condescended to stop crying and eat a little 'for the baby's sake', she said.

Hardly had she been persuaded into a better humour when young Bill awoke with violent indigestion and started to scream lustily again.

Doreen lifted him out of the cot and patted his back as she had seen the nurses do, whilst Jimmy looked on, thinking sentiment-ally that Dorrie looked sweet with the tiny primrose-coloured head of the infant tucked between her chin and her shoulder. But young Bill did not stop crying, and after a moment or two Doreen laid him back in his cot and then turned to her husband, her face scarlet, her lips set.

'I'm not going to stand this any more. I can't. I just don't know what to do. I know there's something wrong with him. We ought to have the doctor. You must send for the M.O.'

Jimmy looked flabbergasted.

'But, darling, I don't think he's ill. Surely we don't want to drag the M.O. out at this time of night.'

'How do you know he's not ill? You don't know any more about babies than I do.'

'But, darling, I'm sure it's only indigestion. You've been upset today, and you told me that the nurses said that it would affect the baby if *you* got upset, as you're nursing him.'

Doreen started to breathe hard.

'So you are going to blame *me* because he's crying? I've never heard anything so unkind!'

Jimmy put his pipe in his pocket. Patient though he was, he was beginning to near the end of his own tether. He felt that *he* could not stand any more nagging, no matter how dearly he loved Doreen. He opened his mouth to make a sharp retort, which was mercifully prevented by the sound of a bell shrilling through the screams and hiccoughs of young Bill.

Husband and wife looked at each other, then Doreen said:

'That's the front door.'

'Someone's come to see us, probably.'

'Well, this is a nice time for visitors!' said Doreen sullenly.

215

'I expect it's the Malterns,' said Jimmy, both looking and feeling miserable; 'shall I tell them to go away and come another evening?'

'No, let them in,' said Doreen; 'perhaps Mrs Maltern knows something about babies...'

Jimmy was fast learning that the motive at the back of most of his wife's actions was a selfish one, and that if she could use people for her own ends she did so unscrupulously. Feeling more dejected than he had ever done in his whole life he went to the front door and opened it, while Doreen hurriedly powdered her nose and ran a comb through her curls.

The Malterns entered the little flat, which was filled with the sound of young Bill's spasmodic screaming.

Jimmy started off with an apology.

Doreen wasn't at all well ... there was something wrong with the baby ... the damn' *suffragi* hadn't turned up ... it was all a bit of a mix-up, and the rest of it.

Rex, however, walked into the sitting-room with his usual charm and willingness to make himself popular. He had just had a good dinner at the Club, and enough drinks to put him in an amiable state of mind, and was smoking a cigar.

'Rotten luck, old boy. What can we do? Let Phil lend a hand. She's wonderful with kids, aren't you, Phil? Listen to the poor little beggar… There you are, old boy. Worst of having kids. Always a spot of trouble.'

Jimmy looked appealingly at Phillida.

'Well, if you do know anything about babies, do give Dorrie a word of advice, Phil, she's at her wits' end.'

Phillida took in the situation at a glance. The distraught-looking Jimmy, the disordered flat (the sitting-room was full of half-opened trunks and a variety of articles spread over sofa and chairs), and the baby's screams which were now frantic.

Then Jimmy's wife appeared, looking, despite her efforts to 'smarten up', rather bedraggled, and having been obviously crying, and started to voice her complaints. And at once Phillida was deeply sorry for them both … for different reasons. Mrs Angus was undoubtedly the helpless type, and Jimmy had not the first idea how to cope with such a domestic crisis. Neither, of course, had Rex, who, in Jimmy's place, thought Phillida, might have stopped trying to cope and fled from the scene long ago. He abominated weeping babies. This 'poor little beggar' stuff he was putting over was all for show. But Phillida was genuinely concerned at what she saw and heard.

All this week she, herself, had been profoundly unhappy. She had wakened this morning with such a blinding head and feeling of sickness that she had had to close the shutters and stay in bed, refusing her breakfast. Madame Martial had kindly offered her lunch, but she had rejected that, too. She occasionally got these sick head-aches at home; more often than not when she was especially worried or upset. She knew that this particular attack was caused by the poignancy of her feelings about Rex and Rebecca, and her bitter disappointment in the reunion which she had so hoped would be a great success.

But she had struggled up before Rex came home, and without complaining accompanied him to the Club and did her best to be bright and to eat something so that he would not be bored.

She had had a bad week on the whole. Rebecca did not come into it much, because Squadron-Leader Rendledon had returned and Rebecca was once more seen at his side. Rex had had to retire from the scene. In consequence he had been rather irritable and was at his best only when they were in a crowd where he could 'show off'. It had been a week of bitter revelation for Phillida. But she had done nothing and said nothing … she sat back and watched and listened. She was still unwilling to admit that there was no hope left of happiness with Rex. He had moments of being charming and lover-like, and she clung to them desperately.

She walked with Doreen Angus into the bedroom to see the baby.

'You know I meant to be here to help you today, Mrs Angus, but unfortunately I got a touch of liver and had to stay in bed,' she said.

The other girl was prepared to be amicable.

'Oh, do call me Doreen! I've heard so much about you from Jimmy, and it's so nice to have a girl-friend. I miss all my friends and relations in England so much.'

'Poor you! And what bad luck your *suffragi* not turning up!'

Doreen felt better already. She liked the look of Rex's wife. She seemed sympathetic. Doreen was hungry for sympathy and attention. She lifted her baby out of the cot.

'I just can't stop him crying, and he had a good feed a couple of hours ago, so he can't be hungry yet... I'm so dead tired. Still so weak, you know, and I simply can't bear the Middle East...'

All the grievances poured out once more. Phillida listened, one eye on the tiny convulsed features of the infant. In actual fact she knew little about babies, and did not understand why Rex had said that she did. But during the summer at Alvercombe last year she had seen quite a lot of a woman who was a friend of Gamma's, and who had a married daughter with a new-born infant staying with her. Rex had been right to say that Phillida loved babies. She loved them as she loved puppies and all small, helpless things, and to have a child of her own had been one of her secret ambitions during the years while she waited for Rex. She had often visited the young Alvercombe mother, who was very efficient with her baby.

She could see without much difficulty where Doreen was wrong and how she mishandled Bill.

'Give him to me,' she said.

Willingly Doreen surrendered the baby to Phillida's outstretched arms. Immediately young Bill was sick over Phillida's crisp, white blouse and grey flannel skirt. Doreen, with a little scream of horror, rushed for water and a cloth. But Phillida was unperturbed. She was using her common sense and what little knowledge had been imparted to her at Alvercombe. There was no need for a doctor here and she knew it. There was nothing wrong with Bill except that he was wet and uncomfortable, and had far too many blankets over him. The soft, silky head was damp with perspiration.

In a few moments Phillida had him clean and dry, and then, having brought up the wind, put him back in the cot with only one fleecy blanket over him, and gave him a few drops of cool water. After a few whimpers, he slept.

Doreen was genuinely grateful, and from that moment Phillida Maltern became a valued friend.

'You were simply marvellous!' she exclaimed. 'I don't know how you did it.'

'I did nothing, really,' said Phillida modestly.

'Oh, how I wish you lived nearer me!'

'While Rex is away I can always come down and give you a hand,' said Phillida, which was exactly what Doreen had wanted her to say.

'Oh, I shall be so grateful!'

She led Phillida back to the untidy sitting-room. Jimmy was enjoying a well-earned glass of beer with Rex. Doreen explained how 'marvellous' Phil had been.

'You ought to have seen how she managed Bill.'

'Phil's good at anything she does,' said Rex.

Somehow this praise did not bring much pleasure to Phillida. She knew that it did not come from Rex's heart, and it was merely because he liked her to 'shine' before his friends. But Jimmy's round, blue eyes looked at her with heartfelt gratitude.

'Peace reigns at last. You are, indeed, a good angel,' he said.

'She's going to come down and give me a hand tomorrow,' said Doreen eagerly, anxious not to let Phillida forget her offer.

Rex eyed his wife covertly. When Doreen called Jimmy out to help her a moment in the kitchen to find some orange squash for Phillida, Rex took his cigarette from his mouth and whispered to his wife fiercely:

'For heaven's sake don't get too involved with that whining little fool. She'll only take advantage of your kindness. You're too damned good-natured. I don't want you here minding her blasted baby.'

Phillida flushed.

'There's nothing against my helping her while you're at work,' she answered, in an undertone. 'I'm rather sorry for her, coming straight out of hospital and no help at all.'

'Well, she bores me stiff,' muttered Rex, 'and I only brought you here because Jimmy's on the same job at B.T.E. as mine in Fayid and we're always in contact. Also there's some talk at G.H.Q. of him being made a Major although he doesn't know it yet. It'll be just a temporary rank, but he's considered pretty useful, and is in with the Brigadier, so it might pay me to keep in...'

He said no more. They could hear Jimmy's footsteps in the hall. Phillida sat down feeling slightly nauseated, as she always did by this attitude that not only Rex but other Army men seemed to take up. Knowing and being nice to someone because it 'paid' seemed to her so hypocritical, so unattractive.

Jimmy and Doreen appeared with some lemon squash and iced water; everybody seemed more cheerful and talkative, and the atmosphere was decidedly less strained than it had been when first the Malterns arrived.

When Phillida returned home that night her head had begun to ache again, and she was only too thankful to crawl into bed and shut her eyes and relax. Rex, after a few more uncomplimentary allusions to Doreen, stretched out on his side of the bed and went to sleep.

For a long while Phillida lay sleepless, staring out at the white moonlight and listening to the incessant chirping of the crickets. She was lonely – horribly lonely – in body and in mind. She felt as though she lay beside a stranger, cold, sexless, indifferent to her, as oblivious to her mental isolation as he was of her physical presence.

She thought of Doreen and the wailing baby in that awful little flat.

She could not admire Doreen. She was almost all that Rex had said about her ... a whining, insipid little creature who lacked courage, and yet Phillida found it in her heart to be sorry for her; to comprehend her homesickness, her rather pathetic fear of this strange land, and the life for which she was so ill equipped. Poor Doreen! In her shallow, cowardly little soul no doubt she suffered acutely. And Jimmy suffered because he loved her. Poor, patient Jimmy!

'And I,' thought Phillida, 'am suffering too. But Rex is all right ... he takes with both hands and gives nothing ... utterly indifferent to the miseries of others. And he is the man I have married, whom I loved and for whom I have waited for three long years!...

She lay sleepless, staring with dry and desolate eyes at the bright Egyptian moonlight.

The next morning, with that quiet, determined streak which few discovered on first encounter with the shy and gentle Phillida, she went down to the Anguses' flat to help Doreen with the baby.

11

Three weeks later Martin Winters walked into the French Club, where he was meeting his friends the Pentyres. It was the Brigadier's birthday, and it was to be a party.

Martin was unaccountably depressed, and he had not, he told himself, 'the party spirit' this evening. Perhaps it was because he knew that Mabyn had invited Phillida Maltern and her husband to join them, and that the invitation had been refused. A few days ago, when he had seen his old friends, Mabyn had said:

'I've tried once or twice to get hold of your little friend, but the husband always seems to be engaged. He must be a very busy young man!'

The touch of sarcasm in those words did not escape Martin. Personally he reviewed the whole situation with apprehension. He was sure somehow that Phillida herself would have said yes to each one of Mrs Pentyre's invitations. It was Maltern who made her refuse them.

Martin wondered why.

He had an uncomfortable feeling that things were not going too well for that girl

who was so like Bridget. It worried him un-
duly, for she was still nothing but a stranger
to him, and she was a married woman in
whom he ought to take no particular
interest. But after that episode on the night
of her arrival – that glaring revelation about
Maltern and the Syrian girl – it seemed
obvious that Phillida, poor child, must be
floundering in deeper waters than she could
swim.

Since his posting from Port Said to Fayid,
Martin had driven over to Ismailia quite a
lot more often than he used to do. And each
time that he dined here he saw the Malterns. Always he stopped to speak to them.
Once or twice he asked them for a drink. At
such times he fancied that he saw a shy
pleasure in the girl's grey eyes and a willingness to talk to him ... but that Maltern
accepted his drinks and returned them in an
off-hand manner; even with reluctance.
There was a slight insolence about that
young man which made Martin secretly
long to kick him. And whether it was
genuine or not, Martin did not know but
Rex assumed an extra proprietary air with
Phillida as soon as they all got together, and
stood with an arm around her shoulders, or
took her hand in his while they were talking
to him, Martin; as much as to say, 'She
belongs to me and you'd better remember
it, old boy...'

Rex Maltern had the most unusual effect on Martin. As soon as he got within an inch of the man he felt his usual good-humour and friendliness vanish. Quite frankly he detested the man, and had it not been for Phillida and the memories which her extraordinary likeness to Bridget evoked in him he would not have bothered his head about either of them any further.

But in that young and touching way she had, Phillida always seemed to want to talk to him ... and when he was with her he was conscious that there was no other girl in the place with whom he would more willingly converse. But the whole thing was futile, and friendship seemed impossible because he and Maltern could never be friends. It seemed a pity.

Tonight he was here a good half-hour before he had been invited. It had been a hot day in Fayid, and with that usual spirit of depression weighing him down, he had decided to come into Ismailia early and perhaps have a drink and a chat with old George, and try to get himself into a better frame of mind for the birthday party.

The first person he saw, the moment he walked into the cool room, was Phillida Maltern.

She was sitting alone in a basket-chair with a book in her hand. She had on her glasses. The fair hair was looped at the back of her neck, and she wore a grey dress with a crisp white collar. She looked like a little Puritan, he thought, very grave and studious with her book and her glasses. As always, when he saw her, he was immensely drawn to her.

He was almost at her side before she recognised him, then she raised her head and he could not but be gratified by the sudden lighting up of her whole countenance, and the deeper pink of her rather pale face.

'Oh, hello, Martin!' she exclaimed, taking off her glasses.

He saluted her. He was in uniform tonight. They were 'dressing' for this dinner party. It was the first time Phillida had seen him in that blue uniform and she thought how extremely well it suited him. He looked so fresh and wholesome, and such a typical sailor, with his fair, shining head and the deep blue eyes, and the brown face, which looked so very brown in contrast to the white shirt and collar.

'You're all dressed up,' she smiled.

He grimaced. 'Birthday honours for old Brig. Pen.'

'Oh, yes, of course,' she said, and a slight shadow passed across her face. Now she remembered that she and Rex had been asked to this party, and that Rex would not let her accept.

He had already invited Squadron-Leader

Rendledon and his wife to dinner, he had told her, and stubbornly refused to alter the date in favour of what he said would be only '*one of those sticky b—y awful shows that I can't take*'.

'May I?' asked Martin, touching the chair beside her.

'Oh, yes, do sit down,' she said, 'please.'

'Your husband hasn't come yet?'

'No.'

Martin signalled to one of the waiters and opened his cigarette-case. 'Is he working?'

'Yes,' said Phillida. 'I've just walked down here but Rex said he'd be late. He didn't go to Fayid this morning. As a matter of fact he was in Cairo yesterday on a job and stayed the night, and he still isn't back, but he 'phoned to say he'd be here by eight o'clock, because we ... we've got people to dinner...'

Martin ordered his usual pink gin, and a tomato juice for Phillida. Then, lighting his cigarette, he said:

'I was sorry you couldn't join the Brigadier's party.'

'So was I,' said Phillida.

There was an awkward silence. Martin added:

'So you were all alone last night?'

'Yes.'

'I'm sorry I didn't know. You might have dined with me.'

'I'd have liked that,' she said simply.

229

And she was not a little disturbed to think how much she would have liked it. She always felt so peaceful and contented in Martin Winters' company.

She had been in Ismailia for over a month now. A month of disillusionment and difficulty, a month full of confused impressions, of black moments with Rex, interspersed by occasional gleams of hope, then back to a state of doubt and suspicion again. Finally the certain knowledge that unless something happened to save this marriage of hers it would soon be on the rocks. For Rex was steering both her and himself towards those rocks with ruthless disregard for her feelings.

She was never sure in what mood he was going to come home to her these days. But she could be certain that whatever she did would be wrong in his eyes, and that if there was anything she wished to do, he would not want it.

There seemed to be nothing of their old comradeship left. Occasionally he was charming. Occasionally he seemed to want to make love to her, but she had long since given up hoping that those spells meant anything like real love. He did not love her. But he knew moments of passion when he took ruthlessly all that she had to give. That was not what she wanted. That did not begin to make a real marriage for her. And she was fast reaching a pitch when she did not want any longer to be made love to by Rex. Kisses from him when they were followed by hours of complete neglect or harsh criticism held no comfort, no sense of security. And there was always the shadow of Rebecca between them ... the thought which she had left unspoken so far, because she shrank from the consequences which might follow an open accusation on her part.

But the atmosphere between them was wretchedly unsatisfactory for Phillida. She had a perpetual struggle not to let her disappointment and despondency master her. She forced herself to write as cheerfully as possible to her grandmother and her friends. And out here she had no friends because Rex would not let her make her own, and she did not care for those whom he chose for her.

In fact, the person whom she knew best and saw most of was the unhappy Doreen, who clung to her piteously. Without saying much to Rex, Phillida went regularly to the Anguses' flat and derived a certain amount of pleasure from minding the poor little baby or shopping for Doreen.

But she did not really like Doreen. One had to 'give' to her all the time. Phillida, with that bitter sense of loneliness deep down inside her, craved for affection and understanding – for real friendship. And in Martin Winters, with his gentle manner and old-fashioned courtesy, she knew she could have found both.

But Rex would not accept any of the invitations which either came from Martin or included him. He seemed to have a devilish wish to frustrate her desire for a platonic friendship. At the mere mention of Martin's name he became churlish – or made mock of Martin; called him 'her boy-friend'; persisted in saying that if she wanted to go out with him she could go alone.

She was not going to do that ... she was not going to give him a chance to cast aspersions on her so that he could feel free to behave as *he* wanted, and she knew now, despite all her reluctance to admit it, that that was at the back of his mind.

While Martin sat here talking to her this evening she was almost happy, until he said:

'It is really about time we had that dinner – you and your husband and myself.'

'Yes,' she said hurriedly, 'one day it would be marvellous...'

Martin saw the hot colour and noted her discomfort. He thought: 'So that's it! It isn't that Maltern is busy. He just doesn't like me.'

He wanted to drive that troubled, cornered look away from Phillida. All the time he was talking to her he was conscious of the change in her since that day of her arrival in Egypt. Then she had seemed so eager, so full of hope, and so much in love. Now … she was like a trapped animal. He could only guess, vaguely, the nature of her unhappiness and the blows that had been dealt at her by life – and the fellow she was married to. The more he sensed the misery in Phillida, the more intensely he disliked Rex Maltern.

But he steered the conversation away from herself and personalities to the subject of Egypt as a country and the Egyptians. He made her forget her embarrassment, and held her interest. She was surprised by his intimate knowledge of the country and the people. He did not condemn them or their methods wholesale as did the unthinking crowd of visitors who completely failed to understand the native mentality. (This included Rex with a vengeance – Rex, who was always rude and derogatory about all foreigners.) Martin had studied the people – and the real Egypt. She found herself listening entranced to his account of a trip he had taken across the desert to Baghdad when on leave last December.

He knew a lot about the vegetation and the wild bird life of the Nile Valley. He told her that now these were the beautiful spring days, cooled by a perpetual breeze, but that soon it would grow hot and humid in the

Canal Zone, and she might feel the heat, but that there would be compensations. Picnic parties, swimming on the French beach, which was called the *Jardin d'Efants* – a pleasant stretch of sand with little huts built to protect people from the sun – open-air dancing both here and at the United Services Club, which had a lovely garden leading down to the blue waters of Lake Timsah.

'One way and another you'll have a grand time,' Martin said cheerfully.

But he said it without any conviction and without any real cheer. For she sat there listening, her big grey eyes so gravely watching him, and he thought that she looked lost and desolate behind her smile.

'How can I help her?' he wondered. 'I wonder if, in fact, it would be better for her if I kept away?'

Now in that hour he became aware that if he went on seeing Phillida Maltern he would grow to love her. Love her not only for the sake of his lost sweet Bridget ... but for her own sweet sake; he would have no right to feel any such love, because she belonged to Rex Maltern.

Hastily Martin smothered these thoughts and ordered a packet of cigarettes from a passing waiter.

'Life's the devil,' he thought.

Aloud he said: 'By the way – are you still with the Martials?'

She nodded. Yes, they could not find a flat at the moment, she told him. Rex hated the modern block in which his friend Captain Angus lived because it was so noisy and the rooms were so small, and anything else that they had been offered which was bigger and better was too much rent. Then she went on to tell him about the Martial family. Suddenly the 'lost look' was replaced by that charming gaiety which he had noticed once before in her. The dimple reappeared deliciously at the corner of her mouth. She showed herself in a new, amusing light, as she imitated young Pierrot's broken English, then recounted a story of how Hassan, the Sudanese boy, had been ordered to make a mayonnaise for one of the meals. And how Madame had returned from a two-hour shopping expedition to find him still patiently and diligently beating the mixture in a bowl, having reduced it to a curdled mess, but, undaunted and smiling, he persisted in continuing with the process.

'Madame Martial thinks he would still be beating it if she had not stopped him,' Phillida ended, with a laugh. 'It really was funny.'

Martin thought, as he had done before, that Phillida ought always to laugh. It made her really beautiful. There was something so simple and guileless about this girl. (Bridget, my Bridget, you too had that strange innocence and simplicity and it went to my heart!)

He pulled himself up with a jerk. And at that moment Rex Maltern walked into the Club. His handsome face wore a thundercloud expression, which darkened as he saw his wife and the tall fair man in Naval uniform. Somewhat curtly he said:

'Good evening, sir...' Then to Phillida: 'Our party's fallen through. I've just seen the Rendledons. At least I've seen Kipps. Becki's laid up...'

Phillida, like Martin, had risen to her feet when her husband joined them. In a flash her laughter and sense of fun vanished. She said quietly:

'I'm sorry, Rex.'

Rex muttered something and added that he 'badly needed a drink'. He had only just got back from Cairo and had 'the helluva bad driver'. He wouldn't have rushed it if he'd known the dinner was off. And so on. Grumbling. Discontented. Martin Winters, as always, froze in the presence of this egotistical and bombastic young Captain. He was so infernally casual about his wife, Martin thought. There was no suggestion that he might have hurried back in order to dine with *her*. So it was the Rendledons with whom they had been dining! Rebecca again. Poor little Phillida! And that was why Maltern had turned down Brigadier Pen's

236

party. It would seem that, after all, there lay some truth in all the rumours. Maltern made little effort to conceal his *penchant* for the Syrian girl.

Rex eyed the tall, fair sailor sullenly.

'What about coming to the bar for a drink, sir?' (He was nettled because he too was in uniform, and had to acknowledge the seniority of Phillida's friend.)

'Thanks, but I won't have another just now,' said Martin. 'I think my party will be here at any moment.'

'You coming, Phil?' Rex turned to his wife.

It was the last thing she wanted to do. To go to that bar and start the dreaded drinking session with Rex – Rex in a poor humour. She was also almost ashamed of the fact that she had been so happy during the last half-hour with Martin. Somehow or other she managed to smile up at the big man and appear casual and gay.

'Well, good-bye, Martin. I expect we'll see you sometime.'

Martin, who was the most unmalicious of men, looked down into those troubled, soft eyes, and suddenly had a sardonic desire to pin Maltern, and pin him properly, this time. He said:

'What about this dinner with me, Maltern? It's high time you allowed me to return your hospitality of the other night.'

Rex stiffened.

'Very nice of you, sir.'

'Well, I can get over from Fayid any time these nights,' said Martin easily, 'and I'd rather like to make up a little party for dancing one Saturday night. Would Saturday week suit you?'

Phillida looked at her husband, her heart jerking. She knew only too well what was passing through his mind. But he had no choice this time. Without being openly rude to Martin he could not refuse the invitation. He mumbled:

'Thanks very much, sir. We are free, aren't we, Phil?'

'Yes,' she said, with a little gulp.

'Grand,' said Martin. 'Eight o'clock, here, then, Saturday week, if I don't see you before?'

Then he caught sight of the Pentyres; Mabyn, in a long, floral evening dress, looking radiant and young, followed by a pleasant-looking woman and a tall man with a crown on his shoulder. Martin said good-bye to the Malterns. For the fraction of a moment his gaze held Phillida's, a steady gaze from him, as though he said, *'Courage, my dear...'*

She felt his warmth, his kindliness, flowing from him towards her, and it gave her a choking sensation in her throat. She knew suddenly that she was alone in Egypt ... absolutely alone except for Martin, and that she needed the encouragement that he was silently imparting to her.

She turned slowly from him and followed Rex towards the bar.

He did not speak to her until he had gulped down two strong whiskies. She, too, remained silent, having refused the soft drink which was offered her. She was all too conscious of the Pentyre party which was now foregathering in the Club within sight of them. She felt horribly embarrassed. Then Rex turned to her and said:

'Let's get out of here.'

She slid off the high stool and only too gladly walked with him through the big room. She could not bear to look in the Pentyres' direction, although she knew instinctively where they were. She certainly did not want to meet the steady and all-too-discerning gaze of Martin Winters' blue eyes again this evening.

The March night was warmish and the stars glittered overhead. A soft, romantic night. But there was little romance in it for Phillida. Once in the little M.G. and Rex had driven away from the Club, crashing the gears, the storm broke.

Dumbly she sat and listened to a torrent of abuse from him.

Why the hell had she got him into that spot with that damned stick Winters? Why hadn't she reminded him yesterday that tonight was the date of the Pentyre party, then he wouldn't have gone to the French Club? He didn't care tuppence what Winters thought, but he didn't particularly want to rub that old fool Penwiper up the wrong way. He must have seen them there alone and wondered why they hadn't accepted his invitation in the first place.

Rex ended furiously:

'And I don't even believe that Becki is all that ill. I reckon that b—y idiot Kipps has had a few words with her and just wouldn't let her come tonight.'

Phillida listened, breathing rather quickly, her cheeks crimson with mingled resentment and mortification. She was growing rather tired of Rex's childish outbreaks of temper. She knew that the whole source of his irritation tonight sprang from the fact that Squadron-Leader Rendledon had for once exercised his authority and put his wife in her place.

Suddenly Phillida, too, lost her temper.

'How *dare* you speak to me like this, Rex! You've no right to ... you've been away in Cairo for two whole days and I've been alone, and then you come back and go for me just because you can't get your own way. You didn't really mind me talking to Martin ... and you know perfectly well that I met him there by accident, and that I didn't deliberately put you "on a spot". You've been horribly rude about all his invitations, and personally I think it's awfully nice of him to bother to go on asking us out.'

Outside the Greek Club, Rex pulled up the M.G. with a slurring of tyres. Then he turned and in the semi-darkness glared at Phillida.

'You must take me for a fool,' he said. 'Do you think I don't know that Winters goes on asking because he wants to see you?'

'Even if that were so,' she retorted hotly, 'I might point out to you, Rex, that you only asked the Rendledons because you wanted to see Rebecca. You can't bear Kipps. You've often said so.'

That floored Rex for a moment. He blinked and fumbled for a cigarette. He was not used to Phillida standing up for herself. Then he muttered:

'All right. Then let's agree to go our own ways. I'll do what I want about the Rendledons and you can go out with Winters and his friends for all I care.'

She grew suddenly cold and still.

'No, Rex,' she said slowly. 'I know that's what you're trying to manœuvre. But I'm not going to be a party to it. We've been married for over three years and we've only lived together a couple of months. It seems quite too terrible to let our marriage drift so soon into *this* sort of thing. I won't countenance it...'

So coldly, so decisively, did she say those words that for a moment Rex Maltern was reduced to speechlessness. He was also surprised and a little dismayed to come up against this unexpected obstacle which she was placing in his pathway of ruthless egoism. This was a Phillida he had not bargained for. Then he said suddenly:

'Well, we'd better go and eat. I'm tired and hungry and not very keen on listening to wifely recriminations outside the Club.'

She said no more. But her heart went on beating with a resentment and indignation which was, tonight, transcending all her normal shyness and reserve.

Later, after a few more drinks and some food, Rex condescended to address her in a more conciliatory fashion. He leaned across the table, put out a hand and looked at her with a touch of the old charm.

'I say, Poppet ... let's be friends. We can't sit here like this, just hating each other.'

She raised her clear grey eyes and looked at him with an expression which made him feel genuinely ashamed of himself.

'Do you hate me, Rex?'

He coughed, cast a quick frowning glance around the crowded room, thick with a haze of smoke, noisy with chatter and laughter, and the clattering of dishes redolent with the odour of rich food, then turned back to meet the serious gaze of his young wife.

What an uncomfortable way she had of looking at a chap, he thought. He said:

'Don't be so damn' ridiculous. You know I don't hate you. It's just my way of putting things. I mean that I don't want us to go on fighting. *You* don't hate *me*, do you?'

'No. But I soon shall, if you go on like you have been doing.'

He coughed again, awkwardly, and jammed his cigarette-end into a saucer. He was not enjoying himself at all.

'Now, if you're going to nag...'

'I'm not going to nag,' she broke in, 'and I don't want to talk to you at all, if you don't want to talk to me. But I'm just *not* going to be kicked around by you every time you come home. And I know it's because you're no longer in love with me.'

He stared at her. 'Who said I wasn't?'

'Well – are you, Rex?'

His gaze wavered before that disconcertingly steady gaze of hers. 'You're so frightfully romantic, Phil,' he mumbled. 'A chap doesn't have to go on saying *"I love you"*, or quoting poetry and holding hands in order to prove that he loves his wife. We did all that sort of stuff when we first fell in love, but damn it ... you don't expect it from me now, do you? Except at suitable times.'

Phillida sat still for a moment. Her heart seemed to be dying within her. Yet she felt curiously detached and able to look at the handsome, familiar face of the man who was her husband, and whom she had once thought so marvellous, without any particular pain. It was as though every word that he said had a numbing effect. She fully realised how little he must love her or he could not have spoken to her this way.

'And what are the suitable times in your eyes, Rex?' she suddenly asked him.

'Oh for heaven's sake, don't let's be analytical!' he snapped.

'All right,' said Phillida, and it was as though something welled up from deep down within her and could no longer be restrained. She felt herself trembling. 'All right, Rex, then we'll come down to brass tacks. There's no question of you being in love with me any more because you're in love with somebody else ... somebody you have no right to love because you are married and so is she.'

Phillida paused, choking a little.

Rex stared at her, the red creeping up under his tan, his pulses jerking uncomfortably.

'May I ask to whom you are alluding, my dear Phil?'

With quivering lips she blurted out the name:

'Rebecca ... Rebecca Rendledon, of course. It isn't just a guess on my part. Everybody knows it. Everybody in Ismailia is talking. Why, the very first night I arrived some woman didn't realise who I was and pointed you and Rebecca out, and said that you two were having an affair. It's beastly, absolutely beastly. I've tried to make myself believe that it isn't true... I've never asked you about it. But now I've finished. I'm not going to go on like this, with you so casual and hateful to me, and just living for the dates you make with that girl. I won't put up with it!'

The words were brimming over with all the bitterness and humiliation that she had endured. Then she stopped, terrified that she was going to break down and cry in public. She added, in a suffocated voice:

'Please pay the bill, Rex, and take me home.'

He did so, completely at a loss for words. He had been thunderstruck by Phillida's revelation. He had not dreamed that she suspected Rebecca and himself. Nor was he aware that people were talking. His first reaction was not one of shame or pity for his disillusioned young wife, but of fear for himself. If gossip was really rife in Ismailia he would have to look out ... he had his career to think of ... it wouldn't do if his C.O. got to know that he was chasing the wife of another officer, he thought. It certainly wouldn't do for Phil to get her back up too far or she might go home and take legal steps, and that would be fatal for his reputation as an officer. In fact, he would have to be damned careful in future.

They sat silent now, without looking at each other, while Rex waited for his change.

Phillida was slightly overawed by her own temerity, and she wondered what good she had done in laying all her cards on the table at last. But Rex's mind seethed with thoughts and ideas mainly connected with the methods whereby he could put things right with Phil and yet continue to see Rebecca.

This was the second time that he had been badly upset and frustrated tonight. On his return from Cairo, when he had called at the Rendledons' flat, he had been received very coolly by Kipps and told that Becki was in bed with an attack of 'gippy tummy', and that he could not see her. But from Kipps Rendledon's manner Rex had gathered that more than the colic lay behind the cancellation of the dinner party. Kipps had had a row with Becki – over him. He had left the flat in a bad humour, fretting because he had to wait until tomorrow morning, when Rendledon was at work, to find out what had really happened. Not that he worried much about Kipps. Becki had had rows with him before, but had always managed the poor 'mutt' in the end.

But this sudden show-down with Phillida was a different matter. As they walked out of the Greek Club he eyed the slim, straight figure and fair head of his wife with a new respect. She wasn't quite the 'yes-girl' that he imagined.

He drove her back to the villa, rehearsing what he would say and do once they were at home.

As soon as the door was shut and they were alone in their bedroom he held out both hands to her.

'Poppet,' he said, 'come here…'

She shook her head. She felt desperately tired and wretched. She began to take off her dress.

'Leave me alone, Rex. I'm going to get into bed.'

Nothing daunted, he seized her, pulled her down on to the edge of the bed and held her there, one arm imprisoning her.

'Listen, darling, this is ridiculous. We can't go on like this. Poppet, it isn't true that I don't love you. I *do!* I swear it!'

She shook her head, trying to free herself.

'I can't believe you, Rex,' she said. 'How can I believe you, after all you've said and done?'

'Darling, I know I've been rottenly bad-tempered. It's chiefly the climate. Everyone gets nervy out here and I had two years in Burma before coming to the Middle East. I dare say it's time I went home. I assure you a lot of chaps 'go round the bend' after they've had years out here. You must make allowances for me; you really must.'

She looked at him with forlorn gaze. Rex was so plausible, and so uncertain. She never knew what to believe or which way to take him these days. She only knew that his caressing hands held no particular meaning for her any more. In fact, she wished he would let go of her. She could not bear him to make love to her tonight.

But Rex continued to hold her and to pour out excuses for himself. Finally, perforce, he came to the point about Rebecca.

'I think it's damnable if people are gossiping about Becki and me. Kipps is a pal of mine. He knows that I take Becki out when he's away ... or used to before you came. Surely, Phil, you're a woman of the world enough to know how people talk when there's nothing in it. In a place like this a fellow and a girl have only got to be seen together more than once and everyone says they are sleeping together.'

She tried again to move away from him. It seemed suddenly that his face was no longer attractive. Handsome, yes, but growing heavy and sensual. The eyes and mouth were without tenderness. It seemed, too, for some unaccountable reason, that in that moment the face of Martin Winters came in between them – that fine-drawn and frank face, with the blue eyes which had looked at her tonight so compassionately and given her so much spiritual comfort. She realised that she was no longer in love with her husband. He had killed her love. Steadily and remorselessly he had been murdering it ever since her arrival in Egypt. Tonight she was like a stone in his embrace.

He went on pleading with her; attempting to exonerate, to whitewash himself. In a tired way she wondered how many lies he uttered. Again and again he swore that there was nothing between him and Rebecca Rendledon. She amused him, he said. He found her good fun. They had some good times together, but there was no question of a serious affair, and Phil *must* believe it.

'As for Martin Winters,' he added, forcing a laugh, 'don't you realise that I've been a cad to you about him just because I'm jealous? I think he's keen on you, and I'd be terribly upset if I thought you looked twice at him or any fellow. But I know you wouldn't. I know how loyal you are. You're much too good for me, of course. I'm a rotten cad. My poor little Poppet ... I'm frightfully sorry for everything I've done to make you unhappy. But I'll be different. I tell you it's just the climate and too much drink. If you'll help me I'll pull myself together. We'll be as happy as we used to be. When we dine with Winters I'll show him that I'm not such a bad chap. And we'll go and call on the Pentyres... I'll even stick a session with old Penwiper if you want me to, darling...'

He worked himself into a state when he really began to feel remorseful and anxious to make amends; he was even half ready to convince himself, as well as Phillida, that his friendship with Rebecca was purely platonic.

At last he stopped speaking. Phillida, by this time, lay supine in the curve of his arm, too tired to argue further, the tears rolling silently down her cheeks. At last she said:

'Oh, I don't know, I don't know!' and began to cry pitifully.

'Don't cry, Poppet, *please* do believe me and let's start again,' he beseeched her.

No answer. Only a sob.

'Poppet, please! Give me another chance. You haven't quite stopped loving me, have you?'

He drew her closer, stroking the damp, fair hair back from her forehead. He was quite anxious in that moment she should tell him that she still loved him. When Rex Maltern could not have a thing, he wanted it. He wanted to be in favour with Phillida again tonight – for many reasons. The image of Becki's dark, voluptuous beauty faded somewhat into the background. In this hour he was genuinely interested in the fair-haired, slender girl who was his wife and who wept so desolately in his arms.

He began to kiss her, seeking to rouse an answering passion in her.

'Poppet, love me again! Forgive me, please, darling!' he entreated her.

She did not know what to say or do. She only knew that she could never again love him as once she had loved because he had forfeited her respect, and that despite all his explanations and excuses she could not wholly believe in him. But because she was so lost and lonely and so desperately anxious that they should make some sort of effort to preserve their marriage, she finally surrendered.

He had never been a more passionate lover than he was that night, and she had never loved him less.

PART II

1

During the first week in June two long letters were written respectively by Phillida Maltern and Martin Winters and sent by air mail to England. The one from Phillida was to her grandmother, Mrs Millverton. It was a letter which she had begun towards the end of May and to which she had added a bit day by day in diary form.

Gamma, darling, I expect you will think I have neglected you lately, but I have really not felt up to writing to anybody. I didn't want you to be worried about me, so I didn't tell you how sick and rotten I've been. But now that I know the reason why I can tell you more fully about it.

Gamma, darling, I'm going to have a baby.

I've been to see an awfully nice woman doctor in the Garrison Hospital and she tells me that it's about three months on its way. So in December I shall be a mother of a son or a daughter – I wonder which?

Will you forgive me for making you a great-grandmother when you're still so young and sprightly? But that's just a joke – I know you will adore it. You've been such a good granny to me and you'll make such a marvellous great-granny to my child.

Wouldn't Mummy and Daddy be thrilled? I've been thinking a lot about them lately, and how sad it is that they didn't live to see my baby.

I think Rex is pleased, although a little alarmed at the new responsibility of being made a father. I don't think he really believes it is true yet. We have only just written to tell his people.

I'm not feeling quite so bad as I did, but it's beginning to be awfully hot in Ismailia. It's the humidity that devitalises one out here. If you sit in the garden at night you get quite wet in spite of the heat and the moonlight … just as though a terrifically heavy dew descends on you. One has to very careful to avoid chills.

I was sorry to leave the Martials' villa the other day. Sophie and Emile and little Pierrot have become great friends and I still see them, of course. Sophie comes down to the town with her shopping basket and does little things for me. But once I knew about the baby I felt I must get a settled home of my own, so Rex made an effort, and we found this funny little house that we're now living in. You will have got my cable with the change of address, but I feel so much better today that I'm going to give you a description of my surroundings.

This is a sort of bungalow with a verandah and a little garden in which there are two trees, and it is right in the middle of a narrow street in what they call the Greek quarter. It was let to us by a Greek who is getting a much bigger rent for it than it is worth. We have a sitting-room – rather shabbily furnished with cheap stuff – a double bedroom and another room which I'm going to turn into a nursery; also a kitchen and a somewhat dilapidated bathroom. In the winter one heats the water by oil on a primitive primus affair, but at this time of year it is so hot that the water runs warm out of the tap, and anyhow one longs for cold showers.

We have a suffragi – Ahmed – who is a Sudanese and he cooks fairly well and does everything for us. But as he only speaks a few words of French and no English, I have to give my orders with signs and gestures. However, we get on quite well, and he is an improvement on the first one whom we had to dismiss because he was so dirty. In this country it is essential to clean everything. One has to cope with enormous cockroaches – horrible big brown things – and wage perpetual war against microbes – and the sand!

It is noisier and less pleasant in this part of Ismailia than it was up in the French quarter where the Martials live. I could have had a quarter in Fayid, but Rex didn't want to have one room in the camp which is all that would have been allotted to a married Captain working at G.H.Q. At least I can make a home out of this bungalow. The other day we bought a very nice rug, and I found some beautiful glass, and with the help of a little Maltese sewing girl I've made some quite charming curtains out of the pretty cotton material which one can get out here – not too dear.

You never need worry about my being alone because I have heaps of friends. Brigadier Pentyre's wife, Mabyn, is terribly good to me and already is knitting madly, as she calls it, for my baby. She and the Brigadier are darlings. And Steve Cubitt comes over from Fayid and sees me once or twice a week when she can cadge a lift, as her husband hasn't got a car. She is a great friend of mine these days. Poor Doreen Angus comes in and out. She wails and moans perpetually, and that wretched baby of hers is always ailing. It quite upsets me to see how thin his little legs are for a child of four months. I hope mine won't be the same. But it is a trying climate, and Doreen is one of those people who can't stand the sticky heat.

You will remember that nice Naval commander friend of mine – Martin Winters – he often rolls up in his little car and brings me an odd bunch of flowers or a book, and he seems to get on better with Rex nowadays. I think he is a good friend for us both to have so I'm glad.

I would love you to see Ismailia just now. The boulevards and the gardens along the Sweet Water Canal are the most incredible sight, with the purple jacarandas in full bloom, and the most marvellous trees called 'flamboyants' which have huge scarlet flowers. It's all most exotic.

I have taken Sophie Martial's advice and keep my windows shut and shuttered from early morning till late afternoon, which helps to keep the house cool. If you open up the air is like a furnace blast and I'm told it will be hotter next month.

G.H.Q. hours are more difficult just now, and three days a week Rex has to be in Fayid all day, and doesn't get home until nine at night, which is pretty exhausting for him.

Well, Gamma, this is the longest letter I've ever written to you in my life, but I wanted to make up for all the scrappy notes you've had from me lately. Take care of yourself and don't overdo it in the garden. How I wish I could see you and Alvercombe! Sometimes when it's very hot and breathless I lie on my bed and dream of the cool breeze that blows from the sea down there in our little bay. One day I shall bring my child home and I shall teach it to love Alvercombe as I do.

All my love. Tell Patsy that I shall think of her on her wedding day next week, and wish her all the happiness in the world.

Your devoted Phil.

The second letter was written by Martin to his aunt, Mrs Mackay, and went to Killoun Castle in Ayrshire.

I haven't written much to you lately, dear Aunt Kate, because I have been rather busy settling down at my Fayid job which I find quite interes-

ting, although on the whole I preferred Navy House and Port Said. I'm a sailor, used to the sea, and I don't think I shall ever quite appreciate the desert as I should. The trouble is that this isn't the real desert – only the fringe of it. But I'm quite sure that I should like to go with some of these chaps who trek across the Sahara. There, one would get away completely from civilisation and I would probably have the same sort of feeling there as at sea. But Fayid means a lot of dusty roadways – huts and tents; tents and huts – German prisoners of war in their thousands behind barbed wire, or working in the camp ... and this new town which is springing up for Army Families – little rows of quarters where a lot of rather brave women are trying to create the home atmosphere and make an English garden out of a sandy waste.

Apart from my job I have been worried, Aunt Kate. Your nephew is now going to get down to it and tell the truth. You've always been so wonderful to me and we've never had secrets from each other. When Bridget died I don't think I would have wanted to go on living but for you and your understanding, and dear Killoun.

It was good, by the way to read from your last letter that despite these troublesome times you still fare well in the old home, and that there are still some big fish in the river. I hear all round that it is a good year for the salmon and it's hard to have to wait till my next long leave before I can take old Macdougall down to the Pool and *sit beside him on the green bank on a quiet evening and watch, before putting on my waders and going out to the 'battle royal'.*

But now for my news.

Aunt Kate, I've fallen in love.

You won't like it. I know that you've wanted me to find what you call 'a bonnie girl' and bring her home to Killoun. I know that you've thought it a pity that I should spend the rest of my days living with a memory – much as you loved Bridget. In the five years that have passed since she died I haven't really looked at another woman nor dreamed of replacing her.

And now by the irony of Fate I've found someone uncannily like her – someone whom I think I could love very deeply. But she's married.

I've already mentioned her name to you – Phillida Maltern – and how some strange fate arranged our meeting at Port Said on the day she landed. I told you how we spent the day together trying to get in touch with her husband, and in one or two subsequent letters I believe I mentioned them both.

I have an overwhelming desire to write and tell you what has been happening since then. Even when I was a kid I used to come and confess things to you that I wouldn't tell another living soul, and you always understood. You'll understand this, won't you?

It isn't only that Phillida looks like Bridget (you'll see it for yourself from the enclosed snapshot which I took of her and her husband on the Plage a few weeks ago). That in itself, naturally, affects me. And apart from the same slender build and long, fair hair, and graceful hands, she even has one or two of Bridget's mannerisms. That sudden, rather lost, lonely look for instance, which Bridget used to get at times, and which goes to one's heart.

But Bridget, thank God, was happy until the day of her death. And this child, Phillida, is desperately unhappy.

She came out here, Aunt Kate, bubbling over with enthusiasm at the thought of rejoining her husband after three years of separation. She was very much in love with him. And on the first night she arrived she found out that he was entangled with the Syrian wife of one of the R.A.F. types out here. I won't go into details. I know how things like that nauseate you. You were always a great believer in loyalties and never very tolerant with slipshod morals and the way in which so many young people today slide in and out of matrimony. I agree. But I also see that the long years of war and forced separation have done a lot of damage. Phillida Maltern, was able to stand up to the long waiting, because she is herself an essentially loyal and decent person. But Maltern is a weak, vain sort of fellow whom women run after because he's good-looking and amusing when he sets out to be; and he can't resist them. He let his wife down, and he's continued to let her down ever since she *arrived in Egypt.*

From the moment that I saw how badly things were going with her and how it affected me personally, I realised the danger. Not from her side because she had no particular interest in me, only the wish to regain her confidence in her husband. All her efforts obviously failed. One could see it when they were together.

She never uttered a word of complaint. She wouldn't. Aunt Kate, you would be full of pity and admiration for her – like I am. Poor Phillida! She hadn't a hope. The Syrian girl had got her claws deeply into Maltern long before his wife came out, and she wasn't letting go.

But I'll spare you the sordid side of the story.

To continue about Phillida. For a few weeks I didn't see much of her. Maltern rather ostensibly ignored me. Our dislike was mutual. But once or twice I spoke to Phillida and she was always so pleased to see me. She was heart-breakingly homesick and lonely. She loves England. And she liked to hear me tell her about Killoun. She knows as much about country life and loves it as much as little Bridget used to do. She is absolutely out of place amongst all the good-time girls who hang round the bars and the beaches wearing as little as they can, and making a bid for any fellow available – all too easy in a place like the Middle East where there are thousands of bored young men and only a handful of pretty girls.

Maltern ought to have welcomed that wife of

his and worshipped her. But he seems to have no sense of values and quite obviously she bores him. She is too quiet and serious. So the trouble between them grew and grew. I saw Phillida at intervals – occasionally sat beside her and talked – and bit by bit I watched her growing thinner and more miserable, although she still tried to smile. One never heard a single word from her lips against the man.

Aunt Kate, that fellow's conduct has been unbelievable. There have been nights at the Club ... parties thrown by Maltern or one of his pals ... including the Syrian when her husband was away, which he often is ... when Maltern has openly affronted his wife. I've seen her try to laugh it off. I've watched her making hopeless efforts to get him away from the bottle (he drinks far too much). I've seen how she loathed the whole show, especially the efforts of one or two imbecile young men to get too familiar with her. Once when I was at another table I watched Maltern – semi-intoxicated – disappear from the dance floor with some enthusiastic young female who thought him attractive, and Phillida, after waiting for him to come back, get up and go home alone. I offered to take her, but she said just that she had a headache and asked me to find her a taxi. She looked so exhausted – and so ashamed. My heart ached for her. And that, Aunt Kate, is the trouble – my heart has gone on aching for her, and I can do nothing really to help. For I fully realised that if I butted in it *would give Maltern a chance to justify his own actions, and try to pin something on his wife.*

It went on like that for a bit. Each time I saw Phillida she grew dearer to me and I felt more and more frustrated because I could be of no real use. Once, when we were alone and she was waiting for her husband (which she used to do interminably), she shyly thanked me for my friendship. She said it meant a lot to her. That's the only thing she's ever said to me. Sometimes I've looked into those very grey eyes and seen the mortal hurt in them, and, Aunt Kate, it's made me feel murderous towards Maltern.

Then something happened between the two of them. I can't tell you what. Perhaps they had a show-down. But he changed his tactics. He became a good deal more pleasant to her, in public anyhow, and even accepted a dinner invitation from me. He made himself quite agreeable. I loathe the man but I recognise his charm for women... When he sets out to be charming ... nobody can be more so. He plays the piano, too, like a professional – swing music – and at any party he is a great asset. He's a good raconteur and he dances like a gigolo. In my opinion he ought never to have been in the Army, but he's a curious fellow – he has a sort of dual nature – because I've heard from one or two chaps at Fayid that he is first-class at his job.

But as a husband for a sensitive and rather noble creature like Phillida he is wrong from every angle, and I don't think she has any illusions left, poor child. She made a ghastly mistake by rushing into marriage with him during the war.

They moved into a little bungalow some time ago, and asked me there to a cocktail party one evening, and then Phillida told me that she is going to have a child – in December. It gave me a sort of shock. I know it's wrong of me, Aunt Kate, but I don't want her to have Maltern's child, and she is looking shockingly ill. Mabyn Pentyre went to see her one day recently and told me the girl wasn't really fit to have a baby. She is in such a low state of health, a lot of which I put down to her mental condition, all her worry and unhappiness.

But when she told me about it she seemed quite pleased that she was going to have the child, so I gave her my congratulations. I half made up my mind not to go back to the house, not to see her any more. Anyhow, I felt that the fact that she was having a child put her completely out of my reach.

All I wanted was that she should be happy. I had no idea what her life was like in private, but I was thankful to see Maltern paying her a bit more attention, and I've been hoping that he's had the decency to chuck the Syrian girl and behave as he should.

When I left that party that night I made some remark to Phillida such as, 'Well, I don't suppose you'll want to be worried with visitors from now onward' – a rather stupid, senseless remark, but

I made it. And then to my concern and, Aunt Kate, I have to admit, my pleasure too, she gave me a quick, pleading sort of look and said: 'Oh yes, I will, Martin. I mean please don't stop coming to see me. Please don't!'

Twice she said those words – 'please don't'. It quite startled me. It was as though she had been behaving the whole evening with a mask over her face and then the mask dropped. I could see all the old misery naked there in her eyes. The advent of the child hadn't made any difference. It seemed that she was positively frightened at the idea that I might not go back to see her.

That decided me, Aunt Kate; I knew then that I could never keep away from Phillida so long as she wanted me or had the slightest use for my friendship.

Aunt Kate, rightly or wrongly, I haven't kept away. And, well, Maltern, whether with an ulterior motive or not – I don't know – has always received me cordially – even encouraged my visits. What he's up to the devil alone knows. I don't often see him.

Phillida is much alone. She's been laid up a lot; once or twice on my half-days I've gone over to Ismailia and taken her in the old Morris down to the Plage. It's much too hot for her during the day, but pleasant between half past five and six to sit in the sun with a breeze blowing across the Canal from Sinai.

Those moments with Phillida, talking about Devonshire and her grandmother, or about my beloved Killoun, have been extraordinarily happy for me, and curiously unhappy. I love her, Aunt Kate – as I loved Bridget. Indeed it is as though Bridget were alive and with me again. And I think if she knew about Phillida she would understand. There was never a living soul more in need of love and gentleness than Phillida.

But naturally I've never told her what I feel. And to her I'm just a chap in whom she has confidence, thank God, and whom she likes to see. The mask that she wears for the outside world is still on and I still don't know what lies behind it or how she feels about her husband or the coming child. (What a sweet mother she will make, Aunt Kate! How I wish that she and her child were mine!) Only once she spoke bitterly. When we were talking about the future I suggested that at the end of this tour Maltern would probably get a job at home. She said: 'Rex hates England, and I don't think he'll ever want to settle there. He'll do his best to get a job abroad again.' Then when I suggested that his mother, when the time came, would surely enjoy seeing a bit of her grandchild, Phillida looked at me and said with the same bitterness: 'She has never been a mother to Rex. She is wrapped up in her new husband, and she has already written and told Rex that she wants nothing to do with my child. She has a horror of being made a grandmother.'

But you, Aunt Kate, have always wanted me to bring a wife and child home to Killoun. Perhaps if Phillida and I had met before Maltern came across her she might have loved me. She might have been my wife, and I might have brought here to Scotland. But that is a hopeless dream. There has never been a word of love between us. Not a suggestion of it.

Aunt Kate, I suppose I ought to walk out right now before the thing gets worse for me and never see her any more. Yet I can't leave her.

Write and tell me what you think.

My love to you and Killoun, dearest,

Ever your
Martin.

2

It was very hot in the Malterns' little house.

Since eight o'clock Ahmed, the *suffragi*, had closed all the windows and shutters to keep out the fierce rays of the sun, but even though it was dim, and a good bit cooler indoors than out, it was still sweltering on this fine June day.

Phillida had been lying down on her bed after lunch, trying to sleep. She lay without clothes on. Her whole body was bathed in perspiration. Despite the morning's effort to spray the room with D.D.T. there were flies which continually pestered her. This being the heart of Ismailia, the noise was incessant. The blare of motor-car horns – the screaming of street arabs – the yapping of dogs.

Phillida gave up trying to rest, had a cool shower, put on a cotton frock, a gay red and white floral affair made by a local dress-maker, slid her feet into white sandals and walked listlessly into the sitting-room.

She pushed open one of the shutters. The strong beam of light that immediately penetrated the gloom hurt her eyes. They were aching. Every bone in her body seemed to ache. She was so completely devitalized from heat and sickness that she could hardly drag her steps round the room.

After a moment she sat down, put on her glasses, and picked up some knitting. She was making a fine shawl for her baby. But after a moment her fingers were so wet and sticky with the heat that she dropped the knitting, took the glasses off again, leaned her head back and closed her eyes. She felt almost too apathetic to think, but she tried to make a mental list of the things she must do; she was always forgetting... Rex got so cross when she forgot things; although she had to admit that he was trying to be more tolerant and understanding these days. He just grumbled.

'Do try to remember what I say. You haven't been out here long enough to develop a Middle East memory; you're letting yourself go,' he said.

But it wasn't so, she thought. She tried very hard to be what he wanted and to do what he wanted, but the heat just didn't suit her. It dragged every ounce of energy from her body, and she supposed it was her pregnancy which affected her, too.

She had had years of active service as a Wren; night watches, broken sleep, hastily snatched meals, and all the nervous reaction of losing her parents in the bombing.

She had begun to realise since she had been out here what a toll it had taken of her, young as she was.

As soon as Rex came home she made a terrific effort to be gay and bright as he liked her to be. That, too, had a nervous reaction. She knew that he had tremendous vitality – he was full of animal spirits. He wanted someone to rush round with him … wished that she was like a lot of other girls out here who seemed to be able to stand the heat, to dance and drink and stay up till all hours of the night; and be equally energetic with their swimming, sailing and picnics during the day.

But Phillida had been so sick, and had fever as well. She wanted to be very quiet. She had grown to hate Egypt almost as much as poor, feeble Doreen Angus hated it. Now that she was going to have a child she would have given her soul to be back in her grandmother's peaceful little cottage in Devonshire. It seemed a paradise out of her reach, far away from the humid, pitiless heat and languor, the flies, the dirt, the sinister undercurrent of feeling which seemed to exist in Egypt these days.

But she made an effort to please Rex, because she believed that he was making this effort to please her. Since that night when she had openly accused him of being involved with Rebecca Rendledon he had certainly been nicer to her. Then … when she told him that a child was on the way …

he had made a show of being pleased and kind. He told everybody about it. He liked to figure himself as the proud father of a wonderful son. He boasted of what he would do for the boy. But at moments he let the act slide, and grumbled about the extra expense that was to be incurred, said what a tie a child would be, and how he loathed the thought of nappies and bottles about the place. He wasn't going to become complaisant and long-suffering like old Jimmy Angus, he said, and when the time came Phil had better keep all that nursery paraphernalia out of his way.

Bit by bit his good humour and thoughtfulness for her because she was ill was giving place to the old selfishness. She could see it. But at least she was thankful that he did not drag her out to too many parties. He let her have meals at home instead of at the Club, and she could keep him more or less happy by entertaining his friends here in the little bungalow. The cupboard was full of bottles. Drink was unlimited out here.

Getting the money out of him to pay the bills, however, wasn't always so easy. Rex was careless about money matters, and mean. Once or twice she had had to nag and nag in order to get the cash to pay the Greek grocer and the laundry whom they patronised. But in the end she got it and silently accepted the abuse which went with it.

Phillida had no illusions left about her husband. The charming young man of Alvercombe days was no more. She was married to a sensualist without a heart; a man whose passions were all on the surface, and who gave only when he was going to get something back. Her own heart was dead within her. She could no longer even pretend to herself that she loved him. But she would rather have died than tell anybody so. And she was as strongly determined as ever to make a success of her marriage.

The real tragedy for Phillida was the fact that she did not want this child. She was aghast at times to realise how little she wanted it. Yet she loved babies and once had longed for one of her own. But she felt almost that this baby had been forced upon her; that she had had no love for its father when it was conceived, and could have neither love nor admiration for him in the future. In this mental state she did not want the child. But she hoped passionately that when it was born it would mean more to her, and might even fill the awful aching void in her life.

The menace of Rebecca Rendledon had been removed with the posting of the Squadron-Leader to Greece. The glamorous and amorous Becki had gone with him. She had relations there.

The week following her departure Rex

had been like a bear with a sore head, and had snapped at Phillida until he reduced her to tears, then he had apologised and said that he had a touch of 'liver'. But Phillida knew that it was because Rebecca had left Ismailia. But she had said nothing to Rex. And he did not mention the name again.

There was another girl now...

Phillida did not know for certain. It was a matter of surmisal. Naturally nobody suggested to her that Rex had found a new attraction; she just knew from various little things he did and said. The girl had just come out from England, fresh from school. A most engaging and amusing young woman of nineteen, daughter of a Colonel stationed at Moascar. She was by no means a 'schoolgirl'. She was already quite sophisticated, and – so Phillida thought – thoroughly spoiled. She had wonderful hair – pure Titian red – green, long-lashed eyes, and a complexion which retained its creamy pallor. She was very tall and slim, and had magnificent health; she played excellent tennis, dived like a professional and could swim as far as any man in the place.

'Copper' they called her. Already Copper was a great favourite with the boys, and a particular favourite with Rex Maltern, whom she, in her turn, found vastly entertaining. She openly declared that she liked men much older than herself, and the fact that Rex was married and that Phillida had a baby on the way seemed to cut little ice with her. There was a good deal of Becki's unscrupulousness in Copper, but a good deal more freshness and youth, which was only an added danger.

Rex was very reticent on the subject of Copper. But Phillida noticed that she was in every party that he planned, and although he was older and more subtle in his behaviour the young girl made little effort to conceal her infatuation.

Once, after a party, when Rex and Copper had danced together most of the evening, Phillida spoke to her husband quietly.

'Don't you think it rather a shame, Rex, to let that little Deacon girl get talked about? She's only nineteen and hasn't a clue how to behave, and you're only encouraging it.'

A cunning look came into Rex's handsome eyes. He immediately roared with laughter, patted Phillida on the back, and said:

'What absolute nonsense, Poppet! Copper's only enjoying herself, like a kid. There's nothing more in it. I like to hear her giggle. Of course one gets tired of her. I couldn't "take it" for more than an hour or two at a time. But she's amusing to dance with. You don't mind, do you?'

Phillida looked at him steadily, and said:

'It's up to you, Rex. I don't wish to control

your actions. As a matter of fact I was thinking of it from the girl's point of view – and her people. Mrs Deacon is rather worried about Copper because her head has been turned since she came out here. I just don't think you ought to help turn it.'

Rex roared with laughter again, and the subject of Copper was dropped.

But Phillida was beginning to know her husband; and she read the swift desire that sprang into his eyes when he saw Copper appear in one of her fresh flowered dresses at the Club, or lay on the Plage in a green silk two-piece bathing-suit that concealed little of her exquisite body.

Rex was in love again... Phillida knew it and kept it bitterly to herself. *He* called it love. She knew now that the feelings that engulfed him were as hot and swift-passing as the *khamsin* wind, devastating everything that it touched.

She knew that she, personally, only bored him now. At the moment she was, of course, looking her worst. She was thin and hollow-eyed, her skin was dry, her hair limp and lustreless. Sometimes she thought of cutting the long, blonde tresses as they were so much bother to wash and brush and keep in order in this heat. When she had asked Rex he had evinced little interest. He had yawned and said:

'I don't care what you do with your hair,

275

Poppet. Please yourself.'

But curiously enough, when she had mentioned it to Martin Winters that same day, he had said quickly, in a tone of dismay:

'Oh, Phillida, *don't* cut off your lovely hair. I think it's so beautiful. And so individual. It would be a crime to cut it and go about with short curls like all these girls.'

Somehow that had warmed her heart. She did not contemplate cutting her hair off again.

Dear Martin! He was her great friend amongst all the men out here. Sometimes when she was feeling very ill and Rex was busy playing tennis or swimming, or doing things she could no longer do because the doctor had warned her to keep very quiet at the moment... Martin helped relieve some of the lonely and monotonous hours. She was never without a book – specially chosen by Martin. They liked to read the same things; tales of the sea or of the country. C.S. Forrester ... Henry Williamson ... magic stories to take her out of herself ... and a long, long way from Egypt.

At least she could be thankful that Rex was no longer unpleasant about Martin, nor did he make it difficult for her to ask him to the house. And when once or twice Phillida had not felt too ill, and they had been Martin's guests at the Club, Rex had been quite affable.

Nor did he insult her these days by suggesting that Martin was 'a boy-friend'. He dared not. She was having his child and he knew perfectly well that he had no cause to taunt her.

So she could only suppose that he suffered Martin's visits because he was glad to 'get her off his hands' and not be made to feel that he was neglecting her whilst he enjoyed life in his own carefree fashion.

This afternoon Phillida sat here in the shuttered sitting-room of her Ismailia home and struggled to remember the things that she must do as soon as she had had tea and could venture out.

There was Rex's white dinner-jacket to be called for from the Sphinx Laundry, where it was being pressed.

There was the beer to order, which she had forgotten this morning, and he had said that he was bringing two of the chaps back from Fayid for drinks tonight.

There was a food parcel to pack up ... she had been meaning to pack it the whole week, and the tins of food were still lying there in a box, in the corner. They were for Rex's mother ... she had a birthday at the end of next month. Rex, in his usual heartless fashion, had said:

'For heaven's sake send something to Mamma to keep her sweet. That was a damn' good cheque she sent us when I told her little

Rex was on the way, and I think both she and step-pop will go on paying me if only to keep the little brat out of their way. They both like these food parcels. Get cracking on it, Poppet.'

But he hadn't time to pack one up himself. He was much too busy even on his half-days. Busy doing what? Playing tennis with Copper, or going down to the Plage to join one of the picnic parties at which he was so popular because he was such good fun.

Phillida racked her brains again ... what else had she forgotten? Oh yes, to go to the French Club and book a table for Saturday night. They dined and danced out of doors there now, with lights glowing from the beautiful scarlet flamboyant trees, which were in full flower. Friends like Patsy, now happily married to her N.O., wrote from England and said: *It all sounds so glamorous. What a wonderful time you must be having!* And Gamma had written: *What a joy it must be to you giving your dear Rex a child, my darling Phillida!...*

Glamour! Joy! Wearily Phillida asked herself this afternoon if she would ever know the meaning of those two words again.

Thinking of Saturday she could only pray that she would be able to sit through the whole evening and not annoy Rex by wanting to go home because she felt that awful nausea which took the pleasure out of everything. The very sight and smell of food revolted her, and she had been forbidden to dance. The doctor had, in fact, told her that she might not be able to see this thing through unless she took the utmost care, because of her low state of health.

But she had not told Rex so. He had no time for sickness. It bored him. He flung her a few words of sympathy at intervals and then capped it by adding:

'Of course I don't know what this fuss is all about. I always thought that having a baby was a natural affair. You must be peculiar, Poppet...' And then he went on to illustrate the argument by mentioning the wife of one of his brother officers who was having a baby out here and was still swimming and going to parties.

Phillida did not exert herself to argue; to point out that the said girl was as strong as a horse, and that *her* health had not been particularly good when she came out here, and that since her arrival it had rapidly deteriorated. She condemned Doreen Angus for whining and making Jimmy's life a misery, and so she, herself, made a vast effort to hide what she felt from Rex.

But she felt decidedly bitter when she compared her lot with that of Doreen, to whom Jimmy devoted his whole time. He waited on her hand and foot. Things were really quite easy for her nowadays. For the last two months her sister Peggy had also been out here with her, and in her capable and devoted fashion was looking after young Bill, and had settled down quite remarkably well to the change of climate, which did not seem to affect her, despite her infirmity. So Doreen these days, what with husband, sister and a good *suffragi,* exerted herself very little. But she continued to air her grievances and dislike of Egypt.

'Perhaps,' Phillida thought, 'if I could air mine I'd feel better. If I could bring myself to tell somebody, other than the doctor, how bad I feel ... if I could tell Patsy that my marriage is a grim failure ... or Gamma that I don't want this baby because it's Rex's child, and I can't bear the idea that I might produce a son who will grow up to break another woman's heart as Rex has broken mine.'

But she kept these things to herself. Even to Steve Cubitt, who was her closest woman friend out here, she did not speak of her intimate life. Steve, being shrewd and observant and very fond of her these days, had once or twice hinted that she 'feared things weren't too good' with Phil.

'You've changed so completely since those days when we first met coming over on the trooper. Is it only the infant on the way that is making you like this?'

But Phillida laughed and said:

'I expect so...'

She wondered if Steve was deceived. She felt that neither of the Cubitts liked Rex, who in his turn labelled them as 'the usual dull prigs' that his wife chose for friends.

Anyone, in Rex's eyes, who did not drink to capacity and produce 'the party spirit' in non-working hours was priggish. He had no repose himself, and no time for books or the quiet evenings of thoughts and ideas. As far as Martin Winters was concerned, he spoke of him now as he would of someone to be pitied.

'I pity these quiet, shy chaps. They don't know how to enjoy life.'

Phillida said nothing. Yet she knew that Rex was the one to be pitied. Yes, she could be almost sorry for him. He was putting on flesh rapidly, and she could picture him in the future, a fat caricature of the handsome boy that he had once been; a Rex without the energy of youth, too out of condition to play games, too out of date to fascinate young girls any more. Then what would he have left? Nothing to fall back on ... no spiritual comfort ... not even the love of an English garden, of home life, the things that *mattered*.

But Martin, whom he pitied, would have all these things. Martin, even if he were stricken down with some malady which might chain him to a couch for the rest of

281

his days, would still have his books, his big receptive mind, his interest in, and sympathy for, humanity.

She had grown to respect deeply Martin's character. And to rely, more than she cared to admit, on the friendship he gave her. Sometimes when she fancied that he might be posted elsewhere it wrenched her heart. She did not really know how she would get on without him these days. Sometimes, when she was feeling at her lowest ebb, and he came and sat with her, she would feel the strength and comfort stealing back into her. She would feel, after he had gone, that she could carry on. And yet why? They never discussed her private affairs. Never once had Rex been mentioned between them more than casually. Perhaps it would be just that he spoke of Killoun ... read extracts from one of Aunt Kate's delicious letters. She had a great flair for descriptive writing, and some of her accounts of the magic spring days down by the salmon river or in the Castle grounds helped Phillida to feel that she herself was there. When Martin read the words, expressing his own delight, it was as though he carried her along with him into the realms of pure enchantment.

He had a beautiful speaking voice, and read well.

Sometimes it would be she who told him the latest news of Alvercombe. He was always so interested and he was as distressed as she to hear how the hard winter had destroyed many of the more frail and treasured plants in Gamma's precious garden.

But Phillida no longer bothered to tell Rex such news. In the early days out here she used to give him her letters to read. And he yawned and said:

'You know I'm not keen on gardening ... it bores me stiff, Poppet.'

So now she left him to flip through the pages of *Esquire* and make amusing remarks about the glamour girls.

How could two men be so different? she sometimes wondered, when she dared allow herself to make comparisons. For it was not that Martin lacked humour. He, too, liked his 'pink gin', a pretty girl, an amusing story. But it just wasn't the whole of his life, in the way it seemed to be Rex's. For Rex 'all the goods were in the shop window'. For Martin there were treasures hidden away, stored.

Sometimes these days, struggling with her sickness and low spirits, Phillida looked at the big, fair sailor or watched him stretch his long legs and smoke his pipe, and thought, '*Poor little Bridget ... you have missed so much by dying ... Martin would have made you the most wonderful husband in the world.*'

Ahmed brought in the tea. She noticed that his *gallabiah* was torn and stained. He was not looking fresh or wholesome these days and he was growing cheeky. She wanted to get rid of him. She did not think he was a good servant. Mabyn Pentyre, who came here to lunch last week, and was, as usual, frank, spoke her mind on the subject. He was a rotten *suffragi,* and she wouldn't have him in the house, she said. But Rex would not dismiss Ahmed. Ahmed waited on Rex in a servile and fawning manner that appealed to his vanity. He did little for Phillida but saw to it that the Captain's shoes were beautifully polished and that he was there when Rex wanted him. Only last night when Phillida had said that she would like a nicer type in the house, especially when her baby was born, Rex had said:

'Oh, Ahmed's all right. You just don't know how to tackle these Arabs. And women are zero in their eyes, anyhow. *'I'm* the big noise in this house. You leave Ahmed to me.'

As usual Phillida was too tired and too defeated to protest further. But she had begun to dislike Ahmed. And she had a morbid fear, perhaps due to her present condition, that he might try to poison her. It was a ridiculous fancy and she knew it, but she could not quite get it out of her head.

In consequence, she eyed all her food with distrust, and was not eating enough.

She had just started to drink her tea when Martin came in.

The moment Ahmed showed him into the

room Phillida experienced that complete sense of security and relief which the big fellow's presence always brought her. She began to struggle up from her chair, but he shook a finger at her.

'No ceremony. Don't get up, my dear, please. How are you today? I'm going to dinner in the Garrison with the A.Q., and I thought if I wouldn't be in the way I'd like to sit a bit with you. Is Rex in?'

Phillida sat back in her chair and smiled up at Martin. She thought how nice and cool he looked in his light gabardine suit and cream silk shirt. Martin always wore such nice silk shirts and ties. She said:

'Rex is doing some special job. I know it's his half-day, but he said he has to go to Quassassin.'

Martin raised an eyebrow. He could see no possible reason why Rex should have a special job in Quassassin; added to which, driving from Fayid to Ismailia, he thought he had seen the M.G., which was a distinctive little car, with Maltern and that Deacon girl in it. There was something pretty distinctive about *her,* too, with her flame-red curls.

His dislike of Rex Maltern was no less than it had been months ago. In some ways it had increased. The man was not only a fool to chase these females the way he did and get himself talked about, but a knave …

considering that he had a wife like Phillida. Particularly at this time when all was not well with her. Little doubt he had got out of spending a quiet afternoon with Phillida by creating a job for himself at Quassassin and possibly he was on his way there just now, or on his way back – *with* Copper Deacon.

Young Copper had the same effect on Martin as Rebecca Rendledon. He saw her attraction, but for other men, not himself. Copper had looks and was, perhaps, less sinister than the Syrian girl because she was English, and to be pitied because she was very young and had had her head turned. But in Martin's opinion she wanted spanking.

He looked at Phillida. She had risen and pushed open the shutters so that the room was filled with light.

The little room, shoddily furnished though it was with cheap wood, and with one or two ancient Victorian pieces which the Greek owner had dragged from heaven knew where, nevertheless had taken on some of Phillida's own personality. The curtains were fresh and pretty. There were roses on the mantelpiece, a big bowl of vivid-coloured Zinnias on the Moorish table in the middle of the room. More roses on the bureau alongside a photograph of Rex as a sub-altern; looking much thinner and better-looking than he was these days. There was also a photograph of a sweet-faced, white-haired woman ... Phillida's grandmother. Over the fireplace Phillida had found a painting of the sea ... an English scene that she had found in Cairo, when Rex had taken her there to shop before they moved into this bungalow.

Martin noticed that Phillida's gaze often wandered to that picture. He knew how she hungered for her Devon home. And he pitied her from the bottom of his soul. For he, too, loved the sea and was weary of the desert sands. As for Phillida, he had likened her to a flower when he first met her, and now it seemed that the flower, uprooted from an English garden, was wilting, dying in the heat.

He was growing very concerned about Phillida. He wondered if the doctors were doing all they should. He felt sure she ought not to be as ill as this. How he wished he could take her back to England ... to Aunt Kate ... take her up to Scotland ... to Killoun Castle, where she could sit with him by the river on one of those cool, enchanted evenings near the Pool wherein the big fish rose to the mayfly and the sunset over the hills was a miracle of loveliness. How she would love it! The moorland air, the peace and beauty of Killoun, would soon cure her ills, both mental and physical.

He looked at the white young face and

big, shadowy eyes and knew that he could hardly bear the thought that she was carrying Rex Maltern's child within her; that soon that slender frame would thicken perceptibly, and she would grow heavy and more listless, and then suffer in order to bring into the world what might be a replica of that detestable fellow.

But it was no good thinking that way. And when his mind so worked he tried to remember what Aunt Kate had written in answer to that very long letter which he had sent, telling her about Phillida.

With that sweet understanding which he had expected from her, she had sympathised about his feelings for Phillida.

She must be a very sweet girl, and as she is like our darling Bridget used to be I know I should love her too. But, my dear boy, try to remember that she is another man's wife, and that you must not think of her as more than a friend. I beg of you to do this for both your sakes. You have always been straight and honourable, Martin, and would hate yourself if you were the cause of trouble between these two. You would only make it worse for her. I can fully see that it is not the case of you coming between a happily married couple. She must be very unhappy, poor child, but do not let her rely too much upon you, nor must you grow to feel too tenderly towards her.

He had that letter still in his pocket. He knew that his aunt was dead right, and God alone knew he didn't want to make things harder for Phillida. But while she seemed so lonely and always had so touching a welcome for him, he could not bring himself to break away.

As far as he himself was concerned, Aunt Kate's warning came too late. Already he thought of Phillida far too tenderly for his peace of mind. But he was not vain enough to imagine that Phillida had grown to rely too greatly upon *him*. He was sure that Aunt Kate was wrong there.

He handed Phillida a plate of sandwiches which Ahmed had brought in on the tea-tray.

She shook her head.

He cocked an eyebrow at her in a characteristic way, with that friendly and extraordinarily sweet smile of his.

'You must eat, my dear.'

He saw a peculiar look come into her eyes – such big, sunken eyes, these days. And now, with a pathetic expression of doubt and apprehension which he did not understand, she reached for her horn-rimed glasses, put them on, opened one of the sandwiches and peered into it.

'Now come on, don't be fussy,' he teased her, 'they look extremely good.'

She put the sandwich back on her plate

and removed her glasses, still unsmiling.

'No. And don't eat that one, Martin. I don't want you to.'

He stared. 'Why on earth not?'

She looked over her shoulder in a nervous way, then said in a low, confidential voice:

'I'm not sure that Ahmed isn't trying to poison me. *I hate him.* He frightens me.'

Martin's smile vanished. He saw suddenly that this girl was in the worst possible state of nerves, which could do no good to one in her condition.

'Look here, Phillida,' he said quietly, 'you're letting things get on top of you. This is all nonsense. Why should Ahmed want to poison you?'

'I don't know.'

'There's no possible reason. And if you have taken a dislike to him, sack him, my dear. You can always get another *suffragi*.'

Her lower lip quivered piteously.

'Rex likes him. He'll do anything for Rex. It's me he dislikes. Rex says the Arabs look down on women and only like taking orders from men.'

It was on the tip of Martin's tongue to say that he had never heard such nonsense. But he restrained himself. All too often he found himself in the position of wanting to air an honest and not too complimentary opinion of Rex Maltern, but had to forget it. He said:

'Oh, I think that's a little exaggerated. The Arabs look down on their own women, but most of these *suffragis* make very devoted and respectful servants. Aren't you getting things a little out of proportion?'

'I don't know!' she repeated, and suddenly lost her control. Perhaps it was the culmination of a hot day following a sleepless night, and that awful incessant nausea, which was not helped by Rex being so difficult to deal with. She covered her face with her hands.

Martin put down his pipe, leaned forward and looked at her with the utmost distress. To see her like that, the bowed, fair young head, the slender shaking hands, and know that she was silently weeping, wrenched his heart. He would have given anything on earth in that moment to take her in his arms and say:

'*My darling, my poor little darling, don't be afraid. I'll take care of you…*'

But he could only sit there helplessly, with his old violent dislike of Maltern inwardly eating at him. Then, after a pause, he said:

'You must never let life defeat you, my dear. You're so brave as a rule. It will be all right. You'll be feeling better after a bit. It's just this infernal heat and the country, generally speaking, and you not being well, and so on…'

He broke off, embarrassed, chafing because he could not comfort her as he wished. He was at least rewarded when she raised her head and gave him the faintest of smiles. But again his heart was torn by the sight of the tears rolling childishly down her cheeks. He pulled a large white handkerchief out of his pocket and handed it to her.

'Clean this morning,' he said, 'and I haven't used it yet.'

She gave a feeble laugh, took the handkerchief and wiped her eyes. When he put the handkerchief back in his pocket he was disturbed to find that his own fingers were shaking. He went on talking to her in a light vein, trying to pull her out of the despairing depths into which she seemed to have fallen.

He even managed to persuade her to eat one of the sandwiches.

'Just one, and I'll devour the rest. I promise you I shan't pass out and you won't even have a tummy-ache,' he said with a wry smile.

So she ate a sandwich and lost that hunted look. Then he sat back, drank his tea and told her the latest news from Scotland. He had sent Aunt Kate some of the snapshots he had taken on the French beach of a picnic party which included Phillida.

He added: 'She thinks you're very like my Bridget used to be.'

'Oh, am I?'

Now he avoided looking at her.

'Yes, very.'

The silence that fell between them then was rather strained.

Then Martin added, with a humorous twist of the lips:

'Except that she didn't go around refusing to eat very nice sandwiches because she thought they were poisoned.'

Now Phillida laughed outright.

'Oh, I *am* idiotic! No wonder Rex gets annoyed with me.'

'Rex,' thought Martin grimly, 'ought to be strung up and thrashed. This girl's very ill – both in body and mind – and he ought to send her home right now, or she'll have a complete breakdown...'

But for the moment she seemed happier and more normal. He even made her laugh more than once, and was delighted to see that enchanting dimple reappear at the corner of her mouth. It was so often like this; when he first arrived he would find a wretched browbeaten little thing, and after an hour with him she became a different person. It was flattering, but it brought him little satisfaction. She was Rex Maltern's wife and she was having his child, and Maltern did not know how to treat her. What in God's name could he, Martin, do about it? Nothing!

By six o'clock Rex had not yet returned

from Quassassin.

At a quarter past six Martin regretfully rose to his feet and announced that he must depart. It was then that Phillida put her hand to her mouth and said:

'Oh dear!'

He smiled at her.

'Now what?'

'Rex's white dinner-jacket. I promised to fetch it.'

He frowned.

'Send the Arab for it. You don't want to go out in this heat if you're still feeling rotten.'

'It's Ahmed's night off. He'll have gone. He goes at tea-time today. But I must get the coat. We're dining out tonight.'

Martin kept the usual control over his tongue, but he would have given a lot to tell her what he thought of this sort of thing. What kind of a fellow was Maltern? No doubt he would be full of life and charm tonight, and keep the party laughing, and all the girls would think what an amusing chap he was, but his wife ... poor little Phillida ... ought to be in bed or lying down here in peace and quiet, with somebody to wait on her.

He said:

'I'll get the coat. I've got the Morris outside.'

'Oh, I can't ask you...' began Phillida.

'Little Wrens don't argue with Lieutenant-

Commanders,' he said.

'Oh dear!' she sighed, and laughed. 'What a long way away my Wren days seem to me now!'

'Well, sit down and relax, and I'll be back with the coat in a moment. Where is it?'

'The Sphinx Laundry.'

'I know. Got a ticket?'

'Yes...'

She went to the bureau and found the ticket. Martin looked tenderly towards the young figure in the short floral dress.

'Tidy girl,' he said.

She did not tell him that it would have been more than her life was worth to lose that piece of paper. On one occasion, through her carelessness, two good shirts of Rex's had got mixed up with somebody else's laundry, and had not been recovered for forty-eight hours; during which Rex had nagged at her so incessantly that she had vowed never to repeat the mistake.

Dear Martin ... what a comfort he was! More than that. *Oh, much more* ... but here she checked herself and would not let her thoughts go further.

Martin came back with Rex's coat, then bade her good-bye.

For an instant her long, slim hand lay in his big one. She said wistfully: 'Come again soon.'

'Of course...' He glanced at his wrist-watch. 'I hope you won't be alone too long. But I'm sure Rex will be back any moment.'

'Oh yes, I'm sure he will,' she said, with a brightness she was far from feeling.

After Martin had gone the little bungalow seemed to her very quiet, and very sultry. She went round the house pushing open shutters and opening all the doors. At this hour very often a little wind sprang up to relieve the closeness of the atmosphere. And it was good to get a draught through the house.

She sat down by the sitting-room window and picked up her knitting again. She wondered why Rex was so late. She wished that she had not got to dress and drag herself out to the Club tonight. She wished she could get over her stupid dislike of Ahmed. She wished so many things…

And then she remembered her momentary breakdown in front of Martin, and her cheeks reddened at the thought. She was ashamed of herself. But who else would have been as understanding, as gentle as he?

Knit one, purl one … the knitting needles clicked. She dragged her thoughts from the past and the present to the future, and tried desperately to believe everything would be better once her baby was born.

3

Phillida sat in a deck-chair just inside the shade of one of the little round huts, down at the *Jardin d'Enfants* on the Plage facing the Canal.

She was watching the rest of the party bathe. She was still feeling ill, and the doctor had forbidden her to swim, although now in the second week in June it was so hot, and the water was so warm and looked so blue and inviting, she regretted her inability to join the others. But she had been trying all this week to take Martin's advice and not allow life to defeat her. She had even succeeded in conquering, a little, that foolish fear of being poisoned by Ahmed, and had tried to eat more. But the nausea was still prevalent, and she was so listless, so drained of life, that she could hardly drag her steps one in front of the other.

The Plage was crowded this Sunday morning. She could see Rex's dark head bobbing in the water. He was holding on to a bright orange-coloured rubber dinghy in which two girls, Copper and a friend of hers, were lying. Phillida could hear them laughing and screaming. Doreen and Jimmy Angus were swimming too. And a new friend of Rex's, a Major Gayter, from G.H.Q.

Phillida disliked Harold Gayter. He was a big, red-faced man, with a heavy moustache, and eyes that leered rather than looked at a girl. But he was a bachelor of means, and had a magnificent English racing car out here, and, as Rex put it, 'threw wizard parties'. Rex was more often with Gayter nowadays than with Jimmy Angus. He had long since decided that Jimmy, apart from his interest in cars, was 'wet' and 'dull', and Rex was trying to drop the Anguses altogether. But in her quiet fashion Phillida continued to go on seeing them. She liked Jimmy, and she had become a friend of Doreen's simply and solely because the baby, and the subject of babies, bound them together. And Doreen by this time had become genuinely attached to Phillida, whom Peggy, her sister, also openly adored. This morning Peggy had taken young Bill into the gardens near their flat. She considered the beach too hot for so small a baby.

Doreen was the first to come out of the water. She threw herself down on the sand in front of Phillida and started to rub her hair with a towel.

'Oh, that was scrumptious!' she said. 'The bathing's the only thing that's worth while in this miserable country.'

Phillida lay back in her chair and looked at Doreen through half-closed eyes, smiling wearily.

'There are other things, I suppose. Martin always finds them. He thinks it is a marvellous place in its way. The real Egypt, I mean. He says the life we Army wives lead and the things and people we live amongst are all artificial.'

Doreen winked good-naturedly at her friend.

'Your Martin!'

Phillida coloured.

'Hardly mine, my dear.'

Doreen put her tongue in her cheek.

'But he'd like to be.'

Now Phillida was crimson.

'Doreen – you mustn't say those things.'

The other girl turned and patted Phillida's lap.

'There! I was only ragging. I wouldn't say it to anyone else. I know what a lot of miserable gossips they are here. But he obviously adores you, Phil.'

Phillida gulped a little.

'Really, Doreen.'

'Oh, I know he's an angel of a man and wouldn't tell you so. But he does. Jimmy and I both think so.'

'Well, I don't want you to say it, Doreen,' said Phillida, and reproached herself because her heart was beating so quickly and her cheeks – her whole body – felt hot.

Hastily she changed the subject.

'You promised to show me that pattern for an infant's vest.'

'Yes, I've got it all ready for you at the flat. But I keep forgetting to bring it round.'

'I'm glad someone else forgets things sometimes,' said Phillida, with feeling.

Doreen glanced round the Plage. A variety of people in a variety of costumes sat round in the little huts. Some Army, and some Air Force, with a sprinkling of French. The gay costumes and swim-suits worn by the women made a vivid splash of colour. There were many children both in the water and on the diving-boards. Even at this early hour of eleven it was baking hot. The sky looked pale with heat. Across the shining waters of the Canal lay Sinai … a white blue of sand, veiled by the heat. Now and then a great felucca with spread sails went by. Already one of the biggest of troopships had passed them, gliding down towards Port Said. Languidly from her chair Phillida had waved to the troops who waved back to the cheering children. As usual it brought a lump in her throat to see a troopship home-ward bound. It always made her long desperately for England. Just as this gay Plage held no interest for her. She yearned for the little cool, sandy beach at Alver-combe, for the sound of the Devon seas breaking gently on a summer's day over the seaweed-covered rocks.

She closed her eyes. Doreen went on chatting. Bits of gossip about the other 'wives'; complaints about the high price of food; of the 'thieves' in the Rue Negrelli, and an account of some stupid thing Jimmy had done. Jimmy was rarely in favour, though on the whole Doreen was more content now that she had her sister to wait on her and mind the baby. After a pause Phillida opened her eyes and said:

'Be nice to old Jimmy. He is so devoted to you. You're a lucky girl, really, Doreen.'

Doreen bit her lip. She was lying on her back now, smoking a cigarette.

'Oh, I know I am. But he's a bit "soppy", Phil. I suppose I'm a little beast, but I do get fed up with him.'

Phillida gave an ironic smile.

'We none of us seem very satisfied.'

Doreen looked up at her friend's haggard young face. Poor Phil! Everyone thought she was looking ghastly. She was having the hell of a time with this baby. And everyone thought Rex pretty difficult and spoiled. But he *was* so handsome and entertaining, Doreen thought. How he had made them all laugh at that party in Captain Williams's flat the other night! He had sat at the piano for an hour singing naughty songs. He *was* so amusing! She wished Jimmy was like that. Of

301

course, Rex was a bit off-hand with Phil, but Doreen rather fancied a man with a mind of his own who didn't get 'soppy' like Jimmy. Then again everyone was talking about Rex and that youngster, Copper Deacon. And *that* wasn't really fair on Phil. But Doreen, finding excuses for the charming Rex, decided that it was Copper who was chasing *him,* and so forgave him. She said:

'Well, even if you get fed up with Rex sometimes because he leads you a song and dance, he's fun to live with, I should think. I'll give you Jimmy if you give me Rex...' She giggled.

Phillida stayed silent. Her lips curved into a bitter smile. Doreen – with the rest of the women – was, of course, all for Rex. Rex was never the *real* Rex in public. And she, loathing women who were publicly disloyal to their husbands, never complained about his behaviour at home. So they didn't know. Nobody knew.

After a pause, she said:

'You stick to your Jimmy, and don't be horrid, Doreen.'

'I like men with a bit of devil in them.'

'Oh, Doreen!' sighed Phillida, shaking her head. 'You're hopeless.'

'Well, don't you? I mean, look at men like your Martin Winters.'

'Don't keep calling him "mine". And why should I look at him?' said Phillida, in an unusually cross voice.

'Because, darling, he hasn't got eyes for anyone else in Ismailia, and you know it. But he *is* terribly proper and conventional, and therefore, in my eyes, a bit of a bore. I tell you I like the devil in a man.'

Once again Phillida was reduced to silence. With that increase of tempo in her heartbeats over Doreen's frank statements about Martin's regard for her, she thought of him, and those thoughts were not as guarded as they might have been. For deep in her heart she was saying:

'You are not a bore, Martin. You are the most interesting man I have ever met. A man who reads and studies and thinks ... and yet you can be gay ... you can make me laugh ... you are all that a woman really wants a man to be ... but Doreen doesn't know the real you. And I ... God help me ... when I chose Rex ... I didn't know the real Rex. I was blind. I should have waited... And now, Martin, even if you do care a bit for me, it is much too late. I am bound for always to Rex and his child...'

The force of such feelings, surging within her, never to be expressed, rarely even to be allowed to enter her mind, made Phillida feel quite faint for a moment. She closed her eyes and gladly let Doreen chatter on in her frothy, meaningless way.

Then when she opened her eyes once more she saw Rex and Copper Deacon coming out

303

of the water towards them. Phillida took off her smoked glasses, and blinking in the strong light watched the two advance. How superb Rex looked still, despite his increase in weight, she thought. Like this, with chestnut hair curling, wet with salt water, and every inch of his body so beautifully bronzed, he was, indeed, any girl's idea of a Greek god – one of the immortals! An intense sadness gripped her. It was awful to *know* that behind that brilliant façade there lay such a meanness of spirit, such egoism ... a character that might almost be called cruel, in its complete disregard for others.

Rex paused to light a cigarette for the girl at his side. Phillida had to admit they made a striking couple. Young Copper (Phillida, barely four years older, felt so old and tired compared with her these days) was as glowing, as Greek-like, as Rex, with her short Titian curls and lovely features, only she had not had time to get so burned by the sun. Her diminutive emerald-green two-piece swim-suit was fashioned to reveal as much as possible of her gorgeous creamy body. She moved with the undulating and rather studied grace of a mannequin. She knew perfectly well that every man on the beach was eyeing her, and thoroughly enjoyed the fact. Now, with a pretty show of sympathetic concern, she moved forward, threw herself on the warm sand at Phillida's feet, and said:

'Oh, it *is* a shame you can't come in with us, Phil. You must get so hot, poor thing.'

Phillida looked down at her. Copper's eyes were really quite green, she reflected, and she was so youthful, so healthy, so much more attractive in every way than Rebecca Rendledon. Phillida would understand a man 'falling for her'. She knew, too, that she was no longer jealous ... no longer cared, from a personal point of view, what Rex did with other women. It was only the fact that it made her look cheap; dishonoured their marriage and destroyed his reputation, as well as that of the foolish girl; and because of these things she hated to see how things were shaping between these two.

Sheer pride in front of Doreen made her force a flippant reply to Copper. 'Oh, I'm too lazy to get into a bathing-suit and walk to the water. That's it, isn't it, Rex?'

He, sitting now on the sand beside Copper, vigorously rubbing his handsome head with his towel, turned to give his wife a patronising smile.

'That's it. Poor old Phil! Doesn't feel up to much these days.'

'She doesn't look up to much, either,' said Phillida, and laughed.

'Oh, I think you are always lovely,' said Copper, with an enthusiasm which Phillida felt to be hypocritical.

Rex now made his own show of concern for Phillida.

'Okay there where you are, Poppet? Or would you like me to run you back to the house? It's getting a bit hot.'

She regarded him gravely.

She knew how little he would like it if she said yes and he had to change out of his swim-suit and drive her back into Ismailia, so she said:

'Oh, don't trouble, please, Rex; I'm all right.'

'Well, I think she looks very white,' put in Doreen, wishing to champion her friend – mainly because she could not stand Copper Deacon.

Rex glanced at Doreen, and said acidly:

'Well, Phil knows she has only to say the word.'

'I see Jimmy coming over here ... *he* will run her back if she wants,' said Doreen.

Phillida's pale, thin cheeks grew hot. She said:

'Oh, please, everybody, don't worry about me ... I'm all right, really...'

Rex, feeling Copper's green eyes upon him, lifted one of Phillida's limp hands and put it against his cheek.

'My poor Poppet isn't having much of a time just now...'

Her muscles tautened. She was conscious of sudden irritation because Rex was putting over all this charm and sympathy just for his girl-friend's benefit. She tried not to snatch her hand away, but Rex's gesture, holding it like that, gave her no pleasure whatsoever.

It had the required effect upon Copper, however. She sighed and said, in a languishing voice:

'Oh, you *are* lucky to have such a sweet husband, Phil!...'

Phillida stayed silent. Rex, his tongue in his cheek, dropped Phillida's hand and grinned at the young girl, who had now stretched her long, creamy body on the sand close to his. Little devil, he thought, she really had a wonderful figure with that small waist and those long tapering legs. And what a mouth! She wasn't at all experienced. He had already kissed that fresh, ripe mouth a good many times and found that she was really still a child, but willing enough to learn. And he was finding it decidedly exciting to teach her. Becki was a thing of the past. And as for poor old Phil ... well, it wasn't any fun being married to a girl who was always ill. Not that it was her fault. He was responsible for the child that was on the way.

Sometimes he thought it might be rather amusing to have a son or daughter a reproduction of himself, to satisfy his ego ... but he had no patience with all this 'palaver' before it was born. He really wished he hadn't lost his head that night of reconciliation with Phil. It hadn't improved relations between them. He could see that their marriage was 'washed-up' and he felt rather aggrieved at the thought that he must be responsible, morally and financially, for Phil and the child for the rest of his life. Unless, of course, she chose to leave him in time to come. But she wasn't the sort to quit on a marriage. She had such high ideals.

He was really amazed these days to think that he had ever married Phil. She was very sweet, and all that, but so colossally boring. He couldn't 'take' all that high-minded stuff; that intellectual side which she sometimes so astonishingly produced. She was extraordinarily well-read, much better educated than himself. He fully realised that she ought to have married a chap like Martin Winters. He would have suited her down to the ground. It was a damn' nuisance that they didn't fall in love and bolt, the pair of them. But, of course, they wouldn't. And *he* wasn't going to do anything of the kind and be forced to pay out a third of his income for the rest of his days. Anyhow, there could be no question of a divorce now because of this child. He would just have to go on enjoying life as best he could. He had firmly made up his mind that he would not allow Phil to drag him down to old Jimmy Angus's level, anyhow … pinned to the domestic hearth, always fussing around with prams and babies' bottles. No sir! And suddenly, as though these thoughts were eating at him, Rex began to hum:

'No, no, a thousand times no,
I'd rather die than say yes...'

Copper giggled.
'You'd rather die than say yes to what, Rex?'
He rolled over on his stomach so close to her that his breath fanned her cheek.
'That's what the young maiden said to the wicked old gent who threatened her honour,' he said, with a broad grin.
She eyed him through her lashes.
'And very proper, too.'
He suddenly lowered his voice so that the others could not hear. 'I'd like to threaten *your* honour, you little green-eyed devil!'
'Go ahead and threaten,' she whispered back, her body quivering with mirth.
'Next time we're alone...' He paused significantly and blew a cloud of cigarette-smoke straight into her face.
Phillida, from her deck-chair, could not hear what they said, but she saw the expression on both their faces, and could guess what sort of a conversation was going on between them. Suddenly she wanted to get away from the pair of them; from everybody on the Plage. She said:

'Look, Rex, would it be an absolute bore if I did ask you to run me home after all? I don't feel too good.'

He dragged his gaze from the girl with whom he was flirting so outrageously and sprang to his feet with a nice show of willingness to comply at once with his wife's request.

'Sure. I'll nip over to the shower and be back in a jiffy, darling. It won't take a second to get you home...' Then to Copper: 'I'll come back and fetch you, you awful child. Here comes old Harold... Harold, keep an eye on this brat while I'm gone. She needs a padlock and chain. I promised her mother to take her home for lunch.'

'Oh!' said Copper, sitting up suddenly. 'Mummy told me to take you and Phil back to lunch with me. We've got a goose. It was alive when Mummy bought it in the Negrelli, and last night our boy cut its throat and we all heard it squawking...'

She giggled and stopped. The giggle gave place to an expression of dismay, for Phillida Maltern, having risen to her feet, suddenly put a hand to her head and swayed.

Doreen Angus sprang up and put an arm around her.

'She's going to faint!' Then to Copper, in an undertone, 'You are a little idiot, talking like that when you know how she's feeling...'

'Oh, I'm sorry,' said Copper lamely.

Rex, thoroughly annoyed, because there was nothing he disliked more than a scene of this kind, seized Phillida by the arm and said:

'Buck up, Poppet. Don't pass out on us. Let me help you straight back to the car. I can drive back like this – I'll just slip a coat on.'

Phillida made an effort to recover. The sunlit world had suddenly swum around her, accompanied by the dreaded nausea. Copper's joke had had rather a poor effect on her ... a joke which brought all too vividly to mind a live bird, its white plumage spattered with blood. She could *hear* those dying squawkings. She had seen so much cruelty to animals out here. Birds crammed together in cages and left to die in the hot sun. Little thin donkeys straining to pull loads far beyond their strength; lean, pitiful horses with their ribs showing through ... mangy, skeleton-like cats slinking around the garbage in the streets ... and the miserable, lean, famished pi-dogs that kept her awake at night with their hunger cries. She could not bear the suffering of dumb animals, and in her present condition Copper's thoughtless story had been too much for her.

She just managed not to faint. Once in the car, driving away from the Plage with Rex, she apologised.

'I'm so sorry … do forgive me, darling.'

He scowled ahead at the white, sandy road fringed with trees circling the banks of the Canal. They were passing the Timsah Leave Camp which lay in the shade of a dark, restful-looking wood on the other side of the water. He said:

'Oh, that's all right. You couldn't help it. But if you feel as bad as this you shouldn't come on picnics and parties.'

She stayed silent, hands, trembling a little, clasped in her lap. He had forgotten that only the other day when she had begged to be allowed to stay at home he had said:

'I think you ought to make more effort. Other women who are expecting babies don't make all this fuss. I'm sure you'd be better if you got out and about a bit more. What you want is to practice a little Christian Science, my dear Poppet.'

She had not argued or pointed out that the M.O. was most insistent that she should keep very quiet because the heat, added to her pregnancy and her low state of vitality generally, was making her unusually ill. She had not wanted to come to the beach this morning. But remembering his little lecture she had dragged herself out. This was the result.

He alternated between grumblings and sympathising with her in a grudging sort of way until they reached their bungalow. As he helped her out of the car, he added:

'I tell you, here and now, if I'd known it was going to affect you like this I'd never have let you have this baby. It isn't much fun for either of us.'

With sudden bitterness she said:

'Well, I'm glad you include me.'

At once he saw a chance to be nasty, and took it.

'There you are! That's what I get when I try to be nice to you. You're always saying that I'm so bad-tempered. Well, you're enough to make any fellow bad-tempered.'

Her heart sank.

'Oh, please, don't let's begin a fight, Rex, I really don't feel up to it.'

'Well, I just think you're making the most of this baby business so as to get at me,' he snapped. 'It's all jealousy … that's what it is. You didn't like me enjoying myself this morning with Copper. I know how your mind works. You attached a sinister meaning to the most innocent flirtation. It's all jealousy.'

She walked into the house with slow, heavy steps.

'Do you really think I brought you back here just in order to get you away from that girl?'

He followed her into the sitting-room, which was shuttered and dim, feeling frustrated; a man trapped by marriage. He flung a hot, resentful look at Phillida's drooping figure.

'I wouldn't put it past you.'

She started to laugh, a wave of hysteria engulfing her.

He shouted down her laughter, in one of his quick, violent rages. 'I don't believe you're as ill as all that. And to create a fainting scene because Copper said a few words about a b—y goose ... honestly, Phil, you're enough to give any man a headache and...'

Now Phillida broke in, turning like a creature at bay, nerves frayed, patience at an end.

'Oh, don't nag me! I can't stand it! Go back to your Copper. Say what you want, do what you want, only leave me alone. You say you wish you hadn't let me have the baby, and so do I. *So do I...*'

She dropped into a chair and burst into tears, great hiccoughing sobs shaking her body, face buried in the curve of her arm. For a moment Rex stared down at her, his mouth pulled down, angry. Suddenly the best side of him temporarily asserted itself. He marched out of the room, fetched some cognac, came back, knelt beside her and began to pour out apologies in his facile, moody fashion.

'Hush! Don't cry. I'm an absolute cad. Drink a little of this, darling ... I ought to be shot... Come on ... stop crying ... you know I want the baby, and I didn't mean to be a brute...'

But Phillida was not to be comforted by that spate of words nor the encircling arm and the brandy. For she knew that she could not believe a word that he said and that there was no stability, no real warmth, nor kindliness, behind his change of demeanour. It was just his usual line of conduct after they had had a row and he had driven her beyond endurance. For the moment he felt ashamed and wanted to put himself right in her eyes. But it meant so little. And nothing, nothing that he did or said, could put Rex right in her eyes again.

4

Towards the end of that next week Rex announced that they had been invited by his Brigadier to a dance at one of the Social Centres of the Married Families' Quarters in Fayid.

'It won't particularly amuse me,' said Rex, 'but I think we ought to go, and' – throwing the invitation card to Phillida – 'the whole of my crowd will be there.'

Phillida glanced at the card and then up at Rex. She was still in bed. It was half past six in the morning. Rex had just come out of the bathroom. The French windows leading on to the verandah were open and the sunlight poured into the bedroom. Already it was hot. But at this hour there was at least a breath of fresh air.

Phillida had had one of her restless nights. She was languid and heavy-eyed, but she smiled at Rex. Since her breakdown, after the episode on the Plage last Sunday, he had been making another of his efforts to be amiable. Not that she had seen much of him, and in her disillusioned state of mind she often asked herself cynically if his geniality was due to the fact that he was having a good time and seeing plenty of his new girl-friend behind his wife's back.

She said:

'I'll certainly go to the dance with you, if you think I ought to, darling. But I don't look my best.'

He flung her an indifferent glance.

'Oh, you've still got your figure – except for the odd inch here and there, nobody would know you were having a baby,' he said. 'Put on that black dress. That makes you very slim. And do your hair in that big plait which always suits you.'

'Does it?' said Phillida, a trifle wistfully.

He struggled into khaki drill shirt and shorts. He had his back to her now, no longer interested. She never felt that he was interested in her these days. She said:

'It's only the long drive into Fayid that I rather dread. The M.G. jolting makes me feel so sick.'

It was on the tip of Rex's tongue to tell her to stay at home and he'd take someone else. He would far rather have spent the evening, for instance, dancing with that gorgeous girl, Copper Deacon. It could be amusing at the Fayid Officers' Club, too, on a moonlight night; and having done all the duty dances at the Social Centre he could have slipped down to the Club with Copper and spent a very amusing hour or two on the beach and under the stars.

But he knew perfectly well that he had to take his wife to a formal show given by the Brigadier, and that was that. His good humour, easily banished, cracked a little at the thought of a duty dance at Fayid, anyhow, with an ailing wife. His handsome face assumed that irritable look which Phillida knew and dreaded.

'When are you going to stop feeling sick?' he grunted.

'I really don't know,' said Phillida, and added dryly: 'I haven't had a baby before.'

He eyed her gloomily. She looked washed out, he thought and certainly not at all attractive.

He muttered:

'Sometimes I think you ought to go back to England.'

She flushed, sat up and slid her arms into the thin cotton dressing-gown which she had made a month ago to replace the satin one which Gamma had given her, and which was now too thick and warm. (It was rather dreadful remembering all the pleasure she and Gamma had had preparing her 'trousseau' for Egypt. There was nothing left of all that eager love and enthusiasm.) Rex added:

'For two pins I'd send you home, only it's so darned expensive, and in the Army, when one has to keep up two homes, it's ruinous. You lose allowances and so on.'

Her large, sunken eyes rested on him with

318

faint bitter humour.

'Well, that wouldn't do, would it? I don't want to be a financial burden amongst other things. Besides, now I've come out I feel I ought to stay and make a go of it. I expect I'll be much better soon. Just be patient, Rex.'

'I didn't know I was ever anything else,' said Rex, in an aggrieved tone. 'But we seem to have got off the point. Shall I accept this dance for you or not?'

'Yes, accept if you like, and if I feel too awful on the day you must just make excuses for me.'

She looked so small and forlorn sitting there on the edge of the bed with her long, fair hair floating down her back that Rex's ill-humour gave place to a vague pity. He felt so magnificently well and glowing himself.

'My God! Who'd be a woman!' he exclaimed. 'I'm damned sorry for you. Well, so long. I must get cracking... Ahmed!' He raised his voice to a shout... 'Breakfast.'

Phillida called after him:

'What time will you be back today, Rex?'

'It's a late night,' he called back; 'don't wait supper for me.'

Her heart sank. Rex's late nights were so very late. She could never understand what kept him out so long after other men seemed to have finished work. And he never offered anything but the excuse that 'he had been kept'. It always filled her with doubts and misgivings, and she did so hate being alone in the bungalow after dark. She was still faintly suspicious of Ahmed, although Martin had almost persuaded her that he was harmless, and that it was her own nervous condition which made her frightened. But the long hours after sundown dragged, especially now when she was not well. Her eyes, always weak, were not reacting well to the strong glare out here, and very often in the evenings they were so sore that she could not read or sew for any length of time.

After Rex had gone she thought over his remarks about her going back to England. She could think of nothing nicer than returning to the heavenly solace of Alvercombe Cottage and her grandmother's loving care. She would miss nothing out here, nobody except Martin. (But she mustn't allow herself to miss or want *him* too much.) But she could not go home, she reflected. Not only because of the financial situation, but because she did not want to accept defeat. Her marriage was turning out badly ... and if she left Rex alone in Egypt now, anything might happen to him. He seemed to have become so weak over drink and women ... she was sure that she ought not to leave him here by himself. And she kept hoping that once the baby was born he would be different ... he might take an interest in his child, even though he were no longer interested in *her*, his wife.

Wearily she dressed and faced up to another long, hot, aimless day.

At eleven o'clock she met Doreen at Antoinette's, where they sat under an electric fan and drank iced coffee. Phillida listened patiently to the usual long list of complaints from the other girl, but this did not make her feel any more cheerful. And five minutes' walk in the heat and glare of Ismailia's noisy, crowded little shopping thoroughfare drove her back to the comparative coolness of the darkened bungalow.

Her cotton frock was wet, sticking to her, when she got back. She had a shower, put on another frock and walked into the sitting-room.

She sat down to write to her grandmother. She owed one or two other letters to people at home, but she had so far not had the energy to write them. She hoped that Rex would remember to bring home some post from G.H.Q. tonight. All her correspondence went through the Army Post Office. Sometimes Rex left the letters lying on his office desk. He admitted that he forgot to bring them back. That meant she went without news for days on end. He, of course, was not personally interested in home news. But Phillida hungered and thirsted for every word that was written from Alvercombe. The one thing she had in common with Doreen Angus was her continued homesickness.

She wondered if Martin would come and see her today; then remembered that he, too, would be working late at G.H.Q. tonight. It was a whole week since Martin had called here. It was rather awful, she reflected, that she should miss him, and want to see him again so much.

Ahmed served her lunch. She did not fancy it. She forced herself to eat a little, then abandoned the effort. Just as she was going to lie down Ahmed approached her, showing his white teeth in a grin.

'Me go off today. Want *feloos* (money). Captain no give *feloos* many week,' he said.

Phillida felt her colour rise. The old story! Ever since she had been out here she had struggled to make Rex pay his bills, and it was always a struggle. He was enormously generous with his entertaining, his drinks, his presents … in a good mood he would come back with an armful of the beautiful roses and carnations which grew so profusely out here, or a bottle of her favourite perfume. But he seemed to hate paying the necessities of life.

She told Ahmed to wait, made a search in her own bag and found that she had fifty *piastres* and no more. Rex had not given *her* the usual allowance this week. Each time she asked for it he said she should have it the next evening. She hated having to go back to the Sudanese and tell him that with her, too, it was a question of *'mafeesh feloos'* ... no money!

Ahmed's smile vanished.

'Must have,' he said stubbornly.

She bit her lip. Some of her old fear of the man returned. Her heart began to beat faster. She thought:

'Perhaps I could borrow from Doreen ... it looks so awful to let people know I haven't got any money ... but the man is justified in wanting his wages. It's so awful of Rex ... I must get it.'

She asked Ahmed when he was going out. He did not understand. He could speak a few words of English, but rarely understood. In despair she said:

'Come back later... Captain will be back... *Later,* Ahmed.'

She did not know whether he understood or not, but he walked out of the room. With troubled gaze she followed the thin angular figure in the long white *gallabiah,* then went to her bedroom.

She could not sleep. Apart from the heat and the oppressive atmosphere she was worried now about Ahmed's money. She lay staring hopelessly round her room. Then she got up and dressed again, and put on her big straw hat. She would go and see Doreen and try to borrow a pound.

Ahmed appeared in the hall. He seemed to slink out of the shadows. He always startled her. One of his eyes was malformed, and the other regarded her malevolently today, she thought. He did not even grin as usual.

'Must have *feloos*,' he said.

In an instant her whole body was bathed in perspiration from heat and nerves.

'Yes, Ahmed ... I go ... I go to get *feloos*,' she said.

'*Kwayis*,' he said, and she knew by that word 'good' that he understood and would wait.

She walked along the hot, glaring street, round the corner to the Anguses' flat. She toiled up the stairs. She knew the climb was bad for her. She was gasping when she reached the top. To her dismay no answer came to the bell, which she rang repeatedly. Then she remembered that Doreen had told her this morning that she and Peggy were spending this afternoon in the house of some French people who had children and with whom they had made friends.

Phillida walked down the stairs again. She now felt sick and rather stupid. And she still had no money for Ahmed. Neither did she know where to get it. She returned to the bungalow. Ahmed was there, waiting for her. He grinned.

Helplessly she looked at him.

'*Mafeesh feloos* ... must wait for Captain,' she said.

He said:

'No *feloos?*'

'Must wait for Captain,' she repeated, her heart thudding. The sweat rolled down her cheeks.

He said nothing more, and turned and vanished into the kitchen.

She went back to her bedroom and with trembling hands took off her dress and rubbed her body dry. How ill and tired she felt! And what a nasty look there had been in that eye of Ahmed's! She really did not like being alone with him under these circumstances. If only someone would come and see her ... if only Martin would come!

She did not dare go into the kitchen, nor ring for Ahmed to bring tea, but she knew that he was still in the house because she could hear the occasional clatter of a dish. Perhaps he did not mean to go out until he had got his pay.

She sat alone in the sitting-room. She tried twice to write a letter and failed. At six o'clock she knew that Ahmed was still in the house, waiting ... and the thing began to get on her nerves. It would be another three or four hours at least before Rex came home. If she had to wait here all that time alone with Ahmed snooping in the background she would go crazy, she thought. She could not even be sure that Rex would come back at the appointed time. She could not, *could not,* wait about like this, endlessly.

Darkness fell. She opened her shutters and let in some air. With it came the noise of the busy streets and the sound of a radio blaring an Egyptian song. The harsh, strident voice singing it brought her no pleasure. Everything seemed sinister and frightening. She felt that very soon she would be like Doreen, scared of her own shadow. She, who had never been afraid...

She decided that she must go out, that even if it meant climbing those stairs to the Anguses' flat once more she must do so and borrow the money for Ahmed.

As she passed into the hall she saw the Sudanese. He was wearing his *tarboosh* now instead of the little round white cap which he put on the back of his woolly head during working hours.

He said:

'Captain no come? No *feloos?*'

So it was beginning again, thought Phillida. She couldn't stand much more. She said:

'I go now to get *feloos...*'

Ahmed came nearer her.

'Must have...'

She caught her breath. He had a queer look ... she had heard tales of these natives

326

smoking *hasheesh* ... it made them excited and violent. Perhaps Ahmed had got hold of some. That one eye of his was glassy and staring ... his breath stank. She had always loathed and feared him. Tonight suddenly her courage cracked. She turned and began to run towards the front door. As she ran her bag slipped from under her arm on to the floor. Ahmed stooped down and picked it up. Possibly he did not mean to attempt any violence, but only to attract her attention. He caught hold of her arm. It was enough to finish Phillida after the long hours of loneliness and apprehension. A long, thin scream came from her lips. She shook herself free of the man's fingers. She screamed again and again, hysterically.

A car drove up and stopped in front of the little bungalow.

The very tall figure of Martin Winters stepped out on to the pavement. He was still in uniform. He had just come from a conference at B.T.E. Moascar. On his way back to Fayid he had decided that he must drop in and see Phillida.

Two things had kept him away from her this last week: excess of work and the force of his own feelings for her. He wanted to see her too much. Deliberately he schooled those feelings, reminding himself no matter how much it hurt that she was married to Maltern, and that she was going to have a child.

But tonight, driving the little Morris to Ismailia, he had not been able to quell the desire to go and see that tragic young figure, the memory of which haunted him so continually. Now as he walked up the steps on to the verandah and heard that high, hysterical screaming, his heart gave a great lurch and his whole body went hot.

In God's name what was happening here?

He tried to open the front door. It was locked. He beat on it with a clenched fist and rang the bell.

'Hi! What's the matter? Hi! Let me in! Phillida, is that you? Let me in!'

The door was flung open. He caught a confused glimpse of an ashen young face that was a mask of terror, and of the Sudanese standing gaping open-mouthed behind her. At the sight of the tall naval officer Ahmed dropped Phillida's bag and turned and fled to his own quarters.

Martin caught Phillida in his arms. She literally fell into them. He could feel her slight body shaking, drenched. Her screams died down to low, gasping moans.

'Oh, Martin! Oh, Martin, *Martin!...*'

He picked her right up and carried her into the sitting-room. He did not begin to understand what had happened. He only knew that she was in an extremity of fear and exhaustion. His own control snapped a little. He pressed his cheek close to hers.

'Darling … Phillida darling. It's all right … it's all right, my dear, I'll look after you. There's nothing to be afraid of. Nothing… Hush, darling.'

She turned her face to his shoulder and cried brokenly.

He sat down, holding her in his arms, waiting for her to quieten down. The fair, silky hair had broken loose from its combs and tumbled down her back. He smoothed it back from the flushed, tear-wet face. He could not now control the longing to kiss her. Without passion … tenderly … he kissed her forehead and soothed and comforted her.

'It's all right. You're all right now,' he kept repeating. 'Darling, don't be frightened any more. Ssh, don't cry. Tell me all about it. What happened? What frightened you?'

For a long time she could not speak coherently. She clung to him like a desperate child. His heart ached with pity and love.

'Thank God I came in just at this moment,' he said; 'thank God!'

Gradually her tears ceased to flow and her body to tremble. At length, quietly, still held in the blessed security of his arms, she lay still. And now that the hysteria had passed, and she could think more normally, she whispered a repetition of his words.

'Thank God you came just at this moment, Martin.'

For a while they both sat on the sofa with their arms around each other. She felt his lips against her hair. She shut her sore eyes. A languid happiness and contentment replaced the misery and fear within her. It was a moment of pure bliss for her; of ineffable relief. Martin, who was so strong and sane and wise, and so very dear.

His gentle fingers passed sensitively over her hair, her cheeks, smoothing, stroking her. She heard him whisper:

'Poor little darling ... poor little thing. What happened? Tell me...'

She began to explain, rather disjointedly, how Ahmed had demanded his wages – her fruitless attempts to get the money and the subsequent events. In a shamefaced way she ended:

'I expect I exaggerated his attitude towards me... I know you'll say it's all nerves. Rex says I don't understand Ahmed... Oh, Martin!'

She broke off. Martin's lips tightened. His very blue eyes looked beyond Phillida's fair head into space. He thought that if ever he had wanted badly to thrash Rex Maltern it was now. In all their talks, Phillida had never so much as hinted that Rex had kept her short of cash. That was to be added to the count against him. As for exposing her to this sort of thing with a native servant ... it was monstrous. Martin said through his teeth:

'You've got to get out of here ... out of Egypt.'

'I can't,' she whispered. 'How can I?'

'Go home, Phillida. Go back to your grandmother.'

'I don't feel I ought to leave Rex.'

'Why ever not?'

'My place is here, with him, isn't it, Martin?'

He found that abominably hard to answer. With all his love for her surging up in him, it was almost too much. Suddenly he got up, set her gently on her feet, and stood for a moment with his hands under her arms, supporting her.

'Better not ask me that, Phillida. I'm not the one to ask,' he said, in a curt voice. Then he added, gently:

'I think you ought to go to bed. No, I won't leave you alone with Ahmed. I'll kick him out, and you can lock yourself in. Then I'll go and fetch Doreen Angus's sister. I'll ask her to come and sit with you until Rex comes home.'

No longer in the safe curve of his arms, she felt suddenly lost and unhappy again. With all her strength at lowest ebb, both her mental and physical courage failing her, she whispered:

'Don't go ... Martin; please don't go!'

His face flushed deeply under the bronze. He caught her close, and said:

331

'You mustn't ask me to stay. I love you, Phillida. You know it.'

The world seemed to spin around her. For a moment she was up in the stars, in realms of undreamed-of ecstasy.

'I love *you*, Martin,' she whispered. 'Oh, Martin, Martin, I love you, too!'

He let his lips rest on her hair for the fraction of a moment. It was hard to summon the control he needed. Now that he actually heard, from Phillida's own lips, that she loved him, he wanted to say: 'Then come away with me... I will adore you and take care of you for ever.' But he had always to remember that not only was she Maltern's wife, but the prospective mother of a child. It bit into his soul – like acid – that destroying thought. He held her close a moment longer, then he put her gently from him. Taking her arm, he led her to the sofa, sat down beside her and kept a protective arm about her quivering shoulders.

'Darling,' he said. (He was more moved than he had been since the day Bridget died.) 'Darling, this is a bad show. We love each other. I think we have known it for some time – don't you?'

She raised her large, sad eyes to his.

'Yes,' she whispered. 'I think so, Martin.'

'It's the devil, Phillida. We couldn't be in a worse position. But I want you to know that if you hadn't been having this poor, unfortunate infant I would have asked you to leave Rex and come away with me. I wouldn't have minded about the scandal – or grieving people like my aunt and your grandmother. I would have thought only about you. I'm going to be frank now about Rex. You two are through – aren't you? I mean – you're struggling very bravely because of the child. But he – even if he's struggling – is fighting a losing battle. You don't want to live with him any more.'

'No, I don't want to live with him any more!' She repeated the words passionately. With one slender hand she hung on to Martin's hand, as though her life depended on it. 'But I've got to. I've *got to!*'

He set his teeth, his gaze looked beyond the bowed fair head into space... His mind was in a daze. He, usually so clear-sighted, so composed, could not think straight.

He said:

'I don't quite know how I'm going to sit by and watch you suffer like this.'

'I'll be all right,' she said, in a muffled voice. 'I'll … perhaps I'll go home. Rex himself suggested it this morning.'

'Suggested sending you back to England?'

'Yes. He said he couldn't afford it, but that he thought it might be best for me to go and let my grandmother see me through these next few months.'

Martin looked down at the hand he was

holding, then raised it to his lips.

'Phillida, I'd like you to go. Personally, I shall hate saying good-bye to you, but I shall be glad for every other reason. The sooner you are home, and away from this soul-destroying life you're leading now in Ismailia – the better.'

'I don't want to stay,' she said, in a choked voce. 'I can't bear Rex any more. Oh, Martin, I can't *bear* him. It may be disloyal … and he is the father of my child … but he's killed every ounce of love I ever felt for him. I have tried, Martin. I *have!*'

His arm tightened about her shoulders.

'Sweetheart, I know you have.'

The tears gushed into her eyes, blinding her.

'I'd like to get back to Gamma and Alver-combe and have my baby there. I'll beg Rex to find the money and send me home.'

'He'll damn' well have to find the money,' said Martin grimly.

She added miserably:

'Yet I wonder if I ought to … if he'll drink too much … when I'm gone … get mixed up with all these girls … there are so many problems, Martin.'

He thought it wonderful of her that she should still consider the blackguard who was responsible for all her misery. He said:

'I don't think you need worry too much about Maltern. He can take care of himself, and if he can't – it's just too bad. You've got to think of yourself now, Phillida.'

She was silent a moment, leaning against his shoulder, the tears still rolling down her cheeks. She felt comforted like this ... secure in the strong clasp of Martin's arm. She would have given half her life to know that she belonged to him; to have waited for this hour ... never to have known or loved Rex. Suddenly she voiced the thought, in a low, impassioned voice: 'Why didn't I wait for you?... Oh, Martin, Martin ... why didn't I wait?'

'No use thinking those things, my poor darling. I wish them, too. But, strange to relate, had you never married Rex you'd probably never have met me.'

'That's true...' Her voice came in a broken sob. 'And I thank God I met you ... I do thank God. You've been so marvellous to me. Even if we never meet again, I'll remember you – all my life.'

He sat silent a moment. Those words gave him a curious shock. He could not easily accept the thought that after she left Ismailia he might never see her again. After a pause, he said:

'One day, darling ... who knows ... we'll meet again... We will keep in touch.'

She nodded. He could see that she was unable to speak. She just sat there weeping. He felt hopeless, impotent to help her. He put both arms about her once more and kissed her hair, then, very, very tenderly, without passion, kissed the tragic young face.

'Be brave, Phillida, my darling. Don't let life defeat you.'

'You said that to me once before, Martin.'

'I'll always say it.'

'I'm not as brave as you are, Martin.'

'You've far more to put up with, my darling. I'm horrified at the mere prospect of all you've got to face. But I shall feel better about you once you're out of this country and with your grandmother.'

'I'll go,' she said, in a choked voice, and pulled a handkerchief from the pocket of her dress and wiped her face; like an unhappy child, he thought. 'Whatever it costs, I'll go ... even if I have to borrow the fare from Gamma. I can't stay with Rex now ... now that I know what *you* mean to me.'

'Perhaps I oughtn't to have told you. I'd hate to feel I'd made things worse for you, Phillida.'

She raised her head and smiled, and it seemed to him like a sudden radiance across the desolate young face.

'I'm so glad you told me. I love you very much, Martin, and shall be comforted by the thought that *you* love *me*.'

He flushed and for a moment held her very close indeed.

'My darling, darling child ... and I am so proud to know you love me too.'

For a moment they were quiet, his lips against her hair, their hands clinging. Then Martin sighed and drew away.

'I ought to go, my darling. I'm due back in Fayid for dinner tonight.'

'Yes,' she nodded.

'Will you be all right now? Do you still feel frightened?'

'No,' she said. 'Somehow I don't think I shall ever feel frightened again. You've given me so much strength. You're so wonderful ... the thought that you love me ... that strengthens me, Martin. And, oh, Martin, if I have a son ... I pray he will be like you and not Rex. I shall *pray* for it.'

Martin – deeply moved – stood up, and pulling his pipe from his pocket stuck it between his teeth. He felt a savage resentment against fate tonight ... the fate that had led him across this girl's pathway so much too late. At length he spoke.

'Thank you for what you say, darling. Now I'm going to look up the Anguses and ask Peggy to come along and stay with you till Rex gets back. I don't want you to be left alone.'

She was about to answer when she heard footsteps on the verandah. Walking to the window, she looked out and saw the big handsome figure of Sophie Martial, who

337

was carrying the inevitable shopping-basket and a bunch of multi-coloured zinnias in her hand. Phillida, relieved, turned back to Martin.

'Madame Martial has come to see me. She will stay with me. Don't worry any more, Martin.'

Quickly he caught her hand and kissed it.

'Good night, then, and God bless you, darling.'

She looked up at him anxiously.

'You will come again?... Oh, Martin, you won't let the fact that we love each other stop you from being my friend?'

'Nothing on earth will ever stop that, my dear.'

She gave a long sigh.

'Thank goodness.'

He added wryly:

'But get Rex to send you home – as soon as possible.'

She felt a lump in her throat again. Turning from him she walked to the front door. Ahmed had apparently left the house, so Phillida opened the door.

Martin, just behind her, greeted the Frenchwoman, then walked rapidly to his car. Somehow or other Phillida managed to drag her gaze from the sight of the tall figure ... and greet Sophie.

'*Comment ça va, Madame?*'

Sophie's warm brown eyes searched the

young face, which was so haggard, so tear-stained, and immediately her arms opened and her broad bosom received the slender figure.

'*Mais comment* ... what ees it? You are eel ... you are unhappy, *ma pauvre!*' she said, in a shocked voice.

Then Phillida broke down again. Sophie dropped the flowers and half carried, half dragged the young English girl back into the house.

'*Mon dieu* ... but what ees it, *ma chérie?*'

Phillida, lying on the sofa, put her face in the cushions and wept again, holding on to Madame's kind hand. But when she was able to speak it was not of Martin ... but of Ahmed and her fear of him. For what had passed between Martin and herself was their own lovely secret, never to be divulged to the rest of the world.

Sophie Martial listened and learned quite a lot. Then with crimson cheeks and set lips she nodded her head. *She* would deal with the *suffragi,* she said ... she who could speak fluent Arabic. She would soon put *him* in his place. She had never liked Ahmed, and neither had Monsieur. They had always wondered why the *Capitain,* retained his services. And she would tell *Monsieur le Capitaine,* when he came home, what she thought of Ahmed. She would not leave the side of *la pauvre* Phillida until he returned.

5

Rex was very late that evening.

He had had what he thought a 'trying time' with Copper. He had managed to snatch an hour or so with the beautiful young girl who was for the moment the centre of attraction for him. But almost as soon as they were out on the desert road driving in the little M.G. she broke to him the unwelcome news that Major Deacon had most unexpectedly been posted to Palestine, and was leaving Egypt at once. He was in the Police branch and had been allotted a special job in Jerusalem. Copper and her mother were to be sent home.

Copper, now madly in love with the handsome and plausible Rex, alarmed him by suggesting that he should leave Phillida and join her in England as soon as possible.

'But my dear sweet baby,' he protested, 'you seem oblivious of the fact that *(a)* I'm a Regular, and Regulars can't resign their commissions at a moment's notice ... and *(b)* I've no money beyond my pay except a meagre hundred or two ... so that I must stick to my job, and *(c)* my wife is having a child. How the devil d'you suppose I can quit? Of course I'm crazy about you, angel. You know that. But there are far too many obstacles in front of us.'

Copper accepted this speech sullenly and he went on to add that she must try to get her mother to stay on in Ismailia ... so that she could take a job with the Army ... a personnel assistant's job, for instance ... they could then continue to see each other.

Copper then reminded him that first of all she could not type, and secondly she would not be allowed to stay on, anyhow, because her parents both disliked her acquaintanceship with *him* and 'fussed' every time she went out with him.

'Then it looks as though we'll have to say good-bye,' was Rex's regretful comment. And he was genuinely sorry, because for the moment he was very enamoured of Copper's fresh, flaming beauty.

There followed a bad hour. The M.G. stopped by the roadside. Copper raged and wept and finally accused him of having played fast and loose with her. Rex tried to kiss her into a state of passivity and was rejected. He, too, then lost his temper and called her a 'spoiled little brat'.

Copper, her green eyes blazing, demanding to be taken home instantly ... but not before she had in a rage made a number of scandalous comments. She was in one of her tempers, which flared up quickly and as quickly died down. But during them Copper lost complete control.

Rex wanted to get rid of her, she said … he was tired of her … he had sworn, originally, that he was bored with his wife, but now he was using the child as an excuse to get rid of her, Copper. He was a fool if he thought Phillida was such a saint. Everyone was talking about her and Martin Winters. Everyone knew the big Naval Commander was in love with Phillida. *And how,* she ended on a high note of fury, *did Rex know that this child was his?* Perhaps it was Martin's … perhaps Rex had been made a fool of, and the sooner he found out, the better…

But here Copper's rage subsided. For as she screamed the vile words she saw a look in Rex's almond-shaped eyes that frightened her. She realised that she had gone too far. She collapsed and burst into tears.

Rex did not attempt to console her. He had been temporarily shocked into silence by the significance of what Copper had said. Of course he knew that the stupid child had lost her temper and didn't know what she was saying … that she was just frustrated and disappointed because she was being forced back to England and (pleasant thought) was so much in love with him. He knew quite definitely that Phillida was not guilty of infidelity to him … and that this coming child was his. To think anything else was preposterous. Apart from the fact that Phil was the straightest, the most loyal, of women ... he knew that it was *his* child ... that she had never had what he called 'palaver' with Winters. He gave her her due ... handed it to the chap, too... Winters was far too much of a prig ... far too high-minded to make love to the wife of another man. Oh, no ... he didn't suspect either of them of that. Copper was just raving. But what *did* strike him as being the truth was her assertion that people were 'talking' about Phil and Martin. That made him sit up. What *he* liked to do was his affair. A chap's reputation was not so important. But he wasn't going to have his wife discussed. By God, he wasn't going to let her name be linked with Winters'.

It gave him a certain ugly satisfaction to have heard what Copper said. He would now have the right to accuse Phil of getting herself talked about, and forbid the fellow the house. He had always loathed him ... mainly because he knew Winters disliked *him*. Up to now he had half hoped that Phil might hit it off with the chap and leave him. Now he knew that because of the kid she wouldn't. But he wasn't going to let her have it all her own way. He would tell her what he had heard (he wouldn't say that it was Copper who had made the remark, naturally), and he would forbid her to see any more of Winters. He, Rex, had had enough of Martin's unspoken but obvious disapproval.

Copper began to whine; to apologise.

'I don't suppose it's true. I was a little beast to say it. I'm sure Phillida's faithful to you. Rex, don't be angry with me. Rex...'

He gave her a cold smile.

'I'm not angry, my dear Copper.'

'Oh, you are!' she wailed.

'It doesn't really much matter how I feel. You are going back to England and I can't follow, and that's that, my sweet,' he said in an acid tone.

She flung herself into his arms.

'Rex, I'm so much in love with you. I can't bear Mummy to take me away. Rex ... don't you want me any more?'

He did want her. That lovely pliant young body against his was still a temptation. But he was too cunning to allow his desires to make things awkward for himself ... and he was not going to become further involved with the little Deacon girl now that she was about to leave Egypt. It wasn't good enough. Especially as she had produced this scene. It warned him to go warily. She was much less sophisticated than Becki ... and if he were not very careful she'd tell her parents the truth and he'd find himself being called to task by Major Deacon ... and Deacon knew his Brigadier...

He put an arm around Copper and

soothed her with a few well-chosen words. She clung ... and they now embraced and exchanged several passionate kisses. Then he drove her back to Ismailia. He would see her again, he said. Of course he would. And of course he loved her. But they must just be sensible and accept the fact that they must say good-bye.

By the time they were back in Ismailia, Copper, with the resilience of youth, was smiling and happy again. Her emotions did not go very deep. Rex took her to the United Services Club for a drink. He himself had many. And when he actually made a 'date' with her for tomorrow Copper was her old gay, sparkling self. Before parting, she raised red, pouting lips for his farewell kiss.

'Oh, I wish we could have had longer together!' she sighed. 'We have such fun, don't we, Rex?'

He agreed. She was an attractive *bint* (he used the Arabic word for woman). He was glad she meant to be sensible and felt that he had got out of an awkward situation very well.

But as he put the key in the lock of his front door his own gaiety and good humour evaporated. He scowled at his thoughts. Blast it all ... if Copper was going home it would be damned awful ... he'd be tied to Phil's apron-strings again. And thinking of Phil, he remembered Copper's allegations and there began to rise and ferment within him a cold rage against Martin Winters ... a cold cruel wish to put an end to that friendship.

'I'll soon settle *them*,' he told himself darkly. And in that state of mind, inflamed by the whiskies he had tossed down at the Club, he went in search of Phillida.

He found her in bed.

Sophie Martial was sitting beside her. Little Pierrot had come down on his bicycle to join his mother and see what his beloved Madame Maltern was doing, and to show her his latest 'craze' – an American football of which he was extremely proud. He, too, was there by the bedside.

When Rex walked into the room everybody was laughing, including Phillida. The atmosphere was a happy one with her genial French friends and she had felt much more herself, more relaxed; some of the awful depression and anxiety which lately had been weighing her down had lifted. Perhaps it was because she had cried out all her sorrows in the kindly arms of the understanding Sophie. Sophie had put her to bed, bathed the hot, flushed forehead with cool *eau de Cologne,* made her one of her own special omelettes and brought her a cup of real French coffee. Then she sat beside her encouraging her to eat and drink.

Certainly Phillida felt better for these

attentions. But it was the secret thought of Martin and all that he had said to her that had raised her spirits to new heights and brought her such exquisite release from sorrow. True, they had had to part – both of them knew that their love was without hope. But it was marvellous to her just to *know* that he loved her. She almost longed to be alone so that she could close her eyes and relive the moments that she had spent with him, his arm about her, his lips on her hair.

Martin, Martin! She kept saying his name to herself with sweet yet bitter delight. *Martin, I love you. I shall always love you. The thought of you and the knowledge that you love me, too, will give me the courage to carry on...*

But as Rex walked into the room, opening the door sharply, noisily, silence fell amongst the three of them there. Pierrot stood up, his sharp dark eyes narrowing. He did not like *Monsieur le Capitaine*. He had learned to dislike him. Late one afternoon, whilst still living in the villa, Rex had returned home, inflamed by drink, and collided with the small boy, who was bicycling round the garden in his careless fashion. Pierrot apologised, but Rex had snarled at him, using a French oath that shocked the boy. From that moment onwards he had no respect for *le Capitaine*. The same applied to Sophie. At first she had been impressed by the good looks and easy charm of the

Englishman. But after a while she and Emile had both seen some of the weakness of character and the ugliness that lay at times under that façade. They had watched, sadly, the gradual decline of Phillida's spirits and happiness. They, like Pierrot, had no respect for Rex today.

Sophie gave one look at Rex's face and her lips tightened. She responded briefly to his greeting. He was quite affable to her. He never cared to miss an opportunity to 'show off' and he knew that he spoke excellent French. But Sophie, without being told anything by Phillida, had guessed much that was going on here. And now she was not to be deceived by Rex's 'charm'. *'Quelle egoist le type!'* she complained to Emile later.

She said coldly:

'Bon soir, Capitaine.'

Rex said, in French:

'You've been looking after my poor little wife, for which all my thanks, *chère* Madame Sophie.'

'She needs looking after,' said Sophie with feeling.

Rex glanced at Phillida. She returned the gaze, then her lashes flickered and a sudden flush stained her cheeks. He wondered why she looked like that. But he spoke to her quite pleasantly.

'Better tonight, my Poppet?'

'Yes, thank you. I've had a lovely supper.

348

Madame made me an omelette.'

Rex glanced round the room. It was neat and cool-looking, with its white bedspread, white-and-blue curtains and the flowers which Sophie had brought in a tall vase on the mantelpiece. The shutters were opened. The night breeze blew into the room, bringing a delicious freshness after the stifling heat of the long day.

'And where is Ahmed? Why did Madame fatigue herself?'

Phillida did not speak. Her heart began to hammer as always, with weakness and fear of calling Rex's wrath down upon her. But here Sophie intervened. In a few sharp words she told Rex what she thought of Ahmed. She knew these servants out here, she said. Ahmed was not a pure Sudanese – one of the good trustworthy kind. He was a mixture ... a bad type. He had given little Madame Phillida a fright ... behaved abominably ... and she was not in a state to be upset like that ... and so on, while Rex listened. He had lighted a cigarette and seated himself, legs straddled over a small chair, arms folded on the back. When Sophie finished, he thanked her charmingly for the interest she had taken in Phillida's welfare. He quite agreed that Ahmed had behaved atrociously. He would deal with him when he returned, he said.

Madame Martial glanced at *le Capitaine* doubtfully. He was so handsome, so boyish-looking. It was difficult, when one did not know him well, to believe how selfish and hard that young man could be at times, she thought. She looked back at Phillida and saw that the beautiful weak grey eyes no longer held a contented expression, but were anxious and clouded again. She sighed. Oh well, Emile would say don't interfere, much as she desired to be a good friend to the little Madame. She beckoned to Pierrot, kissed Phillida good-bye, and then took their departure.

6

Phillida heard the front door close. Alone for a moment, she gave herself up to the luxury of remembering Martin.

Dear, dear Martin. She could hold the memory of his love and his friendship close to her heart. She would try to be tranquil now, and do her best for the baby ... and pray that Rex would let her go in peace back to England.

Rex returned. He was humming under his breath. He seated himself on the edge of the bed. He had brought with him a gin and orange which he sipped.

'You don't want one, do you, Phil?'

'No, thanks.'

'Why are you in bed, Poppet? Sick again?'

She gave him an embarrassed look, her slim long fingers playing with the embroidered hem of the sheet.

'Y-yes. But it wasn't that. I nearly passed out. I ... had an awful scare with Ahmed.'

Rex raised his eyebrows. He was not hurrying to tell Phillida what lay in his mind ... to air those grievances fostered by the hysterical Copper. He was going warily ... biding his time. He said:

'Always something about Ahmed.'

'Well, Rex, you heard what Madame said.'

'Madame knows nothing about Ahmed and I'd be obliged if you wouldn't tell people outside all our private business. You're as bad as Doreen Angus, whining round the place.'

Phillida went red.

'I didn't tell her until she found out for herself how Ahmed behaved.'

'She couldn't have found out unless you said something.'

Phillida bit her lip.

'Oh, Rex, have you come home just to start bullying me?'

He, in his turn, reddened. He threw her a sulky look.

'Well, I object to Madame or anybody telling me what to do with my servants.'

'Rex, she was worried about me. Ahmed adopted a very threatening attitude and it really frightened me. I may be stupid, but I don't care for it when I have to be alone with him so much.'

'Why should he threaten you?'

'Because you haven't paid him, nor given me the money to pay him with,' she flashed indignantly.

He set his glass down on the table.

'I see. So it's all *my* fault.'

'Honestly, Rex, you don't hurry to pay the bills, do you, and I can't altogether blame Ahmed for wanting his wages. Only I'm not

fit to deal with him – or our debts – just
now.'

Rex's brows drew together. He knew that
he was in the wrong. He also had the uneasy
knowledge that he had considerably over-
spent his pay this month on drink (and
Copper) and showing off in the Mess. He
liked to treat other fellows and look 'big'.
But he was more worried over finances at
the moment than he cared to admit. He
would have to sit down shortly and write
one of his most attractive letters to Mamma,
he thought grimly.

Glancing at Phillida, he relented sufficiently to be sorry for her. She looked pretty
awful again tonight. He said:

'Sorry. I'll find the cash for Ahmed tomorrow. Now don't you nag me any more about
that Arab, for the lord's sake. I like him, and
he suits me, and I think you are just
ridiculous about him. All these fads and
fancies, really – it's time you got over them.'

She stayed silent. Her lower lip quivered.
She could not restrain herself from thinking
how completely different Rex was to
Martin. Martin, whose first reaction to her
story about Ahmed had been that she must
get rid of the man immediately ... for her
own sake.

*Martin, Martin, you are so kind, so under-
standing. Oh, Martin, how shall I learn to live
my life without you?*

353

She spoke to Rex again with difficulty.

'Well, I'd like you to know straight away, Rex, that I have made up my mind to go home.'

He turned sharply towards her.

'Go home?'

'Yes. You said this morning that you thought it would be best for me. I didn't altogether agree then. Now I do. I want you to let me go, Rex. I think it will be better for … both of us.'

An instant's silence. Then he said:

'And what has happened to put this idea into your head, might I enquire?'

She swallowed hard … her long silky lashes lowered.

'Many things, Rex. We … are just not getting on … are we? That … isn't good for me … or for our child. I want to be at peace these next few months. I think it would be wise for me to let my grandmother look after me … in Alvercombe.'

'So … after a few months out here … after all your letters, begging me to get you out … you want to quit?'

'Rex, don't put it that way, please.'

'Isn't it true? You're ratting.'

'It isn't … ratting,' she said awkwardly. 'It's just that I feel ill and am ill, and this heat doesn't suit me. I'm no use to you, Rex, anyhow … and you don't really want me. Why don't you admit it?'

'Why should I?'

She looked up at him, quickly, reproachfully.

'You don't play fair. You always want to blame me for things … never yourself and the way *you* behaved to me!…' She broke off and added: 'Oh, never mind. What's the use? We don't understand each other any more. I will always do my best for you. You know that, Rex. But until our child is born – I'd rather live with Gamma. That's all.'

Then the snake in Rex Maltern struck. He leaned towards her, speaking softly:

'And is the Lieutenant-Commander Martin Winters, Royal Navy, by any chance going back to England on leave at the same time?'

She lay back on her pillows, staring, wide-eyed, cheeks slowly crimsoning.

'*Rex!* What do you mean?'

'Just what I say, my pure and unblemished Phillida. I ask you a simple question. Please answer it. Is Winters going back to England?'

She licked her lips, confused, troubled, unconscious of the way his feelings were turning, fermenting within him. She said:

'Not that I know of. No.'

'When did you last see the gentleman?'

'Rex, what are you getting at…?' she began, her pulses jerking, the old sick fear of a 'scene' descending on her like a black cloud.

He interrupted, raising his voice:

'Answer my question, Phil. When did you last see Winters?'

'T-today,' she stammered. 'Th-this afternoon. He came while I was having that trouble with Ahmed. He ... saved me.'

Rex, delighted with the reply, laughed. An unpleasant laugh. Phillida was afraid of him now; afraid that he had been drinking again. He was so peculiar. He had never treated her in quite this way before ... as though trying to catch her out ... wanting to put a black mark against her. Oh, heavens, was this nightmare of a marriage to go on like this indefinitely? Little wonder she felt so ill and stupid and wanted to go home. Some women could stand nagging, bullying, perpetual rows. She couldn't. She just could *not.*

Rex said:

'So he was here alone with you again today, was he? And he saved you, did he? From what? From one of your darned silly notions that Ahmed was trying to harm you, I suppose. Very nice of the amiable Lieutenant-Commander. But I see through it. It's been cooked up because you want to get the better of me. You and Winters wish to dismiss Ahmed. My wishes don't count.'

Phillida began to tremble.

'Rex, really...'

'Well, let me tell you,' he broke in, 'that

Ahmed stays. And *you* stay … where you belong. Here in Ismailia with me.'

She put both hands to her cheeks. They were burning.

'But why? Why? You don't want me. You are quite happy as a bachelor. You've said so dozens of times … you've kept telling me you were better off – happier with all your girl-friends and parties before I came out and spoiled them…'

He avoided her gaze.

'That's as may be; I've changed my mind. I'm not letting you go off alone to England … I don't trust you any more.'

'Rex!'

'You can say what you like. I don't trust you,' he repeated. 'You may have something against me. But I've something worse against you. You, who are a prospective mother. It's disgusting!'

Phillida's mouth opened. Her large eyes looked at him bewildered, aghast.

'What do you mean?'

'I mean that everyone in Ismailia is coupling your name with Martin Winters and that I'm not standing for it,' he said in a savage voice.

Silence. Phillida's heart beat so fast that she could hardly breathe. She thought she was going to suffocate. She lay gasping, the beads of sweat rolling down her hollowed cheeks. Then she whispered:

357

'It can't be true. People *can't* be talking. There's nothing to talk about. They are just a filthy lot of scandalmongers.'

He admitted that. Then added grimly:

'But unfortunately when an officer's wife gets talked about it is apt to reach the ears of his commanding officer. I'm not going to have G.H.Q. thinking me one of these *maris complaisants* ... and hinting that I look the other way while you carry on a nice intrigue with Winters. No. I'll put paid to that, my dear Phil. Neither will I have you going home now and starting a lot of talk which will also put ideas into the heads of the powers that be. They'll say either that you're going home because we don't get on ... and blame *me* ... or think worse things about you... Either way it will do no good to *my* reputation. So you'll just stay quietly here with me, and we'll show Ismailia what a devoted couple we are. D'you see?'

He had risen and was standing looking down at her, hands in his pockets, his handsome face flushed and unpleasant. She looked up at him, still utterly bewildered. He added:

'What is more, Winters can stay out of this house. You won't ask him here again from now onward ... and when we meet at the Club, and so on, we will just bow and pass on. I'm dropping the Lieutenant-Commander. D'you understand? He's abused my hospitality – got my wife talked about and...'

'Rex, that isn't true!' she broke in now, hot, quivering with resentment. She could not and would not have Martin traduced... Martin, who never until this day had spoken one word of love nor abused in any way what Rex called his 'hospitality'. She added, in a choked voice:

'He is my friend ... he has never done anything wrong. Neither have I. People have no right to talk. And it will be grossly unjust of you to drop him ... to ask me to cut him ... because of some foul gossip. What about you and Copper? I've no doubt half Ismailia thinks you are *her* boy-friend ... and I *know* you are ... but I haven't asked you to drop Copper.'

Rex put his tongue in his cheek.

'Copper is going home ... almost at once.'

'I see... So that's it. You're losing your new girl-friend just as you lost Rebecca Rendledon and you're taking it out on me!'

He glared at her. 'Don't try to switch the issue. We're talking about you and Winters.'

She tried desperately to keep calm, to argue quietly ... not to let hysteria defeat her again in face of this new disaster... She was petrified that Rex would carry out his threat and cut Martin ... insult him ... he who had even on this very day felt guilty for admitting that he loved her ... and had left her ... knowing that she meant to do her utmost as Rex Maltern's wife. There was never a more decent and honourable man alive than Martin, she thought.

She began to speak in his defence.

'I'm not sure it isn't all a horrible fabrication on your part. Everybody here who knows us is my friend... Martin's friend ... they couldn't accuse me of having an affair with him ... when I'm so ill ... carrying your child.'

Rex smiled ... a slow, ugly smile.

'Ah, my dear Phil, but you might have started an affair with Martin earlier on ... mightn't you ... and you see, *somebody* ... somebody whose opinion I value, actually ... intimated *that the child might be Winters' and not mine.*'

That brought a gasping cry from Phillida. She stared wildly up at Rex for a moment, as though she could not believe her own hearing. The insult left her stricken. Then she said under her breath:

'I'll never forgive you for even saying such a vile thing ... or for allowing another person to think it. It's a gross lie ... an unpardonable insult ... both to Martin and me. I shall go back to Gamma now even if I have to borrow the fare, Rex. I won't stay with you now. Never ... after *that*...'

His gaze wavered and fell before the look in her large blazing eyes. He knew perfectly

360

well – had known when Copper had made the insinuation – that Phillida was incapable of such a thing ... and possibly Winters too. He muttered:

'Oh, I didn't say I believed it...'

'But you repeated it to me ... and allowed it to be said. And you are taking away my best friend ... a man who would have been *your* friend, too, if you wanted him...' said Phillida, panting. 'You're suggesting that I'm unfaithful to you, and it's the end. I'm through with you, Rex. I'm going home. I just won't live with you any more.'

He uttered a curse. He hated being put in the wrong. He knew that he had gone too far, said too much and so made a fool of himself. He shouted:

'Oh, shut up ... you'll do as I say and stay where you belong – with me. And if you're all that loyal and devoted you won't mind whether Martin Winters hangs round you any more or not.'

Phillida made no answer. He watched her get out of bed and reach blindly for her slippers. He shouted again:

'Where do you think you're going?'

'I'm getting out of this house,' she said in a suffocated voice. She was shaking violently ... sick at heart ... sick of body. Her mind was in a whirl. 'I'm going up to Madame Sophie ... she'll take me in... I won't stay with you... I'll never lay myself open to such

361

frightful insults again…'

He cut in, gripping her by both arms.

'Oh, forget it, Phil. I'm sorry. I know the child is mine. *Of course* I know it. Look here…'

'Let go of me!' she said, her voice rising, her face deathly pale.

'Phil … hang on a moment! Listen, you can't go rushing out of the house like this.'

'I can. I will. I won't stand it any more…'

'Listen…'

'No…' She tried to shake herself free. 'I've stood enough… Leave me alone, Rex. Leave me alone.'

He said furiously:

'I won't. I won't have people saying that I've driven you out…'

She sobbed at him now, half mad with hysteria:

'Then you shouldn't have treated me like this. It's too late. I don't care what people say … about you … about me … or anyone… Oh, *let me go*…'

She dragged her arms violently from him, then slipped on the polished floor and staggered. She felt a sickening pain wrench her … a hideous nausea … a kind of veil blotting out Rex's angry face. She fell down, moaning:

'Oh, I'm going to be ill … *I'm going to be ill*…'

He leaned over her, scared now, penitent.

'Phil ... oh, God, I'm sorry, Phil ... Phil, are you all right?'

She looked up at him, an expression in her eyes that haunted him for a long time afterwards.

Get a doctor, Rex,' she whispered. 'Quickly, please...'

He turned and fled from the house.

Later an ambulance pulled up in front of the little bungalow, which was bathed in the brilliant Egyptian moonlight. Gentle hands lifted a stretcher into place ... a nurse sat beside it holding the hot feverish fingers of a young girl, clinging to her hand in the extremity of pain.

Later that night a much-chastened Rex was summoned to the Garrison Hospital by the woman doctor there, and told that she had news for him. Mrs Maltern was very ill and there was no longer going to be a child.

7

The news spread round Ismailia like wildfire.

Long before twenty-four hours had elapsed everybody knew ... there was much talking and whispering on the French Beach, in Antoinette's, over morning coffee, and from one Army quarter and one office to another in Moascar and Fayid.

Little Mrs Maltern had had 'bad luck' and was in the Garrison Hospital. They said that she was pretty bad. *Rotten* luck after she'd gone through all those months of misery; now nothing to look forward to. But of course nobody had thought she would see it through because she had looked so ill. Captain Maltern seemed distracted – not about the child, but his wife. Of course there had been some unattractive gossip about him and certain females in the district, but he was all right at heart, and so charming and good to look at. And obviously devoted to his wife.

Jimmy Angus had seen him and told the others that he looked ghastly ... it only showed what scandalous things were said by people. *Of course* he was in love with his own wife.

Such was the trend of gossip in that little green flower-filled town on the banks of the Sweet Water Canal.

Possibly only one or two people knew a little of what had been going on behind the scenes. People like the kindly Sophie ... and Doreen Angus, who, although they had never heard a word of complaint from Phillida's lips, had at times seen for themselves the manner in which Rex Maltern had been behaving, and the effect it had upon his wife.

But none of them really knew what had transpired ... not even Martin Winters; but he knew more than most.

The rumour about Mrs Maltern having been 'taken ill' and rushed to the Garrison Hospital reached Martin when he was in his office at G.H.Q. He heard it without astonishment but with a quick sensation of alarm, of concern for her.

He had had a bad night anyhow ... lying awake hot and restless in his tent until the early hours when he had got up and driven down to the Lido to swim before breakfast. All night he had thought about Phillida ... her wretchedness, her pathetic loyalty to the cad she had married... All night he had remembered the sweetness of her in his arms, her heartbroken weeping ... and, later, that shining light in her eyes ... the sudden radiance on the haggard young face when he had said, *'I love you, Phillida.'*

He wondered grimly what had happened after Maltern came home.

Without further hesitation he rang up the exchange and told the operator to put him through to Captain Maltern's office.

Rex was not there. Harold Gayter, who worked with him, informed the Lieut.-Commander that Rex was not coming in today because his wife had been taken ill.

'So I hear,' said Martin. 'I wonder how she is.'

Gayter answered:

'Don't know any details, old boy, but they say she is bad. Poor old Rex sounded pretty het up.'

'Thanks,' said Martin, and put down the receiver.

For a moment he stared out of the window through a shimmer of hot sunshine at the row of offices in the desert beyond. He felt his heart beating with slow painful thuds. He thought:

'Poor old Rex, indeed! Hell to that! He ought to be het up. He's done this to her, damn him, *damn* him!'

He picked up the receiver again, his hand shaking, his face drawn.

This time he called the Garrison Hospital. The number was engaged. It was half an hour before he got through, time enough for him to let his imagination run riot. Phillida was in such a weak state of health ... and this was a bad country to be ill in... What if this finished her? What if she was going the same way as Bridget had gone? *God in heaven, what a thought!*

It seemed to him that history was repeating itself ... it was as though the years rolled back and once again he was sitting beside a telephone waiting for news of *Bridget.* His agony of mind, his despair, when they told him that she was dead. This time he hadn't even the right to offer more than conventional platonic sympathy. Nor could he tell another living soul what he felt about Phillida Maltern.

He became conscious of a mental isolation, a pain which was almost intolerable. He put his head between his hands and waited for the telephone to ring, thankful that at least he was alone in the office this morning. The fellow who worked with him had gone to a conference.

When the bell finally rang, Martin lifted a ravaged face and answered ... knowing that he was afraid ... mortally afraid.

It took him several moments to extract any kind of information about Mrs Maltern. Finally he was told that she was 'going along as well as could be expected'.

The orthodox answer brought no comfort to Martin. He said:

'Is she ... going to be all right?'

'Who is that speaking?'

'Oh, does it matter?' Martin snapped, his nerves fraying.

An injured voice replied:

'We like to know who is calling. Are you a relative?'

Martin pulled a handkerchief from his pocket and wiped his neck. He could feel the sweat pouring down his face.

'No, I'm a friend. I just want to enquire how Mrs Maltern really is. I ... all her friends are naturally anxious.'

With maddening repetition came the former reply:

'Well, she's going on as well as can be expected.'

Martin nearly yelled, 'And how well is that?' but controlled himself.

The nurse answering the 'phone then added:

'She has a rather high temperature, but she's in excellent hands, and there's no need to worry.'

'I'm more than relieved to hear that,' said Martin, his eyes closing.

'Captain Maltern is here if you would like to speak to him... Can I give him your name?'

But that was too much for Martin. He muttered, 'No, thanks,' and put down the telephone. Once again he wiped his face and neck. Once again his imagination played fast and loose with him. This was hell, he thought. There was nothing he wanted more to do than to take his car and drive straight to the hospital, to see Phillida and make sure for himself that she was all right and that everything was being done for her. Maltern was there. Of course, he was her husband, damn him, *damn him!*

It was one of the worst mornings of Martin's life. It was one of the worst days. A long working day at G.H.Q. And when he couldn't abstract his mind from the thought of Phillida and get down to his job and had those three intolerable hours from two till five to get through before returning to the office, he wondered what in heaven's name he could do in order to keep sane. He could not face a lot of chatter and laughter down at the Fayid Officers' Club. Neither could he rest in the heat of his tent. So he went back to the deserted office and sat there and found himself writing feverishly to the beloved aunt at Killoun.

I suppose I oughtn't to love her like this because she's married to Maltern, but I do, Aunt Kate ... and to know she is so ill and that I can't go to her, or do anything about it ... is hitting me hard. If you'd seen her last night as I saw her, poor little thing...

He wrote no more. He tore the pages into pieces and flung them into the wastepaper-basket. It was no good writing letters of that sort. They did no good to anybody.

When at last the long, hot, intolerable day ended, Martin took the Morris and drove a good deal faster than usual into Moascar.

He went straight to the Pentyres' quarter.

Mabyn Pentyre was sitting on the veran-dah having a coffee, waiting for her husband to join her.

She greeted the tall, fair young man with the special warmth which she reserved for those to whom she was especially attached … and Martin Winters was one of her favourites.

'How *nice* to see you … come and hold my hand and have a drink, Martin,' she said. 'Freddy will be with us in a minute. He's just writing a letter about Income Tax Returns, and I don't want to disturb him because it's taken me weeks to get him down to it.'

Then as Martin drew nearer, and she saw his drawn, unsmiling face, her own smile faded. She added:

'Something's the matter. What is it?'

He said: 'It's no good trying to keep things from you, Mrs Pen … you always know.'

He sat down in a basket-chair and pulled out the much-needed pipe. Yes, Mrs Pen knew… In a quiet voice she said:

'There's nothing to worry about, Martin. Actually I was in the hospital this afternoon, and I saw both the M.O. in charge of Phillida and that horrid Rex Maltern himself.'

Up shot Martin's head. His face flushed.

'How is she, Mrs Pen?'

'She's going to be all right. They've had a bit of trouble. But it's over now. It's just her temperature … but they said that was down this evening. I rang up at six o'clock. Poor little soul, I think she was in a bad way when they got her there.'

For a moment Martin could not speak. He fumbled with tobacco and matches and got his pipe going. Then he said:

'I'm glad she's all right.'

'It can be a tricky business,' admitted Mrs Pentyre, picking up her coffee-cup, 'but she's being well looked after … in a private room with a special night nurse. You know I can't *bear* Rex Maltern, but I must say he's running round the place like a lunatic doing things for her, and seems genuinely upset. I suppose he's one of those men who like to keep a harem but still cares a bit for No. 1 wife.'

Martin's lips twisted. For a moment he had lost his sense of humour and even Mrs Pen's satire could not drag a smile from him. But he was conscious of an enormous overwhelming relief. He had half feared to come here tonight and be told that Phillida

371

was dead.

Mrs Pentyre continued in her cheerful fashion.

'Once the child gets over the shock she'll pick up quickly. And she's young yet. As I said to Maltern, there's plenty of time, and lots of girls go through it...'

That brought an involuntary exclamation from Martin.

'God forbid that she should ever go through it again!'

Mabyn Pentyre gave him a sympathetic look.

'I think I know how you feel, Martin. And we all love her. She's a darling little person ... *perfectly* sweet. And *much* too good for him. But...'

'Mrs Pen, she's had a lousy time lately!' Martin broke in.

'I know. I've seen a bit of what's been going on.'

'The fellow's a damn' bully,' Martin muttered.

'Well, quite frankly, I told him when I saw him this afternoon that I thought the best thing he could do was to send her home as soon as she is better.'

'I'm glad you said that, Mrs Pen.'

She was silent a moment. She, who usually knew what to say, felt awkward in the face of the young man's difficult emotion. She had remarked only the other night to

Freddy that it was bad luck poor old Martin getting so fond of Phillida Maltern; not that one blamed him, but it was so hopeless, and he'd already had one tragedy.

'Oh, well,' she said at length, 'in a day or two you'll be able to run in and cheer her up. I'll let you know when she's able to have visitors, then you come here and I'll pilot you along.'

Martin took the pipe from his mouth, and now the faintest smile – the first today – relaxed his mouth.

'You were always a most understanding woman, Mrs Pen, and thanks a lot,' he said gratefully.

The Brigadier appeared on the verandah, pen in one hand, sheaf of papers in the other, face hot and creased.

'Look here, Mabyn... Oh, good evening, Martin, my boy ... just the chap I want. You're good at figures, aren't you? Come and work this out with me. It's an infernal disgrace this lumping a fellow's income in with his wife's. I reckon that if I divorced Mabyn and lived with her in sin I'd be five hundred a year better off.'

'You immoral, mercenary old man,' said Mabyn, grimacing at him.

The three of them began to talk. A bottle of cognac was produced. As Martin sat with his friends, sipping the brandy, looking out at the velvet, star-studded sky, he thought of the girl who was lying in the hospital just a few hundred yards away … and with all his soul prayed that she was not suffering too badly, and that when she recovered Maltern would indeed send her home.

And now that he knew that she was not going to die, and he could relax after the bitter strain of the day, he felt deep down within him a sudden secret satisfaction that Phillida was not, after all, going to bear Maltern's child. He knew that *she* would be glad. That counted most with Martin.

And while he sat there in the cool of the evening, smoking and thinking, talking to his friends, Phillida lay in the narrow hospital bed, half awake, half in a stupor, still under the influence of the drugs that had been given her to ease her pain. She lay there and listened dully to a never-ceasing flow of words from Rex.

He sat holding her hand. Limp, powerless to resist, her long, fine fingers lay in his. The shaded lamp burned by the bed. The windows, covered by fine wire net, were wide open to let in the night air.

A few moments ago a nurse had removed a gorgeous array of flowers. Everybody knowing the Malterns seemed to have sent flowers this afternoon – as soon as the news of Phillida's illness spread. There was one huge silver basket of roses and carnations, which Egyptian florists arrange with such skill and artistry. That had come with a box of fruit and a note from Captain Maltern himself. The sister in charge read it to Phillida during one of her periods of consciousness.

'Get well quickly for my sake. I love you so much. The child does not matter. Only you, my darling. Your anxious Rex.'

The nurse said:

'What beautiful words! You lucky girl, to have a handsome husband so much in love with you... Now you'll have to buck up to please him, won't you, my dear?'

Phillida made no reply. Perhaps the woman wondered why the beautiful lips, dry, hot with fever, twisted into such a bitter smile. Perhaps she thought it was just that Mrs Maltern was still heavily doped and did not really understand what was being said to her.

Later, other messages had been read aloud to her.

From one:

'All my sympathy, you poor dear...'

To which the sister added:

'But don't worry. You're very young. You'll have another baby, Mrs Maltern...'

And then Phillida's heavy eyelids unclosed. She said nothing. But she stared blindly at the woman and thought:

'Never, never, *never!*'

Never, now, a child of his ... a child who might be born with the cruel, ruthless, weak character of Rex Maltern.

Once she had come out of the clouds of undreamed-of pain following her miscarriage, and when she had learned what had happened last night she had rejoiced ... she could not regret the baby. She did not want to bring a child of Rex's into the world.

But all day he had been in and out of her room, showering her with attentions and imploring her forgiveness. She hardly spoke ... only an odd whispered syllable... She listened and wondered how much was true of what he said ... and how much arose from his usual love of theatrical display. Obviously he had 'put things over' in a big way with the nursing staff. They were most impressed by her 'handsome, devoted husband'.

'If you had only seen him when the ambulance brought you here,' the night nurse had told her early this morning. 'He was like a lunatic, poor fellow! He kept begging the doctor not to let you die.'

Phillida, in extreme bitterness, in agony of body and mind, wondered what the good nurses at the hospital would have said could they have heard Rex *before* the ambulance took her away. But she kept silent. Neither had she any explanation when the doctor asked her why she had allowed herself to get into such a poor state of nerves.

All she wanted now was to be left alone.

But Rex insisted on remaining with her.

'Don't send me away. I can't go back to that damned bungalow alone. It would drive me mad. I'm half mad already with remorse, Phil darling. I'd give my soul to undo all that I've said and done. When I saw you fall and ask for the doctor, I realised ... it all came over me. Phil, I've been crazy ... out of my mind. Now I'm sane again. I realise what you mean to me. Phil, you must forgive me, or I'll shoot myself ... I swear I will.'

One extravagant, exaggerated statement after another ... he covered her hand with kisses ... wiped his eyes. (He had wept earlier today. She had actually seen the tears in those handsome, almond-shaped eyes.) He had knelt at the bed and sobbed, his shoulders heaving.

'Poppet, Poppet, I feel such a swine! Oh, darling, do try to forgive me. It's the drink ... I've been having far too much. Drinking myself into a state ... and I haven't known what I've been doing or saying. Poppet, do try to believe that and forgive me...'

To each one of his impassioned pleas for her forgiveness she said nothing. She had nothing to say. For she felt at the moment that she could never forgive that deadly insult to Martin and herself, apart from all the days and weeks subsequent to her collapse, when he had neglected her for girls like Copper Deacon, and bullied her into a state bordering on lunacy.

Mercifully for her, the doctor and nurses forbade him to stay for more than a few minutes at a time. Most of that long hot day, while Martin, in Fayid, was tortured by doubts and fears for her, she slept, under the influence of narcotics.

Her temperature remained high. Some of the time she was delirious. Once or twice she cried out the name Martin. Pitifully she cried it. But nobody noticed. Those in charge of her mistakenly imagined that it was her attractive and devoted husband whom she wanted, so the crestfallen Rex was allowed into her room more often than he should have been.

Phillida's sudden breakdown had in fact scared Rex into a genuine state of anxiety and self-reproach. His remorse, such as it was, might be short-lived. Most of his emotions were superficial, without roots. But for the moment he was truly sorry for all that he had done. He reverted to his early affection for his young wife. He felt the most impassioned desire for her forgiveness and to regain her esteem.

He worked as hard to regain that esteem as he had done to lose it.

That night he himself actually broached the subject of Martin Winters. Clinging to Phillida's limp hand, he said:

'Poppet, I want to apologise with all my soul for what I said about you and Winters. I didn't actually *think* it. I repeated a scurrilous bit of gossip I had heard. But it came from a quarter that is of no account, I assure you, and I shall take steps to shut up the person concerned, once and for all. I ought never to have insulted you by repeating it. Poppet, I know you are the most decent person alive and that you have always been faithful to me. I swear it. I only ask you to forgive me. And I want you to know that Martin Winters is welcome in our house at any time ... at *any* time in the future. Are you listening to me, Poppet?'

She lifted her lashes. Her eyes were dark, circled with heavy shadows. Her face looked pinched, white as the pillow against which she was lying. Her hair was braided in two long fair plaits on either side of her head. She looked at the man to whom she was married with something approaching cold dislike. Yes, she actually disliked him.

He eyed her anxiously.

'You haven't spoken a word to me today,' he said huskily. 'Oh, Poppet, aren't you going to believe I'm sorry?'

Then she found the strength to whisper:

'It ... doesn't matter ... now.'

'Poppet, why?'

'It's … too late, Rex…'

He coloured and caught hold of her hand now with both of his. He held it forcibly against his lips.

'Poppet … for heaven's sake…' His voice quavered. 'Don't be hard. You were never hard, darling. I tell you it was the drink. I swear that when you come out of hospital I'll never touch another drop.'

Now her lips curved into a faint, ironic smile. As though his kisses on her hand disgusted her, she drew it away and hid it under the sheet. She did not speak. Her silence was so full of contempt that he flushed a brighter red and began to chew hard at his lower lip.

'So,' he said sullenly, 'you won't forgive me?'

'I want to be left alone. Please go away, Rex.'

'I can't until you've said you'll forgive me.'

'What's the use…?' She whispered the words.

'It means our whole life together, darling…' He began the plea for pardon all over again; even now, an egoist in his desire to regain her confidence and affection … mindless as to whether this sort of discussion was good or bad for her while she was still so ill.

She drew a long, bitter sigh. She knew him so well now. He was a cruel, selfish man …

a spoiled child, too ... but pitiful in his fashion ... in this frantic wish to be forgiven.

He added:

'I've said I believe in you absolutely. I've apologised about Martin. You can have him here any time... I'll 'phone him myself in the morning and tell him to come and see you, Poppet.'

Then she roused herself ... sat up on one elbow and looked at him wildly, her face flushed with heat and fever.

'Please don't speak to Martin. Please don't interfere with my friendship with him ... or anybody else. I've finished with you, Rex. I'm going back to England as soon as I can travel.'

He looked back at her, his heart sinking. He was not only anxious to get back into Phillida's good books, but scared now of what he had done. From his own personal point of view it was going to look bad if Phil 'took umbrage' and openly showed her dislike; if she went home, hinting at the reason for her collapse. It would be damned awful, he thought gloomily, if his pals in the Mess and others so much as guessed that it was *his* behaviour which had brought about this state of affairs. He began to whine:

'Don't leave me, darling. For God's sake don't. Give me another chance ... a chance to show you that I *can* be decent, and that I *do* still love you, Poppet. Oh, Poppet...'

His voice cracked again. Phillida fell back on her pillow. Heavens, she thought drearily, fighting against her stupor, her pain, if only he would go away and leave her quite alone! She could not believe half that he said and she had not a vestige of love left for him. Perhaps tomorrow she would think more kindly of him. But tonight ... she almost *hated him*.

She said:

'I want the nurse, Rex. Please go away...'

Scared, he rang the bell. When the night nurse appeared he bent and whispered to Phillida:

'I'll come tomorrow early, before I go to G.H.Q. Good night. Try not to be too hard on me, darling. Send me away with one kind word ... I implore you...'

Phillida made a great effort.

'I'll try ... to ... forgive you. Good night, Rex...'

With that he had to be content. He lingered out on the moonlit verandah that encircled the maternity wards of the hospital... Later he went back to speak to the sister in charge.

'My wife is going to be all right ... isn't she?'

The woman smiled up into the handsome brown eyes. 'My word,' she thought, 'Captain Maltern *is* a good-looker. Lucky girl, Mrs M.'

Aloud she said:

'Oh, she's perfectly all right now, except for this temperature. But doctor's seeing to that. We have special tablets. These days we can cope with her condition. You'll find her much better tomorrow. It's her mental state that isn't helping. She seems to be a bundle of nerves.'

Rex's gaze wavered.

'It's this b——y country ... pardon me, sister, but it just hasn't suited my poor little wife. She's as you say – a bundle of nerves.'

'A lot of women can't stand up to Egypt in the summer. It just depends on the make-up. Your wife is very highly strung, I should think.'

'That's it,' said Rex eagerly.

'Oh, well, you take her away to Cyprus or some nice place like that when she's better,' counselled the sister, and gave the handsome, worried young Captain another soothing smile.

Rex went out into the night. He badly wanted a drink. He drove the M.G. to the 'King George' and had two or three drinks there. He met two pals of his from G.H.Q. and drank with them. They listened to his story of his wife's 'breakdown', were duly sympathetic and offered him another drink. Feeling fortified and more pleased with himself, confident that he would 'manage' Phil tomorrow ... yes, he'd win her round again, the poor sweet (and he'd behave himself this time), he drove to the Anguses' flat. He was received eagerly by Doreen, Jimmy and Peggy, all most anxious to hear first-hand news of Phillida. They thought Rex had never been nicer, and seemed so dreadfully upset about his wife and the child they had lost. He had more drinks with them. After he left, Doreen said to her husband:

'I believe old Rex is really fond of Phil after all.'

'Oh, I'm sure he is,' said Jimmy. Then added: 'I feel sorry for the chap. I know what he must be feeling. If this happened to you, I'd be in an awful way, Dorrie.'

She had one of her rare moments of being really fond of him, and grateful for his faithful devotion. She ran into his outstretched arms.

'Oh, Jimmy … you're a dear … honestly you are. I'd rather have you for a husband than Rex, anyhow. I often think he's a bit of a trial and that he leads Phil a dance. I'd far rather have you, Jimmy.'

He held her close, his eyes shining, his heart beating fast with pleasure. In the next room Peggy was giving young Bill the last bottle. Bill was growing fast, putting on weight and beginning to look like a real lad … with his mother's fair curls and his father's stocky, strong limbs. Jimmy was often hen-pecked and he had not many illusions left... Doreen was a selfish little brat ... but he loved her dearly. And he loved his son. This moment was a precious one. He was one of the happiest men in Ismailia that night.

Rex, full of drink, and swerving mentally between his remorse and his resentment because Phil had refused to forgive him, drove the M.G. through the warm Egyptian night to the French Club. The open-air dancing was in full swing. Many people Rex knew were dining there. George was one of the first to approach and offer Captain Maltern his deep regrets and express the hope that Mrs Maltern would soon be seen back at the *Cercle*. One or two of the French residents whom they knew, and who had heard about Phillida, spoke kindly to Rex and sympathised. Steve Cubitt, who was one of a big party, in evening dress (she and Geoffrey were over from Fayid, celebrating the anniversary of their wedding), left her gay table and came up to Rex as soon as she saw him appear.

'You're just the person I want to see. Is it true about Phil?' she asked anxiously.

'Yes, I'm afraid so. Poor darling...' said Rex huskily.

Steve looked grave.

'I'm dreadfully sorry, Rex...'

'You can imagine what I feel,' he said.

385

She bit her lip. She did not particularly mind what Rex felt. She had never liked him, and lately when she had seen Phil she had *known* instinctively, without being told, that things were going badly for the Malterns ... that Phil was not finding the happiness which she hoped for and had spoken of when they first met on the boat coming out to Egypt.

Steve said:

'I'll go and see her as soon as I'm allowed.'

'Do – most kind of you,' said Rex warmly. 'Phil is so fond of you.'

Steve glanced towards her party.

'If you care to join us, Rex...' she said politely. To her relief he declined.

'Not dressed ... no collar or tie ... as you see. Another time. Night-night, Steve. My regards to Geoffrey.'

He walked away from the dance floor in the direction of the bar, which was on the other side of the courtyard. To the left, a flamboyant tree made a brilliant splash of scarlet in the floodlights. The whole scene was gay and colourful. But Rex felt depressed. He wanted more sympathy, more drinks.

Steve returned to her party, which included some charming Dutch people who also knew and liked Phillida Maltern. They all talked of the Malterns for a moment. Geoffrey Cubitt glanced towards the bar at

Rex's figure. He was sitting on a stool now, glass in hand, talking to an airman. Cubitt thought:

'Humph … that fellow is sinking far too much these days. Let's hope this business pulls him up. He's been giving that child he married a raw deal…'

One of the pretty girls in the party said:

'Oh, I do think Captain Maltern is *so* attractive!'

Steve put her tongue in her cheek.

'Do you?…' she said.

'Don't *you*, Steve?'

'I think he's a cad, and his wife's a long-suffering angel,' said Steve Cubitt bluntly. 'If you want my frank opinion.'

Soon after ten o'clock Martin Winters walked into the French Club. He had left the Pentyres, knowing that the Brigadier and his wife liked to retire early. Still feeling restive and troubled about Phillida, he did not somehow want to go back to Fayid too early and face a sleepless night.

So he decided to spend half an hour at least at the Club, where it was pleasant and he could watch the dancing and distract his mind a little. And one nearly always found a friend there.

He strolled in, conspicuous as usual by reason of his unusual height and that slow, rather stately way he had of walking, pipe in the corner of his mouth, hands in his pockets. He took a brief survey of the dance floor and the lamp-lit tables and saw nobody whom he knew in particular, except the Cubitts, to whom he nodded and waved, then made his way to the bar.

He was almost there before he saw and recognised Phillida's husband. He stood still, taking the pipe from his mouth, every muscle in his body tautening. A slow colour crept up under his tan. So Maltern was here, was he ... and alone ... and he had been drinking. That was obvious from the quite unexpected way in which he welcomed Martin. He hailed him like a long-lost brother.

'My dear chap ... I'm *delighted* to see you. How are you? Just the man I want to talk to. Come and have a drink. I'm feeling b—y. I expect you've heard the awful news about poor Phil.'

Martin's face flushed darker.

'You mean...'

'What happened last night ... you've heard?'

Martin breathed again.

'Yes ... I heard about that. I'm very sorry. Very sorry indeed.'

Rex set his glass down on the bar.

'The same again ... and what for you, Martin?'

'Oh, I'll have a Stella beer,' said Martin with difficulty. He was going to find it hard to talk to Phillida's husband in a normal fashion. Yet he felt the necessity to speak to him … to hear from him direct the latest news of her. For that reason alone he accepted the drink. But he looked distastefully at the younger man's flushed face, loose jowl and eyes that were red-inflamed. The fellow looked as though he had been soaking for hours, Martin thought.

Rex, with a vague notion at the back of his head that he would please Phil and secure her approbation if he was nice to her 'boyfriend', made himself extremely agreeable to Martin. He started a somewhat garbled, distorted version of the facts … said how he had got back home last night to find Phil terribly ill … what a fright it had given him … how wretched he was that the child was not to be, but that nothing mattered save Phil.

'We can have other children, but I can never have another wife like my Phil…' He ended with a hiccough.

Martin froze. The man was nauseating, he thought, and a liar and hypocrite into the bargain.

'How is she tonight?' at length Martin asked.

'Still very ill, old boy. Still very ill.'

Martin turned away and took a deep draught of beer. His heart beat with slow, painful jerks.

'I'm sorry...' He forced the inadequate words.

'But she's going to be all right ... the sister said so when I left the hospital tonight. And Phil, poor little soul, was well enough to speak to me... Honestly, Martin, it's dreadful, old man, to see a woman in pain like that. Shook me to the core...'

Martin thought: 'I could wring your neck Maltern ... willingly... Shaken to the core ... you ... blast you ... *you* caused it all ... you who have broken her to pieces...!'

Rex continued in a maudlin fashion.

'Thank God I was here to be with her. She clung to me ... even when she was half conscious she was calling for me, poor sweet...'

A swift, ice-cold anger shook Martin. He felt no jealousy on account of those words. He knew perfectly well that Maltern lied ... for effect. But he felt the old violent dislike of him ... bitter resentment on account of the things Rex had done to that girl who had come out here, eager-eyed, enthusiastic, wanting to love ... to be loved by him.

As Rex talked on, half deceiving himself into believing that he had saved Phillida's life by being at her bedside today ... it became too much for Martin. He drained his glass, ordered a drink for Rex, then said:

'If you'll excuse me ... I've got to get back to Fayid.'

Rex tried to keep him. When Martin persisted in saying good night he caught him by the arm and said:

'Well, look here, old boy, you'll go and see Phil as soon as she's allowed visitors, won't you? You're one of our best friends... I'll tell them to let you in first.'

Martin drew away as though Rex's hand stung him. He looked with cold contempt down into the bloodshot eyes.

'Thanks,' he said. 'I'll be glad to see Phillida when she's better.'

Rex said: 'I'm going to take her away to Cyprus as soon as she can face the journey.'

Martin, who had been on the verge of moving away, stood immobile now. His face was stony. But his pulses had thrilled with sudden dismay.

'To ... Cyprus? You aren't ... sending her home?'

Rex smiled foolishly.

'Oh, she doesn't want to go back to England ... she won't leave me, you know ... it's just a change of air she wants. She said so...'

'Did she?' The words came from Martin's set lips with obvious difficulty. 'Well, good night again...'

He turned and walked out of the Club.

Was it true? Did Phillida intend to go on living with the fellow ... sacrificing herself ... all over again? And must *he* stand by and watch the sacrifice ... and suffer for and with her, as well as for himself?

In a state of deepest depression, Martin drove the old Morris down the curving, beautiful road beside the moonlit Canal. And his heart was like a stone within him.

8

When Phillida recovered from her illness she did not go to Cyprus with Rex. Neither did she go back to England. It seemed to her that fate did not intend that either her arrival or departure in Egypt should be peaceful and straightforward.

On the day that she was due to leave the Garrison Hospital – Rex was supposed to fetch her in the car soon after lunch – Mabyn Pentyre came to see her.

'Well, my dear, you do have bad luck, but I'm afraid there'll be no Rex to fetch you home this afternoon,' she said after she had greeted the girl.

Phillida was sitting on the edge of her bed, packed and ready to leave the little room in which she had been so desperately ill. She still felt very weak and had none of her old colour or vivacity, but on the whole the enforced rest in bed and complete relaxation had done her good. She had been quite surprised to find that she had put on a little weight, and she had completely lost that feeling of fear, of awful apprehension which had been hanging over her during the grim weeks before her collapse.

Certainly she could not complain of any lack of attention from Rex while she was in hospital. He had been most considerate and, after his fashion, had done his best to prove that he was genuinely sorry for what had happened between them.

She had been quite touched when Martin had come to see her and told her that it had been Rex himself who arranged the visit. And on one or two other occasions when Martin arrived and Rex was with her, he could not have been more affable or diplomatic. Once again he was treating Martin as though he were their best friend.

The only thing that worried Phillida was Rex's repeated appeal to her to let him take her away to Cyprus and give him another chance. He seemed so anxious that she should not return to England.

He assured her that he wanted to recapture their old happiness. He behaved as though nothing had happened to change the association between them. But for her everything had changed ... and every time she saw Martin she grew more aware of it. She was deeply and hopelessly in love with him. And he loved her. But the word 'love' had not been spoken between them since that one night when they had revealed their feelings to each other. When he had first seen her in hospital he lifted her hand to his lips for an instant and said:

'Thank God you're all right, my dear…'

That had been all. That and the look in his eyes and the weak tears that blinded hers as she returned the pressure of his long, fine fingers.

He was taking it for granted that she would not remain in Ismailia with Rex. It had been her full intention to get a passage and go home to Gamma as soon as possible. For the sake of appearances she realised that she might have to go back to the bungalow in Ismailia with Rex at first … but she would not live with him again as his wife. To that she had firmly made up her mind.

Now she looked at Mrs Pentyre and said:

'What's happened, Mrs Pen?'

'Reversed positions for you and Rex,' was the answer; 'you're leaving this hospital and he went into No 19 General last night.'

'Rex – in 19 General!' exclaimed Phillida.

Mrs Pentyre explained. Rex had been taken ill whilst at work at G.H.Q. yesterday. He went along to the M.O. and they found that he had a high temperature, and so took him straight off to the hospital, where he had to stay. It was no more than a bad attack of sand-fly fever, but he was certainly not fit to drive into Ismailia.

'And so,' concluded Mabyn, 'if it's all right with you, my child, I'm going to take you back home with Freddy and myself until Rex is out again. You won't want to stay alone in your place.'

Phillida agreed. Indeed, she had no desire whatsoever to go back to that villa, which contained nothing but the most unpleasant memories of sickness and misery – and her unreasonable fear of Ahmed.

The said Ahmed had, of course, long since gone. Rex had engaged a new *suffragi* found by Mrs Pen herself. Ali was an elderly and well-trained Sudanese of a very different calibre. But even with the good Ali, Phillida did not want to be alone. Gratefully she accepted Mrs Pentyre's invitation. Then added:

'Poor old Rex.'

But even as she said the words, she felt guilty. She knew that it was an enormous relief to her to learn that she need not face a scene with him tonight. She had been dreading it. She had felt that an argument was inevitable. He was making things so difficult for her by being pleasant and anxious to please. But it was too late. Nothing that he could do or say could make her love him again. Nor, for a matter of fact, trust him.

Copper Deacon had gone home. But there would be others… Rex could never be faithful … never keep up this new righteous and sober attitude. She felt cynical and hard about it. And yet she could not for the moment plan any other future … nor visualise a happier existence.

There was always Martin … a deep, ever-increasing love and longing for him in her heart. Once he had said that were it not for the child she was expecting he would take her away. But that had been in a moment of extreme agitation. She would never let him do such a thing. He was an officer in the Regular Navy with an unblemished reputation. Under no circumstances would she allow him to be drawn into a divorce. Besides, there was the old aunt up in Scotland … to whom he was heir … and her grandmother. And Rex's Army career. A dozen obstacles … insurmountable barriers between Martin and herself. Not for an instant did she entertain the slightest hope of things working out so that she could live her life with *him*. It was a hopeless tangle.

But she was not sorry that poor Rex had fever so that she could go and convalesce in peace with the dear 'Penwipers' rather than recommence the old bitter struggle with Rex.

The Pentyres were Martin's friends; which, too, was a comforting thought – apart from her personal regard for them. Perhaps she would see him while she was in Moascar, she thought wistfully. She longed for Martin. Just to watch the tall figure move in that slow, rather stately way that he had of walking … just to see him look down at her with those grave and very blue eyes of his ... just to enjoy a little longer the sweetness and understanding that seemed to flow from him, and reach her very heart whenever they were together.

Mrs Pentyre took her back to her nice cool house later that day. Phillida was touched beyond words to find some beautiful flowers waiting for her ... and many messages from her friends ... and she received a warm welcome from the Brigadier himself.

'Glad you're going to stay with us for a bit. We must put a bit more colour into your cheeks and take that trip to Cairo we once talked about and make ourselves sick with Groppi cakes,' he said.

'Now, Freddy!' admonished his wife, 'I won't have you starting your nonsense with Phillida the moment she gets here. She isn't strong enough to stand up to it.'

But Mabyn Pentyre was secretly glad to see how much better the girl was looking, and to hear her laugh as Freddy continued to tease her. What an absolutely *foul* time the poor little thing had had! And as for Captain Maltern ... words failed her on the subject of that young man. Only out of her affection for Phillida did she receive Rex in her house, and it was always a struggle to get Freddy to be civil when Rex addressed him.

Then there was Martin... Mrs Pen was more than anxious about her beloved

Martin. The whole position between these young people was very delicate and invidious, and Freddy had warned her last night to be careful.

'You know perfectly well that my sympathy is all with that pretty child, and that I think Martin Winters a damn' good chap … but Maltern's her husband. One has to consider the rights and wrongs of it. Whatever they all decide to do, there mustn't be any scandal.'

Mabyn had patted his bald head and said: 'Dear old Freddy!'

And in her cheerful fashion she had teased him. But she knew that he was right. And she was extremely worried as to what to do in order to help these two young things who had fallen so much in love and who must deny themselves the privilege of their loving. She had not one ounce of respect or sympathy for Rex Maltern. But – as Freddy said – he was Phillida's husband.

She decided that the best and most tactful thing was to do absolutely nothing; just quietly watch events, and let the thing work itself out.

But, woman-like, she could not resist asking Martin to dinner. The Brigadier, when he heard that Martin was coming, flung her a quizzical look, one bushy eyebrow raised.

'You're up to no good, woman. Now look here–'

'Freddy dear,' interrupted Mabyn, her blue eyes twinkling, 'you go and take a nice church parade in the morning and leave me to arrange my dinner party, and don't be such an old stick-in-the-mud.'

The Brigadier snorted. But he knew his Mabyn. She always *had* been able to twist him round her little finger.

So Martin came to dinner – two nights after Phillida left the hospital. When he arrived she was in the long, cool sitting-room with its attractive green-and-white chintzes and all the lovely china and glass of which the Pentyres were so proud. Mabyn boated that she took her treasures everywhere that Freddy was posted – even though it meant a dozen packing-cases following them from one side of the world to the other. She had once said to Phillida:

'If an officer's wife doesn't take her things and make a home wherever she goes, she'll never have one. She'll live in digs and furnished flats until the age of retirement. And I like my home.'

Phillida liked it too. It was heavenly here with all the tastefully-arranged flowers, the graciousness and beauty that was to be found in the Pentyres' quarters. And tonight she felt happier and so much more peaceful – despite the ache in her heart – than she had felt for months.

Later she found herself alone with Martin.

The Brigadier had been at a conference in Suez, and had come home late. When one of the *suffragis* ushered Martin into the drawing-room Mabyn had said:

'Give Martin a drink, Phillida, and entertain him for me while I see to Freddy. If I don't go and find his clean shirt he'll never appear. Men are the most helpless creatures!'

And after that sally she departed.

So here sat Phillida on the sofa with an iced orangeade in her hand … and there sat Martin opposite her, with his 'pink gin'. The windows were wide open. Through the mosquito netting they could see a velvet night of crescent moon and a million stars. A cool desert wind was rustling in the trees just outside the window and moving the curtains. Two white moths chased madly round the parchment shade of the tall standard lamp. From the garden came the chirp of the crickets, and the deep, monotonous croak of an old bullfrog.

Phillida met Martin's gaze, and for no reason at all she blushed and looked away. He saw the quick colour and felt his pulses thrill. He knew that under his own exterior of calm there burned an incessant flame of yearning towards her … his little love Phillida, incorporated now in his imagination with the other love so long lost to him. And must he lose this one too? There seemed no hope of anything else. He had thought that when she was no longer to bear a child he might feel her nearer to him ... and yet she remained inaccessible. He had not really known any peace of mind since the hour when he had declared his love for her and heard her response. Every visit to her in hospital ... all the polite, conventional words, the friendly discussions, had masked all his passionate desire to take her in his arms.

And how did she feel about it? That quick-burning flush was eloquent. How marvellous she looked this evening, he thought, in a long white dress, with a pattern of blue flowers, her hair pinned high on her head instead of the usual sedate bun. She still appeared fragile, with her transparent skin and grey shadowed eyes. But there was something warm and lovely about her to-night, he thought ... and she looked actually *happy*. He could not restrain a feeling of satisfaction because he knew *why* she was happy... He knew that she felt liberated, free to enjoy her life for a few days, with no Rex in it.

But what was she going to do about Rex when he recovered from his attack of fever and came home?

He felt that he must talk frankly to her tonight. He could not bear to go away carrying with him the feeling of unrest, of indecision, of intense longing for her which had been eating him up all the time she was ill. He took refuge as usual in filling his pipe, and said:

'It's wonderful to see you looking so much better.'

'Oh, I'm fine now,' she said.

He gave another quick, appraising look at the fair, shining hair and then down at the long, slender feet in slim, white sandals. There were pink roses tucked in her belt. She wore charming ear-rings, star-shaped, fashioned out of ivory. She looked exquisitely cool.

He nodded appreciatively:

'Pretty smooth,' he said.

She laughed, and coloured again.

'Mrs Pen said that she was going to have a smart dinner party, so I dressed up. You're looking rather "smooth" yourself, Lieutenant-Commander.'

He cocked an eyebrow and stuck the pipe between his teeth. He, too, in honour of this dinner party, had 'dressed up'. The well-fitting white mess jacket suited him. His fair hair, like hers, gleamed in the lamplight. Yesterday he had had one of his very bad headaches, and all through office hours had fought against the pain. He had been half afraid that he was going to emulate Maltern's example and go down with fever, and so miss seeing Phillida tonight, but the attack had passed, and he was feeling quite fit again this evening. He said:

'How long do you think you'll be here with the Pens?'

She took a sip of orangeade.

'Depends on Rex. How long do those feverish attacks last?'

'That depends upon how bad he is.'

'Well, I expect he'll be laid up a few days, Martin.'

'I'd like to see something of you. I suppose it would be very much wiser for me to keep away – but there you are – one doesn't do the wise thing,' said Martin drily.

She bit her lip. Dear, *dear* Martin. Being with him was like drawing a breath of champagne air from some lofty mountain-top, she thought ... reviving, strengthening ... his was an extraordinary personality. In such a quiet and unobtrusive way he gave out this feeling of force and, at the same time, serenity. She could imagine nothing more wonderful than being always with Martin.

Impulsively she said:

'Oh, I don't want to be wise. I want to see you *terribly!*'

Quickly he looked at her, and felt the emotion rising between them.

'Darling,' he said, under his breath.

'Darling,' she whispered back – her heart plunging. Then she sank back into a state of gloom and perplexity, remembering the man in the Fayid hospital. The man to whom she had vowed to be faithful 'for better or for worse'. It had been 'for worse', but the contract was still there. And even with her tremendous feeling for Martin, she could not easily abandon the principles of a lifetime. She could hear her own voice reproaching her friend Betty because she had drifted away from her husband. She had been so full of illusions, so sure of herself then. She could hear Betty scoffing at her. Telling her to 'wait until she saw Rex again' ... well, she had waited – and this was the result.

Martin saw the mental struggle behind her silence, leaned forward and gently took her hand.

'Don't worry too much, darling. Maybe we'll be able to do something about it.'

'We can't,' she said, in a muffled voice. 'How can we?' and her slender fingers twined convulsively about the big, strong hand.

'Wait a bit, Phillida,' he said. 'We *must* meet and talk.'

'Any time you say, Martin.'

'Tomorrow's my short day. I'll come and take you out for a drive.'

She nodded, but the old desolate frightened expression had crept back into the beautiful, weak-looking eyes, which always rent his heart. He pressed her hand tighter.

'Don't worry, darling, *please!* All you've got to do now is to get well – completely well again.'

'I don't know how I'm going to be able to go back to him,' she whispered.

Martin set his lips.

He wanted to say:

'Don't go back. For the love of heaven don't lay yourself open to any more ruthless cruelty. He'll only let you down. He's all right for the moment, but he won't stay like it. I know him now. I know what he has done to you. For your own sake don't give him a chance to repeat it...'

But he felt that he had no right to say any such thing. He just sat there holding her hand, looking at her, knowing that he loved her more than he had loved Bridget, more than anything and anybody in the world.

Then he heard steps and voices and gently kissed the hand he held and put it down.

'We'll talk tomorrow,' he said in a low voice. 'Sleep well tonight, my darling. Go on getting better.'

The Pentyres came into the room chaffing each other as usual. At the same time the *suffragi* announced that dinner was ready.

It was a lovely party, with tall candles burning on the table and one of Mabyn's perfectly chosen meals. For Phillida it was a lovely evening altogether, just sitting near Martin, listening to him, watching him, feeling the warmth of love that shone in his eyes when they turned in her direction.

It was the happiest night that she had spent since she arrived in Egypt.

That next morning Mrs Pentyre drove Phillida into Fayid to see her husband.

It was Phillida's express request. In her direct fashion, without frills, Mabyn had said:

'A touch of sand-fly fever won't kill him, and you're not fit to do too much yet. Why not just telephone the hospital and leave a message?'

But Phillida had thought it her duty to go – and she went.

She found Rex a good deal better than she expected to see him. After twenty-four hours his temperature had dropped and although he complained of headache, and every other ache, he seemed to be enjoying life – as only Rex would enjoy it, in his supremely egoistical fashion. In a corner bed of the Officers' Ward he looked as handsome as ever, with an interesting pallor and a wan look in his eyes. He was wearing pale blue silk pyjamas, his chestnut hair curling all over his head. He might have been a film star, Phillida thought drily. And, of course, he had all the nurses running around him – and more attention than anybody else.

He received Phillida with a great show of

warmth and affection. 'Absolutely superb of you to come all this way to see me, Poppet. I really feel ashamed of myself when I ought to have been looking after you. Decent of the old Penwipers to put you up. You must forgive me, but I damn' nearly passed out in the office, and when they brought me here I thought it possible that I was going to be a really sick man. But I have amazing recuperative powers, you know.'

Phillida sat beside the bed and looked at him with her grave, candid eyes. He returned her gaze as frankly as though he had never lied to her in his life. He put out a hand and took one of hers, grinning.

'Aren't we a pair! Anybody would laugh. First of all me at your bedside and now you at mine.'

Then he gave her a quick look, up and down, noting her fresh green-and-white print dress, and the green ribbon tying back the long, fair hair. He added:

'You look ten years younger since you came out of hospital. Quite like the little Wren who used to go touring round with me in the old Alvis. Happy days, weren't they? Ah well, we'll repeat them out here if not back there. Won't we, Poppet?'

She sat very still. It was rather awful, she thought, that all these things he was saying left her so cold and utterly indifferent. Rex was trying to get back into favour, but he couldn't do it … not in the easy way that he wanted; like a spoiled child who expects to be forgiven the moment it says 'sorry'. Her hurt was too deep. All his infidelities, his bullying, his lies, the long-drawn-out mental torture that she had suffered since she arrived in Egypt, had left a mark which nothing could erase.

Rex continued to fondle her hand, grumbling cheerfully about the food, asking her to ring up Harold Gayter at G.H.Q. and tell him to bring some fruit and some papers, complaining that he was not allowed any alcohol and that he was bored. He ended:

'I'm doing well, but my temperature's still up, and with these aching bones sister says if I do get up I'll feel like hell. So I won't be able to be with you for a few days, darling. How do you think I'm looking?'

'Not too bad,' she answered awkwardly. She felt awkward, strained and ill at ease with him. And it seemed so typical of Rex that he should spend half an hour talking about himself. He had not, as yet, bothered to enquire how *she* was feeling.

When at length he remembered to do so he hardly waited for her reply, but went on to say that it was a bit of a godsend that he had got this attack because he was frightfully short of cash, and it would save something with the Penwipers putting *her* up, and himself here. And, he concluded, the moment they both felt like taking a journey, they must fix themselves up in the mountains in Cyprus.

'I'll get a cheque out of Mamma,' he ended gaily.

Then Phillida, her heartbeat quickening, and her cheeks hot, said: 'Look, Rex. I didn't mean to talk to you this morning because I thought you'd be ill ... but as you're so much better – I feel I'd like to be honest with you... I don't want there to be any misunderstanding ... but I don't wish to go to Cyprus with you, Rex.'

He stared.

'Why not?'

She made a gesture of her free hand, and tried to draw the other from his.

'Rex, you really are extraordinary. You seem to have completely forgotten everything that has happened. Just because you choose to be nice to me again now, you expect *me* to forget the past and be equally nice to you.'

He shrugged his shoulders, and laughed.

'Oh, I don't bear malice – why should you?'

He staggered her. She wondered how it was possible for any man to be so shallow, so insincere. He had no sensibility, no comprehension of the hell through which he had put her. Or if he had ... he deliberately avoided the issue and tried to pretend to himself that all was well, and make her play the same game.

'How incredible he is!' thought Phillida, with a sinking heart, as she stared into those handsome sloe-dark eyes which looked this morning as innocent and affectionate as though he had never done a wrong thing in his life. When she remembered the ugliness, the cruelty, behind the mask she could not find it in her heart to forgive him. And with the thought of Martin uppermost in her mind she knew that she could never love Rex again.

She got up, walked to the window and looked out at the desert, the rows of hospital huts, baking under the pitiless summer sunshine. Then she turned back to Rex. In a low voice, so that the man in the bed next to Rex could not hear her, she said:

'I just must tell you straight away that I can't begin again in the way you want me to. I just *can't!* You've killed something in me, Rex. I want to go back to England. There are other reasons, besides *us*. My grandmother isn't very fit. Her last letter quite worried me. I'd like to see her. And I don't think I shall ever get really fit here, with the two worse summer months to face.'

There was an instant's silence. Then Rex said, in a changed sullen voice:

'Of course those are a lot of silly excuses.

411

What you mean is that you won't forgive me. You *are* malicious. I'd never have thought it of you, Phil.'

She said swiftly:

'It isn't a question of malice. I don't feel malicious. I don't want to hurt or upset you. But you just don't seem to realise what you've done to me, and I think it's ridiculous of you to take it for granted that I can slide back into the old state of loving and adoring you ... just as though ... as though... Oh! ... if you don't understand, I can't explain!' she ended with a helpless gesture.

Now he lay in his bed with a scowl, drawing his brows together.

'I see,' he said, under his breath, 'so you mean to quit on me?'

She swallowed hard.

'No. But I'd like to go home. I don't want to stay in Egypt any more, for the present, anyhow. Please let me go.'

He threw her a bitter look.

'And tell everybody that I've been a cad to you?'

'That's childish. I don't want anybody outside to know... They all understand now that I am going home for the sake of my health.'

'I see,' he said again.

In a softer voice, she said:

'Nobody is sorrier than I am for the way

412

things have turned out between us. And perhaps ... perhaps after I've been back with Gamma for a bit it will all work out, and I ... we might reach some sort of understanding.'

It was with the greatest difficulty that she said those words, remembering Martin ... feeling his spirit close to her ... feeling all the tremendous love that had come to life between them. It was as though a knife turned in her heart. What she was saying to Rex was slowly, inevitably, heightening the barriers between Martin and herself. Later she must try to forgive Rex. It was her duty to try. Especially if his remorse and his desire to be forgiven were sincere.

'Rex,' she said, after a pause, 'surely you do understand how difficult it all is?'

But he was sulky now, and eyed her with resentment. He hated to be thwarted, and he had a secret, malignant desire to hurt her again *because* she was thwarting him, to throw the name of Martin Winters into her face, but he dared not. Something in the sheer honesty and decency and gentleness of Phillida made him think twice about repeating that insult.

He muttered:

'And how long, may I ask, will it take you before you deal out the royal pardon?'

She coloured.

'Oh, Rex, don't be like that. It isn't a

413

question of "royal pardon". I don't mean to be pompous or priggish about it– I've got my faults as well as you – but you must admit...'

'That I behaved badly,' he broke in. 'O.K., O.K., I did. But I told you it was the drink. A chap doesn't know what he's doing when he's full of alcohol. You're damned intolerant...'

She would like to have protested against that. To have reminded him of the many times she had shut her eyes to his misdeeds ... of the way she had put up with Rebecca Rendledon, with Copper, with all the other unpleasantnesses. But she felt too languid in this heat, and still too weak in herself, to embark on a battle with Rex.

'Don't let's argue now,' she said; 'just ask Movements to get me on to the first ship they can. That's all I ask.'

He flung himself back on his pillows, turning his face from her.

'Well, that's nice! And I'd planned a tremendous reunion.'

'I'm sorry,' she said, in a low voice.

He eyed her covertly over one shoulder.

'And when I leave here in a day or two, and we go back to our bungalow, are we to have separate bedrooms, may I ask?'

She coloured hotly. Her body was damp with perspiration, and her heart thumping. If this sort of thing was going to begin all

414

over again with Rex, she knew she would very soon crack under it. She could never, *never* face another long spell of his selfishness and tyranny.

She said: 'Yes, it does mean that. And you can't blame me. You *can't!* If you want me ever to start with you again I suggest that you give me breathing space ... a chance to get over it... Please try to be reasonable ... and ... and so will I.'

She broke off, her face screwed up as though she were going to cry. Controlling herself, she whispered, 'Good-bye', and turned and walked out of the ward.

9

'So you see, Martin, how hopeless it all is. Quite, quite hopeless!'

Phillida said those words in a voice of despair.

She and Martin were sitting together in the old Morris which he had drawn up under a flamboyant tree in one of those quiet shady streets in the French quarter, *en route* for the Plage.

They had meant to go to the Plage, but they had both had a sudden reluctance to run into a lot of people whom they might know down there on the beach, and be drawn into aimless conversation. They were both too depressed this evening. Phillida had slept all the afternoon, exhausted after her trying morning in Fayid. Then Martin had arrived and they had had tea with Mrs Pentyre, after which he had brought her here. Now it was nearing seven o'clock. That blessedly cool wind was blowing across the desert, relieving the intolerable heat of the day.

For an hour and a half they had sat here unnoticed, hand in hand, talking over the whole thing again and again.

They loved each other. They were both of them quite sure of that. There was more than ordinary love between them. There was understanding and sympathy and friendship. But she was married to Rex and he wanted her to go back to him. That thought to Martin was intolerable, and to Phillida a nightmare. Yet there seemed no way out.

'Nothing will ever induce me to run away with you and wreck your career,' she had said, right from the start.

His first reaction had been to protest ... to say that he could not let her go back to martyrdom as Maltern's wife and that he would take her away, no matter what the cost. But later, perforce, he had come round to Phillida's way of thinking. Even in these modern days divorce was not a pretty thing ... and it would certainly be frowned upon for a Regular Naval Officer. Nobody knew the real facts. It would merely be taken for granted that Martin had stolen the wife of an Army colleague. He would lose his job – possibly, in the long run, his commission.

'You love the Navy, Martin. And it loves you. You've always valued honour and decency. I can't – I won't – let you push it all to one side for me,' Phillida said again and again.

When he protested that it would all be worth while for *her,* she put his hand against her cheek in an exquisitely tender gesture and shook her head at him.

'No, Martin, not in the long run. There's something in you which would hate dishonour, and most of all you'd hate it for me. The things that people would say about me. Bridget has remained an ideal to you. You wouldn't want to lower the standard. It wouldn't be a good beginning for us. The trouble is, Martin, we've both got consciences. We'd both worry, and ... oh, it's out of the question! Even if I don't go back to Rex I shall never let him divorce me on account of *you*.'

'I think,' said Martin, with a long, deep look at her, 'that you're the most wonderful girl I've ever met. I would like Aunt Kate to have heard every word you've been saying.'

'And I would have so much liked to have met your Aunt Kate, and to have seen Killoun,' she said wistfully.

Martin clenched his hand.

'It's damnable, Phillida, when I think that *you* could have divorced that fellow – not once but many times...'

Her head dropped.

'Yes, I suppose I could have done. But you know what I feel about marriage. Divorce is such an ugly, sordid affair. Rex's father and mother split up – and look at the result. I think poor Rex's upbringing is a great deal responsible for his character now.'

Martin smoothed one of her long, slim

hands with his own. He said:

'You talk about me having ideals ... you're full of them, darling. God alone knows why you haven't lost them after what you've been through. You're an amazing little person.'

Then suddenly she turned to him, lips quivering, eyelids stinging with unshed tears.

'I'm not. I love you. I love you so much that I can hardly *bear* the thought of leaving you. Oh, Martin, *Martin!*'

Then he caught her close. For the first time they kissed as lovers ... passionately and hungrily... For Phillida that moment was unimagined bliss and she came nearer in that moment to forsaking her ideals, to giving up the fight, than she had ever been.

For a moment or two they were both lost in the ecstasy of their mutual love. With clinging lips and straining arms they whispered their tenderness, their passion, for each other.

The swift darkness blotted out the brilliance of the day. Time ceased to be. For a while longer Phillida and Martin sat together. Now without passion, but with desperate tenderness, they rested in each other's arms, cheek to cheek. He could feel the hot tears rolling down her face and her trembling form against him. He whispered:

'Oh, my love, my little love ... what a damnable thing to have happened to us! We might have been so very happy, you and I.'

'I'll always be glad that this happened ... that we met and loved,' she whispered back.

'So shall I, Phillida, my darling.'

'Do you remember that first day when you found me in Port Said, struggling with all the natives...?'

'I remember everything...'

'Will we ever meet again, once I leave Egypt?'

'I don't know, Phillida. I suppose it would be better if we didn't. If you mean to come back to the Middle East to rejoin your husband it would be best for me to have a discreet word with old Mortel (he deals with our postings out here) and try to get myself out of the Command. I know they are wanting fellows in the Far East. I shall apply to go there.'

She pressed her eyes against his shoulder.

'Oh, Martin, so far away!... You wouldn't see Killoun for so long!'

He gave a sharp sigh.

'It might be for the best all the same, much as I'd hate it. It would be far worse to hang around here and watch you struggling with Rex.'

She shut her eyes, and he felt her shudder.

'It wouldn't be easy, would it ... for either of us?'

Martin's face had a strained look. He dropped a kiss on Phillida's hair then put her gently away from him.

'Go back to England as soon as you can, darling,' he said abruptly. 'You're very brave and you're much too good for *him*, but there's a limit to everybody's courage and I advise you to stay with your grandmother as long as you can, and get absolutely fit first of all.'

She nodded. Miserably she passed a comb through her hair and wiped her tear-wet face. It was going to be like death saying good-bye to him. But this parting seemed inevitable now. She must go quickly – and eventually – if and when she came back – Martin must not be here.

Last night she had felt peaceful, even happy. Tonight everything was dark and full of despair.

Suddenly, in a broken little voice, she said:

'It's like the *khamsin* ... yes, that's what my life out here has been like ... a *khamsin*, a "wind from hell", isn't that what they call it? Evil and destructive, blotting out everything that's good and beautiful ... that's what my life with Rex has been like ... a *khamsin*, Martin. Oh, *Martin!*'

He put his arm around her again to comfort her, trying to protect her from her own sense of loss and desolation. He himself had never felt more wretched. After a long silence, he said:

'The *khamsin's* come and go, my darling.

421

And after they are over everything is quiet again. And sometimes it rains and the air is deliciously cool, and you can take a long breath of it and feel that all the evil is passed. It will be like that for you, my darling Phillida. Everything will pass – life will seem better after a while. Try not to be too unhappy. I can't bear to think that you are unhappy. You look so beautiful when you smile.'

She looked up at him in the dimness of the little car and saw that his blue eyes were smiling down at her now, and suddenly she smiled back, comforted.

They did not speak any more. In silence he held her hand, tightly and reassuringly, as he drove her back to Moascar Garrison, and she was comforted.

She did not see Martin again that week. She knew that it was for both their sakes that he did not come. But she was not allowed to sit alone and think too much, because the moment her physical strength returned to her and she was able to lead a normal life, Mrs Pen saw to it that there was plenty to occupy Phillida's mind.

She gave a special cocktail party for her, asking all the nicest people she knew, including the Cubitts from Fayid, and Jimmy Angus and Doreen, and (it was typical of Mabyn Pentyre's kindness to remember the crippled Peggy) Doreen's sister came too.

Young Bill was left in charge of a friend that night.

It was the evening before Rex was due to leave the hospital. Tomorrow Phillida must start her life with him again in the bungalow. But she was still determined to go back to England. And still determined not to live with Rex as his wife. She had seen him every day that he had been in hospital and every day he had pleaded afresh for a complete reconciliation. But this was one of the times when the stubborn streak in Phillida asserted itself. Every time he argued with her, she said:

'Let us be friends, Rex. Let me look after you and do everything I can for your comfort. But please give me a chance to get over ... what has happened.'

When he had flung it at her that she had only herself to blame if he found another girl-friend, she gave him a look of silent scorn. And when he drove her by further threats to a further response, she said:

'You're awfully weak, aren't you, Rex? And you're being awfully stupid, too. If you want me back, this isn't the way to do it.'

She, who did not believe in wives discussing their husbands and private affairs with the lack of delicacy that so many women displayed in a colony like this, felt the need to find a safety-valve for some of her bottled-up emotional problems tonight. She snatched a moment alone with her friend Steve, sitting in the garden where Mrs Pen had arranged small tables under the trees, which were gaily illuminated by coloured lights. The verandahs were lit up, crowded with people. There was a gay babble of voices and laughter, plenty to drink and good things to eat.

Phillida had received a great many compliments. She had never looked better, her friends maintained. On the thin side, perhaps, but charming in a dress of soft blue silk. She wore little blue-flowered earrings to match, and the golden hair was looped back into the demure knot which Martin loved.

But Martin was not here.

That spoiled the party for Phillida, even though she knew why he had not come; she had known when Mrs Pen told her that Martin had gone to bed with one of his bad heads. She had thought: 'I've got to get used to it. I've got to live my life without him, so I might as well start now.'

Wistfully she looked at Steve, who had told her tonight, for the first time, that she hoped to give Geoffrey a son and heir at Christmas-time.

Steve's strong, boyish face was happy and tranquil. She had no complaints about life. It was going to be a bit of a 'squash', she said, with themselves and an infant in one room … their quarter at Fayid. But they didn't mind. She could stand any amount of discomfort for the sake of being with Geoff and they were both eagerly looking forward to having their baby.

'Lucky Steve,' thought Phillida. 'I, too would gladly share a hut with Martin. It must be wonderful to have the child of the man you love … so different from the other thing.' When Steve turned the conversation to herself Phillida spoke more frankly on the subject than she had ever done before.

'Do you think me very cowardly to run away, Steve? You know I always used to tell you on the boat coming to Port Said that I hadn't your confidence in life or myself; that I haven't your strength. Is it awful of me to go?'

Steve said: 'I don't think you realise how strong you've been, my poor little Phil. You certainly do not need to call yourself weak. There are a good many women who couldn't have gone through what you've been through. They'd have quit at the start.'

'It hasn't been easy, Steve.'

'Don't I know it, my sweet. Geoff and I have always known. Quite a number of people are taken by your handsome husband. But not us.'

Phillida's lips twitched. She looked towards the crowd … so many nice people who had been so kind to her. She had a sudden mental flashback to the day when Rex had refused to come here ... 'that old bore Penwiper', he had called the Brigadier. Their 'sticky crowd'. She remembered some of Rex's friends, the hard drinking, the aimless, frivolous parties. She said:

'I just don't understand Rex any more. We don't speak the same language. My marriage has been a mistake, Steve, and to you alone I admit it.'

'And you love Martin Winters,' said Steve bluntly, and he's the salt of the earth, and you ought to have had *him* for a husband. Yes. It's darned bad luck, my poor Phil.'

Phillida flushed and for a moment she did not speak. Her slender fingers twined nervously together in an effort to control her emotions. Then in a low voice she said:

'So you know that too?'

'Yes. I hope you don't mind, Phil.'

'No ... I don't mind...'

'I wish something could be done about it.'

'Nothing can,' said Phil, 'but I want to get back to England and stay with my grandmother, and perhaps come back here in the late autumn and start with Rex again.'

Stave cast an anxious look at her friend.

'How is Rex taking this?'

'Badly,' said Phillida, with a short laugh. 'He wants me to carry on now as though there hadn't been anything the matter...'

'I must say that young man has the most

426

gorgeous conceit,' said Steve dryly. 'However, don't you do a thing you don't want to do, Phil. Every time I've seen you following him around in a state of nervous exhaustion my blood has boiled. Until you go home you just keep your end up and let Master Rex stew a bit. He deserves it.'

'Oh, I do hope everyone hasn't seen what's been going on!' exclaimed Phillida.

'What if they have? Although there are still plenty of girls who will fall for Rex every time.'

Phillida bit her lip.

'It's just that he's ... a good soldier... I ... I don't want his reputation to get so bad that he'll be chucked out or anything. And he expects his promotion any moment. He was acting major in Burma, and then went down a pip, but he ought to be getting it again.'

Steve said:

'Land sakes, you're loyal to that guy! If he treated me as he's treated you I wouldn't mind if they flung him out of the Army and kept him out.'

A moment's pause, then Phillida said:

'And more than anything I don't want *Martin* to get talked about because of me.'

Steve patted her shoulder.

'You needn't worry your little head about that, although I don't doubt there's been a bit of gossip. There always will be where

Army wives are gathered together, my lamb. Everybody likes and respects Martin Winters, and they think a great deal of you. Now stop worrying about other people, and concentrate on yourself. Can I do anything for you tomorrow when you leave here?'

'There's nothing to do, Steve, thank you. I saw Ali this morning. The house is quite ready, and I'm going over to Fayid tomorrow to fetch Rex. He's all right again. Just a bit washed out by the fever. I don't suppose he'll start work for a day or two.'

Steve saw Mrs Pentyre approaching with a tall Major whom, undoubtedly, she wished to introduce to Phillida, so their *tête-à-tête* must end. But as the two girls rose to their feet Steve hastily whispered:

'Remember what I've said, and be firm with Rex. Don't let him get away with it.'

Phillida remembered those words.

She remembered and profited by her friend's counsel. She knew her own softness of heart, her dislike of hurting anybody, or being ungenerous. And when Rex went on pleading it wasn't easy to go on being hard… But every fibre of her being shrank from the thought of renewed intimacy with him. She needed that interval at home … she needed to put thousands of miles between Martin and herself first of all. She knew that he was going to try to get a posting away from Egypt. Perhaps by the time she came back to

Ismailia, and Martin was not here, she would be able to bring herself to live with Rex again.

Their home-coming was not a happy one. Rex was in a bad mood, bored by his sojourn in hospital, and furious because he had been unable to make his young wife change her mind. He did not for a moment see why she should harbour resentment against him. Her stubbornness infuriated him. What little he had felt of real affection and pity for her during her breakdown had by now vanished into thin air. He wanted her in his arms solely because she did not want to walk into them. Rex liked to believe himself irresistible.

So he adopted an injured pose. He refused to respond to Phillida's efforts to be cheerful and friendly. He was short and surly on their first night back in the bungalow.

Everything looked nice. Phillida had arranged the flowers and ordered Rex's favourite meal and a bottle of wine to welcome him. Ali was excellent. Phillida kept up a running flow of conversation about Ismailia, and last night's party, but received only curt replies from her husband. When it came to opening the wine, he scowled.

'I don't know who you think's going to pay for this. I'm broke for the moment,' he said.

She gave a faint smile. Rex was reverting to type. Somehow it made her all the more determined not to do exactly what he wanted *when* he wanted it. Now that she was well again she felt so much calmer and stronger than she had felt before. She answered Rex coolly:

'I'll pay for it if you don't want it, Rex. Now how do you feel ... ought you to go to bed, or shall we drive down to the Club for some coffee?'

He eyed her resentfully, pushed back his chair and got up.

'You'd better ring up Martin Winters and ask him to take you out. He'd be more popular than I would. I realise that I am out of favour.'

Her hands clenched. She fixed her serious grey eyes upon him.

'I hope you're not going to begin *that* ... Rex...'

He broke into a tirade. What did she think? Why should he put up with her treatment? All this haughty, chilly nonsense! How could she expect him to be pleasant? A fellow wanted to come home and find a loving wife, not a damned schoolmistress, and so on, while Phillida listened in silence. Then she, too, rose. Her lips were firmly pressed together. He saw a new, strong Phillida, not that one could bully and reduce to tears. In a clear voice she said:

'I'm sorry if you find me not to your liking, and if you don't think I've given you a friendly welcome home, Rex. And I'm sorry if you've been expecting more. But I thought I'd made it quite clear to you that I was not going to rush into your arms. If you want our marriage to survive, you'll leave me alone. I'm just not made so that I can be dropped and then picked up again. Which is what has been happening. No – you've got to be reasonable.'

'Oh, go to hell!' he snarled.

With sinking heart she watched him march into the hall and shout for Ali.

She followed him.

'What do you want, Rex?'

'I want my shoes. I'm going down to the Club.'

Her pulses quickened.

'I suggested that we should go down to the Club…'

'*You* can stay where you are. I'm going alone.'

'Rex, *do* be reasonable… I've been through a very bad time… I just can't get over it so quickly. *Do* try to understand…'

He gave her an ugly look.

'Do as you like, my dear Phil, I won't stop you. And you needn't try to stop me. You want your own bedroom. Have it. And I'll do what *I* want. That's fair, isn't it?'

Despite all her efforts to be calm she felt the old awful tremor of fear and misery that used to shake her body when he twisted her statements and tried to defeat her. She said:

'Rex, it's not my intention that we should go our own way like this and make a mockery of our marriage. I *want* to put it right ... but if you'd only *wait* a while...'

But he had gone. Gone into the bedroom she had prepared for him, and slammed the door childishly.

After a moment he passed her again in the hall without looking at her, marched out of the villa and slammed the front door.

Slowly she went back to the lamp-lit sitting-room where Ali had placed a tray with a cup of Turkish coffee for her. He asked her whether she wanted anything more and she said no. He went out and shut the door. He was a gentle, courteous Sudanese, of whom she had no fear. In silence and solitude Phillida sipped her Turkish coffee.

She was feeling tired now. The day had been long and hot, and there had been all the business of getting the house ready and Rex back. She looked at her flowers. They were already dying in the heat. She thought: 'If Rex had only been different ... friendly, understanding, tonight ... we might have got a little nearer each other. Now we're farther apart than ever.'

Uneasily she thought of him at the Club, drinking alone. Oh, how weak he was! How exacting and utterly self-centred! What was

432

she going to do?

Go home, Martin had said, *go home as quickly as you can.*

Go home, Steve had counselled her last night, and Mrs Pentyre, too.

Phillida gave a long, bitter sigh. She wanted Martin so terribly badly. She put on her glasses and picked up some long neglected mending.

She thought:

'When Rex comes back I'll make another appeal to him.'

But when Rex came back he refused to speak to her. He went into his own room and shut the door.

She knew then that he was not going to try to be friends: that he would accept no truce. And now she could not view the future with anything but complete despair.

10

The morning was particularly sultry and oppressive.

It was one of the rare grey days on Ismailia. The sun beat down through sinister-looking clouds, and the humidity was extreme. From the time that Phillida got up she was dripping with perspiration.

Old Ali, when he brought in the early tea, had said, pointing in the sky:

'*Khamasin* come today.'

The *khamsin!* Martin had explained all about it to her during one of their interesting discussions. *Khamasin* was the real Arabic word, but it was better known among the Europeans as *khamsin*. Fifty days of stormy weather... The swirling yellow sands from China that came at the time of the Indian monsoon. That terrible 'wind from hell' rising suddenly with demoniacal fury lasting perhaps an hour ... perhaps a day ... leaving a trail of havoc behind it.

Like her own life, she had said to Martin. The life and love that Rex had destroyed.

And he was still bent on destroying it. They had been back in their home for a week, during which time she had made numerous efforts to get some sort of friendly and understanding response out of him. But each time she had failed. He was trying a new line of tyranny now. Instead of bullying her he was cutting her; treating her as he would a stranger. He refused to speak to her. He would have no meals at home. He went out to them all. And once when she had protested that Ismailia would gossip he had turned on her, and said:

'And whose fault is that, my dear, sweet wife? You've set yourself up as a judge, and you don't think I'm fit to be your husband any more, and if Ismailia thinks we're washed up it won't be far wrong, so I couldn't care less.'

She did not argue. She knew that he did care but hoped to drive her into his arms by this form of persecution. But she was determined not to be drawn into any scenes with him. Only once when she asked him to stay in and talk, and he snapped:

'Have your pal Winters in. Pray don't sink to my level. It might hurt you...'

The rudeness stung her to a retort:

'You seem determined not to give yourself or me a chance, Rex. Well, if that's how you want it, I'll go home and stay home. But you needn't include Martin's name in any of our discussions because I'm not seeing Martin any more. He's asked for a posting to the Far East. And I hear from Mrs Pen that he's likely to get it...'

Sheer curiosity then drove Rex to enquire: 'Why has he done that, and why aren't you speaking to him?'

Phillida looked at him fair and square in the eye, her fair head erect.

'Because we like each other very much – too much – Rex, that's why. And because we both happen to respect marriage vows, even though *you* don't. That's why...'

Rex stared, his face slowly reddening. Then he gave a short laugh. 'You're too good to be true,' he said; 'I can't take it. It gives me indigestion. Pardon me if I go in search of more humble fare...'

With which remark he turned on his heel and left her.

She knew what *that* meant. Already it had come to her ears through Doreen, who could never keep a secret, that Rex was being seen quite often with a married woman who had rooms in Ismailia, and whose husband was at the moment in Kenya. Phillida had seen the woman, Mrs Channery – her other name was Jacqueline (they called her Jackie) – when she was with the Anguses on one of their Sunday picnic parties on the French beach. She had been pointed out to Phillida ... a little older than Rex, with an extremely fine supple figure, a brown, rather ugly face, big mouth and turned-up nose, and a lot of dark, untidy hair. But she had magnificent eyes – wicked eyes – as Doreen described them rightly; a masculine love of hard drinking, a man's sense of humour, and an undisguised interest in good-looking officers, other than her own husband. She found Rex Maltern just what she needed and had Rebecca's disregard for Mrs Rex Maltern. In any case, Phillida surmised that Rex had woven a story about how badly his wife was treating him, and Jackie was ready to believe it, and offer her sympathies and attempt to distract the 'poor boy'.

Rex was, in other words, in the teeth of a new affair.

This week had seemed to Phillida like the lull before the storm. She was sure that something would happen … that Rex would 'break out' before long. He was not capable of continuing this silence, this haughty and rather ridiculous indifference to her presence in the house. When she spoke to him he answered curtly, avoiding her gaze. He seemed disinterested in what she did or how she was faring. When she invited friends to the house, he was absent. She made pathetic excuses for him. But she, too, was being obstinate, and she was not going to give way to him.

This morning, after she had dressed and walked on to the verandah on the shady side of the bungalow where Ali laid breakfast, she was quite surprised to find how much better she was feeling, despite the heat. Once again, physically, she felt her age, young and able to cope with life. Never again, she told herself, would she let any man in the world reduce her to the condition in which she had been this summer. She felt that she had recovered completely from her illness. Yesterday, for the first time, she had bathed with the others on the Plage, and felt fine. She was beginning to get brown and strong again.

She walked on to the verandah. Rex was already there reading the Egyptian *Mail*.

'Good morning,' she said.

Without looking at her, he mumbled a reply.

'Ali thinks all these clouds and this awful dim heat mean a *khamsin*. It's late in the year, but the weather seems all upside down these days,' she continued. 'We've never had a really bad once since I've been here, have we?'

Rex grunted and went on reading his paper.

Phillida seated herself, poured out her coffee, then added:

'Is there any news of my passage home, Rex?'

He looked at her over the rim of the paper. He resented, rather than enjoyed, the fact that she looked particularly attractive this morning, in her freshly-laundered green

438

cotton frock, which had a pattern of small white flowers. She had pinned her fair hair high on her head to keep it off her neck. He had not seen her look so well or so pretty since she first came out here. Despite himself, a pang shot through Rex Maltern. Why the hell, he asked himself, had he ever behaved so rottenly to this wife of his? Why did he prefer a trollop like Jackie ... yes, that's all she was ... damned attractive, but coarse and not fit to do up the strap of Phillida's sandals. What was there in himself that made him lean towards that sort of woman and be bored by decency ... by that curious virginal purity which belonged to Phillida despite the fact that she was a married woman? He felt that if she had so much as held out a hand to him he would make an attempt to behave himself. But she was keeping her distance, and he felt malicious because of it. He said:

'You'll have to wait for your passage; the boats are crammed.'

'You are in touch with Movements, aren't you?'

'Yes,' he said shortly, and returned to his newspaper.

Phillida ate her breakfast, and resting her chin on one hand looked out through the apricot trees in the little front garden, through the iron gate to the street. A bedraggled old man with a dirty turban was

439

leading a tiny donkey to which was attached a far too heavy cart laden with huge green watermelons. After them crept a lean-looking mongrel, its tongue lolling out. Both animals were probably hungry, and certainly they were exhausted by the heat. She reflected sadly:

'What an awful lot of suffering there is in the world for both men and beasts!'

Then her thoughts turned to Martin. It was a terrible deprivation not being able to see him. He avoided Ismailia. Somebody had mentioned to her on the Plage yesterday that the Lieutenant-Commander had been seen with another Naval Officer at the Fayid Officers' Club. Phillida knew that Martin disliked that crowded spot, and that, like herself, he craved for the trees and the green shade which made Ismailia more bearable than most places in the Canal Zone. But he dared not see her any more. *Oh, Martin, Martin, my love!*

Another long, hot day stretched before her. It was Sunday; that was why she and Rex were breakfasting together. Jimmy Angus had said that he would come later to fetch her in the car, with Doreen. Peggy and young Bill, and they would all go to the *jardin d'Enfants* to swim early, before it got too hot.

She glanced at Rex. As usual he was strikingly good-looking, with that bright chestnut head of his, and the rich bronze of his skin. He wore shorts and an open necked white shirt. Despite his increased weight, he might have been a handsome schoolboy, ready for a day's sport. And she thought how tragic it was that once she had loved him very much and that to be with him alone like this, in their own home, would have seemed heaven itself.

A man in khaki, wearing a red tarboosh, came up to the gate on his bicycle – the postman. Ali went out to meet him and came back with four letters. Three for herself and one for Rex.

Phillida put on her glasses and eagerly opened her mail, the first being from her grandmother. Poor old Gamma had been so dreadfully anxious about her, and now was so relieved to know that her darling was recovered. But she still did not know the real reason why Phillida was returning home. She wrote:

You will hate leaving your darling Rex, but you are quite right to come back. It must have been a great strain on you and a bitter blow to you both...

Sadly she looked up from this letter. How ironic those words seemed in face of the facts, but she was glad that Gamma had been spared the disagreeable truth. It would have broken her heart to know what Phillida had been through. The letter continued on a happy note, with the latest news from home. It ended:

Alvercombe Cottage waits for you, my precious girl. You know what your home-coming will mean to me. Don't worry about funds. We'll manage somehow to raise your fare back again, if poor Rex is hard up. Give the dear boy my love…

It was typical of Gamma to be so generous. She would sell her last, her only, diamond ring, if she thought it necessary to her granddaughter's happiness.

Phillida had a swift vision of the dear little village of Alvercombe, with its winding, cobbled streets, the slope leading down to the tiny quay and the beach; the greeny-blue sea lapping creamily against the rocks; the red cliffs and the spongy turf starred with sea-daisies. The little ships wherein she was so well known; the fishermen on the quayside, mending their nets. The cottage itself, which would be so heavenly with all the roses out at this time of year. Rain pattering on the roof, grey mists and seagulls crying. Everything that was *England.* There came upon her a sudden rush of homesickness, a craving for all those things that she had left because she thought she loved Rex Maltern.

Yet on the day on which she embarked from Port Said she would be leaving Martin. Therein lay fresh bitterness.

With a sharp sigh Phillida dragged her thoughts from Alvercombe and Martin, and opened a second letter. That, too, was from Alvercombe, from the local doctor's wife. She had heard of Phillida's illness and written to sympathise. She had known Phillida since she was a child. Her husband was Gamma's doctor.

Now Phillida lifted the third letter and regarded the envelope curiously. All her post nowadays came by civilian air mail to this address. When things started to get bad with Rex she had stopped people at home from writing through the Army channels, because Rex so often forgot to bring home her mail. This was a sixpenny air-letter addressed to her in a fine slanting hand which she had never seen before. Then suddenly her heart missed a beat and her cheeks deepened to a bright pink because she saw the postmark *Killoun.*

Rapidly she slit the edges of the envelope and turned to the signature. *Katherine Mackay.* Martin's Aunt Kate!

She read it eagerly. It was a short and rather formal little note, and yet it gave Phillida exquisite pleasure. It brought her suddenly near to the Scottish castle about which she had heard so much and where so much of Martin's boyhood had been spent. And it showed her that Mrs Mackay took a friendly interest in her.

I was exceedingly sorry to hear from my nephew of your serious illness. He has spoken so much of you and I am sure your friendship there in the Middle East has meant so much to him. We have never met, but I shall hope that one day you will come to Scotland and pay Killoun a visit. I wish that you could see it now for we are having a little heat wave, and it is all so fresh and green in the woods and on the moorland, and the river is at its best. It is so sad Martin cannot be here to have a day's fishing which he loves so well...

There was not much more than that, and a courteous wish for her complete recovery. Tears stung Phillida's eyelids. She folded the letter and felt suddenly heartbroken that she would never now see Killoun Castle nor meet Martin's Aunt Kate, nor stand with *him* by the willows looking into the crystal-clear pool wherein the great silver-speckled fish lay waiting...

A sudden grunt from Rex. 'Well, that's *that.*'

She looked up and saw him tearing his letter into pieces. He scowled at her.

'Mamma's in one of her worst moods. I presume Jack has annoyed her so she's taking it out on me. I wrote and told her I

444

was hard up after your illness and wanted *feloos,* and she just won't play; says she's overdrawn herself at the moment.'

It was the longest speech Rex had made to Phillida this week.

She said:

'I'm sorry, Rex, but surely the Army paid for my illness?'

'Well, I didn't have to tell Mamma that, did I?' he snapped.

It seemed to her typical of Rex's warped nature.

'Oh, well, Gamma says she'll try to pay for my return passage at the end of the year,' she said quietly.

Rex pushed back his chair, stood up and lit a cigarette.

'Shouldn't bother to come back, if I were you,' he said nastily.

She flushed.

'You know perfectly well that I intend to come back and that I want everything to be different,' she said.

He opened his lips as though to make a reply, then shut them again and shrugged his shoulders. Hastily, because she wished to avoid a fight this oppressive grey morning, which seemed so much hotter than a normal day of sunshine and blue sky, Phillida said:

'Won't you come on to the beach with me this morning, Rex?'

'I've got a date, thanks.'

She knew that it was Jackie. She gave a gesture of hopelessness. Rex seemed determined to get himself talked about. He walked into the house then called back to her in a haughty voice: 'Can I offer you a lift to the beach or are one of your friends calling for you?'

She joined him in the dim coolness of the shuttered sitting-room. She said:

'Rex, please, can't we be friends? It is so senseless going on like this. And so crazy of you to start a scandal.'

'It'll be your fault if I do.'

'Oh Rex! Do be fair!'

He looked her up and down, his eyes narrowed.

'What, may I ask, are *you* doing to foster friendliness between us?'

'Everything I can, except...'

'Except that you don't think me fit to sleep with,' he said brutally.

She flushed to the roots of her hair.

'You know what I feel about that, and anyhow, why is it so important? Aren't I worth anything to you as a friend? In any case, you aren't ... you aren't really in love with me...' – she stammered over the words – 'you know it's only because you want to get the better of me. You're far more attracted at the moment by this woman Mrs Channery...'

It was his turn to redden. In the face of such truth he had little arguments, but the fact that Phil 'had him taped' lately made him feel savagely irritable and disinclined to give way to her.

'I'm not going to spoil my day by arguing,' he said. 'I'm going sailing. See you later...'

Now she suddenly remembered what Ali had said.

'Rex, Ali thinks there'll be a *khamsin*. There are some awfully black clouds around. And it feels – awful – sort of ominous. Do you think you ought to sail? People have been drowned on Lake Timsah in these storms.'

He was silent a moment. He felt a curious desire to burst out laughing. Phil was such a funny little thing, when all was said and done. Why should she worry if he was drowned in a *khamsin*. Her goodness was transparent and somehow at this precise moment, as she looked at him anxiously with her grave grey eyes, he felt a momentary softening towards her.

'My dear girl, I can swim. Don't waste your anxiety on *me*. I know all about sailing, and if there's a *khamsin* I couldn't care less... Bye-bye!'

Whistling, he walked into his bedroom. A moment later she heard him go out and start up the M.G.

She sighed and returned to her bedroom to get her swimsuit and towel ready before

447

Jimmy called for her.

But when Jimmy came it was to tell her that he had taken one look at the weather and cancelled Doreen's plans for a picnic on the Plage.

'I spoke to a chap who knows this country well and he says these *khamsins* blow up with tremendous speed and violence, and during the last one several of the huts on the Plage were blown away. I'm not going to risk it with young Bill. Dorrie says come and lunch with us in the flat.'

He looked round the room, and added awkwardly, 'Where's Rex?'

He *felt* awkward. Everybody knew that young Maltern was making a fool of himself over Jackie Channery and behaving in the most stupid fashion possible about his wife. Jimmy had not liked Rex for a long time. Now he positively hated the fellow.

Phillida made one of her usual attempts to hide the facts.

'Rex and another man have gone sailing.'

Jimmy Angus took his pipe from his mouth and pointed with it towards the sky.

'With this brewing, the fellow's crazy.'

'I told him so,' said Phillida. 'Ali says there's bound to be a *khamsin* today.'

'Oh, well,' said Jimmy, 'come along to us when you feel like it, Phil.'

Then, as he walked out, he turned back and with a smile of pride added: 'Dorrie's told you, I suppose, that young William's cut his first tooth?'

'Yes, isn't it marvellous?'

'Well, cheerio,' said Jimmy, and went off leaving Phillida standing on the verandah.

He carried with him a vision of a wistful young face and that lonely figure. What a damned shame, he thought, that Maltern was being such a cad! That nice girl deserved a better fate. Doreen said that Phillida was in love with Martin Winters; and talked a lot about broken hearts. Women were like that ... they loved to cook up romances and tragedies ... especially Doreen. Nevertheless he was damned sorry for Phillida Maltern, and as far as he was concerned, Rex could go and drown himself in Lake Timsah and he couldn't care less.

That thought, lightly conceived, was destined to have a sinister development. It was shortly before midday that the *khamsin* struck Ismailia.

Phillida was just preparing to walk round to her friend's apartment when she saw the gigantic black cloud which seemed to be descending rapidly upon the town. It was so dark and hot and still now that she could scarcely breathe. The humidity was terrific. Then suddenly Ali came running and begged her to go indoors.

'In, madam, plees... In quick. Ali shut all windows and doors...'

Phillida hesitated. But at that moment there came a terrific wind; a swirl of dust and leaves, a whirlpool, sucking up the filth of the streets as it gained speed, tearing through the town. She had a brief glimpse of a flamboyant tree swaying violently, and of scarlet blossom being tossed wildly on the pavements ... of Arabs covering their heads and faces with their *gallabiahs*, running for cover.

Then Ali called her again, and she went indoors. He shut everything. Every window and door. She stood at one of the windows watching, her pulse quickening, suddenly frightened. It was frightening, and in the closed house it grew oven-hot. Now and then she put a handkerchief up to wipe her streaming face and throat.

This was the *khamsin* ... blotting out Ismailia in a thick veil of yellow dust and sand ... sand that crept through the crevices into the bungalow ... grit in her mouth, in her eyes ... coating everything in the room.

And as she listened to the rising crescendo of that hot savage wind she had a momentary, horrified recollection of Rex.

Knowing him, she was quite sure that he had taken out the little sailing boat which, a month back, he and Harold Gayter had bought between them. Gayter was an experienced yachtsman, but Rex was an amateur. She had often heard Harold chaff

450

him about his lack of control of the boat. And Harold wouldn't be on it today, because Phillida knew that he had driven to Port Fuad with a girl-friend, for a picnic.

Rex would have gone down to the U.S. Club ... without a doubt accompanied by Jackie. Phillida had before now seen the famous Mrs Channery dressed up for a day's sailing in white linen slacks and grey shirt, dark curls tied up in a scarlet bandana. She was like a man, hauling up a sail with a cigarette in the corner of her mouth, laughing and joking.

The boat was only a Dorey B., a frail craft, servicable in a normal wind on mild water, but Phillida could not imagine it standing up to a demoniacal gale like *this*.

She heard a crash ... some shouting ... saw that a piece of scaffolding had been torn down in front of a shop window. The heat was suffocating, and her whole body was wet. She did not know why she felt so afraid. But it was not for herself. It was for that crazy, reckless, handsome husband of hers. Yes, in this very moment there came upon her a strong presentiment of catastrophe.

The storm raged on. Despite the intense heat, the breathlessness, she endeavoured to do some sewing, but her hands became sticky and wet and her glasses steamed over, and after a moment she took them off, laid down the sewing and walked to the win-

451

dows again and peered anxiously out.

Now she saw something which she had not seen since her arrival in Egypt: the rain.

It came down slowly at first, in great heavy drops, then in a torrent pouring from the angry, sun-charged skies. The wind had died down. In a few moments a sheet of rain obliterated the landscape. It drenched the streets and purified them. The water gushed down the roadway carrying with it the sand and the dirt, bits of paper and melon-rind, the scarlet petals of the flamboyant flowers, the yellow-green leaves of the mango trees – a sodden mass, swelling as the downpour increased in velocity.

Phillida flung open the shutters. The air she breathed in was exquisitely cool after the suffocating heat. It was a rich odour, not altogether pleasant, but she found it heavenly and drank it in. She wiped her forehead with the back of her hand and drew one deep long breath after another.

The *khamsin* was passing. It had lasted for nearly two hours. It had been violent and rather terrifying, as though a living thing had torn through Ismailia and devoured it, and now had gone again; so thought Phillida as she stood there at her open windows drawing the rain-cooled air into her lungs.

After a moment she heard Ali opening the other windows. The rain ceased as suddenly and as rapidly as it had come. The clouds raced across the sky and the sun broke through ... that hot, remorseless sunshine which Phillida had grown to dread. Soon it would be hotter than ever, she told herself ruefully. Already the wet road had begun to steam. A crowd of little Arab boys, their torn *gallabiahs* tied round their waists, splashed through the puddles, their thin brown legs ankle-deep. They screamed joyously, rolling their great eyes at each other.

As quickly as they had emptied before the storm, the streets filled up again. Crowds came out to enjoy the aftermath of the rain – so rare in this parched land. Phillida turned and walked into her bedroom. She would get her big straw hat and walk round to the Anguses' flat for lunch. It was growing late.

Her thoughts turned to Rex again. She wondered how he and Jacqueline Channery had got on with their sailing.

She told Ali that she would be back for tea. It was his day out but he would leave it all prepared. Mabyn Pentyre was coming to see Phillida and bringing with her a new young 'wife' who had just arrived in the Garrison, and whom she wanted Phillida to meet.

Certainly it was hotter than ever, with a lot of humidity, now that the sun was scorching down upon the wet streets again. She walked towards the small gate. She had put her big hat on the back of her fair head, and tied it under her chin with a ribbon, which made her look extraordinarily young.

At that moment a jeep tore down the road. It belonged to the R.A.F. Military Police. There were two men in uniform riding in it and a third in civilian clothes. Phillida put on her dark glasses, looked, and recognised the civilian. It was Captain Blacker, one of the medical officers of the district.

Phillida was surprised when the jeep drew up in front of her bungalow. Captain Blacker sprang out and came towards her. She took off her glasses and greeted him. He looked worried and had no smile of greeting in return for her. Now, again, a deep fear of impending catastrophe made her heart plunge.

'Hello, Captain Blacker,' she said.

He had never attended her medically – his work lay mostly in Timsah Leave Camp – but she had met him at parties.

He cleared his throat, coughed, looked more than embarrassed, and mumbled:

'Can I have a word with you, please, Mrs Maltern?'

'Of course, come in, won't you, please?'

He followed her into the little villa, and facing him in the sitting-room she noticed how untidy and strange he looked. His hair was bedraggled and his shirt damp. He must have been out in the rain.

'Sit down, Mrs Maltern,' he said, 'there's something I've got to tell you … it's not so very good… I…'

He broke off as though words failed him. He was quite young. Not so long ago a student from a London hospital, now mobilised into the R.A.M.C. He had a nice boyish face, which was red and puckered with trouble.

Phillida grew cold and very calm.

'Captain Blacker,' she said, 'there's been an accident … my husband was sailing, wasn't he? Something has happened to him.'

The young doctor pulled at the lobe of his ear and avoided her gaze. 'Yes, Mrs Maltern, yes,' he said.

'He went sailing just before this *khamsin*. I warned him not to go…'

'A lot of them went. Quite a number were caught out on the lake. It all blew up very suddenly.'

'What has happened? Please tell me.'

Still he could not bring himself to look at her. He avoided the issue.

'Some of the chaps managed to get their sails down in time. It appears that your husband didn't … the boat capsized … nothing could stand up to that hurricane. And of course there's a strong current … in the water…' He broke off, pulled a handkerchief from his pocket, and wiped his neck.

Phillida stared at him. She felt the colour

draining from her cheeks and the very marrow of her bones freezing as a kind of slow horror crept across her.

She said in a clear, high voice: 'Have you come to tell me that my husband's drowned, Captain Blacker?'

Then he looked at her in an agony of embarrassment. He was a qualified doctor, used to death, to the disasters, the grim tragedies of the casualty wards. But he had never found a mission more trying than this. He cursed the hour that had led him to take his wife over to the Blue Lagoon this morning in spite of the threatening weather. But Barbara had wanted to keep her appointment with the wife of a Squadron-Leader who was a friend of theirs. It was lucky *they* had managed to get off the beach and take cover before that infernal storm really got going. He would never forget the horror of watching some of those little sailing-boats capsize out on the lake … and the way the wind had uprooted one of those bathing huts and tossed it across the Plage as though it was a ball. It had been a regular typhoon.

He wiped his neck again. Now he forced himself to answer Mrs Maltern. He found it the very devil. He did not know her or Maltern at all well, but no doubt they were a devoted couple and this was going to be a ghastly shock to the poor girl.

456

He blurted out his story. Phillida listened, the points of her nails digging into her palms. She had to do that in order to keep herself from trembling too violently. It was all so horrifying. And it was just as she had imagined...

Rex had taken that Dorey B. out, refusing to listen to any of the warnings and not alone in his obstinacy. But the others had had more luck ... or else were better yachtsmen. Rex and Jacqueline Channery, alone in the Dorey B., were out in the middle of the lake when the *khamsin* struck... Blacker himself had seen the boat heel over. He knew no details after that, beyond the fact that the woman had managed to keep afloat, and swum towards the lagoon. She was a particularly strong swimmer. For quite a long way out from the shore it was shallow enough for her to wade, and some of the R.A.F. went out to bring her in. She was unhurt, just exhausted and hysterical. The only thing she had been able to tell them that Rex had been swimming alongside her quite well, then had screamed that he had cramp, and sunk like a stone.

Physically sick, Phillida listened. Her all too vivid imagination drew for her the spectacle of Rex drowning, the bright chestnut head disappearing under the treacherous water. Oh, poor, poor Rex! No matter what he had done she could not want him to suffer like that ... those agonising moments of cramp before the water sucked him under and silenced his voice for ever. She said in a hoarse voice: 'Of course he's dead – *he's dead!*...'

Blacker eyed the girl anxiously and wondered if she were going to faint.

'We don't know yet ... we haven't found ... I mean he may yet come ashore ... but I rather fear...'

She broke in on his stammerings:

'No. He was drowned. He'll never come back. I know it.'

He put out a hand and took her arm to steady her.

'Is there any brandy in the house...?'

She shook her head. The room had spun around her for an instant but now she was quite composed again.

'You'd better take me down to the beach,' she said.

'It isn't much use,' said the young officer; 'much better stay here. Tell me whom you'd like to see ... I'll fetch one of your friends. There's no use harrowing yourself down there by that lake. I've got an official report to make ... your husband was from Fayid, wasn't he?'

Was. That little word, the past tense, sounded horrible to Phillida, and it put Rex so very far away. He *was* ... at Fayid. A few hours ago, alive and buoyant, magnificently healthy, enjoying life in his own way. Now he was dead. His girl-friend had swum ashore, but he had been drowned in the *khamsin*.

Long ago Phillida had stopped loving him. She could not be hypocrite enough to pretend now that this meant what it would have meant when he had still retained her love and her faith. But she had been his wife, and once she had lain in his arms and he had meant everything in the world. It was terrible to know that he had died. For *him* she felt the deep bitter tragedy of death, because he had been young and had loved life.

Captain Blacker was trying to soften the blow by suggesting that Rex might yet be alive. But of course he could not be. They would wait for his body to be washed ashore. They would not know where or when, but it would come … as in those other ghastly accidents which she had heard about … other deaths by drowning during a *khamsin*. The bodies were always recovered hours later.

She heard the M.O.'s anxious voice:

'Do sit down and let me get you a drink, Mrs Maltern.'

Her grey eyes looked into his blindly. The shock was beginning to tell on her now. Her legs were trembling under her. She let the doctor lead her to a chair. He went out and found the *suffragi* and ordered some brandy.

459

She had only a confused recollection of drinking some of the stimulant and of giving Captain Blacker Mrs Pentyre's telephone number. She wanted Mrs Pen here ... that most sensible, understanding woman.

After that she found herself alone, lying back in her chair, eyes shut, breathing hard. Once again she imagined the awfulness of the thing that had taken place. So many times she had watched Rex and Harold Gayter take that boat out on the lake, although she had rarely gone with them herself, because she had been so ill lately. But she could see it all ... *see* Rex – brown, gay, cigarette in his mouth – sitting in the stern holding the tiller. He had always looked marvellously handsome. And this morning Jackie would have been with him. Probably they were laughing together just before that storm, with all its terrifying swiftness, broke over them.

Rex was dead. He had been seized with cramp and drowned.

He would never again enter this house. He had gone beyond mortal aid into that other world which he rarely discussed, for he had once told Phillida in his flippant fashion that he only entered churches for weddings, or, perforce, on Church Parade. He had no religion. It struck her in that moment what a fearful thing sudden death must be ... for a man without faith...

Her mind went on spinning, working. She reflected that some say that just before a man drowns he sees the whole of his past life in a flash. How much of that was true? Had Rex thought of himself, and his fear and horror as he was sinking … or had he remembered *her* … had he had one moment of remorse and of love for her?

She had tried so hard to put things right between them … tried and tried before his cruelty had driven her near to hatred for him. Death had cancelled her hatred. She told herself that she felt nothing but tremendous pity. She wished passionately that he had not left her this morning sneering, still antagonistic, and that he had taken her hand in a friendship – if only for a single instant.

She could not begin to think of Martin or her liberation from the yoke that had bound her in misery to a man who had persistently betrayed and hurt her. She remembered only the fact that Rex had been her husband … and the horror of his sudden death.

A long time afterwards the door opened and Mabyn Pentyre came hurrying into the room.

'My dear! I'm absolutely shocked…' she began.

But she stopped. Phillida looked up at her with an expression which forbade further speech of that kind. Mabyn Pentyre afterwards said to her husband: 'I think the most wonderful thing about that girl is her sincerity...'

For Phillida said: 'You mustn't sympathise with me, Mrs Pen. I can't be a hypocrite. I can't pretend that this is a terrible loss to me. But I *did* love him once and *his* is the loss. He has lost all his chances in life. It's like a terrible punishment ... oh, poor, poor Rex!'

Mrs Pentyre sat down and took Phillida's hand and held it. But it was not Phillida who cried. Dry-eyed, stonily she stared out at the sunshine, thinking of Lake Timsah which would be blue and beautiful and smooth as oil in the glittering of the sunshine again. And of Rex's dead body drifting with the current...

It was Mabyn Pentyre who for the first time for years felt the tears rolling down her face. They were not tears for Rex Maltern. She could feel no grief for the man who had done his best to wreck Phillida's life. But she wept because of all that this girl had suffered, because of her courage and her loyalty, her honesty now. She wept with *relief* because Phillida need suffer no more.

But the name 'Martin' was not mentioned between them.

11

Martin sat in the Pentyres' drawing-room, long legs stretched before him, pipe in the corner of his mouth, talking to Mrs Pen. It was nearly three weeks after Rex Maltern's accidental death on Lake Timsah.

Martin had not seen Phillida since the fatality of the *khamsin*. He had been away on a long, difficult court-martial in Greece. He had heard about it, of course, when the news reached G.H.Q. on that Sunday night. Like most other people, Martin was hardly able to credit it. It didn't seem possible that Maltern could be dead, and would never again enter his office at G.H.Q., or be seen in the N.A.A.F.I., or at the Officers' Club, or driving his M.G. at breakneck speed down the Canal Road.

The death by drowning of Maltern had been a shock to everybody. And of course everybody knew that he had been out on the lake at the time with Mrs Channery, and that she was now in hospital suffering from shock and fever. But nobody minded about her. She was new to the district and had caused a lot of unfavourable comment since she arrived. But Rex had been at G.H.Q. for a long time. He had been good at his job and made several friends, with his facile charm and generous offering of drinks all round. But he also had his enemies and had been harshly criticised for his recent treatment of his wife. For all that, he was a well-known figure and on that Sunday night the news of his death had cast a gloom, and quite a lot of morbid interest, through the camp.

Martin's feelings had been indescribable. It was too difficult for him to believe that Fate had swept Rex Maltern off the earth just as a careless hand brushes a pawn from a chessboard in the middle of a game. It seemed to Martin that his end was certainly grim retribution for all that made Phillida suffer.

But Martin, being honest, indulged in no hypocritical grief for Maltern. It meant that Phillida was free and that her troubles had come suddenly and dramatically to an end. For that reason alone Martin was supremely thankful.

He had not time to do more than write a short formal note to her telling her that the news was 'grim and distressing' and that if she wanted anything she had only to let him know. He had only returned to Fayid from Greece last night.

There were plenty of people in the Mess ready to give him the latest details about the

Maltern tragedy.

Maltern's body had been washed up at the Blue Lagoon two days after the *khamsin*. They said that poor little Mrs Maltern collapsed after identifying him. She was now staying with Brigadier and Mrs Pentyre in Moascar, and they were putting her on the first possible boat for England.

That was all that Martin knew about his beloved Phillida. He did a morning's work at Fayid then drove to the Pentyres' house this afternoon.

Both the Brigadier and Phillida were still in their rooms having their siesta when Martin arrived. It was Mabyn who welcomed him and told him all that he wanted to know.

Naturally the whole thing had been a shock for Phillida, but she was not doing at all badly, Mrs Pen assured Martin. She was not, for instance, in that same nervous condition that the poor child suffered just before her breakdown. On the whole her health was improving. But naturally it had been a grim affair for her.

Mrs Pen had gone with her and 'held her hand', as she put it, during the wretched but necessary business of identification. Poor little Phillida, she had turned deathly pale and nearly fainted. A drowned body in this country after two days in the water was not a pleasant sight. The once handsome Rex had been almost unrecognisable. But she had got through it, then gone home with her friend and been very ill all night. On the next day she recovered and seemed quite normal. She had not mentioned Rex's name, and nobody had mentioned it to her. She had just stayed quietly in the house and written a lot of letters to England.

'The morning after it happened, Freddy and I cabled Rex's father, and this mother of his who is married to someone else,' Mrs Pen told Martin. 'From what I can gather, neither of them had much interest in him. And, to be quite frank, Martin, apart from the sort of cheap popularity which he had with a certain type out here, it appears that he has nobody in the world who will really, sincerely, mourn him. It isn't a pretty thought, but he was an unpleasant type.'

Martin took the pipe from his mouth and regarded it thoughtfully.

'Yes. And in a few short months he managed to create havoc ... worse than that ... absolute *hell* for Phillida.'

'She knows it. But she was loyal to him while he was alive and she's been loyal to him since his death. I haven't heard her say one word against the fellow. She just says, "Poor old Rex..." Isn't that typical of her, Martin?'

'Yes,' said Martin in a low voice, 'it's typical of her, Mrs Pen.'

Mabyn Pentyre's bright blue eyes, which made her weather-beaten face so young and alive, looked with affection at the big fair man. 'I'm glad you're back, Martin. Phillida needs a little happiness. You'll look after her now, won't you?'

Martin coloured under his tan.

'You know it has been my dearest wish to do that for a long time. Only I never dreamed...'

'No, we none of us dreamed,' put in Mrs Pen significantly, and there followed an eloquent silence. Then Martin said:

'When does she expect to go home?'

'Next week, they think.'

'Well, I've got a piece of news for her – and for you, Mrs Pen,' said Martin. 'I think my own posting's coming through at the end of the month.'

'Oh, Martin, not the Far East?'

'No. By the grace of God they didn't take any notice of my suggestion that I should go there,' he said with a faint smile, 'but there seems to be a job they want me to take up in Gib – right out of this Command.'

'Gib!' said Mabyn. 'Good gracious! The old Rock! That won't be too bad, Martin.'

'No, it's not far from England,' he said.

And again they looked at each other in silent understanding.

Then Martin got up, knocked the bowl of his pipe against an ash-tray, and added:

'It might appear that things are going to work out; which will be a pleasant change. I don't know how Phillida feels, but...'

'You needn't worry about that,' Mrs Pen finished for him cheerfully.

'Has she ... spoken about me at all?'

'Several times. She asked Freddy if he could find out when you were due back from Athens.'

Martin looked absurdly pleased – so pleased that Mrs Pen had to laugh.

'Well, now, you can take some of the responsibility off me. You'll be able to get a nice day off and drive her to Port Said and put her on the boat yourself.'

'Put her on the boat, eh,' said Martin reflectively. 'H'm – just as I more or less took her off, when she first arrived. It seems a devil of a long time ago.'

'I should think it's seemed like one long nightmare to *her*.'

Martin was about to reply when the door opened. The subject of their discussion came into the room.

Mrs Pentyre gave one look at the two young people, then slid tactfully out of the room, murmuring that she must go and wake Freddy. Phillida and Martin faced each other.

His first impression was how well she looked – much more tranquil and normal again. She was brown from the sun. The grey eyes were brilliant and held no look of strain. She wore a floral cotton skirt and a crisp white blouse. She seemed to him fresh and flower-like, and altogether adorable.

Phillida looked back at Martin and felt her heart plunge with the wild excitement of seeing him again.

It had been very trying during the past three weeks, and yet with every hour that had passed she had grown more and more conscious of liberation – and she began to appreciate it, almost with a sense of guilt – because she could not truly mourn for Rex – and because he, in losing his life, had unwittingly given life back to *her*.

Looking upon his dead body had been a horror. Now that horror had passed, and with the kindly help of her friends she had got through the funeral (he had been buried with full military honours in the little cemetery at Fayid), and after that it was as though she walked out of darkness into light … and a terrible burden had been lifted from her.

Of course, during those three weeks Martin had figured in all her thoughts and dreams.

And here he was, looking down at her from his great height with those warm blue eyes, smiling … holding out both his hands.

She went to him without hesitation. His arms encircled her. With a little smothered cry, she put her own arms about his waist and buried her face against his shoulder.

For a few moments they stayed in that close embrace without speaking. All the old warmth and understanding and deep affection flowed between them. Then when she lifted her face, he kissed her on the mouth and her eyes closed and she knew that she had reached the summit ... the end of the long bitter uphill climb to happiness.

'Phillida, Phillida, my very dear!' Martin's deep voice whispered against her ear. He pressed his cheek against hers, which was carnation-pink and warm, then turned his lips again to her soft mouth, insatiable for her kisses.

At length, more tranquilly, they sat together on the sofa with locked hands, looking into each other's eyes. And Mrs Pen's green-and-white sitting-room was Paradise. And for the first time for many bitter months Egypt seemed to Phillida a pleasant place. The sinister shadows had receded into the background.

It seemed that centuries had elapsed rather than three weeks since the *khamsin* and Rex's fatal accident.

'I suppose I ought to feel a bit guilty about being as happy as this ... so quickly...' she said to Martin, holding one of his hands against her cheek. 'But there it is! Rex and I had been strangers to each other for a long time and all that time I had *you* in my heart, Martin.'

'And you've been very much in mine, sweetheart,' he said.

And I don't need to feel too guilty, do I?'

'On the contrary, you went through hell you have a right to happiness now,' he said.

'It's so wonderful to be able to say that I have the right to love *you*, Martin.'

'It's a miracle to me, too, darling.'

'Oh, Martin!' she said with a long sigh.

He looked with passionate tenderness at the fair silky head, then down at the exquisite fingers with their rosy polished nails. He thought in that moment of Bridget. He said:

'Bridget will be glad about this ... if she knows.'

She nodded.

'Perhaps Rex will be glad, too. He wasn't *all* bad, Martin. There was some good in him somewhere. But the other side conquered. Poor Rex!'

Martin dropped her hand.

'Sorry, darling, but I can't feel a vestige of pity for a fellow who did what *he* did to you.'

She could understand that. She liked Martin's honest defence of her. She said: 'In time ... all that will be forgotten.'

He turned back to her, took her hands and kissed them each in turn.

'I'd like you to be able to forget it, Phillida.

I'd like your marriage to him to be wiped out of your life. I want you to begin a new one with me.'

Her pulses thrilled.

'Darling Martin, that sounds very marvellous.'

He told her about his possible posting to Gibraltar.

'I'll have to let you go home alone,' he concluded, 'and there must be an interval for everybody's sake. People who don't know the facts are bound to talk, and I'm not going to have one word said against you. You'll stay with your nice grandmother, won't you? And I'm going to ask you also to go up and stay with Aunt Kate. Then I shall come back on leave, and we'll be together for a bit, and afterwards I'll start my job in Gib. Perhaps next spring you'll come out to me there – will you, Phillida?'

She was too moved to speak for a moment. Events had moved so rapidly ... they were almost too precipitous ... she was left breathless. With a catch in her voice she answered him:

'Any time you say, Martin ... I'll just be ... waiting for you.'

'God, darling,' he said huskily, 'it seems too good to be true! You and I together ... *you*, as my wife ... it seems a hellish long way before the spring, but as far as I'm concerned it's so tremendously worth waiting for.'

'For me, too, Martin.'

He gave her a long, deep look.

'You won't be afraid to take a second plunge, will you? I won't let you down, darling. I swear it. I'll live only for you ... for you and my job ... you believe that, don't you?'

Her heart beat with a strong, glad rhythm.

'I believe it. I *knew* it, and I shan't be afraid.'

'And when I get back on leave we'll spend a little time in Killoun together... Oh, my dear, what a wonderful thought. You in Killoun. You walking with me along the river ... as my future wife.'

'It sounds rather like a fairy tale,' she said.

'It's going to come true. Phillida, my very dear,' he said, and added in Arabic: '*El Maktoob*...

'What does that mean?'

'It means,' said Martin, 'our Fate is written.'

They sat together, talking, planning, dreaming.

Possibly he would follow her home in late August or September, Martin told her. And he began to describe Killoun in the autumn, and she could see it all, the beeches turning to red and gold, the moors purple with heather. They would walk down to the big salmon pool; he would show her all the places he loved when he was a boy ... introduce her to the old Scots farmers who had been tenants on the Laird's estates all their lives; and who would have a warm welcome for the Lieutenant-Commander and his lady. Almost, Phillida could smell the heather, warm from the sun ... and hear the plaintive cry of the plover ... and smell the rich odour of leaves in the Castle grounds ... the tang of smoke from the bonfires after the gardeners had cleared the lawns.

On the wings of his eloquence she was transported to Killoun – the place which one day – oh, miraculous thought! – would be hers and Martin's home. She lay in his arms, listening, now and again turning her lips to meet his kiss.

She thought:

'What a lot I shall have to tell darling Gamma ... what tremendous readjustment it will mean to all our lives...'

Then, perforce, they had to return from the world of fantasy to fact.

The Brigadier and his wife were coming downstairs. They heard the footsteps and voices. Martin dropped a quick kiss on Phillida's hair, lifted her left hand, glanced a moment at her wedding ring, and said:

'I shan't be really happy until the day I put mine there in the place of *that*...'

'I know, darling ... I feel the same, but I'm all yours, now and always,' she whispered.

The door opened and Mrs Pen appeared with a shopping-basket over her arm.

'I'm dragging Freddy to the N.A.A.F.I., he's furious.'

'What does she think I am?' snorted the Brigadier, 'a little Arab boy to carry her basket?'

Phillida and Martin laughed. Mrs Pen cast a quick look from one to the other and felt satisfied that her two favourites had said all the right things to each other. She said:

'I must order some more gin. Freddy won't mind that part of it. And how about fixing a little dinner party the night before Phil sails ... just a quiet, private one, with her special friends? We'll have the Cubitts, and Jimmy Angus and Doreen (she's improving, that girl) ... and that poor Peggy ... she does all the work ... and we might try to induce Monsieur and Madame Martial to come and add a touch of French piquancy to our dinner. What do you say, Phillida?'

'I think,' said Phillida, 'that it sounds lovely. They've all been so sweet to me. But *I'm* going to give the party, Mrs Pen. You and the Brigadier have got to be *my* guests.'

'Sorry,' said Martin. 'It's going to be *my* party. I shall hold it in this house, if Mrs Pen permits.'

Mabyn turned to her husband.

'Looks as though we're going to get out of this cheap, Freddy. We shall enjoy a good party and they're going to pay for it.'

'Well, after looking at my Income Tax Returns...' began the Brigadier.

He was not allowed to finish. His wife bundled him out of the room.

'Ring for some tea, you two. Freddy and I won't be back, we're going down to the U.S. Club,' she said as she vanished.

But Phillida and Martin did not ring for tea. They had far too much to say to each other. They were still sitting there, with linked hands, after sundown and it had grown dark in the flower-filled sitting-room.

Mustapha, the Pentyres' head *suffragi*, came in to see if anything was wanted but retired noiselessly, went into the kitchen and addressed the cook who was beginning to prepare the evening meal:

'The English lady whose husband was drowned is once more content,' he observed. 'It is good, for she is good and lovely.'

'*Aiwah*,' said the cook.

'There will be no more *khamasin* this year,' added Mustapha.

'Naturally,' said the old cook, looking at the younger man severely, 'there will be no more *khamasin* for the days of the storm are over.'

'*Aiwah*,' said Mustapha, 'they are over.'

476

The publishers hope that this book has given you enjoyable reading. Large Print Books are especially designed to be as easy to see and hold as possible. If you wish a complete list of our books please ask at your local library or write directly to:

Dales Large Print Books
Magna House, Long Preston,
Skipton, North Yorkshire.
BD23 4ND

This Large Print Book, for people
who cannot read normal print,
is published under the auspices of

THE ULVERSCROFT FOUNDATION